THE

Birthday Scandal

Also By Leigh Michaels

Regency Historical Romance

The Mistress' House
Just One Season in London
The Wedding Affair

Contemporary Romance

Assignment: Twins!
Baby, You're Mine
Backwards Honeymoon
The Best-Made Plans
The Billionaire Bid
The Billionaire Date
The Boss and the Baby
The Boss's Daughter
The Bridal Swap
The Bride Assignment
Bride by Design
Bride on Loan
Brittany's Castle
Capture a Shadow
Carlisle Pride
Close Collaboration
Come Next Summer
A Convenient Affair
The Corporate Marriage Campaign
The Corporate Wife
The Daddy Trap

Dating Games
Deadline For Love
Dreams to Keep
Exclusively Yours
The Fake Fiancé
Family Secrets
Garrett's Back In Town
The Grand Hotel
Her Husband-To-Be
His Trophy Wife
House of Dreams
Husband on Demand
The Husband Project
The Husband Sweepstake
An Imperfect Love
Invitation To Love
Just A Normal Marriage
Kiss Yesterday Goodbye
The Lake Effect
Leaving Home
Let Me Count The Ways
The Marriage Market
Marrying the Boss!
A Matter of Principal
Maybe Married
A New Desire
No Place Like Home
O'Hara's Legacy
Old School Ties
On September Hill
Once and For Always

The Only Man For Maggie
The Only Solution
Part Time Fiancé
The Perfect Divorce
The Playboy Assignment
Promise Me Tomorrow
Rebel With A Cause
Safe In My Heart
Sell Me A Dream
Shades of Yesterday
A Singular Honeymoon
Some Kind of Hero (novella)
Strictly Business
The Takeover Bid
Taming A Tycoon
Temporary Measures
Ties That Blind
Touch Not My Heart
Traveling Man
The Tycoon's Baby
The Tycoon's Proposal
An Uncommon Affair
The Unexpected Landlord
The Unlikely Santa
Wednesday's Child
Wife on Approval
With No Reservations

Non-Fiction

On Writing Romance: How to Craft A Novel that Sells
Creating Romantic Characters: Bringing Life to Your Romance
Novel
For the Love of Tea
Focus on Photos
Illustrated Review of Ottumwa, Iowa 1890
Ottumwa (IA) (Postcard History Series)
1904 St. Louis World's Fair

THE
Birthday
Scandal

LEIGH MICHAELS

Montlake
Romance

Text copyright © 2012 Leigh Michaels

Published by Montlake Romance
P.O. Box 400818
Las Vegas, NV 89140

ISBN-13: 9781612184760
ISBN-10: 1612184766

Dedication
For Ashley and Karina

Chapter 1

Lady Emily Arden added up the column of household expenditures in her head once more, scarcely able to believe that the total could be so high. She had just dipped her quill in the inkstand to write the sum at the bottom of her list when Mrs. Dalrymple tapped at the door of her tiny sitting room and begged an audience.

"I don't mean to intrude, my lady." Mrs. Dalrymple's voice was even fainter and more breathy than usual. "But it *is* important, and you did say that I might have a few moments after breakfast."

"Indeed I did, Mrs. Dalrymple, and I must beg your pardon for the oversight." Emily pushed aside her account books; the horrid truth would still be there, glaring at her, whether she took a moment to listen to her companion or not. "What did you wish to bring to my attention?"

"I took the liberty of asking Sally to bring fresh tea," Mrs. Dalrymple went on. She fanned herself as if stunned by her own daring.

Emily was a bit startled, too. Mrs. Dalrymple was such a tentative sort—so eager to please, so terrified of offending—that Emily was often annoyed by her companion's failure to show the slightest initiative. But of course Mrs. Dalrymple would start to request luxuries at the very

1

moment her employer was making a concentrated effort to cut expenses...

Emily shook her head a little at her own foolishness in thinking that a single extra pot of tea would make any difference in her financial situation. Letting her companion go, on the other hand, would eliminate one mouth to feed and one salary to pay, and it would make the situation significantly easier in the tiny cottage.

But she dismissed the idea almost instantly. She had accepted responsibility when she hired Mrs. Dalrymple, and it wasn't as if a middle-aged and completely ineffectual companion had a great many posts to choose from. If Emily were to let her go, even with an excellent reference, the woman would be fortunate to find any employment.

Mrs. Dalrymple's eyes grew huge. "I was so afraid I might be overstepping my place! Shall I run to the kitchen to cancel the order?"

"No—why do you ask?"

"You were shaking your head, my lady."

"About something else entirely. Of course you must order tea when you want it. Now, what is it you wished to speak to me about?"

"Oh, my lady, you are so good to me. I can hardly bring myself to ask...but I did swear that I would, and..."

Emily's head was starting to throb. If past experience was any guide, Mrs. Dalrymple might take half an hour to come to the point, and even then she was apt to leave her listener not quite certain of what she was trying to say. Tea was sounding better by the moment. At least Emily would have something to do while she waited.

"It's the squire, you see. Sir Cedric. It happened as we were making the last arrangements for the village flower show. Quite a surprise it was—a shock, in fact." Mrs. Dalrymple blushed and stammered a little. "And...and he...he wished to know if it could be announced at the show next Saturday."

Emily settled back in her chair to wait out Mrs. Dalrymple. Despite her best efforts, her mind wandered back to the list of expenditures—she was already doing without new clothes, and it wasn't as if she kept a carriage or a full staff of maids. She'd chosen this path herself, and she'd known from the outset that her limited resources couldn't be stretched to luxuries. But if she even had to give up things like tea and sugar...

Sally appeared, laden down. "There's a couple of letters as has just come, my lady. I put them on the tea tray."

Emily's gaze wandered to the folded pages lying next to the hot water jug. The handwriting on the top one was a dark and spiky slash—her father had obviously been feeling particularly unsympathetic toward his wayward daughter when he'd dashed off that missive. She didn't have to read it to know that much; if it was ordinary business, the Earl of Chiswick turned the matter over to his private secretary. He only wrote to her himself when he was angry or in a mood to issue orders. And since she hadn't done anything for at least a month to make him angry...

I wonder which family he has in mind this time to marry me into.

She set the earl's letter aside and glanced at the other one. Mrs. Dalrymple set the teapot back on the tray. "That's the duke's handwriting, is it not? It looks strange somehow."

3

Emily put out her hand for her cup. Her companion was right; the Duke of Weybridge's fist was not the confident sprawl she remembered. The address looked cramped, almost painful, and even the scrawled *Weybridge* that franked the corner of the letter wasn't quite as strong as she remembered it. "I wonder if Uncle Josiah is ill."

"You must not wait to find out, my lady."

"If you don't mind…" Emily broke the wafer and spread the sheet on her knee, trying not to listen to Mrs. Dalrymple's fluttery and repetitive exclamations that of course she understood, yes indeed she did.

> *My dearest Emily,*
>
> *Time marches on, and I will soon celebrate my seventieth, and I suspect my last, birthday. My various complaints are too numerous for me to list and too tiresome for you to read, so my energy (and this paper) are better spent in other ways. It is sufficient to say that at his every visit—and they are growing more numerous—my doctor shakes his head in despair.*
>
> *I hope you will find it possible to visit me for my birthday. I suspect you may be in shallow water by now, with only your mother's legacy to draw upon and your father no doubt still determined to bring you to heel. Therefore, I have given orders for a post-chaise to arrive the day after this letter, so you may make the journey in comfort.*
>
> *Since I will not long need my worldly goods, I have no wish to collect more birthday trinkets. Perhaps this year we shall play turn-around instead. I have it in mind to make a gift to you and spend my remaining days watching and enjoying your happiness.*
>
> *Your loving great-uncle, Josiah Weybridge*
>
> *P.S. I do hope you believe me, dear Emily, when I say that you have always been my favorite of my niece's children.*

Emily put the letter down, biting her lip. "He sounds so very low. It's quite unlike him." Her gaze sought the calendar on her desk. "His birthday is just a week away—no wonder he's sending for me tomorrow."

"Tomorrow?" Mrs. Dalrymple's hands fluttered to her face. "But how shall we get all your packing done in so short a time?"

"I'm certain we'll manage. But you were telling me about the village flower show and the squire."

"Oh, that doesn't matter now, my lady! Shall I go and tell Sally to start packing your things? Or shall you want to check every garment beforehand? Oh, dear—I never know what to do. But in any case, you need me now more than ever, and Sir Cedric will simply have to wait."

Mrs. Dalrymple flitted out of the room, leaving Emily shaking her head and wondering if she should call the woman back and set her to some other task. Mrs. Dalrymple was a great deal more likely to get in Sally's way than to assist—assuming, of course, that she didn't mangle the message altogether.

But what was all this about Sir Cedric having to wait? Some detail about the village flower show, no doubt. Which reminded Emily that she must arrange for someone to step into her shoes to do the judging next Saturday.

She picked up her second letter and cracked the wafer. Even if her father had issued his usual blast of orders, she found herself feeling a bit more sanguine about the situation.

I have it in mind to make a gift to you...

Of course, Uncle Josiah could simply mean he planned to present her with his late wife's pearl earbobs, since he had no daughter to inherit them. Still, Emily couldn't help but feel better. Even distracted by his own illness, Uncle

Josiah—wise man that he was—understood that her inheritance from her mother would stretch only so far. The Duke of Weybridge was well known to be plump in the pockets, and not just in landed estates; she had heard him expound many times on the benefits of investing in the Funds.

If only he were to settle some money on her, Emily could safely continue to ignore her father—and everything would be all right.

*   *   *

The company was lighthearted and gay, the accommodations sinfully comfortable, the entertainments truly amusing, and the hunting reasonably enjoyable. Despite all of that, Lady Isabel Maxwell was miserable. Simply keeping a smile fixed on her face was the most difficult thing she had done in months, because it was all too clear that the rest of the company would have preferred it if her husband had been the guest at the Beckhams' hunting lodge instead.

"Too bad Maxwell couldn't join us," one of the gentlemen had said just that morning as they'd finished the hunt and called the hounds to heel for the ride back to the lodge. "He's a bruising rider—we wouldn't have seen *him* going around by the fields."

"I do wonder, Lady Isabel," one of the ladies had said slyly yesterday, "that you can bear to be away from your husband for so long. He's such a *masculine* man. But perhaps that's why you need a little time away from his…demands?" And then she had held her breath as if seriously expecting Isabel to answer.

And last night as Isabel passed a half-open bedroom door, she had overheard a fellow guest speaking to her maid. "I do so admire Lady Isabel for not feeling the need to bow to the demands of fashion," the woman had said. "She dresses instead in what is comfortable even if it is not in the first stare. Though I find it no wonder her husband has strayed."

Isabel had gritted her teeth and gone on down to dinner, where she smiled and flirted and silently dared anyone to comment to her face that her dress was at least two years old.

If only her early departure wouldn't cause so much comment, she would call for her carriage and go home right now. But that was impossible. For one thing, she didn't *have* a carriage, for she had come up from London with a fellow guest. Too short of funds to afford a post-chaise, she was equally dependent on her friend for transport back to the city when the hunting party broke up.

And secondly, of course, there were only two places she could go—Maxton Abbey, or the London house—and her husband might be at either one. Unless, with her safely stashed at the Beckhams', he had accepted yet another of the many invitations he received.

But she couldn't take the chance. After little more than a year of marriage, the pattern was ingrained—wherever one of the Maxwells went, the other took pains not to go. She could not burst in on her husband; what if he were entertaining his mistress?

Better not to know.

She might go to the village of Barton Bristow, descending on her sister. But Emily's tiny cottage was scarcely large enough for her and her companion, with no room for a guest—and Mrs. Dalrymple's constant chatter and menial deference was enough to set Isabel's teeth on edge. In fact, the only nice thing Isabel could say about being married was that at least she wasn't required to drag a spinster companion around the countryside with her to preserve her reputation, as Emily had to do.

Isabel turned her borrowed mount over to the stable boys and strode across to the house, where the butler intercepted her in the front hall. "A letter has just been delivered for you, Lady Isabel, by a special messenger. He said a post-chaise will call for you tomorrow."

She took the folded sheet with trepidation. Who could be summoning her? Not her husband, that was certain. Her father, possibly, for yet another lecture on the duties of a young wife?

She broke the seal and unfolded the page.

My dearest Isabel,

You will remember from happier days that I will soon celebrate my seventieth birthday...

Uncle Josiah. But her moment of relief soon passed as she read on. The Duke of Weybridge *dying?*—Impossible. True, he had looked old to her from the day she first remembered him—but through all the years since, he had seemed to stay exactly the same.

Her eyes skipped down the page.

...I suspect you may be in difficult straits, with only pin money to draw upon and, I imagine, no sympathy from your father regarding your marital arrangements. Therefore, I have given orders for a post-chaise...

She couldn't help but feel relieved at such a marvelous excuse to leave the house party early—even while she scolded herself for thinking such a thing. It wasn't as though she *wanted* Uncle Josiah to be ill.

...I shall not long need my worldly goods, and I do not wish you to devote even a pittance to a birthday gift for me. This year I shall enjoy making life more pleasant for you instead.

Your loving great-uncle, Josiah Weybridge

P.S. My dearest hope, Isabel, is that you believe me when I say that you are my favorite of Drusilla's children.

Well, that was clear enough—and very welcome, too. If Uncle Josiah were to offer her a bit of cash, Isabel would swallow what pride she still possessed and accept. Some extra pocket money would come in handy indeed—since it seemed she had no option but to continue to play her role as the Earl of Maxwell's inconvenient wife.

* * *

Lucien Arden had started the evening at one of the few theaters that remained open despite the fact that London was thin of company in early autumn. He went not as a fan of the art but because there was a new face in the chorus, and rumor—in the person of his friend Aubrey—said she was a promising possibility as a mistress. And indeed she was, Lucien had to admit—at least, she would be for Aubrey, who had come into his title and had full control of his fortune. But not for someone like Lucien—a young man on a strict allowance and whose title of Viscount Hartford was only a courtesy one, borrowed from his father. Being *my lord* was, he had found, one of the few benefits of being the only son of the Earl of Chiswick.

"She's quite attractive, as game pullets go," he told Aubrey carelessly after the play, as they cracked the first bottle of wine at their club. "Have her with my blessing."

Aubrey snorted. "You know, Lucien, it's just as well you're not looking for a high-flyer, for you damned well couldn't afford her."

Lucien forced a smile. "She's not my sort, as it happens."

"Balderdash—she's any man's sort."

Not mine, Lucien thought absently. He might have said it aloud if the sentiment hadn't been so startlingly true. How odd—for the chorus girl had been a prime piece, buxom and long-limbed and flashy, as well as incredibly flexible as she moved around the stage. How could he not be interested?

Aubrey was looking at him strangely, so Lucien said, "If she's so much to your taste, I'm surprised you didn't go around to the stage door after the performance and make yourself known."

"Strategy, my friend. Never let a woman guess exactly how interested you are." Aubrey waved a hand at a waiter to bring another bottle, and as they drank it, he detailed his plan for winning the chorus girl. "It's too bad you can't join the fun, for I'm certain she has a friend," Aubrey finished. "The gossips have it that your father is never without a lightskirt, so why should he object to you having one?"

"Oh, not a lightskirt. Only the finest of the demimonde will do for the Earl of Chiswick." Lucien drained his glass. "I'm meant to be on the road to Weybridge at first light—for the duke's birthday, you know. A few hours' sleep before I climb into a jolting carriage will not come amiss."

"Too late." Aubrey tilted his head toward the nearest window. "Dawn's breaking now, if I'm not mistaken. You won't mind if I don't come to see you off? Deadly dull it is, waving good-bye—and I've a mind for a hand or two of piquet before I go home."

Lucien walked from the club to his rooms in Mount Street, hoping a fresh breeze might help clear his head. The post-chaise Uncle Josiah had ordered for him was already waiting. The horses stamped impatiently, snorting in the cool morning air, and the postboys looked bored.

Nearby, Lucien's valet paced—but he brightened at the sight of his master. "The trunks are already strapped in place, my lord. The moment you take your seat, we can be off."

Lucien rubbed his jaw and thought longingly of his bed—or failing that, at least a hot towel and a close shave. But in good conscience, he couldn't keep the team and the boys—or Uncle Josiah—waiting any longer, so he climbed into the post-chaise and settled into the corner.

Sleep eluded him, and the sway and bounce of the springs made him feel like casting up his accounts. *I must change clubs. The wine there is frightfully bad, to leave me with a head like this.*

As they left London behind to bowl along the Great North Road, he looked across at his valet, who was sitting primly upright on the opposite seat with his back to the horses. "I assume you brought the letter?"

"Of course, my lord." The valet drew it from a small hand valise.

Lucien had read the duke's message so often in the last two days that the words felt engraved on his brain, so he skipped to the most interesting parts.

My dear Hartford,

My birthday is next week, and though my doctor does not actually say it will be my last, his opinion is clear...

As one man of the world to another, I understand how you must feel about your father keeping you on such a short leash. I have told him many times how unwise he is not to allow his heir adequate means to sample all the temptations of the city, but Chiswick was always better at giving advice than taking it...Since I shall not long be in need of my worldly goods, I look forward to making it possible for you to take your proper place in society. And if my gift allows each of us to put a finger in your father's eye, so much the better.

Your devoted great-uncle, Josiah Weybridge

P.S. I hope you will believe me, Lucien, when I say that you have always been my favorite of your mother's children.

Uncle Josiah, Lucien thought sleepily, was the best of sports. Too bad that his only son had died in infancy. Then the rest of the family had succumbed one after another, and now the dukedom would fall to the most unlikely of fellows, a cousin from a branch so distant that Lucien hadn't even known they existed. Some blighter from the former colonies would be the next Duke of Weybridge, he had heard—and a bloody great time it had taken the solicitors to find him there, too, with yet another war dragging on. It was over now, finally—but what was wrong with those American fellows, anyway? Did they like fighting so much they simply couldn't walk away from a tussle?

No wonder Uncle Josiah was giving away his personal fortune rather than leaving any more than he must to this unwelcome heir, the new Marquess of Athstone. A strange sort of duke the fellow would make; he was probably bragging to his fellow colonials about being a duke in waiting.

But at least, Lucien thought with a yawn, this new cousin was related only through Lucien's mother—and therefore he would never be the head of the Arden family. Though, come to think of it, even an odd American could hardly be worse to deal with than Lucien's father was.

Good old Uncle Josiah. Lucien suspected it wasn't just the Earl of Chiswick who would end up feeling he'd had a finger stuck in his eye, but Josiah's heir as well.

❀   ❀   ❀

With the windows of the Red Dragon's best private parlor standing open to London's September sunshine, Gavin Waring, the new Marquess of Athstone, could almost have closed his eyes and imagined he was back in Baltimore. From the street, shouts resounded as carriages jockeyed for position, while horses snorted and costermongers called their wares. And as for the smells...

From his place on the most uncomfortable settee he'd ever encountered, Gavin looked up at the small, trim man who stood facing him. "Benson, is it?"

"Yes, my lord. Here are my references, for your review." Benson held out a sheaf of paper.

Gavin took the small bundle, but he didn't look at the pages. "The names won't mean much to me. I assume you know I'm not exactly English."

"Yes, my lord. It was mentioned."

"And if you hadn't been warned already, the way I talk would have told you. I don't know the men you've worked for, or whether they're gentlemen or bounders, so I haven't any idea whether their recommendations are reliable."

The small man stiffened slightly. "I assure you, sir—"

"So let's just get to know each other a bit, shall we?"

"As you wish, my lord."

"*Sir* will do, Benson. This *my lord* business makes my ears tired. Please sit down."

"I prefer to stand when receiving instructions, sir."

"I don't blame you. I can't think the chair would be any more comfortable than this settee is." Gavin pushed himself to his feet and walked across to a table where a decanter stood. "I don't suppose you'd like a glass of Madeira, either?"

Benson's face was wooden. "Certainly *not*, sir."

Gavin set the decanter down without pouring. "You're the seventeenth valet I've interviewed, by the way."

"You must be very hard to please, sir, if not a single one of them met your expectations."

"It was more a matter of me not meeting theirs," Gavin said pensively. "They…er…tended to look down their noses at me, and I'm afraid I could not support that attitude every morning before breakfast."

"I understand, sir."

"Do you, I wonder? I'm looking for something more than a gentleman's gentleman."

"More, sir?"

"I am not a lackwit, but there are many things I don't know."

"May I assume, sir, that one of those things is how to get on in English society?"

"Yes, exactly. It's different where I come from."

"I should think it would be, sir. For a start, I believe we shall require a different tailor." Benson cleared his throat. "If, that is, you should choose to give me the position."

"There's no time for things like that. I arrived in London only two days ago, and I am to leave the day after tomorrow for the duke's birthday celebration."

"Lack of time is not an issue for a gentleman, sir. Not when the gentleman is the Duke of Weybridge's heir."

Gavin tapped his fingers on the table. "Very well, Benson," he said finally. "You have the job. Go forth and start working your magic."

"I shall be pleased to do so, sir." Benson bowed and half turned, then paused. "If I may say so, sir, you are far more English than you think. Despite the accent, you have a manner of command, of ease, which comes naturally to those of noble blood."

Gavin eyed him narrowly. "Don't overdo it."

"I shall exercise caution, my lord." The valet went out so quietly that Gavin, picking up the letter from the duke that had been awaiting him when he arrived, had to look around to be certain he was alone.

With a snap of the wrist, he unfolded the letter and read it once more.

Athstone,

I understand from my solicitors that you have at long last seen fit to darken England's shores with your presence. It is to be hoped that in making this journey to the land of your ancestors you have come to terms with your heritage and plan to embrace your future.

It is my wish that you attend me on the occasion of my birthday, and therefore I have arranged for a post-chaise to bring you to Weybridge Castle. Please do not interpret this as permission to invite others to accompany you. The castle will be yours soon enough to do with as you will; for now my word is law here and I expect you to act accordingly.

Josiah Weybridge

P.S. My health is not good, and there is much for you to learn before you step into my shoes.

"What a lot of damned cheek," Gavin muttered. What did the duke expect—that he would arrive with a ship-load of drunken sailors whom he'd met on the voyage over? Or a bit of muslin to share his bedroom? And as for answering to a damned title, instead of his perfectly good name...

He frowned. The duke might be crotchety because he was ill. It must have cost Weybridge dearly to add that last sentence. And he *was* sending a post-chaise...

"Benson," he called. When the valet silently appeared in the doorway once more, Gavin folded the letter and slid it into his pocket. "When a gentleman prefers not to spend a day or two cooped up inside a post-chaise, how does he go about getting himself across England?"

"A curricle and team, sir. But the skill required to drive such an equipage—"

"Never mind that. Can you get me set up by the day after tomorrow?"

The duke had made clear that his word was law in the castle, but he hadn't said a thing about what went on outside the walls. Gavin figured that as long as he didn't drive the curricle up the stairs and through the public rooms, how he got to the castle was his own business.

Even more important, as long as he had a means of travel he could call his own, it would be his choice—and not the duke's—as to how long he stayed.

Chapter 2

The Beckhams' hunting lodge was only a few hours from Weybridge Castle, so Isabel's post-chaise swept through the gates with a flourish and pulled up in the huge inner courtyard by midafternoon. A footman paid off the postboys, and by the time the housekeeper had come to greet Isabel, her single trunk had been brought in.

"You'll be in the green suite as usual," Mrs. Meeker said. "And may I say, my lady, how good it is to have you here? It will be a tonic for His Grace to have the family gathered once more."

"Then we're all to be here? Hartford and Lady Emily as well?" She hadn't seen her brother since the Season ended months ago—not that she had encountered him with any frequency even then, for Lucien had no patience with musicales and soirees. And as for Emily—the last time Isabel had seen her sister had been more than a year ago, not long after the calamity.

"Yes, my lady. Would you like tea brought to your room right away?"

"No, later in the drawing room will be fine. But I haven't even asked after my uncle. How is he, Mrs. Meeker?"

The housekeeper's face tightened. "Dr. Mason shakes his head, my lady, but His Grace has a strong will, so we must hope for the best."

"Just let me wash the road dust from my face, and I will go and make my curtsey to him."

"He left orders for no one to disturb him. He is resting now so he will be able to come down for dinner."

"I see," Isabel said slowly. Even the duke's letter hadn't made her believe the situation was truly dire; she supposed that was because he had written it himself rather than turning the matter over to a secretary.

The footmen had already brought up her trunk, and her maid was unpacking when Isabel reached the green suite. She washed her face slowly, enjoying the restoring touch of warm water against her skin, and decided not to take the time to have Martha brush her hair. Instead, she captured the loose ends that had slipped out of the knot at the back of her head, tucking them back in place and smoothing the blue-black strands until they gleamed once more. She was about to go downstairs when she heard a soft tap on the door.

"Are you in there, Isabel?"

Isabel waved her maid away and opened the door herself. "Emily? I thought I was the first to arrive. How long have you been here?"

"No more than half an hour. I heard a ruckus in the hall and knew it must be you. I thought we might meet up on the road."

"Traveling together would have been fun—but I didn't come from Maxton Abbey. I was at a hunting party."

"At this season? What on earth were you hunting?"

"The Beckhams are training a new pack of foxhounds—though the best I can say for the sport is that the pursuit was never predictable." Isabel held her sister by the shoulders and studied her. Emily was even more slender than she'd been the last time Isabel saw her, but her golden-brown hair displayed a healthy glow and her dark-brown eyes sparkled with the reflection of her butter-yellow dress. "I still think it unfair that you grew two inches taller than I am. But Emily, you look wonderful! What is your secret?"

Emily laughed. "I find it helps not to read Father's letters. They all say the same thing anyway. *It is past time to give up these crotchets and come home. I've arranged for you to meet a man of good character who will overlook your past...*"

Isabel gasped. "As if what happened was *your* fault! I can hardly believe he's still trying to marry you off."

"Quite seriously, too. He's run through the entire roster of unmarried earls and viscounts, and most of the barons. In fact, his last letter mentioned a plain mister—but one of *excellent* family, I assure you."

"I thought you said you didn't read his letters."

"Well, there's always the odd chance that someday he might say he's sorry for how the last betrothal he arranged for me turned out. I wouldn't stake my jewelry on it even if I still owned any, but..."

"Oh, Emily. I was so afraid—" Isabel broke off.

"That I would go into a decline over Rivington?"

"That you would be haunted forever by this misfortune."

"Not I," Emily said.

But on closer inspection, Isabel thought a shadow lay deep in her sister's eyes, and Emily's smile was not quite as sunny as it once had been.

Emily took a deep breath. "Has Mrs. Meeker told you about Uncle Josiah?"

"Only that he's resting this afternoon. Have you seen him? Is it as serious as he seemed to think when he wrote?" Belatedly, Isabel noticed that her maid was listening. "Martha, go and get settled. You can finish unpacking later. I'll wear—oh, let's see. The blue, I think, for dinner tonight."

"Yes, ma'am. I'll take it down to press." Martha removed the dress from the sparsely filled wardrobe.

As the door closed behind the maid, Emily tipped her head to one side and regarded the meager contents remaining in Isabel's trunk. "That's all the clothes you brought? I thought you said you were at a hunting party. Didn't you have to change your dress four times a day?"

It was silly to feel so sensitive in front of her sister, but Isabel wasn't ready to admit what a very tight budget she was on. "I would have spent the week in perfect comfort if my favorite dinner gown hadn't suffered an unfortunate encounter with a glass of red wine on my first evening with the Beckhams. Then a clumsy young man trod on a hem while we were dancing. Anyway, this is only family, and no one will care if they see me in the same few garments over and over."

"And here I was hoping to supplement my outdated wardrobe by borrowing your magnificence, Lady Maxwell!"

"*You*, outdated? Only because you live in the tiniest village you could find, I'll wager, with no dressmaker at hand."

"You would lose, for I've no money for new gowns. Even a cottage is expensive when you must pay for everything yourself. At least you have a home."

Maxwell provided her with a place to live, that was true—but neither Maxton Abbey nor the London house had ever felt like home, and Isabel expected they never would. But allowing herself to think like this would only make her maudlin, so she forced a smile. "If we get too bored, we shall exchange dresses. At least then we will each have something different to look at."

Emily laughed. "Come, Isabel, I'm longing for my tea. I do hope the tray is already waiting." She linked her arm in Isabel's.

"Is Mrs. Dalrymple resting from the journey, or shall we collect her before going down?"

"Now there's a story," Emily said. "She isn't here."

"Your faithful companion has deserted you? She can't have been offered a better job."

"The local squire has proposed marriage—and though Mrs. Dalrymple protested that she could not abandon me at such a time, I insisted you would be a perfectly adequate chaperone. I was assuming, of course, that you would be here—though my answer would have been the same even if I'd known you were not."

"Mrs. Dalrymple, *married*?"

"It hardly seems fair, does it—that she has a second husband? I grant that Sir Cedric is red-faced and quite square in shape, and his laugh sometimes sounds as if he's braying. But I've never heard that he's been unkind to a single soul—and I suppose that is more important than his personal oddities."

Isabel felt something like envy flicker deep in her stomach. "More important indeed," she said softly as they strolled down the wide staircase to the main drawing room.

Unlike the original section of the castle, this wing had been added within the last hundred years by a previous duke who had thought himself something of an architect. With defense against siege no longer a priority, he had lined the outer walls with windows rather than arrow slits. In the winter, Isabel recalled, the fires at either end of the room had to be kept roaring just to hold frostbite at bay.

But on this pleasant late-September afternoon, the windows were open to the terrace and the room was flooded with fresh air and sunlight so strong that Isabel had to stop in the doorway to let her eyes adjust. A light breeze stirred the draperies and carried the scent of newly cut grass across to her, along with a heavier, spicier scent that was only vaguely familiar. She'd have to ask one of the gardeners which flower or tree it came from.

She was startled to see a tall, silent figure silhouetted by the window. Not the butler; Chalmers would have spoken immediately, and he wouldn't have stood there staring across the grounds anyway. And not a maid, for this shape was definitely male. It must be Lucien, though she was surprised he could have come all the way from London by now.

"Is that you, dear brother?" Emily called gaily.

The man at the window turned, and Isabel's throat dried up. Lucien didn't move like that, with the sinuous grace of a wild animal.

She knew now what the scent had been and why she had almost recognized it. It was not a tree and not a flower—at least not directly.

It was the cologne favored by the Earl of Maxwell.

His deep voice reached out, curled around Isabel's heart, and squeezed. "Good afternoon, Lady Emily. How kind of you to refer to me as a brother. And Isabel— my lovely wife. Shall I do the pretty and say that it's a pleasure, or would that be just a little too much, under the circumstances?"

* * *

Lucien managed a tankard of ale whenever they stopped to change horses, and he swallowed an ill-assorted repast—no one with the slightest claim to sensibility could have called it a meal—at the journey's midpoint. When he suggested that everyone would benefit from a longer rest at the coaching inn, however, the senior postboy—a man who looked twice Lucien's age—shook his head and said flatly, "It's more than my position is worth, my lord, if I don't get you there on time to suit the duke."

So much for being a man of the world, Lucien thought glumly as he climbed back into the post-chaise. He couldn't even seem to give orders for his own journey. Someday, by Jove, he'd have a stable of his own, with a new team of high-steppers and a different well-sprung vehicle for every day of the week. He occupied himself with choosing possible paint schemes for the curricle of his dreams as well as selecting the perfect team to pull it, and ultimately he nodded off. The nap at least made the remaining hours pass more quickly, though his troubled sleep left him feeling groggy, as well as hungover and rumpled, when the post-chaise finally drew up in front of Weybridge Castle's front entrance.

He'd barely crossed the threshold when his youngest sister descended on him. "One of the footmen spotted your chaise approaching across the valley," Emily said. "Come and have tea. You must be starving after traveling all the way from London."

"And not a thing fit to eat on the road," Lucien agreed. "But Uncle Josiah won't like me appearing like this—I'm not fit for company." He turned toward the stairway.

"Uncle isn't coming down this afternoon. It's just us— Isabel and me, and Maxwell."

Lucien stopped in midstride and gave a low whistle. "Isabel and Maxwell are in the same room?"

"Now you know why I want you."

"All right, then, I'll come—but only because I have to see this, and since it's obvious you haven't freshened up or changed, either. I'd swear I've seen that gown before."

"You have indeed, but it's unkind of you to point it out, Lucien. What inspired you to travel across England dressed like *that*, anyway?"

"Not my choice—and it's not a story that's fit for your ears." He offered his arm.

Emily wrinkled her nose but let him pull her hand through the crook of his elbow. "You smell like the taproom, you know. Or is the smell of ale covering up something even worse?"

"Wouldn't you like to know? Conditions must be pretty tense in the drawing room, if you're so anxious to have a distraction that you're willing to put up with my dirt. Lord and Lady Maxwell sniping at each other, are they?"

"They're being so polite it's almost worse than insults." As they reached the drawing room door, Emily called out, "Look who I found, Isabel—and do make him tell why he's wearing evening dress at this hour of the day. Lucien says it's too scandalous a story for me to hear—as though I haven't any idea what sort of pranks he's capable of. But since you're

25

married, he might take you off in a corner and whisper the details. And then you can tell me."

"It's too warm a tale even for a married lady," Lucien said. His sisters would no doubt leap to conclusions that there must be a woman involved, but there was no harm in a man burnishing his reputation, especially when he was telling no actual lies.

Lucien leaned over to kiss Isabel's hand.

She made a face and pulled away, her hazel eyes narrowing. "You need a shave. Have you fired your valet, or has he lost his mind, letting you rattle around the country looking like that?"

Now that was just plain unfair, Lucien thought—taking potshots at him, when Isabel obviously hadn't changed clothes herself. Her pink traveling dress was crumpled and creased from hours of sitting in a chaise, and there was so much dust on her slippers that she might have walked all the way from the village. He opened his mouth to protest and then thought better of it.

Lucien had barely noticed the Earl of Maxwell until he bowed in greeting. But the earl addressed Isabel instead. "What a comfort it is, my dear wife, to know that you still appreciate good grooming. One would never guess it from observing you."

Isabel glared at him. "How strange to find it is my appearance which offends you, sir. I thought it was my mere existence."

Lucien pretended not to hear them. "Good to see you well, Max." He snagged a cake from the nearest stand and consumed it in one bite. "You said there was no sniping," he muttered to Emily.

She shrugged. "Apparently, they progressed while I was gone."

"It's going to be a warm few days at the castle. By the way, do you have any notion how long this house party is supposed to last? My letter didn't say."

"Nor mine."

"Well—that's a bit inconvenient, not to know when I might be back in the city."

"Why? Are you anxious to get back to your friends, or afraid your ladybird will find another protector while you're gone?"

"Not a ladybird." But Lucien said it with a mischievous smile.

"You needn't think I care," Emily sniffed. "All men are alike. You and your mistresses—"

Belatedly, Lucien recalled what had happened to Emily last year, and sobered. "Not the same thing," he said hastily. "Even if I did have a ladybird, it would be nothing like what Rivington was up to." He eyed her carefully. Emily didn't look as though she was still suffering—in fact she appeared to be blooming. But you never knew, where ladies were concerned.

"That's a comfort—for despite you being an annoyance, Lucien, I should not like to see you end up as Rivington did."

Lucien took another cake, more because he didn't know what else to say than because he was hungry. Appetite had fled with the reminder of Emily's ill-fated betrothal.

Emily had moved to the window that overlooked a corner of the great courtyard and the valley beyond. "Are we expecting anyone else?"

27

"I don't think so," Isabel said. "Uncle Josiah is hardly in any condition to plan a gala for his birthday. Why?"

"Because here's another carriage pulling up."

Lucien joined her, his cake forgotten. "Another post-chaise? I wonder who…By Jove, what a bang-up job that is!"

The curricle of his dreams stood by the front door. The vehicle was perfect, right down to the colors he had envisioned—deep green with black accents. Though now that he saw the combination for himself, Lucien decided he might have had the wheels picked out in gold instead.

The driver had already climbed down, for a groom was holding the tired horses, ready to lead them around to the stable.

Had Uncle Josiah read his mind and ordered this setup for him? What a wonderful birthday-gift-in-reverse *that* would be!

Emily jabbed him in the ribs. "You do realize you're drooling, Lucien?"

The drawing room door opened to admit the butler. "Lady Maxwell, the Marquess of Athstone has arrived." He faded away, leaving a gentleman standing on the threshold.

The pieces fell into place in Lucien's mind. *You should have expected him to turn up.*

Envy surged from the back corner of his mind, swamping his better nature. The heir of the Duke of Weybridge could afford the best—or, more accurately, he didn't need money, for he would have no lack of credit with which to buy curricles and horses.

Lucien told himself to be sensible. It wasn't as if the new Marquess of Athstone had pushed him out of a title or an estate; since Weybridge Castle belonged to Lucien's mother's family, it would never have come to him even if this chap had not been born.

Besides, Uncle Josiah had said Lucien was his favorite. No American upstart—a mere twig on some far distant branch of the family tree—was going to come between an uncle and the nephew he loved.

Lucien realized—just as the marquess's gaze came to rest on him with something like astonishment—his momentary irritation and envy had caused his hand to clench hard on the cake he held, turning it into paste that oozed through his fingers and dripped down the front of his coat.

* * *

Isabel had tried her best not to even look at her husband. Instead she had concentrated on pouring tea and then chatting with Emily. But no matter how hard she tried to exclude him, the Earl of Maxwell was not to be ignored; he asked Emily about her journey, and he politely requested a report from Isabel on their mutual friends. The moment Emily left the drawing room to fetch Lucien, Isabel turned to glare at him.

That was a mistake. He was just as handsome as he had ever been, tall and lean and dark, and so perfectly turned out that he seemed to have just stepped from his tailor's hands. But there was an edge about him now that she'd never seen—a glint of danger in his eyes. Had she missed that before, or was it new?

"Just why are you here, sir?" she demanded.

The earl, who had risen politely when Emily got to her feet, sat down again and picked up his cup. "I was invited, like the rest of you." A look of concern crept across his face. "Were you invited, Isabel? Or is *bribed* a more accurate term?"

"I don't know what you mean."

"I'm not suggesting that you aren't fond of your uncle, only that there might have been some additional inducement to encourage you to leave your chosen party behind to join this one instead. Your fellow guests must have been devastated to lose you, to say nothing of your disappointment at having to come away to a dull family gathering."

Not for the world would Isabel admit to her husband that she hadn't enjoyed herself to the fullest at the Beckhams' party. "Quite true," she sighed. "It broke my heart to leave my friends. And of course if I'd known you were to be here, I might have chosen differently."

"No, you wouldn't. I'm guessing your uncle offered to settle your debts, since I've made it clear that I will not. So I believe you'd have come no matter who else was invited."

The accusation stung. "I don't have debts," Isabel said crisply.

"You amaze me, ma'am."

His gaze roved over her, sending a wave of righteous anger flooding from her core to every extremity. Her fingertips positively itched with the desire to smack the doubt from his face. How dare he sit there and simply look at her as though she were a piece of merchandise he was thinking of buying? Or—given the circumstances—he might be considering a sale instead!

That thought made her even angrier, but before she could draw breath Emily reappeared, saying something Isabel scarcely heard about evening dress, and Lucien came to bend over her hand. If the earl hadn't been needling her, Isabel would have been too polite to tell her brother he needed a shave—true though it was. For that matter, he could do with a bath. What was he doing racketing across the country in satin knee breeches, anyway?

Then the earl spoke once more and she forgot all about Lucien. "What a comfort it is, my dear, to know that you still appreciate good grooming."

She saw red and snapped back at him about how he might prefer it if she didn't exist at all.

To her regret, the shot bounced off the earl. "Of course, now that I consider the evidence, I believe you do not owe a dressmaker. I should say you have not so much as consulted one in more than a year—since your trousseau was completed."

Isabel's face flooded with color.

"You were always so careful to look your best, Isabel. What a shame it is that you can no longer afford to do so. Your uncle Weybridge might assist...but if not, what will you do?"

"Why do you care, sir?"

His dark, aristocratic eyebrows arched. "But my dear, surely that is obvious. It reflects badly on me when you go around to society parties looking like a ragamuffin."

"Then let me have more than just pin money! I brought you riches, Maxwell—Kilburn must bring in five thousand a year at least. That estate was my dowry, and it should be my marriage portion. *Mine*, do you hear?"

For a moment she thought he hadn't heard her. Then he said, very quietly, "You've changed your tune since our last discussion of the matter. Perhaps you've found your principles to be less comfortable than you expected, in the absence of adequate funds?"

Isabel bit her lip. "All I ask is my fair share."

"Fair? I seem to remember telling you on the day after our wedding that you could have the benefits of marriage only if you were willing to honor your obligations. My stand has not changed, and under the circumstances, I find it ironic that you refer to a marriage portion. But I shall give the matter my attention, Isabel, and let you know what I decide."

Fury beyond any she had ever felt before left a metallic taste in Isabel's mouth. *Honor her obligations?* The sheer arrogance of the man, to put the blame on her!

"Lady Maxwell," the butler said from the drawing room door. "The Marquess of Athstone has arrived."

* * *

Emily wheeled away from the window at the butler's announcement. The marquess...the colonial cousin who would someday step into the Duke of Weybridge's shoes was *here?*

"What could Uncle Josiah have been thinking?" she said—louder than she'd intended.

The marquess's gaze slid from Lucien—now dripping cake onto the priceless carpet—to her, and Emily felt like crawling under a corner of the Aubusson. What had happened to her manners? Of course, listening to Isabel and Maxwell sparring was enough to put anyone on edge. And though the atmosphere in the room was entirely different now that the marquess was taking part, the tension was no less threatening.

"And you would be Miss Emily Arden, I think?" the marquess asked.

"*Lady* Emily," she said curtly, and wanted to bite her tongue. She'd never been a stickler about her title; why had she jumped to correct him?

"I beg your pardon. I am but an ignorant newcomer."

He didn't look it, she had to admit. His boots shone as brightly as just-cleaned silver, and the gold tassels dangling from the top edges still swung with jaunty ease. His broad shoulders must have been a tailor's dream. His pantaloons were cut tight, showing off strong thighs; his linen was snowy white and perfectly creased, and his hair was brushed smooth so that a random ray of sunlight cast a golden gleam over his chestnut curls.

If he'd planned his entrance to be theatrical, he couldn't have done better. From the corner of her eye, Emily saw Lucien rub at his stubbly jaw and then try to brush mashed cake off his face, and she had to fight down a hysterical desire to giggle.

"Lady Maxwell," the marquess said, "I beg your pardon for bursting in on you like this."

He didn't even *sound* like an ignorant newcomer, Emily thought with irritation. His tone was neither harsh nor twangy, and his voice neither brashly loud nor self-effacingly soft. Even his accent—though not of English origin—settled on her ears with a strange sort of ease.

This, she thought, was a man who desperately needed putting in his place.

The marquess frowned a little. "Was that correct? Or shall I call you Lady Isabel?"

"She's either," Emily said. "One title by birth, one by marriage. Take your choice."

"I prefer to be called Lady Isabel," Isabel said, with a sidelong glance at her husband. "Would you care for tea, my lord?"

The marquess's face lit with humor, his eyes gleaming like sapphires. "And I prefer to be called by my name. Gavin Waring, at your service. If you can bear it, you must call me Gavin—for we are cousins, are we not?"

Well, *that* sounded like an American, Emily thought. She wondered what Uncle Josiah would make of his heir having such democratic tendencies. "Very distant ones, Cousin Gavin," she said sweetly. "What a poetic rhythm that title has! Allow me to present Lord Maxwell, my sister's husband. And Lord Hartford, my brother. Now, about that tea…?"

"Thank you, Cousin Lady Emily," he murmured.

Emily's jaw dropped.

Before she could correct him, he had continued. "I stopped in the village to remove the evidence of my travel before coming on to the castle, and the landlord of the local coaching inn provided me with excellent refreshment."

"And it wasn't tea, either, I'll wager," Lucien muttered.

"An outstanding ale," the marquess said. "At least, it seemed so to me. But you might accompany me someday, Cousin Hartford, and give me the benefit of your experience."

Emily's back was to the door and all her attention was focused on the marquess and her brother. She considered

34

it an even bet as to whether Lucien would get starchy or invite the American to call him by his first name.

He plumped for friendliness—no doubt, Emily thought, because he was hoping to get a chance to drive that spanking curricle.

She was trying so hard not to laugh that the first clue she had of yet another newcomer was a deep, lazy, drawling voice from behind her. "I wouldn't recommend Hartford's palate, Athstone, because his tastes are unpredictable at best."

Every head in the room abruptly turned in his direction as the Earl of Chiswick added, "How unflattering to find that my offspring are all startled to see me here. Or have you conveniently forgotten that as your father, I am a member of this family?"

Chapter 3

❧

*W*hat a strange family he had been cast into, to be sure. Gavin couldn't help but enjoy the expressions on the faces of his new cousins as they regarded their father. He spotted wariness from Isabel, a strange mixture of trepidation and annoyance from Lucien, and…could that possibly be revulsion on Emily's face? Her expression was gone so quickly that he couldn't be certain what he'd seen, but his amusement fled nonetheless.

The Earl of Chiswick advanced languidly to the center of the room as if he were the major player on a London stage. "A pleasure to meet you, Athstone," he said with a tiny bow. "If it's wine you're tasting, you might allow me to educate your palate. For ale, you can't go wrong with your cousin the duke, who despite his high title is something of a connoisseur of the brewing art. But you must not trust Hartford. No, never Hartford."

The young lord's jaw clenched tight.

"How reassuring it is, my son," the earl went on, "to see that you know how a gentleman dresses for the evening." He raised his quizzing glass. "Even though, judging by the crumpled nature of your garments, it was apparently *last* evening you were dressing for. Whatever salary you pay your valet, it would seem to be too much. Isabel, my love, I do admire that dress, as I believe I have told you each and every time in the last two years that I have seen you wearing it. And Emily—I am touched that you do not seem to have fallen into a paralyzing decline as your letters have implied. But Mrs. Meeker tells me you arrived without your companion. My dear, at one-and-twenty you are hardly on the shelf, and you must not behave as though you are an ape leader with no reputation to lose. But I beg your pardon, Athstone." He bowed his head a fraction. "We must not air family business in front of our new cousin."

He'd been doing a good job of it up till then, Gavin thought. In fact, right up until the moment when it appeared Lady Emily was going to burst out with a reply—and then her father had spiked her guns by reminding her of manners he himself did not employ. That might be why she had worn such a strange expression when she saw her father—because the rules didn't seem to apply equally across the generations.

"Your uncle Josiah has ordered dinner served at eight," Chiswick went on. "He has requested formal dress for the occasion, Hartford, so I suspect your valet will need every moment of the time if he is to present you adequately."

Lucien gritted his teeth, made a perfunctory bow, and went out without a word.

"You seem to know a great deal about the household, sir," Isabel observed. "Have you and Mrs. Meeker been gossiping in the housekeeper's parlor?"

"Josiah told me his plans over dinner last night and requested that no one fuss over him or ask questions about his health…I'm sorry; did I fail to mention that I arrived yesterday? My lamentable memory."

"You should consult a doctor about this forgetfulness of yours, Father," Emily said. "I'm going up to rest, Isabel. Are you coming?"

Isabel leaped up. "I do have a bit of a headache."

Chiswick said, "Maxwell, there's a matter you and I need to discuss. You will excuse us, Athstone?"

"Of course." Gavin noticed that Isabel had paused in midstep to listen, almost pulling her sister off her feet. Emily's skirt swayed, giving him just a glimpse of a slender ankle.

"It's about that stallion you have at Kilburn," Chiswick said. "A friend of mine asked whether you would ever consider selling him."

Gavin followed the ladies out of the drawing room, trying to maintain a discreet distance. But he couldn't help but see Isabel's slumped shoulders and tightly compressed lips as she turned to her sister, and he heard the soothing murmur of Emily's voice as they climbed the curving stairway together. He wondered what Isabel had been hoping her father would say—and why she had felt such pain when he talked of a horse instead. Or was it only her headache that made her appear so miserable?

Left to himself, he wandered, looking around the castle. He poked his head past half-open doors and found a long, narrow room lined with bookshelves, and a small, square room full of plush but uncomfortable-looking chairs. Everything he saw was luxurious, grand, elegant—satin and brocade draperies, rich dark wood paneling, velvet-covered furniture, coffered ceilings, carved plaster friezes, life-sized paintings. The carpets were so thick his feet sank into them, while the black-and-white marble floor of the entrance hall was polished till it reflected sunlight like a mirror.

This luxury was hardly what he'd expected when he'd first heard that his cousin's home was a castle. Where were the staircases twisting down to dungeons, and the huge, thickly embroidered tapestries to keep out the creeping cold in winter, and the fireplaces large enough to roast a full ox? The outside had been promising—stone walls stretching four stories tall, with towers where archers might have lurked and battlements high enough to conceal pots of flaming oil ready to pour down on invaders. But inside…

These fancies of his were getting out of hand. Surely he wasn't disappointed to learn that he would not be sleeping in a pile of furs on a stone floor!

Gavin backed out of the reception parlor and nodded genially to a footman who stood near the front door. The servant's eyes widened in shock. Gavin suspected he was accustomed to receiving no more notice than the furniture; his job apparently was nothing more than to open the door whenever someone wanted to go in or out. It was true that the doors were huge, but Gavin had noticed when he arrived that they were perfectly balanced and seemed to move at a touch. Even Emily—*Lady* Emily, he corrected himself—slender as she was, could have managed them. But no—a servant in powdered wig, heavy brocaded coat, knee breeches, and white stockings was sentenced to stand there and wait, just in case. What a waste of strong, healthy manpower!

Perhaps someday, Gavin could do something about that. But for now, the duke was still in charge—*My word is law here*—and as the heir in waiting, Gavin would do better to observe and think. And be very cautious about what he said. If, that was, he decided to stay at all.

He wandered down a side hall and found a walnut-paneled room dominated by a table with eight places already set. He saw movement in an alcove at one end, and a moment later the butler came into view, wearing an apron and still holding a candlestick and a polishing cloth. "My lord, is there anything you require?"

"No, I was just startled to find such a small dining room in such a very large house." Gavin waved a hand at the table.

"This, sir, is the family dining room. His Grace prefers to use it when the group is to be a small one—that is, fewer than sixteen sitting down at table."

"Of course," Gavin muttered. At Weybridge Castle, *small* was apparently a question of perspective.

"The main dining room is just beyond that door." The butler nodded toward a section of paneling.

To Gavin, it looked exactly like the others that lined the room—some heavily carved, some displaying oil paintings of hunting scenes. There was no knob, and only on close inspection did he see hinges along one side.

"The table there can be extended to seat forty-two," the butler went on. "Larger parties are held in the great hall, in the old wing of the castle. I recall that when Lady Drusilla married the Earl of Chiswick, we seated nearly two hundred for the wedding breakfast. But there has been no celebration as large in all the years since. If there is nothing else, my lord?"

No, that put me neatly in my place.

He went back into the hall and found the other way into the main dining room easily enough. The slabs of mahogany that formed the polished tabletop could have built half a house in Baltimore. Around the next corner he discovered a billiard room and idled away a few minutes with a cue before going up to dress for dinner.

As he stepped onto the gallery that ran in a square around the open staircase, he realized that he had no idea where he was going—and every door was closed. He contemplated the possibilities. He could go down to ask the butler, or he could start knocking at random. Either way, he'd look like a fool, but he'd rather brave the servants than take the chance of meeting the seriously ill duke for the first time by banging on his door to ask directions.

He was starting down the stairs when a door opened nearby and Emily came out. She was hardly his first choice for assistance, Gavin thought, but any port in a storm. "Lady Emily—"

"You're going down already, sir? That is a very nice coat, but if you think it's going to pass inspection with Uncle Josiah as formal evening wear, I'm afraid you're in for a shock." She sounded as if she were instructing a child.

"I would be happy to change if only I knew where to find my room. And thank you for the compliment, by the way."

"Compliment?"

"Yes—to my 'very nice coat.'"

"Oh, that. Well, I suppose it does well enough. Mrs. Meeker didn't tell you which room she'd assigned?"

"The housekeeper? I encountered only the butler when I arrived."

She nodded wisely. "Chalmers can be a bit stiff-necked. Let me take this headache powder to Isabel—she might know." She tapped on a door and went in.

Two possibilities had been eliminated, Gavin noted—her room and Isabel's. That left only twenty or so to check.

Emily returned a moment later, shaking her head. "She thinks it likely you've been assigned the gold suite, since that's the one which has been set aside for the Marquess of Athstone ever since this wing was built."

Gavin said ruefully, "I'm not certain I like that idea. Nothing good ever seems to happen to the heirs around here."

"Superstitious, are you? There's no cause to be afraid of the room, you know—it's only an ordinary bedroom, with no spirits possessing it." She led the way around the corner. "It's all the way around the other side of the gallery, though—just about as far from the duke's rooms as it's possible to get."

Gavin's spine still prickled at the slur. So she thought he was worried about ghosts?

"Besides, the suite hasn't been used in years. Uncle Josiah's son died before he was old enough to leave the nursery, and since then, the heir of the moment has always been treated like any other visitor."

"I thought you said this was the marquess's room."

"I did—but since there was always the possibility that Uncle would have another son one day, the next in line for the title wasn't officially known as the marquess." She looked up at him appraisingly. "Come to think of it, you're the first he's ever referred to by the title, but I suppose that's because he's so ill. You do understand that the title you bear is only a courtesy? It's not as if you have any official function or any power."

"Yes, the solicitors made that quite clear."

"Well, it gives you and Lucien a bit in common—that you both have honorary titles, I mean. Though Lucien's definitely the heir to Chiswick, while you—"

"There is no need to explain to me the possibility that should my cousin marry again and produce a son, I would be...*poof*! Plain old Gavin Waring once more." At the moment, he couldn't think of a more inviting idea.

"Why *Waring*, by the way? The family name has always been Mainwaring."

"Things are simpler in the Americas. It seemed a natural choice."

"No wonder it took so long for the solicitors to find you. Here we are."

The door she had led him to looked no different from the others. "Numbers might be a good idea," Gavin said under his breath.

"Like a common boardinghouse? Then what excuse could a noble gentleman possibly give when he is discovered in the wrong bedroom at a house party, with a lady who is not his wife?" Her voice was crisp.

"Does that happen a lot?"

"Often enough. Well, try the door. Either your valet will be there, or we'll ring for Chalmers." Her brows drew together. "You did bring a valet, did you not?"

Gavin opened the door, and she leaned around him to peer inside the room.

This was what she called an ordinary bedroom?

In the first place, there was no bed. At one end of the room was a fireplace, with a cheerful blaze crackling. At the other end was a massive piece of furniture that looked more like a dining room sideboard than anything belonging in a bedroom. On the far wall two immensely tall windows looked out across a valley where a small lake lay nestled among the hills, like a sapphire in a velvet-green setting. A pair of chairs had been drawn up so that someone sitting there could easily admire the view.

He didn't notice the door that was just beyond the big bureau until it swung open and Benson appeared. Behind the valet, Gavin saw the corner of a tall canopied bed with gold velvet hangings. The gold suite, Emily had called it. Now he knew what she had meant.

The valet bowed respectfully, looked from Gavin to Emily, and said, "Good evening, sir. Your clothes are brushed and laid out, and I am ready to attend you. Unless you and your guest would prefer privacy?"

Emily's face flamed. She muttered something about impertinence and hurried off down the gallery.

Gavin grinned and closed the door behind her. This business of living in a castle might not be quite such a nuisance as he'd thought.

I wonder if this gathering could be considered a house party, where a gentleman can wander into the bedroom of a lady who is not his wife...

❖ ❖ ❖

Isabel's blue dinner gown hung on the wardrobe door, pressed and ready, when she reached her bedroom. She regarded the dress without enthusiasm, already hearing in her head what her father was likely to say about her appearing in yet another old garment. The Earl of Chiswick had long ago perfected the art of paying compliments that cut like the edge of a well-honed sword—the blade so sharp that sometimes seconds passed before the injury was even felt.

His opinion shouldn't matter to her any longer, of course. Once a woman married, not only her property but all responsibility for her well-being shifted from her father to her husband. What she wore was no business of her father's. Most gentlemen probably wouldn't even notice—or remember—what their daughters wore on widely scattered evenings over a period of months.

But the Earl of Chiswick wasn't most gentlemen. So the question was, when he noticed that his daughter was practically dressed in rags, why hadn't he called her husband to task? If he truly cared for Isabel, surely he would question why her husband had not provided a new dress for her now and then. Her mother would have found a way—but then the countess had been gone since just before Isabel's twelfth birthday.

Instead, the earl had flicked her with his trademark sarcasm—as though the lack of variety in her wardrobe were Isabel's deliberate choice. He had scolded Emily for her reluctance to consider marriage—as though the death of her betrothed had been no more important than a breakfast egg being overcooked and should be as easily forgotten. He had sent Lucien to his room as though he were a child.

Some things and some people never changed. And they were all closed up here in the castle with him, for heaven knew how long.

Isabel swallowed the headache powder that Emily brought for her, then rang for her maid and took her time in dressing for dinner. Before she left her room, she made certain that her hair was brushed to a blue-black gleam and every strand was perfectly in order, with every fold of her gown precisely aligned. At least there would be nothing about her grooming for her father to complain of. A few minutes before eight, she draped her mother's Norwich silk shawl over her shoulders and stepped out into the gallery.

A door stood open between her room and the stairs, and just as Isabel passed, the Earl of Maxwell came out. Despite her best intention to walk on without taking notice, Isabel's toes seemed to take root in the gallery's oak plank floor. Her gaze wandered over him. He was soberly dressed in pure black and white, with his only ornamentation being a bit of fanciful embroidery on his white waistcoat and a single flawless diamond in his neckcloth. Even the knee breeches and silk stockings, which often made shorter men look like characters in a pantomime, only made him look more handsome than ever.

Belatedly, she realized that he had come out of the bedroom directly next to hers—the matching bedroom of the green suite. She told herself it didn't matter. By habit and custom they still occupied adjoining bedrooms at the London house and at Maxton Abbey as well. For the lord and lady of the house to move to separate wings would cause comment; servants talked, and soon all of society would know. So on the rare occasions when they both found themselves in the same location, only the width of a dressing room separated them.

After all, sharing a suite was a great deal different from sharing a bed.

Still, her stomach quivered a little at the idea of the earl being right next door. It had been months since the last time that had happened. She had miscalculated the date of his return from a house party and found herself under the same roof, lying sleepless in her bed, knowing that he was only a matter of feet away from her.

Sleepless, she told herself, because she had been worried about what interpretation he might put on her presence. If he had thought her presence in the room next to his was an invitation, rather than an accident…

But he hadn't, of course—and he would take no more notice of this arrangement of rooms at the castle.

Without comment, the earl offered his arm.

Isabel shook her head. "There is no need. I wasn't hovering in the hope you would escort me."

"I am quite aware you're able to walk down the stairs by yourself—but come along so we will not be late. I was beginning to think you might have forgotten the time."

"You waited here to waylay me?"

"Waylay? No. It merely seemed the polite thing to do."

"You aren't known for politeness, sir. Not to me, at least." But there was little point in quarreling over so trivial a matter, so she laid her hand on his arm and let him guide her to the top of the staircase. "What did my father tell you?"

"That he has a friend who would like to buy my stallion—which is not for sale."

"Is that all he said? He did not scold you?"

"About what, ma'am?"

He sounded quite serious—and entirely oblivious. "Nothing of importance." She hated that there was a catch in her voice.

"If you hope he might have been instructing me in how to be a better husband—"

"That would have been amusing to hear," she said bitterly. "The Earl of Chiswick's rules for a happy marriage."

"I would not have paid attention to advice coming from such a source. In any case, I have now considered your request from this afternoon, Isabel."

She had to think for a moment, because so much had happened. Was it possible he was talking about her outburst over the estate that had been her dowry?

Don't get your hopes up, she told herself. *He's probably going to say no—and then congratulate himself about being a modern, progressive gentleman because he gave his wife's opinion a single instant's thought before refusing.*

"And I believe we might come to an agreement," he went on.

Isabel's foot skidded on the marble floor at the base of the stairs. "You...you do?" She felt almost hoarse.

Was it to be so easy? If all she'd had to do was ask...how foolish that she had not done so long before!

"You requested a fair share of the income from Kilburn. I agree—but only as part of a bargain."

Her momentary elation vanished. "What do you want in return?" she asked warily.

"A simple thing."

Something warned her that despite his deceptively calm tone, there would be nothing simple about his request. Isabel wanted to run, but she seemed to have lost control of her body and was inexorably floating across to the drawing room. The voices of the family members who had already gathered for dinner seemed distant, almost blurry to her ears.

"A very simple thing," the Earl of Maxwell repeated, "and no more than you promised me when we wed. I have been patient for more than a year, waiting for you to tire of your principles and live up to your obligations. I want an heir. All you need to do to find me generous, Isabel, is to give me a healthy son."

❀ ❀ ❀

The drawing room seemed to be empty when Lucien came downstairs a few minutes before the time set for dinner. A tray full of decanters and glasses had been set up on a side table, but it had obviously not been disturbed. Apparently he was the very first to arrive.

"A snap of the fingers for my father's opinions about how long it takes me to turn myself out," he muttered, and was startled when Gavin poked his head around the corner of a wingbacked chair. "Oh—you're already here."

"I didn't want to chance offending the duke by losing my way in the corridors."

Lucien poured two glasses of wine and handed one to Gavin. "You'll get the hang of it. First learn how to get around the new wing—well, it's probably a hundred years old now, but that's much newer than the original section, and more important. You can pick up the rest gradually. There's a sort of map somewhere in the library."

"Thank you. I shall look for it."

"Or if you're anxious for a full tour, ask my father. It's not that I recommend spending a morning with him, you understand, but he does know this castle better than anyone save Uncle Josiah. And it would keep him from annoying the rest of us for a while."

Gavin looked thoughtful. "It's not my place to give advice, of course, but it seems to me that the more reaction you show your father, the more he's likely to jab at you."

"Well, not reacting is easier said than done when he holds the purse strings. You'll find that out with Uncle Josiah when he starts pressuring you about making a good marriage."

"Perhaps it would help, when your father is talking to you, if you were to think instead about our trip to the village to test the ale."

Lucien was pleased beyond all reason. "You still want me to go?"

"I can't quite see tucking my cousin Weybridge up in rugs in my curricle to make the trip, no matter how good his judgment where ales are concerned."

Lucien laughed, feeling carefree for the first time in days. "If I allowed myself to think about it, I would envy you that curricle, you know. It's just the sort I'd like to have. May I drive it one day?"

"Of course. But wait till my own team arrives."

"Oh, Uncle Josiah has a famous stable." Lucien heard a rhythmic creak from the hall. A moment later, a footman pushed a wheeled chair into the drawing room. A couple of big dogs followed, flopping down next to the duke's chair with heavy sighs.

Uncle Josiah seemed to have shrunk, Lucien thought— though the fact that the duke was not on his feet no doubt contributed to the impression.

"Uncle Josiah." Lucien gave a deep, formal bow.

"Hartford," the duke growled, but he looked on past Lucien to Gavin. "And you must be Athstone."

"Technically," Gavin said, "I'm not, sir. At least, if I understand the rules from your solicitors' explanations—"

"That's *Your Grace*, to you. Fussy old women, those law readers. I expect they told you all about how you're only the heir presumptive, so if I have a son you'll be out in the cold. Exactly how likely do you think that is?"

"I have no idea, Your Grace," Gavin said. "But it does me no harm to hope for that eventuality."

The duke glowered and then gave a rusty laugh. "You expect me to believe you don't want this? All of this?"

Gavin looked into the distance, almost as if he'd seen a mirage, and for a moment Lucien thought he was going to admit that he'd been lying his head off. But he didn't need to say it; the thing was obvious. Who *wouldn't* want Weybridge, with its thousands of acres of lush, productive land, its woods and fields filled with game, its lakes teeming with fish?

Gavin said, "You will believe as you like, Your Grace. What power do I have to change the mind of the Duke of Weybridge?"

"Trying to smooth me down now, are you?" The duke looked him over closely.

Lucien was impressed despite himself, for Gavin stood perfectly still, without coloring or turning a hair, under the inspection.

"Think you can get round me with fast words, eh?" the duke went on. "What's this I hear about you arriving in a bang-up, brand-new curricle? Do not think to send the bill to me for your affectation. Or for that fine ward-robe—which I'm certain did not accompany you from the farm field where my solicitors found you. I'll give you an allowance—I can do nothing else—but I won't be held up for your extravagance."

Gavin's forehead wrinkled. "Then I suppose you will also refuse to pay for the high-steppers I bought to pull the curricle. What a shame that I asked my other groom to bring them along by easy stages so I'd have them to start the drive back. Well, I might return them to the seller, if I explain the circumstances."

"The circumstances?" The duke sounded wary.

"No doubt someone would like to own the very horses that the cheeseparing Duke of Weybridge can't afford."

Lucien wanted to cheer.

The duke sputtered. "Damned cheek!"

"As for my grooms, I've already suggested they stay in the village rather than come here, in case it was too much trouble for the household to accommodate them."

"You must be in your cups, you chawbacon—suggesting I haven't room for your servants."

Lucien saw the flutter of a skirt outside the drawing room door. That must be Emily, no doubt pausing to listen in the hope that the fireworks—and the volume of the duke's ire—would die down before she had to come in.

"Of course, that wasn't the only reason I left them at the inn," Gavin went on. "They have instructions to watch over my mistress there and keep her out of trouble."

The duke stared, his brows lowered—momentarily speechless.

Lucien gave a low, soundless whistle. "Gavin, ladies present. Well, one lady at least, and she doesn't care for talk of mistresses." He heard the unmistakable timber of his father's voice as the Earl of Chiswick greeted Emily in the hall, and he was not surprised when an instant later Emily stalked into the room and made her curtsey to the duke.

"Miss Emily," Gavin said. "I beg your pardon; I forgot. Lady Emily—"

Her gaze swept across Gavin as if he were empty air. "Since Father tells us we are not to make a fuss over you, Uncle Josiah, I shall only say that I hope your doctor is wrong to think your condition is serious. There—now we shall move on to other things. If we're to remain at the castle for a while, Isabel and I should make calls upon your neighbors. Do you happen to know whether Sir George and Lady Fletcher are in residence at Mallowan?"

"Haven't heard any different," the duke said.

The Earl of Chiswick had quietly followed his daughter into the drawing room. He filled glasses for himself, Emily, and the duke. "They are indeed at home. I encountered Sir George this afternoon on my ride."

"That would be the best place to start, I suppose," Emily said. "I am certain Lady Fletcher will know exactly who else is at home in the neighborhood."

Isabel and Lord Maxwell came in. Isabel looked pale, Lucien thought, and she quickly took her hand off her husband's arm and went to join Emily.

Lucien blinked in surprise. She had been touching Maxwell? No; he must have been seeing things.

Emily plowed on, sounding determined. "Their daughter is just a few years younger than I—surely she has made her come-out by now. Isabel, have you encountered her in London? Isabel, are you listening? Do you recall Miss Fletcher?"

Isabel seemed to shake herself. "She's called Chloe, I believe. I'm certain I heard her name associated with...I don't quite recall who. Mr. Lancaster, I think."

"What a coincidence." Emily looked at the Earl of Chiswick over the rim of her glass. "Didn't you refer to him in your last letter to me, Father? Or was that a different Mr. Lancaster?"

"No, it was the same one," Chiswick admitted smoothly. "Though I have reason to know Sir George is not seriously considering him for Miss Fletcher's hand."

Lucien couldn't help himself. "And how would you know that, Father?"

"Because Father is considering Mr. Lancaster for me," Emily said, "despite the fact that I'm not interested in marrying."

Lucien had to sympathize. He wasn't interested in being married any more than Emily was, but that hadn't stopped the earl from suggesting matches for him, either, so he understood how annoyed she was. Their situations were different, however—Emily was getting perilously close to being on the shelf, but for Lucien there was plenty of time. He didn't plan to set up his nursery before he was thirty, at least—no matter how set his father was on there being a spare, as well as an heir, for his title.

"No, Emily," the Earl of Chiswick said, "that is not the reason. You see, I know who Sir George *is* seriously considering as a match for his daughter."

Lucien felt a sudden urge to look up at the ceiling, fairly sure he'd see a sword there, dangling by a thread and about to fall on him.

The earl let the silence draw out as he moved across the room to refill his glass. "In a word—me."

Chapter 4

The silence in the drawing room was so profound that Emily's ears ached. She waited for someone—the Earl of Chiswick himself, perhaps—to burst out laughing at his jest, for surely he must be joking. At his age, to think of taking a new wife—

"My goodness," Chiswick said gently. "One would think you are all startled by my announcement."

"Startled?" Lucien said. "Smacked in the gob, more like."

"But my son, surely you of all people should have anticipated this. When you refused to consider the *sixth* young lady I suggested as a potential bride, I was forced to conclude that you are not...inclined toward females. It thus falls back on me to make certain our noble house does not end with you."

"Not *inclined*?" Lucien was sputtering. "I'll have you know I am *entirely*—"

"Ladies present," Gavin murmured. "Well, one lady at least." The way his gaze slid over Emily as if she didn't exist, then came to rest approvingly on Isabel, made his meaning quite clear to Emily.

How dare he simply dismiss her when he was the one who had behaved badly? Any man who hauled his

56

mistress along on a journey like this, stashing her for his convenience in the nearest inn, was unfit for the notice of a gently bred female.

Men were all the same. It didn't matter whether they were noblemen, or gentlemen, or men like this creature named Gavin Waring, who was neither noble nor gentle.

But her course of action was simple. She would simply pretend he didn't exist. He was unworthy of attention anyway. Imposing, yes, with his height and broad shoulders and regular, pleasant features. Some women might even call him handsome. Well, it only stood to reason that he must be viewed as attractive, for he'd acquired a mistress awfully quickly after landing in England. Of course there was the attraction of his title. She stole a look at him. Even without the status of a title, she had to admit, Gavin Waring would catch feminine attention. His bearing wasn't rigid enough to seem military, but the way he stood spoke of pride and confidence. Or arrogance, more like. If the solicitors really had found him in a farm field...

She was pleased to see that the interruption had given Lucien a chance to regain control of his tongue, though the distraction had obviously not restored his composure. He was still a bit red-faced and inclined to mutter when Chalmers announced the arrival of the last guest, who turned out to be the duke's physician. Emily was grateful to have a stranger in their midst, for surely that meant her father would mind his tongue.

"Dinner is served," Chalmers announced a few minutes later, and a footman appeared to wheel the duke into the small dining room.

"No quarreling over who outranks whom, now," the duke said over his shoulder. "And no escorting someone you're related to. That leaves Dr. Mason and Athstone to see the ladies into the dining room. The rest of you can just follow along."

Athstone? She'd rather be escorted by one of Uncle Josiah's dogs. Emily put out a hand to summon the doctor to her, but she'd hardly moved yet when she saw Gavin bowing to Isabel and offering his arm. Emily would have sworn he was standing halfway across the room from her sister—far closer to Emily than to Isabel. How had he managed to move so quickly that he had cut the doctor off almost before the duke had finished his sentence?

Not that she was sorry, for the last thing she wanted was to spend all of dinner sitting next to him.

Instead, she ended up seated directly across from him, watching with annoyance as he conducted himself with perfect aplomb throughout the meal. The least he could do was stab his slice of sirloin with his knife like a savage! She dragged her attention back to Dr. Mason and made a half-hearted answer to his question about life in Barton Bristow.

Though she had been away from her cottage for less than a day, her regular life felt almost like a dream. How quickly she had fallen back into the customs of her upbringing—a gentleman holding her chair, the butler pouring her wine, a footman offering dish after dish in a savory feast for the senses. Somehow all this felt so much more real than her cottage in the village—and if it hadn't been for her father and the need to be always on guard against what he might say next, she would have sunk into a pool of luxurious enjoyment.

Enjoy the comforts of the castle while you can. Soon enough it will be back to Barton Bristow...and boredom.

She caught herself up short. *Not* boredom. Peace of mind, the freedom to make her own choices, the surety of not having to listen to her father repeat his opinions every day—those benefits more than outweighed any shortcomings in her cottage life.

Though she had to admit the Earl of Chiswick had surprised her with his announcement. What was he thinking of, at this time of his life, to consider another marriage? Though *consider* was hardly the right word; he seemed to have already made up his mind to wed a girl even younger than his daughters...

As she turned from Dr. Mason to Maxwell, sitting on her other side, her gaze caught once more on Gavin Waring, and she wondered what was going through his mind. Was he feeling overwhelmed by his surroundings? Or thinking of the day when all this would be his? Or wishing he was in the village instead—with the woman who waited at the inn?

His mistress, he had called her—but somehow, the words hadn't rung true.

Come to think of it, surely even a barbarous American would know better than to bring his newly acquired light-skirt to the very doorstep of a duke, especially when that duke had the power to make his life easy—or very, very difficult.

❈ ❈ ❈

Gavin couldn't honestly say that he enjoyed his first dinner at Weybridge Castle, but at least the duke's insistence on formal dress and informal manners kept the evening entertaining. With the numbers of men and women so uneven that all rules of etiquette were suspended, he found himself seated between Chiswick, who talked urbanely of things Gavin knew nothing about, and Lucien, who said almost nothing—still seemingly in shock over the announcement his father had made before dinner.

Isabel, sitting at the end of the table in the hostess's chair, seemed to have received no relief from her headache powder, for she was pale and jumpy and now and then her brows crinkled up as if she was in pain. Mostly she frowned whenever she happened to look down the length of the table to where her husband was sitting. *There* was a story, Gavin would wager.

Directly across from him, Emily chattered to the doctor—about nothing, as far as Gavin could tell. If that was what passed for conversation in this society, he'd die of boredom before the week was out. And on Emily's other side, the Earl of Maxwell chatted easily with the duke and showed not a hint of concern about the dark looks cast at him by his wife...

The whole thing was as good as a play. Gavin was almost sorry when the port was brought in and the ladies rose to leave the dining room. He watched Emily study her sister's face and then turn to the duke. "If you do not object, Uncle Josiah, Isabel and I will retire directly to our rooms."

"An excellent idea to seek your beds early, after the long journey," Maxwell said. "You must get your rest, my dear wife."

Isabel turned brick red.

Gavin made a small wager with himself about how long it would be before Maxwell found an excuse to join her, while Emily looked at her sister in shock.

Now there's a virgin's reaction.

So much for his intention to catch Emily away from the rest and apologize for making that remark in her hearing about his mistress. Tomorrow would have to do—though when he wished her a pleasant rest and got only a stiff nod in return, he wasn't so certain he wanted to apologize.

After the ladies left and the port was on its way around, Chiswick looked down the table at his son. "Oh, do get it off your chest, Hartford. Whatever is bothering you, if you keep swallowing your fury you'll explode."

"*Whatever is bothering me?* What are you thinking of, to make a cake of yourself by marrying a lady young enough to be your daughter?"

"On numerous occasions, Hartford, you have suggested that I mind my own business—so that is what I'm doing. The continuance of the line is my concern, and since you have shown no initiative in that direction—"

"There's plenty of time!"

The earl snorted. "I'm tired of waiting for you to stop acting as if you're still in the nursery and get around to setting up one of your own."

"If you didn't treat me like a stripling—"

"What would it take for you to stop acting like one?"

"Enough!" The duke pushed his wheeled chair back from the table and waved a hand at his doctor. "Mason, you'll come along and see me settled?" His gaze came to rest on Gavin. "I'll expect you tomorrow morning, nine o'clock, in my room. Time we put some matters in order."

Gavin bowed assent. After the duke was gone, he said, "Gentlemen, let's work off some frustrations at the billiard table. Unless you'd rather set up a ring in the stable yard and test who can draw the other's cork first?"

Maxwell laughed, and to Gavin's surprise he came along to the billiard room and played with every evidence of enjoyment and not so much as a glance at his pocket watch.

Probably, Gavin thought, only because he felt too sorry for Gavin to leave him alone with the battling duo.

* * *

At the top of the stairs, Emily offered to come in and brush Isabel's hair. "For it's obvious that you're still in pain, my dear. Send your maid away, and I'll take care of you."

Isabel accepted—not because her head was still hurting, though it was, but for the company. Surely Maxwell wouldn't press for an answer until she was alone, so the longer she kept Emily by her side, the longer she would be able to think over his offer.

Though why she felt a need to think was beyond her. Why hadn't she told him right there in the hallway that bartering over a child as though he were merchandise was repugnant?

His words whispered through her mind. *It's no more than you promised me when we wed.*

True, a lady didn't marry a titled gentleman without understanding the bargain: her only task was to provide him with an heir. She and Maxwell had never spoken of it during their brief betrothal, because there was no need; the expectation was clear.

But that had been before the wedding.

Isabel had always known that he found the marriage contract so inviting only because she brought Kilburn with her. Her father had told her as much. But that, too, was a part of their world—money and property were behind many an aristocratic match.

But when Maxwell had vanished from their new home on their wedding night to carouse and commiserate with his friend Philip Rivington—the same Philip Rivington whose betrothal to her sister, Emily, had been announced that very day at Isabel's wedding breakfast—and then to act as Rivington's second in a duel at dawn over the well-born lady he had tossed aside when he contracted a marriage with Emily...

It wasn't that Isabel had expected—or even dreamed of—love. That wasn't the way of the world; the best a woman could hope for was to be comfortable in her marriage, in the same way her parents had seemed to be before the countess's long illness.

No, Isabel hadn't aspired to love.

But she did require that her husband show the same respect for her good name that a bride was expected to show for her husband's. By standing with Philip Rivington, Maxwell had helped to create the scandal that had so hurt Emily. He had turned his back on Isabel—on every reputable lady, when it came right down to it—to support a cad in his loose behavior.

With that action, her husband had voided all contracts as far as Isabel was concerned—which was exactly what she'd told him on the day after the wedding, when he had finally reappeared. Nothing had happened, in more than a year since Rivington had died in that duel over Lucilla Lester, to change her mind.

Isabel's decision had been made long since. It was time to move on to other things.

Emily ran the brush gently through the long, heavy strands of Isabel's hair. "Am I helping your headache, Isabel? Is it Maxwell who's making you so miserable?"

She had never told Emily that the man who had negotiated the terms of the duel, stood by as Rivington fought, and held him as he died was her own husband. Knowing how Maxwell had betrayed them both would only hurt Emily more.

"Yes, it's much better." Isabel sat up straighter. "Tell me, Emily—what do you think of Athstone?"

"Gavin Waring, you mean—because the thing isn't certain as yet."

"Not certain? Surely you're not thinking that Father's foolishness in planning to marry Chloe Fletcher might inspire Uncle Josiah to do the same!"

"Who's to know it wasn't the other way around and the idea was Uncle Josiah's to start? Now that he's met his heir…" Emily gave a delicate little shiver. "Did you know when the solicitors found him he was working in a farm field?"

Isabel studied her sister's reflection in the dressing table mirror. "I quite like him. He has rough edges, of course, but Uncle Josiah has a few of those himself. Athstone may grow into the role."

Emily sniffed, set the hairbrush down, and began to braid.

"What did he do to annoy you so, Emily?"

"He left his doxy tucked away at the inn." Emily tugged a strand painfully tight, and Isabel protested. "I'm sorry—I forgot your head. You hadn't come in yet when he told Uncle Josiah that his mistress is waiting in the village."

"He said as much?"

Emily nodded.

Isabel would have been amused if not for the over-enthusiastic braiding. "Then I would wager there is *not* a bird of paradise at the inn. It was not well-done of him, of course, to try to gammon Uncle Josiah like that."

"You didn't hear him, Isabel."

"And you're used to thinking the worst of any man. It's true that Cousin Gavin is out of his element. But if he were to marry well—"

The heavy tresses slipped through Emily's fingers and spilled over Isabel's shoulders, but she didn't seem to notice. "*That's* the answer! All we have to do is wave a future duke under Sir George Fletcher's nose. Hint that his daughter might end up a duchess, and he'll soon put paid to Father's notions of marrying her. Think about it, Isabel—we can put a pin in Father's plans and get Gavin Waring settled all in one swoop!"

Isabel laughed. It was the first time she'd felt like doing so since she'd walked into the drawing room that afternoon and found her husband waiting.

By the time Emily left, Isabel was feeling the tight braid more than the residue of her headache, so she released the ribbon and let her hair flow free. By the time she'd unwrapped the last twist, she was even pleasantly sleepy—too much so to bother to do it up again. She climbed into the big bed, blew out her candle, and snuggled under the heavy wool blanket. But a moment later her eyes snapped open and her gaze focused on the door that connected her bedroom and the adjoining one. The room that the Earl of Maxwell would occupy.

Surely he wouldn't dare to simply open that door and walk through. Surely he wouldn't assume that just because he'd offered a bargain she had agreed to it. And surely he wouldn't break the uneasy truce that had lain between them for more than a year, just because he'd suddenly decided his wife should carry out her duties.

But if he did, Isabel knew, he would be completely within his rights under the law.

She slid out of bed and tiptoed across to the door. He wouldn't be in his room yet, of course. Knowing that the ladies were not waiting in the drawing room, the gentlemen would linger long into the night, drinking port and smoking cigars and swapping stories. She was perfectly safe—and quite sensible to turn the key in the lock, just in case there had been even more port than usual.

But the key was not in the lock.

Very slowly and quietly, she turned the knob. Reaching around the edge of the door, she felt carefully for the lock, hoping to touch the rounded handle of a big brass key.

Just as she realized it wasn't on that side, either, the Earl of Maxwell spoke from the quiet room. "How wise of me to pocket the key earlier—for if you were to lock me out, Isabel, I would break down the door, and I cannot think your uncle would appreciate having his castle damaged."

He rose from his chair by the fire. He seemed taller than ever as he crossed the darkened room, his body a silhouette against the moonlight that poured in through the tall windows behind him. He must have come upstairs some time ago, for he was no longer in evening clothes but wrapped in a dark-red brocade dressing gown.

Had he been listening by the door? Waiting for her sister to go away? Giving Isabel time to get settled, before...

Too late, she realized that the rays of silvery light were focused almost on the door, falling past it to rest on her old plain white nightgown. Her action in reaching around to feel for the lock must have been as obvious to him as if she had shouted her intention.

"All I was trying to do was assure that I will be safe in my sleep," Isabel said.

"Then you need have no fear—and you do not need a key, for you are quite safe from me."

Despite his deep, reassuring tone, Isabel had her doubts—especially because he was now close enough to touch if she merely turned her hand.

"While you sleep, at least," the earl went on, "for what I plan to do will be when you are fully awake."

Isabel's stomach clenched. "Are you trying to drive me mad, sir? Are you hoping that I will lose all reason so you can lock me away in an attic somewhere in a far corner of your estates and forget that I exist?"

"That would not get me what I want." He brushed a stray curl away from her face.

Isabel flinched.

"You are my wife. If I am to have an heir, he must be from your body. Those are the simple facts."

"How sad for you. Unless you are threatening to take me by force, sir—and in that case, you are truly a monster."

"No, my dear. If I were to force you, it would be no more than my right and my due. But I have not threatened force, and I shall not. Instead, I have offered you a compromise."

"A *compromise*? Is that what you call it when you make insane demands?"

"I am not demanding. And what I ask is not insane. I have made a simple request, in return for a generous settlement."

His palm cupped her cheek, tipping her face up to his, and he leaned toward her until his lips brushed hers. The contact was so soft, so fleeting, that she couldn't be certain he was touching her—until he spoke and his voice vibrated through her. "Think it over, Isabel—and let me know when you decide to accept the bargain."

❖ ❖ ❖

Emily's mood was in tune with the morning—remarkably sunny and fine—and she ran lightly down the stairs. Her intention was to nip a slice of bread and a bit of ham from the breakfast room and escape to the stables to wheedle a mount from the duke's stable master. She hadn't ridden in months, and the opportunity—as well as the day—was too good to miss.

She pulled up short at the door of the breakfast room, where Gavin Waring was settling himself at the table with a full plate. He leaped to his feet as he caught sight of her. The Earl of Chiswick, sitting across the table and nearly hidden behind a newspaper, only half stood, as though he was reluctant to grant his daughter the status of a lady. Emily decided neither of them deserved more than bare civility. "Good morning," she said coolly and lifted the lid of a chafing dish.

The earl put down his newspaper, and Emily felt an itch creep over her as he inspected her from head to toe. She braced herself for a comment about the age of her riding habit—but at least he could have no disparaging comment about its condition. Since she had little opportunity to ride in Barton Bristow, the garment bore no signs of wear.

But the earl surprised her. "You're already dressed for riding. Excellent. We have calls to make. I trust your sister is not planning to lie in bed all morning?"

"When you're planning an expedition, it would be useful to tell the participants what you expect," Emily pointed out. "I have my mind set on a good gallop this morning to shake the fidgets."

"If that is your goal, then you should not mind galloping toward a specific destination." The earl turned his attention to Gavin. "Weren't you summoned to meet with the duke this morning, Athstone?"

"Yes, sir, but I thought it prudent not to meet a lecture on an empty stomach. Thank you, Chalmers," Gavin added as the butler set a tankard of ale before him.

The prospect of a lecture didn't seem to bother him much, however, Emily thought as he applied himself with steady concentration to his breakfast.

Since her father's presence seemed to put paid to her plan to roam the countryside by herself, Emily decided she might as well enjoy breakfast. She put a spoonful of shirred eggs, a slab of ham, and a slice of toast on her plate and took the chair next to Gavin. He looked startled at her choice of seats, and she wanted to tell him that she'd opted for that position only because it meant he wouldn't be in her field of vision and she could ignore him more easily than if she were sitting across the table. But even though telling him would be satisfying for a moment, doing so meant she'd have to admit that she had noticed him enough to make a deliberate choice.

There were moments, Emily thought, when the simplicity of her life in Barton Bristow looked appealing after all. On the other hand, she hadn't tasted anything nearly as good as the ham, which had probably been cured right on the duke's estate, in as long as she could remember.

She sipped the tea Chalmers had poured for her, spread butter on her toast, and addressed her father. "I assume you intend to call on Miss Fletcher at Mallowan this morning and would like Isabel and me to do so as well. But since you are surely not intending to defer to our opinions regarding your plans to marry, I see no point in going through the motions."

Chiswick's eyebrows rose. "But my dear, it was your own plan to call on Lady Fletcher. To refuse to do so simply because of her daughter makes you sound like a small child throwing a tantrum."

"Correct me if I'm wrong, Lady Emily," Gavin murmured, "but I think that is what's known as being hoist with your own petard." He finished his ale and excused himself before Emily could retort.

"In any case," Chiswick went on, "what could you possibly find lacking in Miss Fletcher?"

Emily dropped her fork. "What on earth are you thinking, Father, to betroth yourself to Chloe Fletcher? Or indeed any other young woman—at your age?" She wanted to say, *"Have you a maggot in your brain?"* and was proud of herself for resisting the temptation.

She thought he would refuse to answer, or snap at her not to be impertinent to her elders. Instead, Chiswick replied quite calmly. "You should not be surprised that the idea of starting a new family has occurred to me, since all my children are unsatisfactory in various ways."

Emily gasped. "And if we're unsatisfactory, whose fault is that? You matched Isabel with a man who wanted her only for the property she brought with her, and then you wonder why it is not a successful marriage. You tried to marry me off to Philip Rivington, and you didn't turn a hair when he was shot in a duel over Lucilla Lester just a day after the betrothal was announced. You've tried to sell Lucien to each empty-headed ninnyhammer who has joined the *ton*, so long as she has a pedigree and an enormous dowry."

"Hartford is empty-headed himself."

"He is not. You haven't tried to know him. Mother would not have allowed—" She swallowed the rest of the protest.

Chiswick seemed not to hear. "Thank you for the well-timed reprimand, my dear. I shall keep Hartford beside me on our ride today so I may discover what is hidden under that fluff of hair." He folded the newspaper with precision and went out.

Emily bit her lip. Not only had she failed to make headway on her main point, but Lucien was not going to thank her if he was subjected to the constant presence of the earl on their ride. It must be six miles across country to the Fletchers' home. She didn't care to think of the number of scathing comments the earl could deliver in the time it would take to ride so far.

As though her remorse had summoned him, Lucien appeared in the breakfast room, and a moment later Isabel came in as well—though she hesitated on the threshold for a moment, looking around.

Making certain Maxwell wasn't there, Emily guessed, and thanked heaven that she herself had escaped the pain of having a husband she despised.

"What's this about a riding party?" Lucien asked. "We ran into Father in the hall."

"Brace up. It seems we're to meet the bride this morning and give our formal approval to his choice."

"Even though we *don't* approve of her?" Isabel poured herself a cup of tea and sat down across from Emily.

"Exactly," Emily said. "Though I imagine we'll find Chloe Fletcher as unobjectionable as any other young lady who has so recently left the schoolroom. Our father, on the other hand…"

"The sainted earl is an arrogant ass," Lucien said, picking up the tankard Chalmers had just set in front of him. "And any female who finds marriage to him an inviting proposition is a dolt."

"Her father's only a baronet," Isabel mused. "She'd be a countess. It's hard to blame her for having stars in her eyes."

Lucien snorted. "Stars? More likely she's seeing guineas, or tiaras and coronets. She might be excited over becoming a countess, but not over our father. How old was he when he married our mother, anyway?"

"Thirty," Isabel said. "Honestly, Lucien, you shouldn't have to ask these things."

"*Thirty?* And he thinks *I'm* wasting time? I'm only twenty-six!"

"Our mother was seventeen," Emily said.

"So I suppose he thinks he's being reasonable to choose a bride who's nearing twenty this time," Isabel mused. "However, as there's nothing whatever we can do about it—"

"There's always the distraction of a duke," Emily said.

"You think Uncle Josiah could stop him?" Lucien looked morosely at his empty tankard. "Where did Chalmers go? If I'm to be civil to my new stepmama, I need another ale."

"Not Uncle—the next duke. Emily's taken a notion that the moment the Fletchers hear about Cousin Gavin, a mere earl will be out of the running. And I must say Athstone makes a tempting prospect."

Emily choked on a sip of tea. "Athstone? *Tempting*? Compared with an earl in his fifties, yes, but—"

"A marquess, soon to be a duke," Lucien said. "If it's a title they're trying to capture, there's nothing higher—except a royal duke, of course."

"What female would *want* one of the king's sons?" Isabel murmured.

"But a duke—or even a duke's heir—marrying the daughter of a mere baronet?" Lucien went to the door and called out for Chalmers.

"Don't be such a snob, Lucien."

"Anyway, he's not a duke," Emily argued. "Or even a marquess, officially. He's an upstart with an accidental title."

"I think he's charming," Isabel said.

Silence dropped over the breakfast room for half a minute. If Isabel was comparing Gavin to Maxwell, Emily thought, she had a point. But in Emily's mind, *charming* and *Gavin Waring* were two terms that could never belong in the same sentence.

"Oh, quite charming," Lucien muttered. "He'll probably end by beguiling Uncle Josiah into leaving him the lot after all, and the rest of us will be just as high and dry as ever."

"Lucien!" Isabel scolded. "I thought the two of you were getting on quite well last night. What happened?"

"Nothing." He had the grace to look ashamed of himself. "Very well—it's Uncle Josiah's money, and we shouldn't count on a thing. But I'm telling you—if we each end up with nothing more than a thousand guineas and Uncle's good wishes…"

"A thousand guineas may not look like much to you," Emily said crisply, "but I assure you it would make a great deal of difference to me in Barton Bristow."

"And to me." Isabel sounded almost absentminded as she stared out the window.

"Besides, Lucien, you're at least assured of the entailed property. Neither Isabel nor I have expectations."

"You know I'll take care of you," Lucien said. "Chiswick will always be your home."

"I could hardly move back to Chiswick if Chloe Fletcher is there. And your resources may be stretched thin if our father has a second family to provide for."

Isabel seemed to shake herself. "Listen to us! We're letting the very idea of a stepmother put us at dagger's point with each other, as well as with our father."

"Well, that tears it," Lucien said cheerfully. "There's no other road I can see but to match her up with Cousin Gavin. He needs a wife. We might be fortunate, if he falls head over heels in love with Miss Chloe."

The idea of the match had been Emily's own—and she still thought it a good one. But somehow, she didn't feel quite as cheerful about the notion anymore.

Chapter 5

At Gavin's request, Chalmers showed him up to the duke's bedroom. Weybridge's valet opened the door and escorted Gavin across a sitting room even larger than the one in his own suite to a corner of the new wing. Up two steps from the bedroom was one of the towers of the original castle. Even larger than it had looked from outside, the tower room was fitted up as an office, with a tidy desk standing near a window facing out over the lake and the valley.

In the huge scarlet-draped bed, the duke was sitting up with a tray across his knees, a stack of pillows at his back. "About time you showed up," he growled.

Gavin bowed but said nothing. The valet brought a small straight chair and set it down with precision beside the bed. The duke waved a hand at it; Gavin waited till the valet had gone before he seated himself. "May I enquire how you are feeling this morning, Your Grace?"

"Well enough that you needn't make plans just yet to change the colors in my bedroom." The duke shifted against his pillows and his tray rocked alarmingly. One of the dogs sprawled in front of the fire got lazily to his feet and came over as if to check for fallen crumbs. Finding none, he studied Gavin with dark, liquid eyes, then poked his cold nose into Gavin's palm.

"Enough, Balthazar," the duke said, and the dog retreated. "The grooms you sent to the village are now housed in the quarters for outdoor servants, in the stable wing. And as for your mistress…"

"I trust she, too, will be adequately cared for?"

"I took care of her, all right." The duke shot a sideways look at Gavin. "It appears you enjoy telling cock and bull stories, because there was no such female at the inn."

"She must have grown tired of waiting for me and found another protector."

"Didn't take her long," the duke grunted. "Twelve hours or so. She must have heard from someone in the village that I'm not expected to die for a few days yet, and thought she might do better for herself." He glared at Gavin. "I'll thank you not to carry on trying to pull whiskers on me, sir."

"I shall bear that in mind, should I be tempted to lie to you in the future, Your Grace."

"Hmph," the duke said. A little silence fell. He twisted his cup round on the tray. "There's something I didn't ask my solicitors to discover. Didn't particularly want them to know."

Gavin listened with rapt interest. Considering all the questions he'd already answered for the solicitors, what could possibly be so sensitive it had to remain between the duke and his heir?

"Were you involved in the late dust-up between our countries? Or I should say, between your former home and this one?"

The duke might not have asked for the information, Gavin thought, but he'd lay odds the solicitors knew. "Would it matter if I was?"

"To the title, no. To me, yes."

"I did not bear arms against England, Your Grace," Gavin said carefully.

"Ah. So you did respect your heritage." The duke leaned back against his pillows and waved a languid hand toward the tower room. "Look in the top left drawer of the desk. There's a red velvet box."

"I did not say I wouldn't have taken up arms, had the conflict continued," Gavin warned. But he rose and went to the desk. He was more interested in the papers spread across the blotter than in whatever lay in the drawer. Taking a quick look wasn't prying, exactly; the pages were right there, out in the open, where he could scarcely avoid seeing them. The top layer appeared to be some kind of map of the estate, with water courses and lanes marked.

The red velvet box was easy to spot, for it was right at the front of the drawer. It was small and square, the sort of box that usually held jewelry. Gavin looked at it with trepidation. So young Hartford had been right about the duke starting to bring pressure on him to marry.

Gavin made a private bet with himself that the ring inside the box would be studded with diamonds, and probably a lot of them. Nothing less would do for a family as grand—or as self-important—as the Weybridges seemed to be.

He carried the box across to the bed and held it out to the duke, balanced on his open palm.

"It's not going to bite you," the duke said. "Open it."

Gavin pressed the catch and popped the lid. The ring inside did not glitter or catch the light from the window. There were no precious stones after all, only a crest deeply engraved in the flat gold surface.

"The Marquess of Athstone's signet ring," the duke said. "Hasn't been out of that drawer since I put it away the day I moved into this room."

When he had become the duke. Gavin stared at the ring. Suddenly it felt heavy—as if the weight of the job had come to rest in the visible symbol cupped in his hand.

"I suppose the scribes at Debrett's, with their long scrolls and dusty record books, would say it can't be official until I actually turn up my toes. But I'd only make myself look a fool if I took a young wife now, and the result would be the same. I must say Chiswick did me a favor there. Not that I was planning to do anything of the sort—though why he's willing to put himself forward as a laughingstock is beyond me. But that brings me to the point."

Gavin braced himself.

"Chiswick does make a degree of sense about the importance of continuing the line."

"I understand why it matters to you, sir." Gavin kept his tone level. "But surely you aren't shortsighted enough to believe that I have acquired the same sense of duty, family, and lineage in a matter of days that has been bred into you all your life."

The duke's beady gaze rested on him. "It'll come with time, and maybe before you expect. Your heritage will win out. In the meantime, look around. Get your feet wet."

"And here I thought you'd demand I marry immediately and start producing little duke-lings."

"If I thought you'd bend to my will," the duke said frankly, "I might. But all I ask is that you remain open-minded and not tie yourself to anyone without consulting me."

"Then we understand each other quite well, Your Grace. What you mean is that I must not tie myself to a woman who doesn't meet your specifications."

"There are good reasons for seeking my approval. You would do well to think of your future comfort when you wed."

Gavin let a hint of irony creep into his voice. "Oh, I shall, sir, believe me."

"I mean in other places besides bed. A woman who knows as little as you do about the society you've entered would be no help to you. You'd end up miserable."

"Am I right in guessing that you have someone already in mind? Your niece, perhaps?"

"Emily?" The duke gave a harsh bark of laughter. "God, no! After what happened to Emily...No, she'll never marry. And it's just as well she doesn't, for she'd make a man's life a living hell."

Gavin didn't doubt it. Lady Emily had started off by snapping at him, and now she was practically ignoring him—which was something of a benefit. The duke's attitude was a surprise, but he was relieved to know that on this one point he and the duke were in agreement.

Still, he found himself wanting to know. *What happened to Emily?*

Before he could decide whether it was wise to ask, the duke had gone on. "This party on Saturday next, for my birthday—"

"There is to be a party, Your Grace? This is the first I've heard of it."

"Must have forgotten to bring it up last night. A garden party followed by a ball, in fact. It will also be a presentation of sorts for you—introducing you to all the families in the county."

Gavin could see the way the wind was blowing. "Including all their daughters, I suppose."

"Wouldn't be much of a ball without young people to dance. You'll do your duty, of course—substituting for me in the host's role, since I can hardly waltz the night away. And if one of them should strike your fancy..."

"I am certain that before the night is out I shall be consulting you about the suitability of my chosen bride," Gavin murmured.

"Don't go trying to run a rig on me now, I beg. And stop dilly-dallying and put that ring on."

"You'll grant, Your Grace, that your plan does sound rather like a fairy tale." Gavin reluctantly took the signet from the box. "Falling in love during a ball."

"Left hand, pinky finger. Easier to take it off to seal your letters, if you wear it there. See if it fits."

Gavin was startled when the ring slid into place as if it had been made for him, for his hands were bigger than the average man's. The gold quickly warmed to his body heat, but he felt as if it had grown hot—a brand upon his finger, marking him for all time.

"Wear it always, and keep it safe, until the day comes that you put on this ring instead." The duke waved his left hand. The signet on his finger—larger and showier than the one Gavin wore—caught the light. "Then stow it away to give to your son when he reaches his majority."

A son who would also have to carry this burden. Gavin tried not to sigh. The duke had been right about his growing awareness of duty, family, and lineage. The weight pressed down on him.

"And now the matter of the name. We've been Mainwarings since the dawn of time, and going around calling yourself Gavin Waring won't do."

"It is my name. My great-grandfather sought a simpler life when he left England."

"Your great-grandfather was a scoundrel who sought to escape the law," the duke said frankly, "so don't tell me he changed his name because he was some sort of idealist. You're a Mainwaring now, and that's the end of it."

"I shall consider the matter," Gavin said diplomatically. "If I might ask a question, Your Grace?"

"I suppose there'll be no stopping you, so go ahead."

"Do the ladies—Lady Isabel and Lady Emily—know that you have planned a ball?"

"No idea. Why?"

"I suspect they have brought no finery they would feel suitable for such an event."

"Why talk to me about it?"

Gavin's self-control cracked. "Well, *I* can hardly provide them with dresses!"

"I should think not. Quite expensive, what the ladies like to wear—as I expect you'd know if you *had* stashed a turtledove at the village inn. Though I must say I like you better for showing a little spirit."

"Surely you do not want your nieces to appear less well turned out than the other ladies at your party."

"So you think I should dress them myself? I suppose you have a point. Speaking of being well turned out, I have reconsidered the matter of your wardrobe. You may give my steward the reckoning for your clothing—I assume you know how much it runs to?" The duke's tone hardened. "And I suppose for the curricle and horses as well."

"Very generous of you, Your Grace," Gavin murmured.

"You may well think so, for it is! But that's the end of it. You'll live within your allowance from here on, or I'll know why—and I promise you'll regret it if you try my patience. Now off with you. I've wasted enough of the day."

Gavin rose and bowed politely. As he crossed the room, something made him look over his shoulder, and he saw the duke lay his head back against the puffy pillows as if he was exhausted.

Gavin ran the pad of his thumb over the band of the signet ring and wondered how long he would wear it before the day came to put it away and don the duke's ring instead.

No matter how long it was, he did not expect to feel ready.

*   *   *

A thousand guineas...

Emily had been right, Isabel thought. Such a sum would feel like a fortune just now.

Yet the reality was that for Isabel—as for Lucien—even a thousand guineas wasn't much. It was one thing for Emily, living quietly in Barton Bristow. But for Isabel, who must keep up appearances, such a sum wouldn't last long. Emily didn't need elegant gowns. She didn't even have to provide vails for servants, as Isabel was expected to whenever she stayed at a friend's country house.

Besides, a thousand guineas was simply a number Lucien had pulled out of the air. It was clear to Isabel from what her brother and sister had said that Uncle Josiah had made no promises to any of them about what they might expect.

Not even the most irritable peer would deliberately impoverish his heir—though of course a thousand guineas given to each of his cousins would leave plenty for Cousin Gavin. But they could hardly hope that Uncle Josiah would be more generous than that.

Still, a thousand guineas—or whatever sum Uncle Josiah might provide—would keep Isabel going for a while, and perhaps something else would happen to make her situation easier.

Something like accepting the Earl of Maxwell's bargain?

For a moment, she didn't even realize the direction in which her thoughts had wandered. Not until she stared out the breakfast room window to the garden, where her husband—resplendent in a dark-blue coat, buckskins, and top boots—was strolling back and forth among the roses. He looked as though he had not a concern in the world. As if he was certain to get what he wanted, just because he wanted it.

Well, he wouldn't—not this time. Isabel would die before giving in to his coercion—and she should have told him so last night. If she hadn't been stunned by the audacity of his demand, she would have spoken up right then and reminded him of exactly why they'd found themselves in this situation to start with. If he hadn't taken sides with Philip Rivington, he would have stayed with his bride on their wedding night. There would have been no betrayal, no white-faced confrontation on the morning after. She would have had no reason to refuse him his marital rights; by now, he might even have the heir he so badly wanted.

No, it was not Isabel's fault that things had gone so badly askew. But now she was caught in a trap. Maxwell had played his cards shrewdly. He had given her a full year—and to all appearances, he had done so patiently and quietly, simply waiting for his unreasonable wife to see the light. Now, if she rejected what he had so carefully called a compromise, she would be the one who was in the wrong. All of society would agree there—for when a wife's only duty was to produce an heir, a wife who stubbornly refused to do so was the guilty party, no matter what her husband might have done. Maxwell might even be able to win a divorce because of her refusal.

Being divorced might not be such a bad thing. At least she would be free of him—unless she was left in such desperate straits that she had to return to her father's house and to her father's control. If she was the disgraced party, she would not even have the little pin money she received now—and as a divorced wife, she could not claim her dower rights. The estate that had been deeded over to Maxwell as part of the marriage settlements would remain in his hands, and Isabel would have nothing.

But there was another way.

Let me know when you decide to accept the bargain, the Earl of Maxwell had said. As though she was only waiting for an excuse to back away from her principles!

But it was a bad bargain when one of the parties had set all the terms. What if she was to do some negotiating of her own? And what if the earl was the one who didn't like the offer? If he refused to meet her conditions...

Isabel stood up so suddenly she almost knocked over her teacup. "If I'm to ride with the party this morning, I must go and change."

"Sorry," Lucien said. "Didn't mean to drive you away."

"No—this is just something I must attend to." She scooped her skirt up in one hand and hurried out of the breakfast room.

"I wonder what bit her," she heard Lucien say.

"You have to ask? The more we snarl at each other, the more we sound like our father. Is it any wonder she's heard enough of that?"

No wonder at all, Isabel thought as she went out of earshot.

She didn't go upstairs to change. She didn't even pause for a hat before going out to the rose garden. Her best chance of speaking privately with her husband was right now—or else late tonight, after the household had retired. And this was not a conversation she wanted to hold in his bedroom, or hers.

He obviously saw her coming, for he paused beside a particularly robust bush bursting with late yellow roses. He might almost have planned the pose, for the light fell perfectly across his face and the yellow blooms showed to advantage against his dark-blue coat and buff buckskins.

"Dare I hope you have a decision to announce?" he asked gently.

Only when she tried to speak and found herself breathless did Isabel realize that she had hurried too much. No doubt he thought she was desperate to seize his offer, in case he might withdraw it!

"Not quite," she managed to say. "I have questions which must be addressed before I can give my answer."

"Then ask away, ma'am." He pulled out a pocket handkerchief and dusted a nearby seat, but Isabel shook her head and remained on her feet.

"You made an offer, sir."

"I did—and I stand by it."

"You said you would give me a portion of the income from Kilburn. What portion?"

"I believe you asked for a fair share."

"And I want to know what you consider to be fair."

"A very wise question—though I could find it in my heart to be hurt that you doubt my intentions to treat you equitably."

As though he had a heart! "Let us stop fencing over the matter," she said sharply. "I will tell you what I consider fair. Since the estate was my dowry, I believe that Kilburn should be mine—*entirely* mine."

He pulled back a bit, as though he found the conversation distasteful.

Good enough. She had startled him into showing his surprise. Press him now, and he would refuse. He might for once even lose that superior air and calm confidence and yell at her. How she wished her father could be present to hear that!

She went on inexorably. "The income, the house, and the lands—without restriction or reservation. Mine to do with as I like—to live in if I wish, and to sell if I no longer want it."

"That is your definition of a compromise? You ask a great deal of me."

Isabel was surprised that he could still sound calm, but she thought she detected a note of stress underneath. "Less than you ask of me. Kilburn is my dowry—therefore it should be my property."

"Let us be perfectly clear, Isabel. You propose that on the day you give me my heir, I sign Kilburn—*all* rights to Kilburn—over to you."

A shiver raked through her. *It will never happen,* she assured herself. He probably thought she was bluffing, hoping he might settle for half. But even half would be more than he was willing to give—she was certain of that. Kilburn was an old and prosperous estate; he would not lightly give up even a fraction of the income.

"Yes," she said.

She heard the stamp of boots behind her on the crushed-shell path, but she didn't blink or look away. Maxwell must not be allowed to think she would weaken. He must be convinced that his only option was to utterly refuse her preposterous demands.

"Isabel, I insist that you go and change right now." The Earl of Chiswick was directly behind her. "The horses are waiting."

"In a moment, Father," she said, without taking her gaze off Maxwell.

Maxwell didn't blink. "I agree."

She almost laughed, because his words were so absurd. "You mean you agree that I should go and change, of course."

"I agree to the terms you have offered," he said softly. "We have a contract—and may I add that I look forward to consummating our arrangement?—Tonight, Isabel. *Tonight*."

*   *   *

Mallowan, the Fletchers' estate, lay a good half dozen miles from Weybridge Castle, a distance that was no more than a pleasant morning's outing for riders who were used to being on horseback. Though Lucien had his doubts about Gavin—particularly after he chose a big, rangy, and temperamental gelding—they were no more than a mile away from the castle before it was clear that his new cousin knew what he was doing.

And a good thing, too. It wouldn't do if their best hope of distracting Sir George Fletcher was laid up in plaster because he'd fallen off his horse. On the other hand...

Emily drew her mare up beside him. "I've seen that look of yours before, Lucien. What devilry are you plotting now?"

"I'm contemplating ways to spook Cousin Gavin's horse."

"It's not that I object in principle, but whatever for?"

"If he were to break a leg somewhere close to the Fletchers' home, they'd have to take him in. He'd not only be on the spot, but as an invalid he'd be far more fascinating than an aging earl. She'd have to fall in love with him."

Emily gave a gurgle of laughter. "Don't let our father hear you say anything of the sort."

"No danger. Isabel's keeping him beside her. That's odd, though—she can't really want to spend the morning with him."

"She's sacrificing herself for your sake, for he threatened to ride beside you all the way."

Lucien shuddered. "And quiz me on matters of land management, I suppose."

"I wonder if that's what Lord Maxwell and Cousin Gavin are discussing. Say what you will about him, I've never heard that Maxwell doesn't take care of his properties."

"Oh, Max is swimming in lard. Not that you'd hear much gossip, stuck away in that tiny village. How do you stand the boredom, Emily?"

She frowned a little. "Routines can be comforting—and one can become accustomed to anything."

"Well, I couldn't. It's London for me. And don't tell me you never miss it, after you cut such a dash through society during your Season."

"Oh, yes—*quite* a dash. No one will ever forget my Season, I am persuaded!"

"I wasn't talking about Rivington, you know. He fooled us all—even Father, I think. I meant before that. How can you *not* miss being the Incomparable?"

"That all seems so long ago." Her voice was wistful. "It's true I miss dancing, and flirting, and parties. But mostly I miss hearing the news. Not many of my friends still write to me. Tell me all about the city, Lucien."

Lucien whiled away the rest of the ride with tales—most of them carefully edited—about the doings in London, and when they came in sight of Mallowan, he was startled at how quickly the time had passed.

The Fletchers' manor house was a square, upright brick structure with no pretense to architectural significance. Solid and unassuming—exactly as he'd always thought the Fletchers were, until they'd started this mad chase after a title.

The Earl of Chiswick must have warned the ladies of his plans, for the visitors were ushered into Lady Fletcher's drawing room without a moment's wait. The introductions left Lucien standing to one side where he had an uninterrupted view of Miss Fletcher.

Now he remembered her. He had never spent a great deal of time at Weybridge Castle, but now and then, on their random visits, there had been some local function in which they had all taken part. More than once, he recalled, the duke had thrown a huge gathering of all the surrounding neighbors. They had wandered around the castle grounds—eating, drinking, playing games.

On those occasions Chloe Fletcher had been a much younger pest who insisted on tagging along after his sisters, who in turn had insisted on tagging along after him. That was all he remembered, but he recognized Chloe's face.

She looked just short of fragile, and she appeared even younger than he knew she must be. Her face was small and triangular—he'd have known her anywhere just from that, for how many females had such a marked resemblance to a cat? Enormous and almost luminous green eyes; a pointed chin; high, classic cheekbones—yes, she was definitely feline in nature.

She was no longer the skinny and awkward girl he remembered, the one who regularly fell over her own feet—or over a blade of grass or a ray of sunlight. She was taller than either of his sisters, and in another contrast she was very fair, with golden hair and pale skin that showed up dramatically next to Isabel's and Emily's darker coloring. Though Chloe was still slender, she had filled out nicely—her muslin morning dress, though modestly cut, was stylish, and it hinted at intriguing curves underneath. Her clumsiness had gone as well; her curtseys were perfect.

If Chloe's mother had groomed her daughter to win a title—as she no doubt had, Lucien thought irritably—Lady Fletcher couldn't have done a better job. No wonder the Earl of Chiswick thought Chloe would make a perfect second wife.

At least, she seemed flawless on the surface. But if someone were to scratch that elegant surface, what would he find? Was it only Lucien's imagination that said she was not attending to the earl but instead stealing looks under her lashes at Cousin Gavin?

"What a shame Sir George is not at home, Lord Chiswick," Lady Fletcher murmured. "His responsibilities as a justice of the peace often take him away, I'm afraid."

"And Mr. Lancaster?" the earl asked smoothly.

"He rode with Sir George, saying he would like to observe the proceedings."

Lancaster? Lucien caught the look on Emily's face and recalled the plain mister that the earl had most recently tried to match her up with.

He strolled across to her and muttered, "He's running for his life, I suppose."

"I should prefer to think he is showing sensitivity to a woman who rejected him by not forcing a meeting," Emily said under her breath.

Well, that was barely possible, Lucien supposed—though if it had been him, he'd have made himself scarce in fear that the lady might change her mind.

"But I have a most excellent notion," Lady Fletcher exclaimed. "You must all come back to Mallowan to dine with us tomorrow—and the dear duke, too, of course, if he is able. We are nearing the full moon, so it should be a wonderful night for a drive. We cannot offer a great deal in the way of entertainment, but we can manage cards and a little music for dancing."

Lucien tuned out the nonsense in favor of closely watching Chloe. She sat near her mother, exchanging a few words now and then with Isabel and Emily. But he noted that her gaze wandered over the group. Maxwell she dismissed with a glance, and so far as he could see she barely acknowledged that the Earl of Chiswick was present.

He thought her pretense of disinterest a little overdone—just a bit too ingenuous to be real.

Only once did she look directly at Lucien, and for a moment her eyes seemed to flash with a challenge. But most often, he noted, she looked at Gavin.

"Miss Fletcher might show us your gardens, ma'am," Maxwell suggested smoothly. "I understand Mallowan has quite an interesting maze."

Lucien could have cheered. But his effort to steer Gavin to Chloe's side went awry when Isabel claimed their cousin instead. Maxwell offered his arm to Emily, leaving Lucien with no option but to escort Chloe.

But that, too, might work out better in the end, he assured himself. If the duke's heir had walked off with Miss Fletcher, Chiswick might have been stirred to jealousy and come along. As it was, the earl agreed with their hostess that a long ride was quite enough exercise for a morning, and he settled next to her on the settee to chat while the young people wandered about.

Though the manor house was nothing special, Maxwell was right; Mallowan's gardens were remarkable. Mostly, Lucien thought, because it would be possible to get lost in them, even without venturing into the maze—where well-maintained old boxwoods had been allowed to grow more than head-high. But the rest of the garden offered private little nooks as well, full of flowers and sculptures and here and there a fountain, with rows of neatly trimmed shrubs screening off each section. What a boon that would be to lovers!

Deliberately, Lucien let their pace lag a little, until they were far enough behind Gavin and Isabel that they could not be overheard. "He'll be looking for a wife soon. Athstone, I mean."

Chloe sucked in a tiny breath that almost sounded like a gasp.

She's startled that I was so direct. But there was no time to delay; once Chiswick concluded his marriage negotiations, no one could back out of the arrangement and it would be too late for them all.

Despite her momentary surprise, Chloe spoke calmly. "Lord Athstone's plan to marry is a matter that is entirely immaterial to me."

"Indeed? I wonder if you've set your heart on a countess's coronet or if—even with all your confidence—you think that's the highest you dare aspire. Is it all arranged, then?"

She did not look up at him, and her voice was wooden. "The matter is far from decided. It would be immodest of me to talk of—or even to know about—what arrangements my father is contemplating for my future."

Lucien started to laugh. "Now there's the biggest fara-diddle I've heard in all my days! Females *always* know—at least my sisters did. And they had a few things to say about the choices, too."

Chloe shot a look up at him, her eyes suddenly shimmering with irritation. "And how well *that* turned out for Lady Emily!"

So the girl had a spark of spirit, did she? Lucien looked at her with new interest. "It makes no sense for you to cling to the notion of being a countess when there's a duke to be had—especially one who's not so well-placed that he can demand a bride of his own rank. Still, there's nothing wrong with Gavin that an ambitious wife couldn't fix." *And you would be the most ambitious wife in England,* he almost added.

"Then I hope for his sake that he does not wed an ambitious wife—for I cannot think it would be pleasant for him to be *fixed*."

Lucien pursed his lips in a soundless whistle and wondered if his father had ever been allowed to see this side of Chloe Fletcher. Doubtful, for she seemed well able to control herself. And a pity it was if she had shown herself only as meek and mild, for this spark of defiance might have given Chiswick second thoughts before it was too late to change his mind.

She added, in dulcet tones, "Lord Hartford, would you like to admire this particularly fine young *senecio jacobaea*?"

"Can't say that I would. Not that it isn't a very good example of its breed," he added hastily, "but I'm not much of a gardener."

"Nothing could be clearer than that, since what I have just pointed out is common ragwort—a weed that has unaccountably escaped my mother's notice." Chloe let go of his arm, wrapped both hands around the offending plant, and tugged it out of the soil with a quick jerk. "There. Now that I have destroyed something, I feel better—but we should hasten to rejoin the others before I am tempted to release my destructive impulses on you for the foolish suggestions you have made today."

Females, Lucien thought irritably. He'd only been trying to do her a favor. Surely there was no call to threaten him with violence!

Chapter 6

*I*f it hadn't been Maxwell who suggested walking in the Fletchers' garden, Isabel might not have been so quick to turn to Gavin for companionship. But her husband had been playing cat and mouse with her all morning—ever since that incredible moment among the roses at Weybridge Castle when he had agreed to her terms. All through their ride he had been just behind her, and she had felt his gaze every second of the way. He had been the one at her side to help her dismount. He had chosen a seat in the Fletchers' drawing room that was so close to her it made Isabel's skin itch.

He was toying with her. He had agreed to conditions no sane gentleman would have contemplated for a moment. He couldn't have truly meant it, for he had agreed far too easily. If only she understood why, and what his game was, she could counter his moves.

She barely saw Mallowan's gardens. The soft caress of an autumn breeze against her face reminded her of the way Maxwell had touched her cheek last night, how his lips had barely brushed hers. The soft rumble of his voice behind her, as he walked and talked with Emily, echoed along her nerves.

What did the two of them have to talk about, anyway? Emily had never been particularly close to Maxwell; in the days leading up to Isabel's wedding, Emily had been busy with her own friends, her own romances, her own budding betrothal. Since then, she had been hidden away in her village. Isabel would have said the two of them were scarcely acquainted. Yet there seemed to be no uncomfortable lapses, no awkward hesitations in their conversation. And once, Emily even laughed.

Isabel wondered if she had made the right choice a year ago, when she had held back from telling Emily about the role Maxwell had played in the disaster.

"Lady Isabel?"

She had the uncomfortable sensation it was not the first time Cousin Gavin had said her name. "I was woolgathering, I'm afraid. Such a beautiful day." How foolish she was, able to think of nothing but sheer nonsense.

She was grateful Gavin didn't push for more, and even more glad when Lucien and Chloe came up to them a few minutes later. Chloe's cheeks looked pinker than usual—with annoyance rather than pleasure, Isabel concluded. Had Lucien done something he shouldn't—or had he not done something Chloe expected? Or was the bride-to-be simply annoyed because she hadn't received the warm welcome from any of the earl's children that she had hoped for? More fool she, if she'd expected them to be pleased!

"The tradition of the Mallowan maze," Chloe said, "has always been for the ladies to go in first, one at a time, and the gentlemen to wait five minutes before they follow. Of course, tradition assumes that the ladies will need—and want—to be rescued, but if you would prefer to stay in a group..."

"What a lovely custom," Maxwell said.

"We must investigate the maze some other day," Isabel said hastily. "It is past time to go, for it is a long ride. We will have another opportunity tomorrow to get better acquainted."

"Very wise, my dear. We do not want you to be exhausted." Maxwell surveyed the others. "I trust you will not take it amiss if my wife and I leave the group and ride back together?" Isabel felt his gaze come to rest warmly upon her as he went on, "I find myself feeling tiresomely romantic."

❋ ❋ ❋

Emily dawdled as long as she could, not eager to get back into the saddle, and by the time one of the Fletchers' grooms led her mare out and helped her to mount once more, Gavin was the only one still in the stable yard. Lucien had been first away, and their father had followed closely behind—something Lucien must not have anticipated, or he'd have been more careful. Though Isabel had lingered, trying to stick close to her sister's side, Emily had watched in bemusement as Maxwell cut his wife off as neatly as if he'd been cornering a fox. Which left only her and Gavin.

Emily adjusted her reins and touched her heel to the mare's side, and Gavin pulled his rangy gelding in alongside her.

They were barely out of sight of the Fletchers' manor house when she realized that the other riders had pulled well ahead. Gavin noticed as well, for he said, "You are setting a slower pace than before, Lady Emily."

"My horse seems a bit tired."

His voice was dry. "I didn't deceive myself that you were enjoying my company so much that you were attempting to draw out our time together. I was merely suggesting that if you are as tired as your mare is, I will escort you back to Mallowan and ask Lady Fletcher to send you home in their carriage."

And then he'd be rid of her. Only a few minutes before, riding along next to him had been the last thing Emily wanted, but suddenly she felt both stubborn and perverse enough to refuse to let him escape so easily. "I am not such a pudding heart as that. It's just that I haven't ridden in some time."

"You do not keep a mount at your home?"

"No room for one in the cottage," she said crisply. "I fear the landlord would object to me turning the kitchen into a stable." The words were scarcely out before she regretted being so sharp—for his question had been a civil one. "I beg your pardon, Cousin Gavin."

"Apology accepted, Lady Emily." They rode in silence for a bit, and then he said quietly, "I wish you would tell me..."

Emily's stomach did a flip. He must have heard something of the truth by now, and of course he was curious. Sooner or later, everyone who knew anything about her history wanted the details. They all asked, in tones that ranged from gentle to horrified to probing, how it felt when one's betrothed died in such a horrid way.

"I wish I knew what stories your brother was telling you this morning."

She turned her head so suddenly to look at him that she tugged awkwardly on the reins. The mare startled, and in an instant Gavin had kneed his horse close enough to lay an iron hand on the bridle, steadying the animal.

"I am quite capable of controlling my mount, sir," Emily said coolly.

"Under ordinary circumstances, no doubt you are. But you said you haven't ridden in a while, and you are tired." He did not back away; the white cuff of his boot top brushed her skirt. Was it her imagination, or could she feel the strong heat of his thigh against her leg?

She bit her lip in aggravation at being treated like a child—but he was right; if she'd been in the habit of regular rides, she would not have allowed herself to be so easily distracted. "If you're interested in hearing Lucien's stories, you should ask him."

He let go of the bridle. "I'm not. But this morning was the first time I have heard you laugh—and it's quite an engaging sound. You may not be aware of it, but your laugh starts out with a sort of low gurgle and builds to a peal of delight that reminds me of church bells."

"*Church bells?*"

"Small and joyous ones, of course. Not the big, deep-toned one they toll for funerals."

She stole a look at him. Was he trying not to smile?

"I thought we could while away the time more pleasantly on our ride if I knew what sort of things you find amusing."

"Was it really the first time I've laughed in two days?"

"In my hearing, at least. Until then I thought you very high in the instep, Lady Emily. Of course you did have reason to be. The statement I made about a certain lady in the village…"

"That is not my business, and I prefer to hear nothing more of the matter." She shook her head in surprise. For a moment there she'd sounded as prudish as Mrs. Dalrymple! "The vagaries of gentlemen are beyond the understanding of mere females like me. Fortunately I shall never need to comprehend them in any but a general way."

"If I may ask—why are you so averse to gentlemen?"

"You have seen my sister and her husband, and you can ask why I do not applaud marriage?" Emily followed his gaze across the valley to where the four riders looked no bigger than nursery toys. Two pairs of riders, rather—Isabel and Maxwell to one side, Chiswick and Lucien to the other.

"They seem to have settled their differences," Gavin said dryly.

"I very much doubt that. In all my life I have known of just one truly happy marriage—that of Uncle Josiah and his wife. Their union always seemed very romantic to me."

"Is that why the duke didn't remarry? Because he was still in love with his wife? How long is it since the duchess died?"

"Only a few years. They had just one son. It was a difficult birth, and the child was never strong. After that—well, the doctors said she should not have more children."

"That hardly sounds romantic," Gavin said dryly. "If a husband and wife can't—"

"You seem to have a habit of plain speaking, sir," Emily said sharply.

"I beg your pardon. We tend to be direct, where I come from. But it's also plain fact. What is romantic about a marriage if a husband and wife can't take physical solace in each other?"

Hints were not enough to give him pause, and she doubted that even refusing to acknowledge him would prevent him from discussing anything he chose. It would be better in the long run not to try to silence him, for his views might pop out at the least suitable time.

Besides, it would be refreshing if she herself didn't need to watch every word for impropriety.

"I mean the fact that they remained happy together," Emily said. "Satisfied with each other. Many an English gentleman would have solved the problem by having a wife at home and a mistress in Town."

"You seem to know a great deal about how men behave."

"I've had a bit of experience along those lines," she said dryly.

"Is that the trouble for Lady Isabel?"

"I have to warn you, Lord Athstone—you must be more careful what you say in company."

He looked surprised. "But I am not in company now; I am alone with my cousin, who understands the rules of society better than I. If I may not ask questions in private, how am I to learn which subjects are better avoided in public?"

Emily sighed. "Very well. You're asking whether Lord Maxwell has a mistress. I am hardly in a position to know— but if he does, I would not be surprised."

"Why? Because it's what gentlemen do?"

"Because he was quite a prize on the marriage mart," she said finally, "and he took his time about choosing a bride. Before he offered for Isabel, his name was linked to several ladies—some of them already married."

"You amaze me, Lady Emily. We may be barbarians where I come from, but our young ladies would not be privy to such gossip."

She stared at him in disbelief. First he nagged her into speculating, and then he blamed her for having done so? He deserved a swift kick to his horse's flank; if the poor beast threw him, she could ride on alone!

She reined in her temper. "Nor here. I beg you will not consider this a fit topic of conversation with—for instance—Miss Fletcher."

"But it's all right to talk to you about it? I'm only trying to figure out the rules."

"If asked, I should deny having this discussion! In any event, my situation is different. I was betrothed myself at the time, or I probably would not have heard the talk. Isabel's marriage contracts were already drawn up, and it was too late for her to break off the betrothal. But I always wondered…" Her voice trailed off.

"You wondered if telling her would have made a difference."

She nodded. She expected him to offer some platitude, and she was grateful when he was silent instead. "Now you understand why I am opposed to the very concept of marriage."

"I suppose so," he said slowly, "though you haven't explained why you were once betrothed, if you're so against the state of matrimony. But that's not what I asked."

Emily frowned.

"I want to know why you're so disapproving of men in general. It isn't necessary to marry a man to make a place in your life for him, you know."

Emily almost dropped her reins. "If you're suggesting I might wish to take a lover..." Too late, she tried to swallow the words. A real lady wouldn't have understood what he meant—or at least would have pretended not to follow his meaning. What a horrible effect this man was having on her! "You forget yourself, sir. Let us carry on as though you said nothing." She took a deep breath. "As long as we're speaking of marriage, what about yours, Cousin Gavin? Were you impressed with Miss Fletcher today?"

He laughed easily—as though she had not just rebuked him. "Oh, no, you're not going to draw me into that bumblebroth. It would be as much as my life is worth to get between an earl and his chosen bride."

Something clicked in Emily's mind. "*That's* what was bothering me. My father didn't act like a gentleman who's newly betrothed...or even one who's about to be betrothed."

"There's a certain way a gentleman is supposed to act?"

"Of course. He should have been satisfied to have the negotiations concluded."

"*Satisfied?*" Gavin sounded disbelieving. "Are you certain you don't mean excited or exhilarated or exultant? Or even just pleased? But perhaps the newness has worn off the match."

She shook her head. "There seems to be nothing firmly settled, or Lady Fletcher would have been...oh, entirely different. She was friendly enough to all of us, but there was no triumph in her attitude as there would have been with her daughter soon to be a countess. If she knew for certain that Chloe was to be our stepmama, she'd have made some clumsy, foolish comment."

"I've been wondering what people who live in a castle find to do all day. Now I know. They study their fellow humans and try to find patterns in their conduct, even if their actions defy all rational explanation."

Emily ignored him. "I'm sure I'm right. There is nothing firm yet."

"Perhaps he's given up the idea."

"So suddenly, and so soon after announcing it? No— they're probably still working out the marriage settlements, and of course they will eventually reach an agreement. My father is an earl, after all, and a wealthy one. Sir George must be holding out for a fortune for Chloe. Hoping for any other outcome would be mere wishful thinking on my part." She took a deep breath and tried to find something good about the situation. "However, at least I shall not have to share a house with the happy newlyweds—and *that* is something truly worthy of celebration!"

❦ ❦ ❦

The first gong found Gavin already dressed for dinner, sitting on the stone rail of the terrace just outside the drawing room and gloomily looking out over the valley. Late as it was, the September sun was only starting to cast long shadows across the fields. In the distance, he could see the last of the farm carts trundling along, loaded with golden grain on their way to the—where did they store grain, anyway? Yet another thing he didn't know about this strange new life.

Lucien peered out from the long windows and came onto the terrace to join him. "Surveying your kingdom, Cousin Gavin?"

Gavin looked out at the valley and the lake, but he wasn't seeing the estate—or even the farm carts anymore. Emily's face flashed into his mind instead.

Only because she represented all the bad things about the position he was caught in, he thought. The rigidity, the hypocrisy, the rules. Even though for a little while today she had talked to him like a real person, just minutes later she'd remembered her position and that she was annoyed at him, and once again she had been Lady Emily.

Lucien leaned against the stone baluster. "There's nobody else out here, is there? Now that you've met Chloe Fletcher, what did you think of her?"

"Are you trying to push me that direction, too? Give over."

"It would be a very sensible match, you know. Sir George's land adjoins yours."

"Weybridge is not mine," Gavin said crisply. "And since what you really want is for someone to detach the lovely Chloe from your father—"

Lucien pounced. "You think she's lovely?"

"She's most likely considered a beauty."

"Maybe, if she never said a word. Once she opens her mouth, all the golden curls in the world wouldn't make her pretty. Do you know what she said to me?"

Gavin smothered a smile. "If you're trying to sell me on the idea of wedding her, you should be rattling on about how sweet she is."

Lucien snorted. "*Sweet?* Chloe Fletcher must have been weaned on a dill pickle. It's a wonder she got through a Season, the temper she has. Though I'm not surprised if my father is the best match Sir George could come up with for her."

"Give it up, Lucien. I'm not tumbling into that tangle."

"I grant you that no gentleman of sense would want to marry her. But it's not necessary to go so far as that."

Gavin turned to stare at him. "Are you suggesting garden-variety trifling with the lady's affections, or outright ruination?"

"Trifling, of course. I mean, no—not *trifling*, exactly. Only making it clear to everyone concerned that a young wife is hardly the best choice for a man in his dotage. What do you think I am, anyway?"

"*Not* a gentleman, that's certain," Gavin muttered. "If you're so determined to see your father's betrothal broken that you're thinking of seducing his bride, Lucien, you're going to have to do it yourself."

Lucien sighed. "Are you certain you're not interested? There's the second gong. We'd better go in, for Uncle Josiah's a stickler for promptness."

Gavin was already on his feet, grateful for the excuse to return to the drawing room—rigid rules or no.

Over the soup, the duke raised his voice and said, "I hope you ladies aren't planning to gallivant around the countryside again tomorrow, paying visits."

Gavin noted that Emily, sitting between him and the duke, seemed to perk up. "We are all bidden to come to dinner with the Fletchers, but if you object, Uncle—"

"No, no," the duke said hastily. "I shan't go, of course—best to save my strength. But the seamstresses from the village will be here bright and early to see to it that the ladies are properly turned out for my birthday party."

"That's very generous of you, Uncle Josiah," Isabel said.

"No, it was Athstone's idea that I provide ball dresses for you, and a thumping good notion it is, too. I've been racking my brain about what to give you girls for the reverse birthday gift I promised, and the answer turns out to be both simple and perfect. Ball gowns," the duke chuckled. "Exactly what you both need."

Emily's small, pearly-white teeth fastened hard on her lower lip, and her big brown eyes flashed irritation as she turned to Gavin and muttered, "A ball gown? What were you *thinking*?"

Gavin swallowed hard. The duke hadn't told an untruth exactly, for the suggestion *had* been Gavin's—and to his chagrin, he couldn't figure out what he'd done to set Emily off again. What was so terrible about suggesting that she and her sister would be more comfortable at the party in new dresses? "Is it bad form to speak of a lady's garments?" he guessed.

"Just what, pray tell, will I do with a ball gown in Barton Bristow? I'll never have cause to wear it again!"

"Astounding," the Earl of Chiswick murmured from Gavin's other side. "I believe that's the first time I've ever heard a female complain about receiving a new gown, or fret because she might not have more than one occasion to wear it. Emily, my dear, I congratulate you."

Her eyes went wide. "I beg your pardon, Father?"

"There are at least three gentlemen of my acquaintance for whom these new economical ways will make you even more of a prize as a wife. I wonder—should I wait to mention it until I encounter them casually, or should I dispatch letters right away?"

*   *   *

Emily was still grumbling about ball gowns when they went upstairs at the end of the evening, and she made it plain she would like to come into Isabel's room to continue the conversation. "The worst of it," she said as they climbed the stairs, "is that Cousin Gavin seemed to expect me to thank him for his thoughtfulness!"

Isabel, however, was scarcely listening. She understood Emily's frustration, of course, for though she hated to think of herself as grasping, she was every bit as disappointed as her sister to find that their uncle's gift wasn't to be a nice sum of cold cash after all.

But Isabel had far bigger problems right now than what dress she would be wearing to Uncle Josiah's birthday ball—though she could hardly admit as much to her sister. Instead, she pleaded a return of her headache and closed the door of her bedroom with a sigh of relief, glad to finally be able to let down her guard.

At least for a little while.

Maxwell had not so much as touched her all evening— yet every time his gaze had rested upon her, Isabel had felt as though her skin was scorching. Just a few minutes ago when she had excused herself to go upstairs, he had been all the way across the drawing room, leaning against the

mantel and talking casually with her father—but the way
he had looked at her as she said her goodnights had made
her feel as if her corset had suddenly shrunk by half.

Tonight, he had said. The mere memory of the word
made her feel shaky, because of the way he had said it—as
though it tasted like sweet wine on his tongue.

Tonight…

Suddenly panicky, she pulled open her door again,
intending to call to Emily to come back and keep her company—for the entire night. But Emily's maid was coming
out of her room, which meant Emily was probably in bed.
Besides, Isabel could hear the rumble of male voices as a
couple of the gentlemen climbed the stairs. She pushed
her door closed hastily, before anyone could glimpse her
standing there.

She did not ring for her own maid. No matter how tight
and uncomfortable her garments felt, Isabel absolutely
refused to undress. If Maxwell came to her room tonight as
he had threatened, there would be no misunderstanding.
He could not possibly pretend that she was willing—much
less that she was trying to be seductive—if she was still
fully clothed.

She sat beside the fire in a big wingbacked chair, stared
at the flames, and waited.

It seemed hours before there was any movement, and
then—because she was half-hypnotized by the flames—she
didn't hear the door between their bedrooms until he was
closing it behind him.

She leaped to her feet, tempted to flee. But running
away would solve nothing, so she squared her shoulders
and faced him.

He crossed the room, unhurried but inexorable, and with every step he took Isabel felt her breath grow shorter, her throat tighter. His very gaze seemed to heat her blood.

"You are not yet dressed for bed," he said. "Should I expect Emily to bob up from behind the curtains?"

Even though she had considered keeping her sister at hand to chaperone, the implication annoyed Isabel beyond reason. "No, for I do not wish a witness to our conversation."

"Conversation?" he murmured. "I'd hardly call it that." He was close enough by then that the firelight gleamed against the metallic threads in his brocade dressing gown and turned his eyes to gold. He reached out both hands to cup her head, his palms barely grazing her hair.

"And as for why I am not yet in my nightgown," she said, "I did not agree to this. So if you expected to find me lying meekly in bed awaiting your attentions…"

"Of course I did not, Isabel. And if you were wearing a nightgown, I'd simply have to take it off—so it makes little difference to me."

She felt the tug of hairpins pulling free, and suddenly her hair spilled down over her shoulders. "No!" But her voice wasn't loud and firm and strong, as she had hoped.

"You made a bargain. You dictated the terms, and I accepted them. The negotiations are finished, and it is too late to say that you want more favorable terms."

"You cannot have taken me seriously."

"Why not? Because you admit your terms were unfair? If you would like to lessen your demands, Isabel—"

"I don't trust you to honor your promise."

His eyes narrowed, and suddenly his voice was edged with iron. "If you were a man, Isabel, I would knock you down for saying that."

She took a step forward and raised her chin. "Go ahead."

"Strike you, so you can fly to your father and brother and uncle for sympathy? No, I have a more satisfying punishment in mind."

He didn't sound angry, but her heart thumped wildly nevertheless. What would be worse than being beaten? Rape, of course. She drew her arms protectively across her body.

But he didn't touch her. Instead, he walked over to the writing desk in the corner of the room, lit a candle that stood ready there, and found a pen and a sheet of parchment.

She should have been relieved—but his very unpredictability frightened her. Who was he writing to? And what was he saying?

He sanded the page, snuffed the candle, and came back to her. "Here are your terms—in writing—for you to hold safely. Now that you have proof, I must live up to our agreement or face the loss of my good name."

If it hadn't been for the crackle of the parchment he pressed into her hand, she would have thought she must be dreaming.

"What I have agreed to is a great deal more than any husband must—and I will abide by my word. What about you, Isabel? Are you willing to stand by the bargain you yourself proposed?"

He had tricked her, leading her step by step into the morass, until she gave her word—and then he had pounced.

She looked down at the paper she held. In the firelight, she could just make out the words. He had written out the terms, clearly and concisely. He had given her a warranty that he would keep his promise. The page she held might not be legally binding, but a gentleman's promise was his bond.

He said softly, "The question now is whether your word is worth anything. Are you nothing but a cheat and a liar?"

Fury surged through her at the accusation—and died away as she realized he had every right to question her integrity. In this game of chess, he had taken her queen. There was no move left but surrender.

Isabel ran her tongue along her lower lip. "I have never broken my word of honor, sir, and I do not aim to do so now."

For a long moment he simply looked at her. "Then come here, Isabel."

He was standing less than a yard away, and yet the distance between them felt as huge and dangerous as a desert—an endless distance too enormous to traverse, especially since her feet seemed to sink into the carpet as if she were standing in loose sand. She hesitated, looking from him to the bed.

"Not yet," he said, and sat down in a big chair by the fire.

The first step was the most difficult. Too soon, she was standing before him, uncertain what to do, what he expected from her. "I can't...get out of my dress by myself," she whispered.

"We'll deal with that in good time."

His hands clasped her waist and drew her close. This was not a great deal different from waltzing, she told herself, but she knew better. She was standing between his knees, looking down at him, feeling the heat of his hands even through her dress and corset and chemise, as though he was burning away the barriers that separated them.

Slowly, he pulled her closer yet, until there was nowhere to go. He drew her down onto his lap, shifting his position to cradle her close. Her head dropped against his shoulder and she tipped her chin down, trying to hide her face from him.

"Look at me, Isabel." His hand rested on her throat, holding her gently but firmly. Slowly he bent his head until his lips rested on hers.

This kiss was nothing like the faint brush of his lips last night. His mouth was firm, strong, warm. Deep inside her something shifted, and her lower lip trembled.

He pulled back a fraction, using the tip of his tongue to soothe the tremor. He traced the outline of her lips slowly and carefully, as though he were thinking of drawing her, and stroked her jaw until her muscles were pliant and her mouth softened under his.

She wanted to taste him, and before she quite knew what she was doing she opened her mouth just a little and the tip of her tongue darted out to sample him. "Yes," he said, and sudden heat swept through her as he deepened their kiss, gently probing. His hand slipped away from her throat, down to rest against the top of her breast, pushed up by the corset—which felt suddenly so tight that she could not breathe. He seemed to understand, however, for his fingertips moved on, over the swell of her breast and then around to rest against her spine.

"Let's get you out of that prison," he whispered against her lips, and suddenly the fastenings at the back of her dress gave way. The low neckline sagged, leaving her breasts almost bare to his gaze, covered only by the sheer lacy edge of her chemise.

She gasped. "How did you do that?"

"I had to distract myself with something throughout the evening—so I made a study of how best to defeat your dress." But then he was kissing her again, his lips even hotter against hers. But not for long, because his mouth trailed down her throat and came to rest like a brand in the little valley between her breasts. She arched her back and felt the pressure of her corset ease—he must have untied the tapes.

Suddenly she found herself standing, the bodice of her dress pooling at her waist—somehow he had shifted her off his lap. But he was standing with her, still kissing her hungrily while he loosened the corset strings, as he pushed her dress down and out of the way, as he stripped off her corset. She sighed a little in relief, and then his hands skimmed over her body and she realized how very close to naked she was, with only her almost-transparent chemise remaining.

She broke away long enough to say, "My nightdress is in the…"

"Unnecessary."

"But I'd like my nightdress. I'm practically—"

"You no longer make the rules, Isabel." He bent and picked her up, lifting her out of the mess left by her gown and petticoat and corset, and carried her over to the bed.

As he joined her there, stretching out beside her, sanity returned. How could she possibly have allowed him to touch her so intimately? Even worse, she suspected that she was cooperating in her own downfall.

Isabel flung her head back against the pillows, staring up at the shadowy folds of satin that lined the great canopy. "Do what you have to, Maxwell. Just get it over with."

He leaned over her and for a long moment he only looked. His gaze swept over her body, from the tousled locks of hair that had caught under her shoulders as he put her down to her bare toes—and how was it she didn't remember him taking off her slippers and stockings? She trembled, still feeling the stroking of his fingers even though there was no physical contact. Then he smiled and said, "I shall," and bent his head to take her nipple into his mouth.

The thin white fabric of her chemise went transparent, and she arched off the mattress as though he'd touched her with a red-hot spark. "You don't need to do...*that*," she gasped. "I'm not a fool, Maxwell. I know how babies are made!"

He cupped his hand around her breast, holding her gently but firmly. He ran his tongue around the margin of the areola and once more drew the nipple gently into his mouth. "I'm only thinking of you, Isabel. It is said that a woman who welcomes her lover conceives more quickly."

Welcome him?—How very unlikely that was!

He turned his attention to her other breast, licking and nipping. Fire leaked through her body, and she moved restlessly, tossing her head and trying to ignore the heat that seemed to pool low in her belly. She was relieved when he moved over her, gently spreading her knees.

Soon this will be over.

She braced herself for invasion, but instead he knelt between her knees, drawing circles with his fingertips on the soft skin of her thighs—circles that gradually climbed higher until each new stroke brushed the dark curls between her legs. She shifted, trying to escape, but he held her more firmly and slipped a finger inside her. She jerked, and he pulled back—but a moment later he probed once more, and this time she was startled when the heat inside her seemed to go all slippery and liquid.

"That's the way." He sounded breathless. He leaned over her, sliding one arm under her shoulders to support his weight. He took her mouth once more, his tongue teasing past her lips to thrust in the same rhythm as his finger. Every muscle in her body tensed, out of control—seeking something she did not understand. "It's all right," he whispered. "I've got you safe."

Safe? What an utterly stupid thing to say.

But she couldn't think clearly enough to speak—or else her voice had quit working. Before she could retort, her body clenched and then shattered, and she sobbed in her release.

He caught her cries against his lips and cradled her close to his body, and only when she stopped shaking did he move again, probing and entering. Still stunned by the storm that had just rocked her, she was only vaguely surprised that there was no discomfort, only heat and slick smoothness as she took his body inside hers.

He paused, and said, "I'm sorry. It will just be a moment." Then he thrust hard, and she shrieked, though more with shock than actual pain. He held himself still until her discomfort passed, and then slowly eased further inside her. With each long slow stroke, her breathing grew tighter, harsher, until once more the storm took her—but this time, he, too, cried out, burying himself deeply inside her at the moment of her release, and his.

Chapter 7

Emily's maid was full of news when she brought up the usual tray of chocolate in the morning. As she bustled around drawing back the draperies and building up the fire to take off the morning chill, Sally rattled on about the grand party that was planned for a few days hence. "And it's not only the ball," she gushed. "There's to be a garden party on the grounds that day, before the ball. All the people of the estate are invited, even the servants. Chalmers and Mrs. Meeker announced it in the servants' hall. They said the duke wants everyone to have a holiday—and we can, if all the work is done."

Emily let the words wash over her while she sipped her chocolate. She was still half-asleep, for she had lain awake long into the night and then tossed restlessly. She felt as though she had only dropped off into a truly restful state about a quarter of an hour before Sally bustled in.

"Not much like Barton Bristow, is it? Oh, thank you for bringing me, my lady. I never thought I'd get a chance to see a castle. What the folks back home are going to think, when I tell them all about Weybridge! It's nothing like they'll ever see—and they'll likely not even believe me when I tell them how grand it all is."

Not much like Barton Bristow... Emily could easily put herself back to sleep by counting the many ways Weybridge Castle was unlike her cottage in the village, starting with the fact that the entire cottage would nearly fit inside this bedroom.

But it wasn't sheer size, or the grandeur of gilt and satin and brocade, or even the glamour of parties that formed the greatest contrast in Emily's mind. Here at Weybridge there was always something going on—some unexpected event to keep her on her toes. And there was always someone to talk to.

Emily had loved her Season—the parties, the shopping, the excitement, the people. Each day had been a new adventure—until everything had come to a crashing halt with Philip Rivington's death, and she had salved her pain by retreating to Barton Bristow.

After the duke's parties, she would once more go home to her cottage, where she would spend her days as she had in the last year, occupied with small housekeeping tasks. She would go to the market and visit neighbors. She would read when someone loaned her a book—for her small income did not allow her the luxury of joining a lending library, even if the village had boasted such a thing. She would sew—though mostly she would mend, since she had no funds to buy new materials.

She thought wryly that she might turn the new ball gown into pincushions and sell them.

It wasn't like her to be at loose ends. She had always been able to entertain herself—but at Chiswick and in London there had never been a shortage of things to do.

When she had first arrived in the village of Barton Bristow, Emily had been in such pain that nothing else mattered. All she wanted was quiet and peace and the opportunity to heal in a place where no one asked uncomfortable questions or expected her to pick herself up and go straight back into the marriage mart to catch another husband.

But now...she must have healed more than she had realized, for after only a few days of being in company, Barton Bristow looked just plain dull. And there hadn't even been parties as yet—only family gatherings and rides and long talks with her sister. Add in the promise of dancing and dining and flirting, and how could Emily possibly go back with a smile to activities like judging the flowers at the village show?

Not that Barton Bristow was a bad place—but the idea of going back to her cottage, to settle down there forever, dragged at her spirits.

There were alternatives, of course. From the safe distance of Barton Bristow, Emily had doubted that the door her father seemed determined to push her through—into marriage—was still open to her. Yet she was an earl's daughter, and to get her off his hands, Chiswick might even increase the dowry that Philip Rivington had been promised. Surely somewhere there was a man who would be tempted, despite the scandal of her previous betrothal.

Never forget how that proposition turned out for Isabel.

No, Emily would not marry to suit her father, and she would not marry in desperation, simply to have a different sort of life. After the debacle of Philip Rivington, she could scarcely trust her own judgment—and even though Rivington had initially been her father's choice, Emily had agreed to the match.

Not even the blessing of a child or two could compensate for the misery which would come of putting herself in the hands of a husband who saw her only as a source of wealth. Rather than take the chance, she would prefer to spend her life alone, relying only on herself.

But being independent was not nearly as inviting as it had been a year ago. With Mrs. Dalrymple going off to marry the squire, Emily would not even have a hired companion to keep her company. Instead, she would go through her life in solitary state—at the breakfast table, in the parlor after dinner, in her bed each night.

If she were a man she would take a lover, and no one would think twice. Why couldn't she do the same? Because an unmarried woman was not allowed to have a lover.

But why was that? Indulging in a love affair would make her unfit for marriage, of course, which was no doubt why the behavior was forbidden. But that restriction didn't apply to Emily. Since she had already chosen not to marry, what possible obstacle remained?

The fact that a woman preferred to avoid matrimony didn't mean she had no longings, no curiosity about what men and women did together. Once, just after their betrothal, Philip Rivington had kissed her. Emily had felt mostly apprehension, for she had never been kissed before—and the way he had poked his tongue into her mouth had frightened her. And yet, there had been something else—a little curl of anticipation, of looking forward to the time when her husband would show her what men and women did together, and why so many of them seemed to like it.

She turned the idea over in her mind, examining it for flaws. Taking a lover would allow her to satisfy not only her curiosity but her physical needs. When she tired of her lover, she could do as the gentlemen did and move on. And there was a bonus—if her father were again to press some worthy suitor on her, she could inform him that she was no longer a suitable bride.

While it was easy enough to make a convincing argument, she knew that finding the right man would not be nearly so straightforward. Barton Bristow was small—the only gentleman in the village was the squire. Even if he had not been her companion's new husband, the large, square, and florid Sir Cedric Reynolds was hardly suitable for the role Emily had in mind.

No other man in the village came close to fitting the bill. The fishmonger's boy was closest to the right age—his title reflected his occupational status rather than his birth date. During the summer, as she walked past the smithy where the blacksmith had shed his tunic to shoe a horse, Emily had noticed that he displayed a commanding set of muscles. But she could not see herself taking either of *them* into her bed.

Perhaps it would be better if the man she chose was not one she would meet on a regular basis. Even a woman of no experience could recognize that it might be awkward to encounter one's former lover at the village market or the flower show or on the walking path. Especially after one had told him the affair was over.

It was apparent this new plan of hers would require some thought.

* * *

Though the duke ordered out his carriage to take them to Mallowan for Lady Fletcher's dinner party, the vehicle was not large enough to carry all six passengers in comfort. Lucien suggested slyly that Gavin drive his curricle and offered to make the sacrifice of riding with him in the open air rather than in the greater luxury of the carriage. "Sacrifice?" Gavin grinned. "I suppose you'd also force yourself to drive."

The two of them had a grand time, taking turns with the reins, catching up with the carriage and passing it, then dropping behind once more, all the way to Mallowan. By the time they arrived, the early evening sunlight cast long blue shadows across the fields, and Lucien wanted nothing more than to turn around and drive straight back to the castle.

"You're a good sort after all, Gavin," he announced as they made the sweeping turn into the estate and tooled smartly up the long avenue of lime trees leading to the square, blocky manor house.

Gavin's eyebrow quirked. "*After all?*"

"You must see that life would have been easier for us—Isabel and Emily and me—if you had been completely impossible. As it is, Uncle Josiah seems quite taken with you."

"And here I thought the way he lambasted me meant he was anything but!"

"You call *that* lambasting? You've obviously never been on Chiswick's bad side. We had hopes, you know. All three of us are suffering a serious lack of resources—well, you obviously noticed that our father's not quick to hand out the funds, and Uncle Josiah had led us to believe…" An innate sense of justice made Lucien start over. "No, that's not fair. He didn't promise anything, I suppose. Still, it came as a bit of a shock to the ladies when Uncle Josiah only plunged to the tune of new ball gowns and not a nice sum of hard cash."

Gavin said slowly, "Is that why Lady Emily has been so perturbed all day?"

"Was she? I didn't notice, so I daresay she wasn't any shorter-tempered than usual."

"I should describe her as distracted. Having something weighty on her mind."

"No doubt it was the weight of the purse she was hoping to get—and didn't." Lucien sighed. "About that other matter, Cousin—are you absolutely certain you can't see your way to sweeping Miss Chloe off her feet?"

"I've already rescued you from a long ride in a closed carriage. That's the extent of my knight-errantry for one day."

"It's not just for my sake, you know. You'd win the everlasting gratitude of my sisters, too, if you broke up that match. Isabel says Chloe is too complaisant to stand up to someone like our father."

"And what do you think?"

Lucien snorted. "*Complaisant* isn't the word I'd have chosen. You should have heard the way she dressed me down yesterday, when all I'd said was…" He caught Gavin eying him. "I might as well tell you the truth, since it's pretty clear you're not of a mind to help us out. Chloe Fletcher is a termagant, and if our father ends up married to her, the match will be everything he deserves."

"You won't attempt to seduce her yourself?"

"And end up caught in parson's mousetrap with that shrew if anything went wrong? Hardly."

"You think it would be all right for me to take that chance, but not for you."

"You're older," Lucien said reasonably. "Much more ready to settle down. Besides, everyone thinks she'd make a good bride for you."

"I'm not that much older than you. I'm also not in such a hurry as you'd like to think, and when the time comes, I plan to do my own choosing."

"I imagine Uncle Josiah will have something to say about that."

"We'll see. Besides, you're the one who said the scheme needn't go so far as actual seduction, so you can carry out the plan yourself. You must only cause her to be so unhappy with the prospect of the earl that she makes a misstep and shows him the sharp side of her tongue. That must be easy enough—I doubt he's felt it necessary to woo her with sweet words. You can do that much without compromising yourself."

Lucien was not convinced, for the plan was seriously flawed. Gavin's lack of experience with the females of the *ton*—and their mothers—was showing. Someone should take the fellow in hand before he set foot in London, just to keep him safe from himself. Without some serious guidance, Athstone would have acquired a marchioness—or rather, some woman would have acquired *him*—before he recognized what was happening.

But Gavin's marital arrangements were a matter for another discussion; Lucien would be well advised to keep his attention on their current quandary instead. The trouble was that every other plan that had been brought forward to separate the Earl of Chiswick from his intended bride seemed just as seriously flawed as the one Gavin had proposed, as well as difficult to put into operation. At least this scheme was feasible.

Very well—he'd give it a try. He would sympathize, taking Chloe's side in any difference of opinion. He would encourage her to openly share her doubts and fears, and agree with them. Hell, he'd toadeat her if it would accomplish the purpose—if only she didn't set him on fire or push him into the nearest fountain the moment he showed his face.

At least this new resolution meant he could face the evening with something less than complete dread. He even summoned up a smile as they were ushered into the Fletchers' drawing room.

Before Lucien could put his plan into effect, however, Chloe Fletcher rose from her seat next to her mother and made a severe, correct little curtsey to the group as she greeted each one by name. "I am pleased to see you again, Lord Hartford." She had left him to the last, and her voice was colorless. Her eyes met his without a hint of the fervor she had shown on the previous day.

Her mother beamed approval.

Lucien was alarmed. He didn't know how her parents could have learned about her little temper spasm in the garden—had a trusted servant listened on the other side of the hedge when she ripped up at him?—but it seemed she had been sternly rebuked. What had they done to her? Beaten her? Locked her in her room until she yielded? Limited her to bread and water?

While Lucien was absorbed in observing Chloe, Sir George Fletcher had greeted the rest of the party, but finally he advanced on Lucien, beaming. "Hartford—so sorry to miss you yesterday when you called. But you'll forgive me for being from home, yes? As they say, we'll all be part of the family soon, so—"

Lady Fletcher went rigid. "Sir George!" she hissed.

The big bluff red-faced man seemed to wilt, and Lucien wondered if Chloe's father, too, would find himself on a bread-and-water regimen for displeasing Lady Fletcher.

He was still wondering when the Fletchers' butler announced dinner. As the couples paired off in order of rank, he found himself offering his arm to Chloe to escort her into the dining room. He supposed he should have expected to end up with her, for the room was full of titles more exalted than his. Come to think of it, the only men who were lower in rank than Lucien were Emily's Mr. Lancaster and their host. And Chloe, as the mere daughter of a baronet, was barely more significant than her mother's companion—who ended up seated on Lucien's other side.

If this dinner had been last night, Lucien reflected, he'd have been annoyed at finding himself stuck with Chloe throughout the evening. But this was the perfect opportunity to put his new plan—well, Gavin's plan—into effect. Their respective unimportance placed them near the center of the table, as far as they could possibly be from Lady Fletcher and Sir George, and from Chiswick, who was seated next to their hostess. With no possibility of being overheard by their respective parents, Lucien would have a couple of hours to plant subtle suggestions about how utterly impossible it would be for Chloe to live in amity with the Earl of Chiswick and how—title or not—she should flee from his offer of marriage.

Subtle, he reminded himself. The trouble was, now that the opportunity presented itself, he couldn't think of a thing to say that might convince her.

"If you plan to treat me to another lecture about why I am not fit to be a countess, Lord Hartford, I beg you will spare yourself the effort," she said quietly as she lifted her spoon to sample the first course.

Lucien turned to stare at her. "Because you're determined to wear a coronet and nothing will change your mind?"

Her eyes sparkled—with defiance, he thought. So they hadn't crushed her spirit after all. Then he realized the gleam was caused by candlelight reflecting against—tears? Was Chloe Fletcher crying?

"Here, now," he said hastily. "None of that."

She was staring at her spoon as if she'd never seen one before, and she had caught her lower lip between her teeth—quite hard, too, he suspected. He wanted to jab her to make her stop. He leaned forward, so his body would block Lady Fletcher's view of her daughter.

"It wasn't my intention to scold you, anyway," he said. "Just to make you understand how miserable you'd be if you married him."

Chloe's eyes widened, making her triangular face look even more feline. She was looking at him so intently that Lucien knew exactly how a mouse felt in the moment before the cat pounced.

He hurried on. "What I mean is, being a countess isn't all sunshine and daisies—not when the earl is Chiswick."

She blinked, finally. "That is why you oppose the match? Your concern for *me*?"

He nodded, but honesty forced him to go on. "It's not the only argument, of course. Stands to reason it couldn't be, for I barely know you."

"What are your other grounds?"

"My father would look a doddering old fool. And—well… I'd just as soon not have a raft of younger brothers and sisters toddling around."

"Brothers and sisters who would eventually need to be established with professions and dowries, of course. I am grateful for your honesty, Lord Hartford. Perhaps…"

The footmen began serving the next course and Lady Fletcher's companion, seated on his other side, claimed Lucien's attention. Chloe turned to Mr. Lancaster, leaving Lucien wondering exactly what she had started to tell him. He found himself answering the companion almost at random as he tried to eavesdrop on Chloe instead.

By the time the conversation turned again, Chloe had herself well in hand once more, with no evidence of tears. In fact, she looked quite cheerful.

Lucien was startled; he hadn't thought Lancaster the sort of man a young female would find so amusing. In fact, Lancaster had been no surprise at all—he appeared to be exactly the type of dull stick that Lucien would have expected their father to try to match up with Emily after the debacle of Philip Rivington, just because he was such a contrast.

Lucien would have sworn the man couldn't hold an original notion in his head. Yet Chloe seemed to have enjoyed their conversation—and a moment later, he heard

Emily's light laugh as Lancaster shifted his attention once more to her. What the devil was the man's attraction? If *Emily* was flirting with him...

Chloe frowned a little, as if she found the mere sight of Lucien sobering. "It occurs to me, Lord Hartford, that you are my best opportunity." Her tone was brisk but low.

Lucien felt as if he'd been stabbed in the back with an icicle. No, a whole row of them—for the chill arched the length of his spine. When a young woman spoke of a gentleman as an *opportunity*, there was only one thing she could mean. He could hear bells—wedding bells—ringing in his ears. "Uh..." His voice didn't seem to work right. "If you have in mind to substitute me for my father..."

"Oh, don't be such a clodpole. I'm not interested in you—for yourself at least. But I do require assistance, and in that regard you *might* be useful."

Lucien cut a bite from his slice of beef, just to have something else to look at, and let irony creep into his voice. "What exactly do you want me to help you with, Miss Fletcher?"

"It is hardly something I can discuss in detail here." She shot a meaningful look past him at the companion and on toward her mother. "I ride early every morning. It is the only time when I am entirely free to come and go—so long as I stay on my father's land. Meet me as though by accident, tomorrow morning at eight, in the linden grove that marks the boundary between Mallowan and Weybridge. You know where it is?"

"Of course," he said coolly. "But—"

She gave a little shake of her head, as though bemoaning his lack of understanding. "If you feel in need of a chaperone, I'll ask a groom to accompany me. But I would prefer not to, so we may speak alone."

All the sympathy he'd felt for her vanished under a wave of aggravation. First she'd insulted him—since his salad days, Lucien had been considered a handy man to have around in a squabble, so her observation that he *might* be useful struck him as faint praise indeed. Then for her to imply that a man like Lucien Arden needed protection from a slip of a girl like her—!

"Do stop sputtering, Lord Hartford. You'll be perfectly safe from my wiles." Chloe sipped her wine and added, so softly that Lucien wasn't certain he'd heard her correctly, "Just as long as you do what I want."

❖ ❖ ❖

After dinner, Lady Fletcher suggested that the company stroll through her conservatory. "To view my orchids, you know," she murmured. "I have a new and quite unusual specimen, and I should like your opinion of it, Lord Chiswick. But I must not hurry you, gentlemen. Take your time, and join us at your leisure."

Isabel wanted to chime in and encourage the gentlemen to sit over their port until dawn—for if they stayed in the dining room drinking, she wouldn't have to deal with Maxwell. Even if she had to listen to Lady Fletcher for the rest of a long evening, the trade seemed to her well worth the cost.

As she meekly followed their hostess out of the dining room, relief surged over her. She'd have a few minutes—an hour if she were lucky—without Maxwell's gaze flitting over her every time he turned his head. It seemed to Isabel that throughout dinner, he'd looked her way a great deal more than was suitable for a gentleman who was supposed to be paying full attention to his dinner partners.

Not that he'd seemed to be enjoying the sight of her, any more than she had liked being looked at. She hadn't expected smiles, of course—but the cool appraisal had puzzled her a little.

Emily linked her arm in Isabel's and said softly, "Since when is our father an authority to be consulted about orchids? The last I knew, the greenhouses at Chiswick grew mainly hothouse grapes."

"He may have a new pastime."

"Or Lady Fletcher is determined to defer to him on all matters. I must warn you—if she starts to consult him about new draperies for her drawing room, I shall not be responsible for what I say."

Isabel was barely listening. The cool air of the hallway washed over her, clearing her head, and the farther she got away from Maxwell the easier it was to laugh at her own foolishness. It must have been her imagination hinting that he was looking at her in a particularly meaningful way. She'd been sitting directly across the table from him; how could he have avoided looking in her direction now and then?

The fact was that the entire day had gone by without a word passing between them—or at least, not a word that couldn't have been overheard by the entire household without embarrassment. Of course, he *had* gone out with her father and a pair of shotguns and spent most of the day away from the castle.

Almost as though he had wanted to avoid her—and though that possibility did not bother her in the least, it did make her curious.

She did not truly remember when he had left her bed, though she had a vague sense that it had not been long after he had finished with her. She had been too stunned, too exhausted, to calculate the time—but this morning she had noted that the sheets had not been crumpled except around her. So though she had slept, it seemed he had not.

Had he found her distasteful? He had not seemed to enjoy their encounter; he had even seemed to be in pain. She supposed if that was the case, he might even intend to wait a few weeks to see whether their coupling bore fruit, in the hope that he might not need to return to her bed.

Not that she cared, of course—in fact, a reprieve should please her. Except that Isabel was reasonably certain he wouldn't change his mind about wanting an heir, and she'd just as soon have the whole thing over with as soon as possible. If in a few weeks she proved not to be with child, and all of this simply started over again…

Her head was spinning by the time Lady Fletcher showed them into the conservatory, where despite the lateness of the hour, the air remained warm and humid. She duly admired the prize orchid and moved slowly on to look—without seeing—as Chloe showed her Lady Fletcher's other pet plants.

"You must like flowers," Isabel said finally. She was annoyed with herself for the inane comment.

But Chloe seemed to take it seriously. "I prefer drawing plants to growing them. But I suppose I shall feel the lack when I am no longer able to ask the gardeners for blooms whenever I like."

For the first time Isabel pushed aside her own concerns and focused on the girl. "You sound quite certain of your plans. Is everything agreed, then?"

Chloe's body seemed to freeze into a statue. "That is not what I intended to convey, Lady Isabel. I only meant that at some time, a girl must leave her father's home."

Emily and Lady Fletcher came into sight around a corner. "And you will be sadly missed, my dear Chloe," Lady Fletcher said, "when the day comes that you remove to... ah, to your husband's home."

Emily took Isabel's elbow and drew her away. "There's something back here you must see, darling." She let her voice drop. "And do keep me away from Lady Fletcher. The hypocrisy of her scolding her husband when she herself has tossed out hints left and right...Thank heaven, here are the gentlemen."

The conservatory seemed suddenly overrun with people. Gavin and Lucien, Mr. Lancaster...and Maxwell. Her husband's gaze captured hers; Isabel's breath caught in her throat and she deliberately looked away.

Mr. Lancaster kissed Emily's hand and murmured something about wishing to have a guide as lovely as the flowers. Emily dimpled prettily as she laid her hand on his sleeve.

Gavin made a sound that could charitably be called a snort and turned away down a winding path with Lucien in his wake, and Isabel was suddenly alone with her husband.

"If I didn't know better," Maxwell said softly, "I'd wonder if you purposely sought out the perfect spot for a tryst."

Isabel looked around. She hadn't realized until that moment that she'd reached the farthest corner of the conservatory. She could barely hear the murmur of voices, for the foliage absorbed sound as well as screening the paths until the conservatory was almost a maze.

He didn't wait for an answer. "You look warm, my dear. Quite uncomfortable, in fact."

"The humidity makes the air heavy."

"Are you certain that is the cause? Or is it the fact that we're alone together which makes it difficult for you to breathe?"

"It has nothing to do with you." She realized that he had moved directly into her path. "If you will step aside, sir—I am perfectly capable of finding my way back to the entrance."

"I don't want to step aside."

"Surely you don't mean that after ignoring me all day—"

He smiled. "Did you not want me to leave you alone today?" He moved closer. "I thought you would prefer if I was not underfoot. I had no notion you would feel abandoned."

Isabel could have bitten off her wayward tongue. "I merely meant—" She tried to move back, but it seemed she already had retreated, for she was standing so close to a glossy-leafed bush that she had no place to go. "You cannot have sought me out here on purpose."

"Of course I have. Come away from that bush, Isabel, before you catch your skirt on the thorns."

"Thorns?" A picture flashed through her mind of going back to the drawing room with a rip in the only decent dinner gown she still possessed, and the looks—and comments—that would evoke. She took a quick step and looked over her shoulder. "What do you mean? I don't see thorns on that bush."

"I was certain I caught sight of *something* prickly. Ah, yes—there's one." He was suddenly so close that the low rumble of his voice made her skin tremble.

Isabel gasped. "Sir! This is not a bedroom!"

"Do you wish it was, my dear?" His lips moved softly up the side of her neck until he could nip at her earlobe.

"I do not. This conduct of yours is perfectly pointless, for it only serves to upset me."

He slid an arm around her, pulling her farther away from the bush. She tried to resist but ended up off-balance, half-afraid that if his hold loosened she would fall. She flung one hand up around his neck to steady herself.

His eyes went dark, and he bent his head to take her mouth. His lips felt hot against hers—but how could that be, when she was already overheated? She held herself rigid. This wasn't happening. It could not be happening.

"Stop pretending to be a statue and let me kiss you, Isabel."

His hold had shifted so she was no longer afraid of falling—but she knew she could not free herself because his arm was locked around her.

She could hear no one else—had they all left the conservatory? She squeezed her eyes shut and shook her head.

"Did you learn nothing last night, my dear?"

"I learned you will not stop at anything to get what you want," she choked out.

"Then why fight me, unless you enjoy being coerced? Kiss me, and I'll let you go."

She stood on tiptoes and pressed her mouth against his, lips sealed.

"Give me a real kiss, or I shall take more."

She was horrified. "Here?"

He gave a low laugh. "You have much to learn about the pleasures of lovemaking." His hands slid slowly down over her shoulders, past her waist, to cup her hips and pull her tightly against him. She could feel the hard bulge of his erection nestling against her belly, and to her shame she felt a rush of wetness between her legs.

She let him nudge her mouth open and she gasped as he explored, his tongue delving firmly and reminding her of a different sort of invasion, last night. He raised his head, and she saw that his eyes were gleaming. "You're not upset, Isabel. You're aroused." His breath was warm on her skin as he traced the line of her jaw with his tongue. He slid his hand under the edge of her bodice and with one fingertip teased her nipple. It peaked at his touch, and he whispered, "You will learn the difference, my dear—with practice."

Chapter 8

By the time the ladies left the dining room, Gavin
was feeling seriously out of sorts. He thought it
bad enough that Lady Emily had been carrying on like a
flirt of the first magnitude all evening, to the point that
the Lancaster chap was barely able to stop himself from
drooling whenever she smiled at him. And as for the way
the man had looked down her neckline every time she took
a full breath—did she not understand what she was doing?
Surely she hadn't changed her mind about accepting him
as a husband. But the duke might have been right, and she
was setting out to attract a man purely to make his life hell.

The Fletchers' butler set out the port, and the gentlemen moved closer to the head of the table, clustering
around their host for easier conversation. Finding himself
sitting beside Lancaster, Gavin twisted the signet ring on
his little finger and concluded it was his duty to drop a
word of warning in the man's ear. "If I were you, I'd watch
myself where Lady Emily is concerned," he said quietly.

Lancaster looked him over with something like pity.
"But then you're not me, are you? You may be in line for
a title one day, which I am not—but the Earl of Chiswick
knows blue blood when he sees it. As does Lady Emily, I

am persuaded, so when she tires of this girlish game, I'll be waiting."

"You think your blue blood is enough to break down her aversion to marriage?"

"She'll marry me," Lancaster said shortly. "One way or another."

Gavin's blood turned so icy that he thought it might just be blue after all, regardless of Lancaster's opinion of him. He drained his glass to give himself a moment to think, and then kept his tone casual. "Her dowry is worth that much, is it?"

"Considering her circumstances, her father has agreed to sweeten it."

"Noble of you to overlook her past." Gavin could feel the pulse pounding so loudly in his ears that he thought it odd no one else seemed to hear. "Lucien, pass the port, will you? Lucien?"

Across the table, Lucien jolted upright, almost knocking over the decanter. "Better watch out for that stuff, Gavin," he muttered. "It's bloody bad, as port goes."

By the time they'd all trailed through the conservatory to admire the flowers, and then dawdled over a tea tray in the drawing room, he had gone from concern for Emily's well-being to barely contained rage at her foolishness. She must be no more than half-witted to lead on a man like Lancaster under any circumstances, but it was sheer madness to make herself so obvious about it that her father was watching her with something like approval.

Not your concern, Waring. He decided that on the drive home he'd bring the situation to Lucien's attention. Surely she'd listen to her brother…though Gavin wasn't altogether certain he'd trust Lucien not to make the situation worse.

But when the company broke up and the carriages were brought to the door, he surprised himself by sidestepping Lucien and confronting Emily directly. "It's a fine night, Lady Emily. Would you care to accompany me on an open-air ride?"

Never taking her eyes off Gavin, she allowed the butler to assist her with her cloak. She looked as though she was contemplating how best to skewer him for his impudence even to have asked, and he felt like a fool.

Then she smiled and said, "It *is* a fine night, with a lovely moon. Thank you, Cousin Gavin—I would enjoy taking the air." She turned away to make her farewells to Sir George and Mr. Lancaster, who had seen them to the door.

Lucien sidled up to Gavin. "A moonlight drive? Are you *trying* to get caught up in a duel? Lancaster looks as if he'd like to call you out right now, and my father seems to be groping for his horsewhip!"

Gavin wasn't about to admit his own conviction that this ranked high among his worst ideas ever. "Your father should keep the horsewhip handy all right, but not for me." He strode out the door to wait beside his curricle.

Emily appeared a minute later with the hood of her cloak already drawn up. She was obviously in the midst of a disagreement with the Earl of Chiswick. "Surely my cousin can drive me in an open carriage, in full sight of the rest of the party, without endangering either my reputation or his," she said with a laugh, and held out a hand to Gavin so he could help her into the curricle.

He didn't speak until they were well down the avenue of lime trees. "The cool air will do you good, I should think, after the very heated evening you have had."

Her face was shadowed by the deep hood, but her voice was light. "Oh, dear. That sounds awfully like a scold. If you'd warned me that you intended to take me to task—"

"In that case, you would no doubt have preferred the company in the carriage. I am certain your father would not have scolded over seeing you bringing Lancaster around your thumb. What were you thinking, to carry on like that?"

"Is it my flirting you object to, or Mr. Lancaster?"

"Both!"

"Flirting, Cousin Gavin, is considered a polite pastime in the *ton*. You would be well advised to cultivate the knack before you go to London to seek a bride."

"We are not talking about me."

"You cannot have such hidebound ideas as to think that a lady of the *ton* must never—"

He cut across her protest. "After the ladies left the dining room, Mr. Lancaster as much as announced that you will marry him."

That silenced her—for a few moments. "If that is what he believes, he is sadly mistaken. I've no mind to marry."

"Then what are you about, tormenting the men like that? You were even flirting with Maxwell, before dinner! Not that he seemed to notice."

"Sadly, he didn't," Emily agreed. "Apparently I, too, need to refine my technique."

Gavin took his gaze off the road to stare at her. "You admit that you were attempting to captivate your sister's husband?"

"Well, *she* doesn't seem to want him. Of course, I don't, either, if it comes to that. Anyway, you're the one who put the idea into my head."

"I am almighty certain that I did *not* suggest you flirt with Maxwell. Or with Lancaster, either."

"Well, no, not exactly. Must you sound like a thundercloud, rumbling and roaring all the time? You did, however, point out that Maxwell might have a mistress already. That's why the idea occurred to me—for if he has one, why not another?"

"And you're putting yourself forward for the position? Lady Emily, have you run mad?"

"Of course I'm not aiming to be Maxwell's mistress. I have merely realized that since I have no need to preserve my virtue for marriage..." Her voice wavered for an instant. "I am free to contemplate taking a lover."

She couldn't be serious, of course. She hadn't actually *said* she was going to take a lover, only that she was thinking about it. And lady that she was, she'd had to work herself up even to utter the words. She was trying to shock him—her sense of humor must be more like that of her madcap brother than Gavin had credited. No doubt she would go off into peals of laughter when he reacted with outrage.

Therefore, he swore, he would not be shocked. He swallowed hard and played along. "Is that why you were going after Lancaster, trying to enmesh him in your toils? Because you believe he might make an adequate lover?"

"I've always wondered," she said carelessly. "What *are* toils, anyway? And don't be silly—Mr. Lancaster was a distraction for my father, no more."

He didn't want to ask what she meant. Was this drive never going to be over? He was beginning to deeply regret putting his oar in.

"It is a beautiful moon, isn't it?" she went on cheerfully. "It could be quite a romantic evening, if only—"

"If only you were with Mr. Lancaster?"

He could hear her smile in her words. "If only you weren't trying quite so hard to correct my flaws."

"I beg pardon, Lady Emily," he said stiffly.

"Accepted." She gave a little sigh. "In any case, I'm not looking for an *adequate* lover. I want a very good one."

Gavin's hands twisted convulsively on the reins, and his team broke step and pulled to the side, almost putting a wheel off the edge of the road. He devoted himself to the horses for a full minute, and wanted to swear when the duke's carriage drew near enough that the coachman hailed him.

"Nothing wrong," he called back, and flicked his whip a bit closer to his team's ears than he was in the habit of doing. The animals picked up their rhythm again and began to draw away from the carriage.

"Very neat driving," Emily said. "You're not quite in the style of the topmost sawyers in London, I believe, and there was that small trouble a moment ago—did your hands cramp for an instant, sir? But overall you're the equal of any whip I've observed."

He thanked her, gravely.

"Think nothing of it," she went on. "We were, I believe, speaking of lovers."

"No, we were not; you were attempting to shock me. I find your choice of subject quite strange, you know, for I'd have sworn you disapproved mightily when you heard talk of a mistress I'd tucked away in the village."

"Such a change of heart would seem odd, would it not? I was only shocked that you dared to bring her to Weybridge village and announce the fact to Uncle Josiah. It was foolish of you, of course, for I suspect he has been keeping you too close to slip away and visit her."

He cursed himself for giving her the opening. She was clearly not going to rest until she had achieved her goal—so he might as well play along. "Tell me, Lady Emily, what are your criteria for selecting this 'very good' lover?"

"Oh, there are far too many specifics for me to list just now. Or hadn't you noticed that we're nearly at the castle? However, I am certain you will be relieved to know that Mr. Lancaster does not meet my standards."

Relieved was hardly the word. Gavin was still concerned about Lancaster's intentions, because she appeared not to take the man seriously. But another part of him was positively giddy—for it was clear now that she was talking only to lead on Gavin himself, to annoy him and entertain herself, with no intention of acting on this foolish plan.

"No," she mused, "Mr. Lancaster is not at all like the gentleman I've chosen."

The curricle drew up in front of the castle's main door, just ahead of the duke's much heavier carriage. Gavin's groom slid off the perch at the back and ran around to the horses' heads, ready to lead them to the stables.

Gavin had to admire her; she had timed her announcement perfectly. But sheer perversity would not allow him to stay silent after she delivered that coup. He would not let her slip away so easily to gloat over her triumph.

"I suppose you prefer not to tell me whom you have chosen—though I must wonder why you would hesitate, when you have shared so much. I must wonder if this paragon among lovers only exists in your imagination." He climbed down and turned to lift Emily from the curricle. Her hood had fallen back, and moonlight struck full across her face, casting a silvery gleam over her golden-brown hair and reflecting from her big brown eyes. She hesitated for an instant with her foot on the step, looking down at him, and then she smiled.

The effect on him was something like seizing a hot ember from the fire with his bare hand. Gavin knew that soon enough it was going to hurt like the very devil, but in the first instant he didn't feel pain, only shock.

"Oh, he exists," she said sweetly. "I choose *you*."

* * *

Gavin's reaction to her announcement was not exactly what Emily had hoped for. He stared at her for a moment, and then he doubled over laughing.

No gentleman in the whole of her existence had ever before laughed at Lady Emily Arden—at least not directly to her face. No *gentleman*, she was positive, ever would; it simply wasn't done, to laugh at a lady.

Besides, Gavin wasn't simply laughing—he was holding his ribs and chortling. As though she'd needed confirmation that he was no gentleman!

"Of course," she said icily, "it was *you* who implied my choice must necessarily be a paragon. I see I was quite mistaken!"

He sobered then—but mainly, she suspected, because the occupants of the carriage had descended upon them. "Do share the joke," Lucien said eagerly.

Emily wasn't about to hover and listen. She tipped her head haughtily and swept through the front door, already untying the strings of her cloak. Handing the wrap to Chalmers, she headed directly for the closest refuge—the library, which would be deserted at this time of night. She would, if necessary, stay there—pretending to read—until the entire household was asleep.

But no sooner had she closed the door behind her than she thought better of the move. Anyone might ask Chalmers where she had gone, and follow her there. Her father, for instance, would not hesitate to run her to earth if he had any reason to suspect her of unconventional behavior—and if seeing Gavin doubled up with laughter didn't make him ask questions, nothing would.

If Emily could just get upstairs, she wouldn't have to face anyone until morning—except Isabel, the only one who would dare to invade her bedroom. But Emily could deal with her sister.

She waited till her heart had stopped racing and her cheeks no longer felt brilliant red, and hoped that the company wouldn't be milling around the hall. Then she tucked a book—selected at random from the shelf—under her arm, opened the door a crack, and listened. She could hear nothing, so she tiptoed down the hall toward the stairs.

The door of the billiard room stood open, and she could hear the solid, meaty thunk of one ivory ball striking another. She hesitated for an instant and then tried to slip past.

Gavin came to the door in his shirtsleeves, still holding his cue. "I thought everyone had gone upstairs."

She took refuge in haughtiness. "That no doubt explains why you are only half-dressed. A gentleman puts on his coat in the presence of a lady."

"And a lady doesn't proposition a gentleman to become her lover, even in jest—*Lady* Emily."

She felt a hot flush rising in her cheeks. "How amusing that a man who feels able to give a lady a scold such as you have delivered to me feels the need to stand on ceremony with her title."

"Very well. We will agree that neither of us can claim such a term of respect. Do you wish to hold this conversation in the hall?"

How was it she hadn't noticed where she was standing? She knew how easily voices carried in this cavernous space. Catching a glimpse of a servant passing by in the shadows under the stairs, she stepped quickly into the billiard room.

Gavin closed the door.

She could barely remember the last time she had been alone behind closed doors with a gentleman. The man had been Philip, of course, and the occasion had been just a few days after he had made his formal offer of marriage. That must have been the day he had kissed her, too.

"What were you *thinking*?" Gavin began. "I only pray you are not considering carrying this clanker any further. You're safe enough with me, Emily, but—"

"That's a pity," she said crisply.

"But if your father should get wind of this—"

"You mean you did not tell everyone I'd made a fool of myself?"

"I said you'd entertained me with a very funny story which would be altogether too difficult for me to repeat in a way others would find humorous. You may wish to supply yourself with a funny story before breakfast, in case someone asks you to recount it."

"Thank you for the warning."

He eyed the table as though judging his next shot. "Mind you, offering to make me your lover was a good joke, even if you carried it a bit too far. Exactly the sort of humor a barbarian colonist could appreciate."

"Is it?" she said drearily. "I mean—of course it would be."

"What did you mean by saying 'That's a pity'? Surely you don't think it's a pity that you're safe with me?"

She bit her lip.

"Oh, no. You're serious?" Gavin laid down his cue, leaned against the corner of the table, and folded his arms across his chest. "I think you'd better tell me the whole story."

"I already have. Weren't you listening?" Emily sighed and started over. "I will never marry. But that doesn't mean I'm not…curious. Since the main reason a woman needs to remain a virgin is to satisfy her husband, and since I shall never have a husband who might object to the fact that I'm not a virgin, then why cannot I satisfy my curiosity?"

"By taking a lover?"

"There seems to be no other option to accomplish my purpose," she said tartly. "There are, however, limited opportunities in Barton Bristow. I am inclined to think it would be uncomfortable to meet the gentleman again afterwards."

"I should think it would be," he said dryly. "So that's why you were flirting with every male at the Fletchers' party."

"I considered each of them, yes. But aside from the practical difficulties—"

"Slipping away with one of them to the conservatory to make love would have presented a challenge."

"The conservatory? Is that even possible? It's such a public..." He started to smile, and Emily felt her face heat. "Never mind. I felt that any of those gentlemen might misunderstand the reasons for my request."

Gavin nodded. "Yes, I can see why a man might be confused about your intentions. He might even suspect you were trying to trap him into marriage, regardless of your protests to the contrary."

"Why must gentlemen persist in thinking that the pinnacle of every woman's dreams is to capture a husband? Then I thought—why not you? You're not at all typical."

"Thank you. At least, I think that may have been intended as a compliment."

"You don't reason in the same way an English gentleman does. You're not hidebound, and you're not a traditionalist— at least I thought you weren't, until you began dishing me that scold. You are experienced with women, which means you're capable of satisfying my curiosity, and just now you must be...uncomfortable."

His eyebrows went up. "*Just now?* If you mean because of this conversation, I've been uncomfortable for quite a while."

"If you haven't been able to visit your mistress, I mean. I understand—at least, I've heard other ladies say—that gentlemen feel out of sorts when there is no outlet for their..."

The barest trace of a smile tugged at his mouth. He had nice, full, smooth lips, Emily noticed. Not red and chapped-looking, like Mr. Lancaster's had been.

She took a deep breath and changed direction. "Also, since there is nothing about me that you admire, you are unlikely to pretend you wish to marry me. Not even to get your hands on my dowry—which as the duke's heir you don't need anyway."

He gave a low, long whistle. "I see you've given this a great deal of thought."

"I had all evening to plan, since I found my dinner partners exceptionally boring."

"That's a facer for Lancaster, who thinks himself a notable swain. One of your objections still applies, however, for you and I are very likely to meet again."

She shook her head. "In truth, only Uncle Josiah's fond memories of our mother have kept the connection as close as it has been in the years since her death. Of course all of us—Lucien and Isabel and I—are very fond of him. But the fact is that once he is gone, there will be no occasions for us to come to Weybridge Castle, and you will hardly be interested in visiting Chiswick. You'll be very busy with estate responsibilities, and you will soon have your own family here. Besides, I shall be living retired at Barton Bristow, so we would not even risk a chance encounter in London during the Season."

He looked thoughtful. As if, she thought, he was nearly persuaded.

"In fact," Emily finished, "you and I shall likely never meet again after this week."

"Then we should by all means take advantage of every moment we have." His voice had a rough edge.

Before Emily had quite realized that he had capitulated, he pushed himself away from the billiard table and caught her tightly to him. His hands slid down her back, pressing her close against him. Her breasts felt as if they were melting from his body heat. Even Philip had never held her like this; no wonder there was a rule about gentlemen always wearing their coats when they were in the company of ladies.

He cupped her derriere and pulled her even closer. She tipped her head back, trying to see his expression, but his mouth came down on hers, so hard and hungry and demanding that her vision blurred.

Her mind was going fuzzy, too, but she retained enough awareness to know that this kiss was so far unlike Philip's that to use the same word for the two experiences was utter foolishness. When Philip had kissed her, she had been puzzled by his actions and a bit put off because he had tasted of stale wine. Now, though Gavin was doing things she had never dreamed of, she was too swept up in the moment to wonder what might be next. And his mouth was the most luscious flavor she had ever tasted, something exotic but so perfectly attuned to her tastes that it seemed she had always known it and had been waiting patiently to sample it again.

He was no longer holding her so tightly; his hands had wandered higher, and suddenly she felt the brush of cool air against her naked skin and realized that he had released the fastenings of her dress. The silk and lace of her bodice whispered down her arms, holding her fast and leaving her breasts open to his gaze—and his touch. He ran his tongue along the edge of her chemise, across the tender upper swell of her breasts, and then around her nipple. She gave a little squeak of surprise as a pleasurable shock shot through her.

She planted her hands against his chest, not to push him away but simply to enjoy the feel of him, the smooth linen of his shirt barely concealing the strength of muscles underneath. She had never touched a man so intimately, but she wanted more. She wanted to rid herself of the last remaining barrier between his flesh and hers.

He nipped once more at her breasts, then picked her up and set her on the edge of the billiard table. Catching the ruffle at her hem, he pulled it up until skirts and petticoats pooled around her waist, then tugged her knees apart and stepped between her legs. The same cool air that had tightened her nipples brushed across her most private areas, followed by heat once more as he pressed against her. The bulge of his erection felt firm and eager against her. "You're not ready for that just yet," he whispered against her lips, "but you soon will be."

His hungry, openmouthed kiss left her panting, and his fingers sliding inside her made her gasp. But when he began to ease her down onto the table, she was stunned. "*Here?*"

"Why not?" Gavin laughed softly. "Oh. My apologies, for I am in truth a barbarian. No, not here." Gently, he pulled her skirt down, smoothing the fabric over her hips, and lifted her from the table. He turned her away from him and cupped his hands over her breasts for a moment before he raised her bodice back into place and refastened her dress up the back. Then he bent to press his lips into the hollow under her collarbone. His breath teased across her throat and down between her breasts, sending a wave of heat over her once more.

"Shall I come to your bedroom, my dear?" he whispered. "Or will you come to mine?" The rumble of his voice against her skin made her entire body resonate.

Emily hesitated, feeling the full weight of this decision. She knew she was contemplating far more than the question of where they should rendezvous. "Yours." Her voice was little more than a croak.

"Then I shall wait for you there." He kissed her once more, long and thoroughly, and his hands roamed over her as if he planned to draw a map of every inch of her skin.

When he released her, Emily fled.

She had won, and she should be celebrating. But she had never in her life been more confused.

❀ ❀ ❀

The evening had been long and wearing, but Isabel was not eager to go to her room. Emily had vanished, however, and Lucien was yawning—though Isabel suspected he was more bored than tired. She was never excited about spending time with her father, and Gavin seemed preoccupied, interested only in billiard balls. Which left just her husband—and though conversation with Maxwell would be preferable to the other activities he no doubt had in mind, she was certain she would not enjoy the topics he chose.

You're not upset, you're aroused, he had told her in the Fletchers' conservatory. A little jolt ran through her at the thought. She was feeling anxious, that was all. Yes—anxiety about the night to come was mixed with some disdain. Even a tinge of distaste.

None of which explained the slight sensation of heaviness in her womb. Was it possible she had already conceived? Surely there could be no physical sign—and yet...

You're not upset, you're aroused.

He must be wrong. Her body was *not* tightening in anticipation of him making love to her again.

The mere suggestion sent a sudden rush of heat through her belly. The reaction took her by surprise, and suddenly she wanted only to be alone. "You may go, Martha," she said, and began pulling pins from her hair. Then she thought better of the command. She couldn't get out of her dress, much less her corset, without help. If her assistance must come from either her maid or her husband, the choice was clear. "No, wait."

Her half-undone hair had fallen over her face. Silently the maid took over the task of searching out hairpins. When Martha began brushing, Isabel relaxed under the gentle strokes and closed her eyes, letting her head tip back.

The door must have opened silently, for she didn't hear Maxwell until he spoke from beside her. "Thank you, Martha. You may go now."

Isabel's eyes snapped open. The maid looked even more surprised than Isabel herself felt. Isabel was more startled by the fact that he knew her maid's name than by his presence, though she had thought herself safe for another half hour.

Martha bobbed a silent curtsey and went out, leaving Isabel annoyed that her own servant had obeyed Maxwell without even a glance at her mistress for instructions.

"I didn't realize you enjoyed acting the part of lady's maid," Isabel said.

"I don't, particularly." He stepped around behind her, laying his fingertips on her shoulders, and studied her in the dressing-table mirror.

Isabel flinched under his touch. Or was that a shiver of expectation instead? No, she told herself. It was only that tonight she knew what to expect, and she was bracing herself for his demands. She returned his inspection, noting that he was still dressed as he had been at dinner.

His hands wandered down across her collarbones and paused over the upper swell of her breasts. He insinuated his thumbs under the lacy edge of her bodice, between her breasts. Isabel sat as still as she could manage.

His hands closed on the fabric and ripped, baring her breasts to his gaze and his touch.

Isabel shrieked. "How *dare* you tear my dress?"

Maxwell shrugged. "I've seen it more frequently than I like."

"You cannot just destroy my wardrobe!"

"Why do you care? You can't be especially fond of this garment, for you've worn it so often you must be weary of it. Besides, our bargain means you will have no shortage of funds to buy new dresses."

"Someday." After she gave him a child...a son to carry the title...How odd, that the heavy sensation in her womb had given way to something almost like a throb. "But in the meantime, if you continue this course I'll have nothing to wear!"

"Then do not keep me waiting, wife—or you shall have to stay naked in my bed."

She jumped up, trying to spin away from him—but he didn't release his hold on her dress, and with a rasp the fabric tore through the rest of the bodice and halfway down the skirt. She stared down at the wreckage in disbelief.

"Have you a pair of scissors," Maxwell said calmly, "so I can cut your corset strings?"

"No! You mustn't, for it's the only one I have with me!"

"That is hardly a reason for me to want to preserve it."

"*You're* still dressed." The protest was no more than a feeble sally.

"Come here," he said softly.

She cast a glance over the dressing table, making certain there was no blade in sight, and warily presented her back. He worked loose the knots in her corset strings and pushed the garment down so she could step out of it. "Thank you for not ruining it," she whispered.

"You're welcome. How do you plan to reward my patience, Isabel?"

She should have known he'd put even such a tiny concession to use. But there was no point in turning this sparring match into a battle she could not possibly win.

As quickly as she could, she unfastened her slippers, rolled down her stockings, and wriggled out of her underthings, till she stood before him in only her chemise. The garment had been washed so often it was growing threadbare, and it was creased against her skin from the tight corset that had fitted over it. Though she tried not to look at him, she was uneasily aware that he had not taken his gaze off her for so much as an instant.

A nightdress lay across the chaise where Martha had left it—but it would not cover her better. Since she could not put it on without stripping off the chemise, she decided not to bother.

As Isabel crossed the room to the bed, she couldn't quite keep her gaze from straying to Maxwell where he stood in the center of the room with his hands on his hips, quietly watching. The blankets were already turned back, and she started to slide between them.

"Not yet," he said. "Tonight I have a fancy to see you wearing nothing."

She wondered if he had read her mind. "But..." His eyes narrowed, and she thought better of protesting. She hadn't brought enough chemises to take the chance of him ripping one.

Before she could raise her hands to the ties of her chemise, he was there beside her, disposing of her last garment by lifting it over her head with a surprisingly gentle touch. She tried to slip between the blankets, but he pulled them back until there was nothing to hide her. He did not take his gaze off her as she lay there, naked and exposed, while he stripped off his clothing.

The previous night she had caught only a glimpse of his body. As he divested himself of his breeches and his erection sprang free, she tried to stifle a gasp.

"Frightened?" he said softly. "You accommodated me quite well last night, and I assure you I am no larger now than I was then."

Suddenly, however, all his urgency seemed to dissipate as he stretched out beside her on the bed and drew her close against him. The soft hair on his chest teased her nipples; his mouth against hers was hot but not demanding; his hands were gentle on her breasts, her belly, her thighs; and when he moved over her, she gave a little sigh and opened her legs for him. Best to get it over with, she told herself, but her heart had speeded up till it was matching the rhythmic pulsation deep in her belly.

The head of his penis nudged at her, and then he paused. "I know you have never taken a lover, Isabel, but you must have been tempted sometimes. Think of one of those men, if you like, while I make love to you. I don't mind if you pretend."

He slid slowly inside her.

If the room had been dark, she might have thought of someone else, but all she could see was him, looming over her. All she could feel was him, sliding slowly in and out, heating her from the inside until she felt she would burst into flames. All she could think of was him, as he seemed to take more than her body…

His face was fierce, and she wondered whom he was thinking of as he stroked her. A woman he had known before her? One he had wanted but never had? Or a mistress he would have preferred to be with now, if not for his need of an heir?

Her child might look like him, with the same fierce concentration, the same determination to take what he wanted. Her muscles clenched around him, pulling him even more deeply inside her.

The throbbing in her womb grew until she could think of nothing else, and an instant later she climaxed just as he gave a hoarse, almost painful cry, and spilled his seed inside her.

A long minute later, he rolled just enough that he didn't crush her. She waited for him to move away as he had the night before. Instead, he cupped one hand over her derriere and pulled her closer, till he was once more buried fully inside her.

Isabel was at a loss. Did he intend to stay here—to rest like this? Somehow, this stillness was even more intimate than the act that had preceded it, as though he was claiming her somehow. His breathing had steadied; hers didn't, for every beat of his heart seemed to press him more closely against her core, reminding her of the rhythm they had shared.

"Does it hurt?" she said finally. "I mean, when you… finish."

He opened his eyes. "Why do you ask?"

"Because you looked as though you were in pain. I wondered why men do it, if it hurts. Women have to—and I suppose men do, too, if they're to have an heir. But that doesn't explain why they set up mistresses, if they don't enjoy…" She saw that he was smiling, and her voice trailed off.

"It only hurts in a good way, Isabel. A very enjoyable way."

"Oh." She remembered that throbbing ache inside her. "I think I see, but…"

He moved then, his penis sliding slowly out of her as he rolled to his side. Isabel knew she should be relieved because her duty was at an end for tonight—but she was a bit fearful, too. She shouldn't have asked those questions but remained silent and unassuming. If he was annoyed…

What a shame it will be if he goes away. The thought came so naturally that for a moment she didn't even realize how odd it was to want him to stay—but she had almost enjoyed lying quietly together and talking.

As if he had read her mind, Maxwell settled back against the pillows and looked at her. All he did was look— but suddenly Isabel's throat tightened and she couldn't quite catch her breath.

He kissed her temple, tasted her earlobe, traced her collarbone. Her breathing grew labored. His mouth moved onto her breastbone, and he nibbled softly at each nipple in turn. She arched against him. He drew a line with the tip of his tongue to her navel, and palmed her hipbone to hold her steady.

Once more he moved over her, and this time she parted her legs for him without hesitation. He smiled as if satisfied, and she saw to her surprise that he was hard once more. But rather than slip inside her, he settled back between her knees, his hands resting lightly on her thighs, holding her open. His gaze still held hers, while almost absently his thumbs stroked the soft curls between her legs.

And then he bent down to her and licked—and Isabel came off the mattress with a surge and a half-swallowed shriek.

Gently but firmly he pushed her down and set about caressing her with hands and mouth until she writhed and wailed. He was utterly relentless as he alternately fondled and tormented. He brought her to the very edge of satisfaction, but just as she reached for release, he backed off and started again—over and over, until ultimately she screamed for relief from a frustration she could no longer bear. Only then did he give her what she begged for, and while she was still quaking with her climax, he slid inside her once more. He took his own pleasure with fast, hard, deep thrusts which would have terrified her earlier, but which now seemed right, and natural, and infinitely satisfying. Before one orgasm had ended, another rolled over her and left her panting and exhausted and trembling.

"You see? It only hurts in a good way," he whispered, and with a great effort Isabel managed to regain enough control of her muscles to nod.

Chapter 9

✤

When Gavin reached his suite, his valet was fussing around with something at the wardrobe. Sorting stockings, Gavin saw when he drew near. "I'm not sure how many pairs you think I need in a single day, Benson," he said, "but surely you don't have to arrange them all at this hour of the night."

"I was merely busying myself until you came in, sir, in case you should need me."

It was an almighty good thing, Gavin told himself, that he'd scared Emily so thoroughly down in the billiard room. At least she wouldn't be popping in at any minute.

"I haven't forgotten how to undress myself," he said dryly. "But I would like a brandy before bed."

"Certainly, sir." In his unhurried way, the valet put aside the last of the stockings, hung up the coat that Gavin had carried upstairs with him, and went out. A few minutes later he returned with a decanter and glass, built up the fire, and took his leave.

Gavin shed his neckcloth and sat down beside the fireplace in his sitting room, sipping his brandy and hoping he would eventually calm down enough to sleep. What kind of fool was he, anyway—deliberately setting out to almost make love to a woman, with no intention of following through?

He supposed he should find gratification in knowing that he'd saved Emily from her own foolishness. After his demonstration in the billiard room, he was reasonably certain he'd frightened all her curiosity away. Since that was exactly what he'd set out to do, he should be pleased at the outcome.

But who would have thought that hoity-toity Lady Emily had it in her to arouse him even more than he'd managed to arouse her? Her kisses had been inexpert, her touch uncertain—but both had inflamed him. He'd pushed her further than he'd intended to because she hadn't reacted as he'd expected. He had thought she would be too much the lady to allow him—or anyone—to touch her so intimately. Instead...

She'd been shocked when he'd begun to undress her— that was obvious—but not shocked enough to call a halt. It wasn't until the interlude on the billiard table, when she'd thought he was going to make love to her right there, that she'd gone all tense and terrified.

He regretted that it had been necessary to frighten her so much. But it was for her own good.

He shifted uncomfortably in his chair. Just thinking about her was keeping him hard. The velvety smooth skin on the underside of her breasts...the surprisingly soft and downy hair between her legs...the feminine scent of her which still lingered on his hands from touching her so intimately...

He drained his brandy and poured a second.

He had acted in her best interests. But now that it was too late, he was suffering deep and painful regret—not for what he'd done, but for what he hadn't. He could have taken her, right then and there. If he had employed a little gentleness—instead of deliberately acting like a demanding cad—she would have given herself to him.

You're capable of satisfying my curiosity, she had said. And oh, how he would have enjoyed satisfying her!

He'd never before kissed a woman who was so naturally responsive. He had almost lost control of himself for a few moments there—he had forgotten they were on a billiard table and not in a bed.

How ironic, considering her low opinion of his manners—which his conduct tonight had done nothing to change, he was certain—that he was too much the gentleman to take what she had offered. If he was truthful, he had to admit that he had been able to stop only because he knew she had no idea what she was doing. Still, he could congratulate himself for showing restraint—even if his control had been minimal and slow to surface.

It was just as well that he'd scared her into giving up on her plan. She would be safe now.

Too safe. He'd lay odds that her determination not to marry would be stronger yet, now that she'd glimpsed first-hand what a man expected. If the Earl of Chiswick ever did succeed in chivvying her into marriage, Lady Emily's husband would have the devil of a time talking his way into her bed.

Gavin smiled. The problems and frustrations of a hypothetical husband were not his concern, though he had to admit, *Oh, lord, how I would enjoy watching that dance play out!*

In the meantime, he was looking forward to seeing her at the breakfast table tomorrow—though he wouldn't be surprised if she had a tray in her room instead, too embarrassed to come downstairs. But she'd have to face him sometime, and he thought she was too much of a lady not to acknowledge that she had been at fault in breaking her promise to come to his room. He was looking forward to hearing how she tried to explain *that* lapse of manners. She'd no doubt be the most proper, upright lady anyone had ever seen…doing her best to hide the shame she must feel.

Whenever she made her appearance, he would be the complete gentleman. He would pretend amnesia about the few dramatic, heated, passionate minutes they had shared. Except he knew that all he would have to do was smile at her, and she would remember and turn that delightful shade of pink that was so becoming to her.

Yes, he would have fun for the rest of their stay, reminding her without ever saying a word.

Also, it was a dead certainty he'd never again feel the same way about a billiard table.

He laughed at himself and went into his bedroom. In the dim glow cast by the fire, he shucked off the rest of his clothes, draping them over the nearest chair for Benson to deal with in the morning. As he did every night, he took the nightshirt the valet had left on his pillow and set it neatly atop the pile on the chair before he climbed between the sheets wearing nothing.

The well-ironed sheets were smooth—but not as smooth as Emily's skin had been. The pillow was soft, but not as soft as her breasts. The blankets were warm, but not as warm as…

He heard something stir in the sitting room. Benson, no doubt, sneaking back in to finish up his project with the stockings. The man never seemed to sleep. Or Lucien, looking for a brandy and a bit of conversation. Come to think of it, the young man seemed to have had something weighty on his mind tonight. He might want to ask advice.

Or, Gavin thought lazily, Emily was coming to keep her assignation.

Wishful thinking, of course. She had practically burst out of the billiard room in her anxiety to escape—it was a wonder she'd stayed long enough for him to get her dress back on straight. And it had been obvious to him why she'd made the choice she had, when he'd asked her which room they should use. *"Yours,"* she'd said—and it had been clear right then that she had no intention of carrying out the implied promise.

Not that the result would have been any different if she'd invited him to her room instead, for he wouldn't have gone. Still, it was far better that he not be the one to break his word. She couldn't blame him if it was her own choice not to proceed—but regardless of the location, he was too much the gentleman to debauch her.

And he'd keep right on repeating that for as long as it took to convince himself.

The connecting door opened. Gavin rose up on one elbow.

Within the half-drawn curtains of the four-poster bed, he was concealed from view, but the same couldn't be said of the figure in the doorway. A pale, billowy shape loomed there; Gavin blinked, and for a moment thought he had conjured up a ghost. Then he saw how the moonlight from the sitting room outlined a perfect shape, easily visible beneath a pale dressing gown and a white nightgown so thin that it seemed no more substantial than a spiderweb.

Unbelieving, he could do nothing but stare.

"Gavin?" Emily whispered. "Are you there?"

*   *   *

For the life of him, Lucien couldn't get his head around what Chloe Fletcher could possibly want, and why she had made an assignation to speak to him alone. A long, comfortable coze about how best to please Chiswick? Tips on how to wheedle her future husband into doing as she wanted? No; the girl wasn't a fool. If she wanted anything of that sort, she'd have asked his sisters. Not that talking to Isabel and Emily would do her any good, but she wasn't likely to realize that.

You are my best opportunity, she had told him…and then there had been that threat about doing what she wanted or else. Or else *what?* It all depended, he supposed, on exactly what sort of intrigue innocent-looking Chloe Fletcher was capable of.

He should just forget about their meeting, stay in bed, and let her steep in her own juice out there in the linden grove at Mallowan. And yet…if her goal had been to fascinate him, she'd managed nicely.

"I've a mind to ride in the morning," he told his valet carelessly. "Wake me early."

His valet looked so startled at the idea that Lucien wanted to curse. Had living in London turned him into such a lazy slug that his valet thought him incapable of enjoying country pursuits? "Oh, go away," he said finally. "I'll get myself to bed."

But despite his early appointment, Lucien sat by the fire for a long while, still mostly dressed and still thinking about Chloe Fletcher.

"I shouldn't be surprised if she aspires to be a wealthy widow," he muttered. "She might wish to be certain of what I'm prepared to do for her, once I'm the earl, in the way of settlements and such—beyond what the marriage contract allows her."

He dozed, and in his mind he saw Chloe wandering among all the interesting plants in her mother's garden, plucking a few leaves here and there, brewing them into tea. He woke with a start. What if she had notions of helping Chiswick along on the journey to the next world? Who knew what poisons were to be found in Lady Fletcher's gardens? Chloe definitely knew her way around all those odd plants...

But if that was what she had in mind, she surely wouldn't admit it to Lucien. In any case, he couldn't quite see Chloe Fletcher as a mad poisoner. No need to go and warn his father just yet.

He sighed and got to his feet. If he could have nightmares while sitting by the fire, he definitely didn't want to go bed. He would raid the kitchen instead. Dinner at the Fletchers' had been plentiful enough, but he had been so focused on Chloe that he hadn't been in the mood to eat.

As he rounded the corner of the gallery, a whim made him stop at Emily's door, knocking softly so he wouldn't rouse the rest of the household. Surely his sister could advise him about how a girl of Chloe's age reasoned, for she wasn't all that much older herself. But she must have been sound asleep already, for she didn't answer.

Worn out with all that flirting, no doubt.

He was just stepping out of the shadowed niche when he heard a door click further along the gallery. A man had come out of the duke's rooms, and Lucien recognized Chiswick.

The earl saw him, too, for he stopped abruptly. "Why are you still wandering around, Hartford?"

Lucien gulped to keep from saying, *Because I have a tryst set up in the morning with your promised bride and I'm nervous about it.* "Unlike Emily, I just can't sleep. If Uncle Josiah is restless tonight, I'll keep him company."

All the way across the gallery, another door opened— and quickly shut again. Odd, Lucien thought, that Gavin would have heard such a small stir from all that distance.

Chiswick shook his head. "The duke has settled himself for the night. He seems a little better and said he'll come down for breakfast if he's feeling up to it. You can see him then."

A breakfast Lucien would miss because he had agreed to meet Chloe in secret.

Which brought him squarely back to the question that was keeping him too riled to rest. What in heaven could the girl want from him?

* * *

The bedroom was utterly still, so when a coal crackled in the fireplace Emily's heart almost jumped out of her chest. "Gavin?" she whispered. "Are you there?"

The sheets rustled, and the bed curtains swung back. Suddenly Gavin was standing in front of her, swathed somehow in a white drapery that reminded her of drawings of ancient Romans. He'd wrapped a sheet around his waist, and it trailed onto the floor. But the rest of him was bare.

"Oh, my," she whispered.

She'd noticed that his shoulders were broad, but a man's tailor sometimes padded his coats to emphasize that feature. Not Gavin's; the width of his shoulders was entirely him. She'd known he was strong, from the way he'd lifted her so easily from the curricle and picked her up as though she'd been a feather to set her on the billiard table. But seeing his bare chest and arms, noting the well-defined muscles under sun-darkened skin, was a different thing entirely. How, she wondered, could a gentleman's chest and arms be exposed enough to the elements to turn that color? He must have spent days outdoors, without wearing a coat or even a shirt...Of course, she recalled; Uncle Josiah had said the solicitors had found Gavin working in a farm field. She knew she was staring, but she couldn't tear her gaze away. She had known he was a big man, simply from standing next to him. But somehow he seemed bigger when she was alone with him in his bedroom, and when he was dressed—or rather undressed—like this.

She realized she was holding her breath and let it out as quietly as she could.

"Emily." He sounded as if someone had hit him in the stomach. "What the hell are you doing here?"

Confusion swept over her. "But you said...We agreed..."

"Oh, damn! I'm sorry, forgive my tongue. But I never thought you would go through with it."

She felt hot color sweep over her. "You weren't expecting me?"

She saw it all, suddenly, as the truth burst upon her. The way he had pressed her—and the discomfort and uncertainty she had felt after the interlude downstairs—had kept her dithering and hesitating in her room. Now she knew he had done all that on purpose. He had acted the part of a rutting cad, trying to frighten her into giving up her idea.

Embarrassment surged through every vein, but it was mixed with a strange sort of confidence. She was only here because somehow she had known, without even realizing she knew it, that the man downstairs—that too-eager, too-presumptuous, too-abrupt man—wasn't the real Gavin. He would never have treated her like that, as though she were nothing more than a convenience. She had known she could trust him. Wasn't that why she'd asked him to be her lover in the first place? Down deep, without even realizing it, she had known he would be careful with her and never speak of their encounter.

But why had he set out to scare her away? Was it because she was a virgin and therefore too much trouble? If that was the case, why hadn't he simply said so?

Or was it because he couldn't bring himself to tell her how foolish and silly she was to think he would want to make love to her under any circumstances? That would be even worse, if he *didn't* find a single thing about her appealing.

"I thought men could always—but if I am such an antidote…"

"*Damnation.*" He came across the room swiftly, his sheet swishing. He should have looked and sounded silly, but instead he looked delectable. Her mouth went dry while her entire insides felt like she'd turned into a puddle—which she supposed meant that she had made a good choice for her first lover.

Except for the inconvenient fact that he didn't seem to feel the same way.

The confidence she had enjoyed a moment earlier was gone. He had done the proper thing—the gentlemanly thing—but for all the wrong reasons, so far as Emily was concerned. He hadn't been trying to protect her after all, only to avoid getting himself stuck with a nuisance.

"How ridiculous of me," she said. Her voice was low, and despite her best efforts it trembled a little. "What a fool I must be, to think that all I had to do was offer myself to rouse your interest. I must apologize, sir, for insulting you."

"Insulting me?" He shook his head a little, as if he was having trouble understanding.

"Yes, by assuming that you would find any female form—no matter whose—adequate to rouse your lustful desires."

"So now you think I find you undesirable?"

"Just as a matter of interest, what makes your mistress more appealing to you than I am? I would like to be educated, you see, so that next time I offer myself to a lover..." Her voice cracked.

"Appealing? For God's sake, Emily, I came near to raping you on the billiard table!" He reached for her.

She put up both hands to fend him off. "I don't need another demonstration."

"Yes, I think you do." His voice was low and rough. "A different sort of demonstration, however."

He swooped upon her, drawing her against the length of his body with one arm, his other hand spread possessively along the side of her throat. His thumb pressed her chin up to an angle where he could claim her lips, but he didn't immediately kiss her. In the firelight, his eyes gleamed as he looked at her—just looked, as if he were staring into her soul. When he bent his head to kiss her, he was almost gentle—his mouth brushing hers softly, asking rather than taking. And yet, this touch was even more masterful than before, for this time he was not pressing her but wooing her, until Emily was the one who asked for more. She arched her spine to press closer against him, flung a hand up around his neck to hold his mouth tighter against hers, darted her tongue against his lips…He let her toy with him for a moment, and then he took control, kissing her long and deeply. He tasted wonderful…but she wanted more still, and she shifted against him and whimpered a little.

"There," he said thickly. "Now are you convinced I find you appealing?"

She considered as she skimmed his body with her fingertips, learning the shape of every muscle. His skin felt hot under her hands—smooth, sun-kissed, stretched taut over hard muscles, as though every sinew of him was tensed with the effort of holding her close. But there was no need, for she was hardly a captive; if he let his hands fall, she would still be pressed against him.

He was putting forth so much effort, she realized, because he was holding her away from him—if only by a fraction of an inch. She stepped back.

"Go to your room, Emily." His voice was taut.

She shook her head and untied the belt of her silk dressing gown, letting it slide off her shoulders to pool around her feet. As she raised her hands to the ties at the neck of her nightgown, he swore again and swooped on her, picking up the dressing gown with one hand—his other was still clutching the sheet—and draping it around her. "I'm trying to be a gentleman here," he said urgently. "But you have to cooperate. Put your arms through the sleeves, sweet."

"You promised you would make love to me." She swallowed hard, trying to keep her voice from cracking.

"No, I didn't. Oh, very well, it might have sounded like a promise, but I didn't mean it. You—"

She turned slightly away. "You mean you don't want me."

Silence stretched out like honey dripping from the comb. "Yes, damn it, I want you. Does that make you happy? I want you so much that I'm going to send you straight back to your room. Just let me peek out to be sure no one is stirring."

She stood exactly where she was, making no effort to put her dressing gown on again. She was stunned, a bit hurt—and yet somehow triumphant, too, for she believed far more in the truth revealed in the rough edge of his voice than in all the smooth words downstairs. He *did* want her.

But he was sending her away—at least, he was trying to. They would see about *that*.

Gavin strode across the sitting room, opened the door a fraction, and peered out into the gallery. In an instant he closed it again—far too quickly, she thought, to have made a full inspection, and before she had finished formulating a plan. He came back to her. "Lucien is out there, wandering around."

Her heart leaped. "That means I have to stay here."

"Only for a few minutes, until he gets settled somewhere."

Suddenly, uncontrollably, she began to shiver.

He wrapped the dressing gown more tightly around her. "Come closer to the fire."

"I'm not cold. I'm…" The trouble was, she didn't know what she was feeling. Embarrassed? Ashamed that she still wanted this so much, if he didn't?

Gavin sat down in a big chair by the fireplace and drew her onto his lap, wrapping his arms around her. Slowly, as his body heat seeped through her, she relaxed, snuggling more closely against him.

"Sit still, please," he ordered.

She peeked up at him, stretched a bit, pressed a kiss against the strong column of his throat. "Since we have to wait for Lucien to go away, we might as well…"

"Even after what I did—how I treated you—you want to go on?"

Since her efforts at being a coquette didn't seem to be working, Emily settled for unvarnished truth. "I trust you, Gavin. And I want to be your lover."

He sighed, and for a moment Emily thought the entire world had stopped moving, waiting to hear his answer.

"I am not a saint," he said dryly. And as he scooped her up and carried her to his bed, his sheet was forgotten.

*   *   *

Gavin almost fell over the trailing corner of the sheet, so he dropped it—and only then realized that despite her determination, Emily might panic at the sudden view of him entirely naked. But though her eyes widened, she made no protest.

Somehow her nightdress landed in the center of the carpet as well.

The big bed was shadowed, the hangings half-drawn. He set her down on the mattress, and Emily stretched out her arms to welcome him. Gavin's head swam. Lying across his bed with her arms upraised, her breasts gleaming in the bits of firelight that flickered past the heavy silk bed curtains, she looked like a wanton impatient for her lover. He scrambled for control and did not do what he wanted—which was to bury himself full-length in her with a single thrust. She was a virgin, he reminded himself. A *virgin*.

An inconvenient shred of gentlemanly honor poked uncomfortably at him. If he took her virginity, she would never be able to marry. She said she didn't want to—but how could she possibly be certain that she would never change her mind? She was still very young; she had been hurt; she was angry at men. With time, her determination might soften, and a lover might not be enough to satisfy. But if she did eventually want to marry, then found she couldn't because of something Gavin had done...

He could not respect himself if he took that possibility away from her. But as long as he left her a virgin—no matter how tenuous the definition was—she would still have the choice.

Of course, there was the small difficulty that making love to her while leaving her a virgin was going to kill him.

Take it slowly. He leaned over her to begin with a kiss. The gesture should have been simple, ordinary, for he had kissed her before. And this time he wasn't even touching her, except for his lips against hers.

He didn't quite know how he ended up half-lying on top of her, his thigh tucked tightly between hers, her arms around his neck.

She squirmed against him. "Oh, that's lovely," she whispered. "Kissing feels so different, lying down—and I don't have to worry that I'll fall over because my knees gave way."

The ingenuous admission rocked him. As though his hand had a mind of its own, he checked out her knee. She bent it invitingly, and—slightly off balance—he slid a little closer, the head of his penis skimming along the silky skin of her thigh.

Time for a new approach. He backed off, ignoring her protest, and bent his head to her breast, focusing all his attention on the rosy, eager tip. If he concentrated on just two square inches of her at a time, he might maintain control.

She arched her back, pressing her nipple deeper into his mouth. Though her movements were unstudied, even a bit awkward sometimes, she was so responsive that she was driving him out of his mind.

He slipped his hand between her legs and discovered that she was wet, and eagerness jolted through him. Carefully he slid a finger inside her, then another. Her body gave a little jerk and squeezed around his hand, and Gavin's mouth went dry.

He kissed her again, mimicking with his tongue the movements of his fingers. He could feel her tension rising, her body growing taut. She whimpered, and breathlessly he said, "Don't be frightened. I've got you."

As she came, he watched the dawning wonder in her eyes, and suddenly all his own urges were as nothing compared to the joy of satisfying her.

❃ ❃ ❃

The linden grove at Mallowan was a landmark, but Lucien had seen it only from afar. He hadn't realized that the grove stretched over a couple of acres, with graceful trees growing so close together that wending between them on horseback was difficult, at least for a man as tall as Lucien was. He finally gave up and slid down off the back of his roan, leading the animal and hoping that he wouldn't miss Chloe Fletcher in the shadows.

After a while, he began to wonder if she had any intention of meeting him after all. Just as he started to suspect that she might be capable of repaying his sincere—though clumsy—interference in her marriage plans with some nasty or embarrassing surprise, or by letting him dangle there in the grove for hours, he heard the muted thump of a horse's hooves against mossy ground. A beautiful chestnut picked its way through the trees opposite him and stopped in a small clearing. Chloe dismounted, landing on a small log with a grace that said she had done this many times before.

Her riding habit was almost the same green as the lindens' leaves, and trimmed in black like the shadows between the trees. She might have blended into the grove if not for a stray beam of sunlight that found its way around the branches and lighted the mass of golden hair peeking out from the edges of the severe black bonnet. For an instant, she was surrounded by light—as though the sun had illuminated a halo. Lucien snorted at the thought of Chloe Fletcher as some kind of angel.

Chloe turned quickly at the sound, as wary as a cat. At the sight of him, she visibly relaxed. "I thought you might keep me waiting. But no matter, you're here." She tied her chestnut's reins to a sapling and sat down on the fallen log, patting the spot beside her.

Lucien approached cautiously. She seemed awfully friendly this morning for a young lady who on the previous evening had had so little to say to him.

Her sudden approachability should make his task easier. *Woo her with sweet words,* Gavin had advised. All Lucien had to do was show her the contrast between Chiswick's attitude and that of a real gentleman, and her dissatisfaction with her elderly lover would take care of the rest. But now that he was alone with her, groping for ways to carry out the plan, Lucien would have given anything to be elsewhere.

What had made him think that talking to her would be easier than outright seduction? It might be a trifle less dangerous—at least sweet words wouldn't likely end with him standing by her side at an altar under the threat of her father's favorite shotgun. And of course, a gentleman wouldn't carry a seduction through—not with a lady, at any rate. He wondered idly how his friend Aubrey was progressing with that chorus girl he'd been chasing. It seemed to Lucien as if weeks had passed since they had gone to the theater together.

"Oh, do come and sit down," Chloe said irritably. "It gives me a crick in the neck to look so far up at you. And if you're worried about your virtue—you're in no danger. You needn't be in the least concerned about how you stand with me."

Lucien's pride tingled a little. There was nothing about him that made her even consider casting out a lure?

"We're meeting alone in a very private spot," Chloe went on. "Whether you are sitting next to me on this log or looming over me would hardly make a difference to my father, were he to discover us here. So you may as well stop trying to look like a Roman statue and sit down. Let's get this conversation over with before there is any reason for someone to come looking for either of us."

For a flighty young miss, Lucien thought, she suddenly showed a terrifying amount of common sense. He sat down gingerly, staying as far away from her as he could on the uneven log.

"Despite what you seem to think of me," she began, "I don't wish to marry the Earl of Chiswick."

"Good judgment there," Lucien muttered.

"But I cannot simply reject the offer."

Lucien had to admit she was probably right on that count. Refusing any request of Chiswick's was a dicey sort of task, and Chloe's father would not be sympathetic to her reluctance.

"I might have an idea, along those lines," he began. Perhaps his seduction notion wasn't such a bad idea after all. She wasn't in the least interested in him, which eliminated most of the danger. If she would agree to play along just a little—flirt a bit, giggle like a girl with a beau, whisper nonsense, send a melting look his way now and then—he was certain the Earl of Chiswick would not only notice, but he'd get on his high horse and break off the entire connection before Sir George knew what had hit him.

Chloe shook her head. "I have a perfectly good plan, and the last thing I need is another one to confuse the situation."

Lucien was almost disappointed. Couldn't she at least have let him explain his idea? "Let's hear your plan, then. If I'm to be involved in this—"

"You're a bigger wet goose than I thought if you believe I'd put myself in your power any more than I must. All I need is for you to do an errand for me."

Lucien shrugged. "I imagine your father has grooms who would appreciate earning a few shillings by taking care of your personal requests."

"Are you *trying* to sound like a dunderhead, Lord Hartford? I need a letter delivered, but it wouldn't take much wit for a groom or a stable boy to realize he could earn a great deal more by taking it directly to my father for a reward, rather than seeking out the person it's addressed to."

"And then you would be in the suds." He eyed her narrowly. This might be the answer to his quandary. If his father was to hear that his chosen bride was communicating secretly, with—now there was the question. *Who?* "It's a letter to a lover, I gather?"

She tossed her head. "Of course not!" Then she bit her lip. "Well—I suppose you would say…"

"I had a suspicion you weren't writing to tell your old governess about your betrothal. I think you'd better tell me all about this plan of yours, Miss Fletcher."

"What is there to tell?" She had turned delightfully pink. "It's a *letter*, that's all."

"If it's so ordinary, send it by the mail coach."

She looked him over as if she'd like to build a fire and turn him on a spit. Then she sighed and went over to her horse. From a saddlebag she took a folded page. "I need for you to hand this letter to…" Her voice dropped. "Captain Hopkins. Jason Hopkins. You must put this into his hands—and only his."

Now Lucien knew what she'd sound like if she whispered nonsense into a man's ear—because that order was just as lacking in wit as any feminine chatter he'd ever half-listened to. "Just as a matter of curiosity—because I haven't officially agreed to be your errand boy, Miss Fletcher—I don't suppose you've thought far enough ahead to tell me where I might find this paragon of the British Army?"

"Of course I have. He's in the infantry, and his regiment is stationed now at Peterborough."

At least a couple of hours' ride, Lucien calculated. And then he would have to turn straight about and ride back. Of course, that assumed the captain was to be found in his quarters or nearby. If he happened to be off on maneuvers or delivering messages for some colonel, it might take days to run him down.

"It won't work," he said. "I can't just disappear from the castle for the better part of a day. Everyone will ask uncomfortable questions about where I went and why."

He thought for a moment she was going to cry, but Chloe Fletcher was made of sterner stuff than he'd expected. "How difficult can it possibly be for you to go for a long ride? All a gentleman must do to excuse himself is to announce that you need relief from your family's constant company. Or you can make up a story. In fact, if you weren't hen-hearted, you could simply go and make no explanation at all."

Lucien's jaw set hard. "Hen-hearted, am I?"

"It appears so. No wonder your father gives you no respect, if you never stand up to him!"

"You and my father have discussed this?" The polite edge to his voice could have peeled an apple.

"I've never discussed anything of the sort with him. We've barely exchanged words."

"Then I hardly think you an expert on the subject of my dealings with my father."

"But your sisters' feelings on the matter are not difficult to read, and they coincide with my own observations."

She was damnably slow to take a hint, Lucien noticed irritably. He nodded toward the folded page in her hand. "What is in this letter?"

"None of your business."

"It is if I'm to be carrying it. Tell me, or I won't help you."

Chloe tilted her head to one side and narrowed her eyes. "Deliver it to Captain Hopkins," she countered, "or I'll do nothing more to stop the wedding. So what about it, Lord Hartford?—for it's entirely up to you. Would you rather be my messenger this once, or my stepson forever?"

Chapter 10

❧

*I*sabel didn't come down to breakfast until late, but she was surprised to find the room crowded. Even the duke was in evidence; Isabel exclaimed in delight to see Uncle Josiah downstairs, with more healthy color in his face than she had seen since their arrival.

"Coming down to breakfast is nothing to make a fuss over," he grumbled.

"He's been growling at all of us," Emily put in. "But I think he looks pleased nonetheless that we're attempting to coddle him."

Isabel noticed her sister's full plate and helped herself to a sizeable pile of shirred eggs. She was considering the relative attractions of beef or ham when she realized that her husband was regarding her thoughtfully down the length of the sideboard, and she almost dropped the serving fork.

She felt her cheeks go as hot as the flame under the chafing dishes as she recalled their uninhibited behavior last night. It all felt like a dream now. Had she really shrieked as she took pleasure in what he was doing to her?—and then, afraid that the household would hear, bitten down hard on her hand to keep from shrieking again? Worse, she was very much afraid that at one point she had been so lost to good sense that she had begged…and then after he had finally done with her, she had tumbled into sleep so suddenly and so deeply that she didn't even know when he had left her bed.

"Let me help you to kidneys," Maxwell murmured. "They are said to be very healthy for you."

Had there been the smallest hesitation in his voice before that last word—as though it was not Isabel's welfare he was commenting on, but that of the child he was so determined to create?

But of course he was thinking only of his child.

She told herself she was not shocked at the realization; she wasn't even surprised. And she definitely was not disappointed to have it made clear that her own health was a concern for him only as it might affect a child she carried.

In fact, she was almost pleased to have the solid reminder of what was important—particularly since a child was just as important to her, now, as it was to him. Once she had embarked on this course, there was no way out but through—so the sooner she was provably pregnant, the sooner this farce would be over, and the sooner she would be free.

Maxwell laid a hand on the back of the chair next to his, as if to pull it out for her, but Isabel shook her head. "I shall sit with my uncle," she said, and took a chair between her father and the duke. Odd, however, that even though she was three seats away from her husband, she could feel him next to her, as though he was still cupping her wrist to hold her plate steady as he spooned kidneys onto it. She could smell his cologne as clearly as if his scent had soaked into the sleeve of her morning dress where he'd brushed against the fabric.

She half listened to the conversation as she pushed the kidneys around on her plate, and thought that Emily, sitting across from her, was being unusually chatty this morning. Her sister was sitting next to Gavin and paying not a whit of attention to him. What a shame that was. If only Emily could see their new cousin as Isabel herself did...

Emily paused midsentence as her gaze came to rest on Isabel. "My dear, what did you do to your hand?"

Isabel glanced down at the shadow of a bruise. "Bumped it, I suppose," she said and prayed that Emily would let the subject drop.

Chiswick turned a page in his newspaper. "Is Hartford still abed? One must wonder what sort of dissipation he could possibly have found to indulge himself in, not to be able to arise at a decent hour of the morning. Not that the rest of you are exactly early birds today."

Isabel felt her face warm. Dissipation—yes, that would be an accurate way to describe a good deal of what had gone on between her and Maxwell last night. She tried not to look at her husband, but she knew that his gaze was resting on her.

"You must have been quite deeply asleep last night, Emily," Chiswick went on, "since Hartford couldn't rouse you."

"Country air," Emily said promptly. "It always makes me rest so well."

Gavin chuckled. The duke looked askance at him, and Gavin added, "A castle was never my idea of the country. If you'd seen some of the small farms around Baltimore—"

"Spare us, Athstone," the duke said. "If I wanted to see agriculture in the heathenish new world, I'd have gone there. Take yourself off and study your ancestors for a while. Surveying the portrait gallery will give you a better understanding of the value of history and family, and help you forget about farms."

"Of course, sir," Gavin said respectfully. He bowed to the company and went out.

Emily pushed her chair back. "The seamstresses will be waiting. If you'll excuse me, Uncle Josiah?"

Isabel stopped stirring her food. "Wait just a moment, Emily, and I'll go with you."

Maxwell intervened. "But you have not yet finished your breakfast. Let me get you a fresh, hot plate, because your food must have gone cold. You must keep up your strength, for the sake of—"

Isabel's face flooded with color.

"—the seamstresses," Maxwell finished gently as he set a plate before her. "You want to be able to stand still long enough that your ball gown will fit properly—don't you, my dear Isabel?"

❂   ❂   ❂

Though Gavin never seemed to be in any hurry, he could obviously move quickly when he wanted to—for by the time Emily followed him from the breakfast room he was out of sight, and it took her a few minutes to run him to earth in the portrait gallery which spanned the width of the second floor of the castle's oldest section.

He was standing halfway down the gallery, contemplating a full-length portrait of a long-dead Duke of Weybridge and idly scratching the ears of Uncle Josiah's favorite dog, when she caught up with him. "Well, I must say this is the last place I thought of searching for you, Gavin—exactly where Uncle Josiah suggested you go."

He smiled a little but didn't take his gaze off the portrait. "A right old tartar *he* looks, doesn't he?"

Emily spared no more than a glance at the old duke in his stiffly whaleboned brocade coat and long, cascading curls before turning back to Gavin. "What were you *thinking*? Laughing at me in front of the entire family for saying I slept soundly!"

"You *do* sleep soundly—and a good thing it is *I* didn't or you'd have still been in my bed when Benson came in with tea this morning."

Emily bit her lip and said reluctantly, "I suppose I owe you thanks for that much. I seem to have been more tired last night than I thought."

The corner of Gavin's mouth twitched. "All that fresh air, no doubt."

"There you go again," Emily accused, "laughing at me. You *must* be more circumspect or someone will guess that we…that we…"

"You mean someone like your father? I should warn you that before you came down this morning, he admonished me to have a care with your reputation."

Emily's heart dropped to her toes. "But how could he possibly suspect—?"

"He told me that after our moonlight drive last night, he is concerned I may not fully appreciate the need to treat an English lady's good name with delicacy."

She could breathe again. "I'd almost forgotten that."

"My heart breaks," he murmured.

"A moonlight drive, in company, is nothing. It's done all the time in the *ton*. And stop trying to distract me. You can't go around laughing at me when—"

"Whenever you tell some gigantic bouncer? Is your behavior at breakfast what you consider being circumspect—chattering at random so no one else could get a word in, and never once looking at me? If that is an example of you being discreet—"

"More discreet than you were," she accused. "And you must have let something slip to Benson."

"I swear on my honor I did not. What makes you think I did?"

"Because he was in the gallery when I came down this morning, and he looked at me in such an impertinent way—"

"That would have been your own guilty conscience speaking, Emily. Benson is only impertinent to people who insult me."

"Me? I haven't—"

He raised an eyebrow.

"All right," she said reluctantly. "Perhaps I have. But—"

"There's an easy solution to all of this, you know. Just don't come back to my room."

Emily was startled. "What?"

"Surely last night provided the answer to your questions. If the possibility of being discovered troubles you so much, and if you feel you cannot trust me to maintain the proper respectful attitude, then you should thank your good fortune that last night is safely past—and not take further chances of discovery."

"Oh." Emily was surprised for a moment that he was being so calm, so straightforward, so clear of vision. She wondered if Gavin had found himself in this sort of situation before—facing down a woman's kinfolk just hours after making love to her.

And his suggestion was quite sensible, she had to admit. Emily had, in her inexperience, underestimated the difficulty of carrying on an intrigue directly under the noses of her entire family. How, she wondered, did the ladies and gentlemen of the *ton* ever manage? But house parties were generally made up of friends, not families—and if all of the guests were following the same set of rules, they would not ask uncomfortable questions of their fellows.

There was no reason to feel irritated at how easily Gavin seemed to have given up the idea of another night together. In fact, it would have been quite embarrassing if he had insisted, or pleaded, or begged, or bargained. She was glad he was being sensible.

"Quite a simple solution," Gavin said.

Emily tried to smother her aggravation. Did he need to sound so pleased that their *affaire* was already finished?

The silence stretched out awkwardly as she considered ways to excuse herself without looking as though she were running away or flouncing off in disappointment.

Gavin gestured toward the nearest oil painting. "Would you care to explain to me who all these worthy ladies and gentlemen are, and how they're related? I'm reasonably certain the duke intends to quiz me."

Emily darted a look at him, suspicious that he was changing the subject in an effort to spare her feelings. But he seemed perfectly earnest. "That's the fourth duke you're looking at," she began. "The artist is said to be Sir Peter Lely, who also painted Charles the Second. His duchess is just over there."

"The one who looks as if her stays are pinching?"

Emily tried not to giggle. Most of the gentlemen of her acquaintance wouldn't admit to knowing what stays were—at least not in a young lady's hearing.

Gavin offered his arm, and Emily slipped her hand into his elbow.

"Standing at her right is her son, the marquess. If you look closely you'll see your signet ring." She pointed.

Gavin twisted the signet on his finger.

"And the next portrait is her daughter," she went on. "That artist is said to have fallen in love with his subject and flattered her greatly."

"She looks like you," Gavin said softly.

And it was a long time and a good many portraits later when Emily remembered that she'd been meant to spend the morning with the seamstresses.

✦ ✦ ✦

Chloe Fletcher's demand had been nothing short of blackmail, and as his mount steadily clipped away the miles that lay between the linden grove at Mallowan and the army barracks at Peterborough, Lucien could scarcely believe that he'd surrendered to her demands. He was not only being held hostage by a pert little miss who probably weighed less than any one of the duke's favorite hounds, but she had used a threat that any fool would know she couldn't possibly mean to carry out. *Run my errand or I'll marry your father after all.*

What had he been thinking of, to cave in to something so foolish?

He whiled away a few miles thinking about what would happen if she acted on her threat. Lucien wouldn't mind watching the fireworks if the Earl of Chiswick came up against someone just as determined as he was.

No wonder your father gives you no respect, if you never stand up to him.

That terse assessment still stung, but it didn't mean she was right. Easy enough for her to make judgments when she was safely on the outside. In the end, however, determined though Chloe Fletcher might be, the Earl of Chiswick would stand for no nonsense from a mere wife. He'd crush her like a grape.

It would be a shame for that to happen—for that spirit of hers to be smashed out of existence. Lucien supposed that was why he had given in to her demands and why he was riding off on this mad errand.

The scent of roasting meat drifted from a wayside inn as he passed, and Lucien's belly rumbled. The horse needed rest, he told himself, so he turned the animal over to the ostlers and went into the taproom for a pint of ale and to check out the innkeeper's wife's skill with a hearty breakfast.

Exactly how mad the errand—and Chloe herself—might be, Lucien wasn't certain. Obviously he was helping to arrange an elopement; there was no room for doubt about that. Captain Hopkins must be more than just a friend, because Chloe had colored a bit when she spoke of him, and there had been that telltale softness in her voice when she said his name.

Equally obviously, Sir George and Lady Fletcher did not approve of Captain Hopkins as a suitor for their daughter. They probably had an inkling of Chloe's feelings—thus her need for complete privacy to ask the favor. The captain's mere existence might help explain why they were so quick to agree to marry off their only daughter to a much older man, earl or not. If Chloe Fletcher had tumbled into an attachment with a soldier who had no family or connections to speak of, her parents would have done everything in their power to stand in the young lovers' way. No doubt they thought that once married, she would be safe from foolish thoughts about a soldier in a bright red uniform.

Now, because of their clumsy handling of the entire affair, she was planning to elope. Could they have made any more of a mull of things?

But was Lucien helping matters? He had agreed to aid and abet a girl—barely past her first Season—who was running away to Gretna Green!

So much for me never going against my father's wishes. If Chloe succeeded in making her escape—or even if she didn't—and the earl found out the role Lucien had played in the scheme…That didn't bear thinking about.

But he might have read too much into the letter that weighed so heavily in his pocket and on his mind. Chloe might not really be planning a flight to Scotland; she might only wish to have the support of her beloved when she made her stand to her parents and the earl. After the way she had scolded Lucien for not voicing his opposition when his father applied pressure, surely she wouldn't simply run away rather than face the music.

He *needed* to know what was in that letter. He'd be in a far better position to offer real assistance if he knew exactly what she was planning.

He pulled the folded page out of his pocket and studied the seal. Was it his imagination, or was it slightly loose on one edge? If he was to slip a warm knife under the wax and pry just a very little, surely it would pop loose without breaking.

It wasn't that he wanted to snoop, of course. His intentions were pure; he only wanted to help. Investigating exactly what she was up to would be for her own good.

❋   ❋   ❋

When he first stepped into the portrait gallery, Gavin would have said the castle housed far too many dark, stiff, and solemn oil paintings of dark, stiff, and solemn people, most of whom looked too much alike to hold his interest. Emily's stories, however, kept him entertained, and by the time they'd circled the gallery he had a fair grasp of the Mainwaring family.

But all too soon they finished with the portraits, and she said shyly, "I should go."

Gavin groped for an excuse to keep her beside him a little longer. "This is the perfect place for a dancing lesson."

"Apart from the lack of music, perhaps."

"You could walk me through the figures. You wouldn't want me to embarrass the duke at his ball, would you, by showing myself as a clumsy colonial?" He did his best to look innocent and helpless.

Isabel's maid found them wheeling around the portrait gallery in a silent parody of a country dance, and with an embarrassed flutter Emily peeled her hand from Gavin's arm and went off to have her ball gown fitted.

Gavin found himself standing once more in front of the full-length portrait of the fourth duke's daughter, who did look amazingly like Emily. He thought, however, that the resemblance lay more in the expression than in the features themselves—a sort of mixture of haughty entitlement and mischief. He wouldn't be surprised if the minx in the painting had deliberately led the artist on so he would flatter her on the canvas.

And what about Emily? In their little dance of enjoyment, he wondered who was leading whom.

❂ ❂ ❂

For a young woman who had been so unhappy about the state of her wardrobe, Emily seemed awfully unconcerned about her new ball gown.

Isabel had plenty of time to consider the matter, since her own fitting was complete and one of the seamstresses was doing up the fastenings of her day dress—her own maid having been dispatched to search the castle for her missing sister—when Emily finally appeared, almost breathless.

"I am so sorry to keep you waiting," Emily said to the head seamstress. "I—well, the truth is I forgot."

The woman bobbed a curtsey. "It's perfectly all right, Lady Emily, but let's get you out of that dress right away so we can see how the ball gown looks."

"It is *not* all right," Isabel said. "How did you manage to forget? When you left the breakfast room before me, you said you were coming directly here."

"No, I didn't." Emily's voice was muffled because one of the seamstresses was lifting her dress over her head. She emerged with her hair askew and her face a bit pink. "I got here, didn't I? Oh, don't give me that look, Isabel—you remind me of Mother when I'd violated good manners, only you don't look nearly as stern as she did. You'll need to practice, so you'll be ready when you have a daughter of your own."

Isabel's stomach did a flip. *A daughter of your own.*

No. Fate couldn't be so cruel. The baby she would carry—the child she might be carrying even now—would be a boy. It *had* to be a boy. Then the Earl of Maxwell would have his heir, and Isabel would have Kilburn and her freedom. But if she were to give birth to a girl instead—a girl who could not inherit...

I will absolutely not have a girl. I just won't stand for it.

"Isabel?" Emily stood stock-still in the center of the room, wearing only her chemise and corset, and waved off the seamstress who was approaching with an armful of frothy deep-pink gauze. "Are you all right?"

"Perfectly," Isabel said mildly. "And I *am* practicing Mother's look—on you."

"Well, you can stop right now. I suppose next you'll be harping at me that I must hire another companion when I go back to Barton Bristow, since I won't have the benefit of your guidance."

"I can't think it matters. Mrs. Dalrymple never seemed in the least able to exert a good influence on you." Isabel sat down so her maid could touch up her hair where the fitting had disarranged it. "What have you been up to, anyway, to make you forget?"

"I found her in the portrait gallery, ma'am," Martha murmured into Isabel's ear. "Dancing—or something like that—with Lord Athstone."

Dancing—or something like that. With Gavin, whom Emily hadn't even spoken to at breakfast. Isabel's gaze went to Emily in the mirror, but her sister was submerged for the moment in pink gauze.

Finally, Emily's face reappeared. "Besides, other than my obvious rudeness to the seamstresses—for which I have apologized—what's the hurry?"

"You didn't hear Lady Fletcher say last night that she and Chloe might come to call on us this afternoon?" But of course she hadn't, Isabel realized, for Emily had been off to the side just then, arranging with Gavin to drive home with him in his curricle. "Mr. Lancaster might come with the ladies." Isabel stole a look at her sister to see if the shot hit home.

Emily shook out the skirt of the ball gown and glanced at her reflection over Isabel's shoulder. "His conversation would be preferable to listening to Lady Fletcher's hints."

"He seemed quite enamored of you last night—and you didn't appear to be put off by his interest. I thought you were determined not to encourage Father in making matrimonial plans for you."

"At least if Father is arranging alliances for me, he won't have so much energy to devote to his own." Emily tugged at the bodice, pulling it down a little lower. "I should be certain to tell Mr. Lancaster what color I'm wearing. He can choose his coat accordingly so that we shall look well together as we dance."

A fitting room full of seamstresses and maids was not the place to take her sister to task for flirting, Isabel reminded herself, and this was hardly the right time to dredge for the reasons why Emily was suddenly so flighty and so brittle.

And in any case, if I pry into her secrets, she may return the favor, and I'd much rather not share mine.

Isabel inspected Martha's handiwork, nodded, and stood up. "Do try to hurry, won't you, Emily?" She didn't wait for an answer.

As Isabel entered the drawing room, Gavin leaped to his feet, but she barely noticed him, for she was no sooner across the threshold than her nerves gave the characteristic thrum she had come to recognize as her own personal signal that the Earl of Maxwell was in the room.

"Gentlemen," she said. "It's not that I wish you to be gone from here, but…"

Maxwell had also stood. Her gaze was instantly drawn to the perfect fit of his dark-green coat, unblemished buckskins, and highly polished top boots.

Especially, she had to admit, the buckskins.

As she saw him start to smile, she dragged her gaze away. "I am half expecting Lady Fletcher to call at any moment."

Gavin looked puzzled.

"If we are here when the ladies arrive," Maxwell murmured, "we will no doubt be condemned to playing the gallants until they say their farewells, because it would be rude to leave them for other pursuits. And since they are coming from a distance, they may well stay for the entire afternoon. However, if we have already gone out when they arrive—"

"I believe," Isabel went on, "that Mr. Lancaster, at least, intends to accompany them."

Gavin was frowning. "Do you truly wish to be left alone with all of them?"

Isabel wanted to say that she would happily entertain an entire army as long as her husband wasn't part of it, but she kept her voice pleasant. "I am certain my father will be able to occupy any part of Mr. Lancaster's attention that is not focused on Emily."

She almost missed the way Gavin's mouth tightened, because only an instant later he said calmly, "Then I am not needed here, and I find myself longing for a ride. How about you, Max?"

The earl didn't answer. "How thoughtful of you, my dear Isabel, to offer Cousin Gavin and me the option of disappearing in such a timely fashion. But are you *quite* certain you would not prefer me to remain to support you?"

"Oh, do go away," she said irritably. "And as long as you're going, be certain to take Lucien with you so I don't have to deal with another of his heavy-handed attempts to show Chloe Fletcher the errors in her thinking."

Maxwell frowned a little. "I have yet to see him today. Gavin?"

Gavin shook his head. "His bedroom door was open and his man was about when I came downstairs, so he's not still abed, or ill. I wonder..."

The two of them went off, and Isabel sank into a chair to enjoy the quiet. At least she wouldn't have to deal with Maxwell, on top of Lady Fletcher and Chloe, and Emily flirting with Lancaster.

Her peace lasted only a moment, it seemed, before the butler announced Lady Fletcher's arrival. Such a short interval had passed that Isabel wondered if Maxwell and Gavin had managed to make their escape in time after all—but they did not reappear in the visitors' wake. Lady Fletcher rattled on, Chloe sat silent and prim as if she were trying to be invisible, and Mr. Lancaster looked around the room, obviously hoping to find Emily hidden in a corner.

Half an hour had gone by and the tea tray had just come in when Emily finally arrived, once more neat and trim. She had changed into a pale-blue day dress, Isabel noticed, one that flattered her golden-brown hair and peaches-and-cream complexion.

Emily fluttered for a moment over her apologies to Lady Fletcher and Chloe—and a more insincere performance Isabel had never seen—and gave Mr. Lancaster a melting glance that summoned him instantly to her side. "Have none of the gentlemen stayed at home to entertain you? I thought Lucien at least might finally make an appearance. But he seems to have gone off on some mysterious errand as well."

Isabel handed a teacup to Chloe just as a wave of pink rose in the girl's cheeks. She looked, Isabel thought, as though the heat of the entire teapot had suddenly washed over her.

"What a pity," Emily went on, "but I shall do my poor best to amuse you, Mr. Lancaster."

Isabel turned to look at her sister, dismissing Chloe's odd reaction from her mind. A bruising ride, Isabel thought grimly, sounded more appealing by the moment, if the alternative was to watch Emily flirt!

* * *

Early afternoon found Lucien once more within a few miles of the castle. As though his horse had sighted the towers and landmarks of home, the animal tossed his head and whickered eagerly. Lucien patted the gelding's neck. "You're tired out, aren't you, and longing to run for your stable? But it's not a good idea to start a race now, after the day we've had."

He had started to skirt the village when he thought better of the idea and drew up in front of the inn instead. Resting the horse for an hour would mean he wouldn't turn over an exhausted mount to a stable master who would without doubt question what he'd been up to.

A coin to an ostler assured that the gelding would be brushed down, watered, and supplied with hay and grain, and Lucien himself went off to the taproom while he waited. He could almost smell the innkeeper's ale all the way from the yard.

Delivering Chloe's letter had not been the simple errand she had seemed to think it would be. Merely finding Captain Hopkins had been a challenge. The army barracks had been full of bustle and noise, and Lucien had had to stop soldiers three times to ask directions. Finally he located his quarry at the smithy, where the captain had been overseeing a blacksmith who was tending to his horse—an animal that in Lucien's opinion was a great deal more show than substance. To add to Lucien's problems, Captain Hopkins had not been of a mind to interrupt his pursuits to listen to the confidential business of a complete stranger.

Lucien's eyes hadn't yet adjusted to the dimness inside the taproom when he heard his name called. "Lucien! Where in the name of heaven have you been all day?"

Lucien strode across the room to where Gavin sat by the window with a tankard of ale the innkeeper had just set in front of him. He plucked the tankard out of Gavin's hand and drained it. "Thoughtful of you to have a drink ready for me, Cousin." He turned to the Earl of Maxwell, sitting across the table, and eyed his tankard as well. "And you, too, Max—I couldn't have asked for more of a welcome than this."

The earl prudently moved his ale out of reach and gestured to the innkeeper. "You don't look as though you've been laboring in the fields all day, Lucien. What causes the great thirst?"

"Never knew I needed a reason to be thirsty," Lucien said. "Especially not when the ale is as good as this." He settled himself at the table as the innkeeper delivered another round. This time he sipped slowly and appreciatively.

He wouldn't have been surprised if the two of them had quizzed him. But Maxwell only raised an eyebrow and Gavin smiled a little, and Lucien relaxed. This might work out for the best after all. They could enjoy their ale, then ride back to the castle together—and with luck no one would ask exactly when he had turned up or where he might have gone before that.

"Are you two escaping the party preparations or the dress fittings?" he asked.

"Riding the estate," Gavin said. "Meeting tenants, seeing the land."

Lucien gave a soundless whistle. "Uncle Josiah approved that? I'd have liked to hear the conversation!"

"He told me to look around, get a feel for the estate."

"It was hardly a formal inspection," Maxwell added, "but enlightening nonetheless. And it fitted well with Gavin's urge to escape Lady Fletcher's call."

Lucien silently gave thanks for the impulse that had made him stop at the inn rather than ride straight on to the castle.

Maxwell consulted his pocket watch. "I suppose if we don't turn up at a reasonable hour, and in a reasonably sober condition, there will be a price."

"Surely not for you," Lucien said idly. "Isabel seems to prefer it when you're nowhere in sight."

Maxwell's hand clenched for a moment on the handle of his tankard, and then relaxed.

Lucien wondered why Lady Fletcher was making the trek over to Weybridge today, of all days. They'd all been together for dinner the night before, and the garden party and ball were tomorrow. Why wasn't she staying at home for once? Surely, just like his sisters, the Fletcher ladies needed to occupy themselves with—oh, things like ribbons and fripperies, he thought vaguely, and whatever else females did all day when getting ready for a big occasion.

Worry gnawed at him. Max seemed to think this was an ordinary call—but then Max had no reason to be suspicious of Lady Fletcher's motives. Surely Chloe would be careful not to let her mother suspect she was up to something— wouldn't she? But they did say mothers had a special sense about these things.

Lucien was just glad he didn't have to face Chloe's dragon of a mother right now—before he had a chance to talk to Chloe herself. He wished he didn't have to wait until morning, when they had agreed to meet once more in the linden grove, to work out a story.

Yes, he was looking forward to their rendezvous in the morning—even though he had yet to decide what he would tell Chloe about Captain Hopkins and his reaction to her letter.

❀ ❀ ❀

When Emily finally flitted into the drawing ro5om, Isabel was just starting to pour tea—which probably meant that the Fletcher party had settled in for the long term. Emily made her curtsey to Lady Fletcher and Chloe, tossed a quick smile and a greeting to Mr. Lancaster, and surveyed the room. A mere glance at the tea tray showed just half a dozen cups and saucers set up neatly in a row—enough for the people currently presently in the room, with only one extra.

So Isabel was not anticipating that the gentlemen of the castle would turn out in force. Emily wondered which of them her sister did expect to join the group. She supposed Isabel might still be hoping that Gavin would make an effort to cement his interests with Chloe—though Emily thought it rather a bad bet.

Isabel handed a steaming cup to Lady Fletcher. "I expect our father will be down shortly. I believe he intended to visit with Uncle Josiah."

"The dear earl," Lady Fletcher said fondly. "Such a lovely man."

Emily swallowed hard in an effort to keep herself from choking.

"And the dear duke, too. We are so fond of him, Sir George and I. Chloe, of course, has always regarded him almost as a grandfather."

Chloe seemed not to notice what her mother had said—or else she had heard but merely had a better command of herself than Emily would have expected. She seemed to be studying the stitching in her gloves, except when she sneaked glances at the tall clock in the corner. Emily could sympathize, for it seemed impossible to her that no more than five minutes had passed since she'd come into the room. It felt like an age.

Lady Fletcher sipped. "Do tell me, my dear Lady Isabel—is Weybridge up to the exertions of a garden party, and the ball? It seems so odd that he would spend his strength to host such a party if he is as ill as it is reported."

"If the choices are to lie helpless and dull in bed," Emily said, "trying to husband one's vital force merely to extend the time one can lie helpless and dull in bed, or to spend one's strength in a last glorious event, I believe I know which I would choose."

"You are so full of the vital force, Lady Emily, that it is difficult to see you doing anything else but living life to the fullest," Lancaster chimed in.

With great effort, Emily resisted the urge to roll her eyes. Too bad Gavin wasn't present to hear that. She wondered what his reaction would be—and whether he'd be able to hide it. He probably wouldn't try. She suspected his eyes would glint and that little half smile would toy with the corner of his mouth. And she might even get a peek at the dimple that occasionally came out of hiding in his left cheek. Such an unexpected thing that dimple was, in such a masculine man—but all the more charming in her mind for being so improbable. And he'd have some unanswerable rejoinder to put Lancaster in his place.

Unless, of course, Gavin no longer cared what she did.

Emily caught herself up short. This arrangement of theirs had never been more than physical. No matter what she did, it would be none of his business—especially now that their *affaire* had come to such a sensible end.

With an effort, she pulled her mind back to the drawing room and to Lancaster, just as he said, "Surely now that you are away from your exile, Lady Emily, you have reconsidered the choice to bury yourself in a village."

She frowned. "Barton Bristow is hardly exile, Mr. Lancaster."

He gave her a small, pitying smile. "I understand the reason for retreating from the world for a while, of course. Such an action made you a mysterious figure to the *ton*—even a tragic one."

She paused with her teacup halfway to her mouth. "You think that was my aim?"

"But you must not expect that society will remember indefinitely, Lady Emily. Past a certain point, you will no longer be considered inscrutable—merely eccentric." His voice dropped. "You may even be seen as *odd*."

"Such a pity that would be," Emily said crisply.

"Indeed it would. The duke's ball is the perfect opportunity to make clear that you wish to rejoin your world, by asking the guests to extend the hand of forgiveness."

"You're suggesting I should *ask for forgiveness?*" Emily could feel heat rising in her face. How dare he suggest that she should beg to be once more part of society? She hadn't been the one who created the scandal!

"You did turn your back on your friends," Lancaster reminded quietly.

Emily's hand was shaking, and her teacup rattled in the saucer. She set it down carefully.

Before she could gather her thoughts and blast him, a footman wheeled the Duke of Weybridge's chair into the drawing room, and the force of habit brought her to her feet to make her curtsey.

The interruption couldn't have been timed better. There would be no convincing Mr. Lancaster that he sounded like a fool, so it was better to leave him entirely alone.

What had she been thinking, anyway, to start flirting with him again? Gavin wasn't present to watch—and what was the point in flirting if there was no audience?

For a moment the thought didn't even register, and when it did, Emily was puzzled for a moment. Why had the mere thought of flirting with one man brought another—very different—man to her mind?

You only did it because Gavin made it clear he doesn't want you.

But that was nonsense, for Gavin hadn't done anything of the sort. He'd just been sensible—pointing out the fact that even a very large castle was no guarantee of privacy when it was full of family members. Emily was relieved to know that he wasn't going to press her for more than she was willing to do.

Really she was.

Belatedly, she turned her attention to the gushing welcome Lady Fletcher was dishing up for the duke. "Your Grace, you are looking so well!" she exclaimed. "I was fearful, after the reports—but indeed, you have seldom looked better."

Emily caught Isabel's gaze. Her sister seemed to feel the same raw astonishment Emily did. Which was foolish of both of them, since the one thing that had been clear about Lady Fletcher from the start was that she had no native tact. To tell a dying duke that he looked quite well was wishful thinking of the highest order.

Emily hadn't seen the Duke of Weybridge since breakfast, and then he had looked pale and drawn...or had he? She had been so caught up in her own ticklish conscience, half expecting someone to guess that she had spent a good part of the night in Gavin's bed, that she hadn't looked closely at Uncle Josiah.

He *did* look better. He seemed rested, and there was more color in his face and a bit of a sparkle in his eyes.

He must be excited by the upcoming celebration. Such a boost might not last, for it was probably not an actual improvement in his condition. But even if that was the case, seeing him lively again—if only for a short while—was enough to lift her spirits. She caught his eye and smiled.

"I had doubts of your wisdom in holding a party," Lady Fletcher confided. "Even a small party—much less two separate ones."

The duke frowned. "Small? Compared to some that have been held here in the past, it could be called small, but this is hardly to be an intimate gathering. The rest of the houseguests should start arriving at any time now, I believe. I hope you and Sir George intend to take part in all the festivities."

"That might be difficult," Lady Fletcher murmured.

"Not at all. You must bring everything you need for the ball when you come for the garden party—so there is no need to go all the way back to Mallowan in between. Of course, you'll stay overnight after the ball as well. No sense in driving home in the dark."

Joy. We'll have Lady Fletcher with us full-time.

Chloe suddenly sat up straighter. For the first time since Emily had entered the room, the girl looked almost excited.

Emily glanced toward the entrance hall, half expecting to see the Earl of Chiswick—for surely only the sight of her betrothed could cause such a contrast in a young woman's demeanor. But it was only the gentlemen returning from wherever they'd gotten to all afternoon—Gavin, and Maxwell, and Lucien. Their boots clattered on the marble floor of the hall, and one of them laughed. That must be Maxwell, she thought, though she did not remember ever hearing him laugh before—but had it been either Lucien or Gavin, she would have recognized the sound.

She realized abruptly that at the first sound from the hall she, too, had sat up even straighter than her mother had always demanded. *No doubt you look just as foolish as Chloe does.*

Deliberately she composed her face and settled ever so slightly back in her chair, and told herself that the mere fact Gavin Waring had finally returned to the castle was no reason for her to feel excited.

Chapter 11

❧

ucien hoped that they had lingered long enough in the village over their ale for Lady Fletcher to finish her call and depart for home. Failing that, he thought perhaps they could slip in a side door and avoid being drawn into the socializing.

But on the ride from the village to the castle, they encountered two carriages full of the duke's guests, and ordinary courtesy demanded that they all proceed together. In the castle courtyard, the footmen helped the guests to climb down. The first one to alight—an elderly lady with a nose so prominent Lucien thought it must precede her into a room—fixed a beady gaze on him and announced, "You're Chiswick's cub, aren't you? I've a couple of young ladies here who want to make your acquaintance."

Behind her, two giggling girls not long out of the schoolroom climbed down from the chaise. Lucien was so unnerved that he almost forgot about Lady Fletcher.

Maxwell tossed a sympathetic smile in Lucien's direction. "Lady Stone, what a delight it is to see you again—and to meet your young friends. I'm sure they will also like to become acquainted with Lord Athstone, if I might be allowed to present him?"

Lady Stone's gaze grew even beadier as her gaze came to rest on Gavin. "Weybridge's heir?"

Under other circumstances, Lucien might have been amused by the smoldering look that Gavin gave Maxwell—but as it was, all Lucien felt was relief. With a duke's heir present, no young woman was going to look at a mere viscount—even if he would someday be an earl.

"Indeed," Lady Stone said, and there was a world of meaning in the single word.

Lucien let out a careful breath, feeling that he'd barely dodged a bullet.

Maxwell seemed to have read his mind, however, for he murmured wickedly to Lucien, "Of course, there are two of them. Plenty to go around."

"Getting acquainted can wait," Lady Stone declared, "while a glass of port to cut the travel dust cannot. Give me your arm, Maxwell. If I can burst in on the duke in all my dirt, you damned well can escort me."

Lucien looked around wildly, hoping that someone from the second carriage might rescue him, but at last surrendered to the inevitable and offered his arm to the nearest young lady. He was pleased to see, however, that she was so busy goggling at Gavin, just ahead of them with the other young lady, that she almost missed the step at the entrance. For a moment she hung heavily on his arm, and then she caught herself, cast a look up at him through her lashes, and murmured something about him being her hero.

"No trouble, miss," Lucien said shortly and hurried her on into the castle.

Once in the drawing room, his gaze was drawn almost instantly to Chloe, who was sitting off to the side, bolt upright. As he came into view, her eyebrows raised a fraction, and there was a question in her eyes. He glanced around, but everyone seemed to be paying attention only to the very assertive Lady Stone—the woman was good for something after all—so he gave Chloe the smallest of nods.

She seemed to sag in relief, closing her eyes for an instant. Then she sat up straight again, looked directly at Lucien, and smiled.

She had never smiled at him before—at least not a real smile, one that wasn't simply a polite gesture. A stab in the heart couldn't have surprised him more. She looked almost gay, relaxed, at ease—as though she was truly enjoying herself. As though she was happy to see him.

It wasn't really Lucien who had put that glorious sparkle in her eyes and sent the warmth into her face, of course, but the news that her message had been delivered. Still, being on the receiving end of that look made Lucien's breath stick tight in his chest. He hadn't realized before that she was more than conventionally pretty, in the unremarkable way that many of the young women of the *ton* were. But the fact was that with joy and liveliness in her face, Chloe was absolutely beautiful.

He wondered if his father had ever seen her like this. If he had, no wonder Chiswick had been stunned enough to begin negotiations to marry her. The earl might be old, but he was still male—and when a woman smiled at him in that way, a man was bound to get ideas.

At least most men would.

Hell, Lucien admitted, even *he* had gone a bit out of focus for a minute there. And if someone as non-marriage-minded as Lucien could be confused by Chloe's melting look and sultry smile, it would be no wonder if an old codger like Chiswick started to believe that in her company he might relive the glorious days of youth.

Chloe gave a discreet pat to the cushion beside her. Lucien shook his head a fraction. He understood she was eager for details, but surely she had more sense than to think a conversation between them could go unnoticed—especially if he strode straight across the room to sit by her.

Chloe bit her lip and her gaze slid to the young woman beside him.

"I am Miss Carew, by the way," the young woman announced. "Lady Stone is a friend of my uncle. You may know him—Colonel Huffington? My sister and I are visiting my uncle, so Lady Stone invited us to come along when the duke's invitation arrived. I am so excited to be a guest at a real castle; you have no idea!"

Lucien was barely listening. He was still watching Chloe from the corner of his eye. And he was wondering whether she was as certain as she seemed that Captain Hopkins would follow instructions. On a whim, he tugged Miss Carew over toward Chloe. "You must meet Miss Fletcher." Belatedly, he realized he had sounded as though he were issuing an order, not making a suggestion—but the girl seemed accustomed to that tone of voice, since her uncle was a military man. She made a pretty curtsey to Chloe.

Chloe stood to return it, but she didn't invite Miss Carew to sit down. A moment later, under the cover of a burst of laughter that drew Miss Carew's attention to a group across the room, Chloe murmured, "All went well?"

Lucien couldn't quite bring himself to agree, so he temporized. "Your letter has been delivered."

Was the relief that flickered in her eyes mixed with something else? Before he could identify the emotion, it had passed and she was smiling again. "Then everything will proceed as I have planned. I thank you, Lord Hartford—I am greatly in your debt."

Up close, Lucien realized, the effect of her smile was even stronger. He felt queasy—but he wasn't certain whether that was the result of her smile or of her words.

She was betting on her soldier to carry out her wishes, and she had tossed all of her chips into this wager. Lucien couldn't help but wonder what would happen to Chloe if Captain Hopkins didn't come through in exactly the way she expected he would.

⁕ ⁕ ⁕

Gavin hadn't exactly ignored what Lucien had been telling him for days now—that as the heir of one of England's wealthiest dukes, he would be sought after and courted not for himself but for his potential title. But he hadn't expected the chase to start here in the castle—a place where, much to his surprise, he had already begun to feel safe and at home.

And he hadn't expected to have so little time before the pursuit grew determined. But the fact was—at least as far as the Carew sisters were concerned—he might as well have a target painted on his chest.

Even as the Carews took turns attempting to enchant him, he found some comfort in noting that Lucien, too, had to fend them off. All through tea, and again as the group gathered in the drawing room before dinner, Gavin's attention was divided between being politely discouraging to the ladies and frankly enjoying watching Lucien.

But even Maxwell hadn't entirely escaped feminine attention, Gavin realized. A particularly lovely young matron whose carriage had arrived not long after Lady Stone's—Lady Murdoch was her name—had been flirting with Maxwell from the instant she'd entered the drawing room. With every passing minute, she grew more animated. Her laugh trilled higher, and her fingertips brushed more closely across Maxwell's sleeve.

And with every passing minute, Isabel seemed to freeze just a bit more solid. Gavin wondered if she realized how obviously her irritation was showing.

What was it Emily had told him? Maxwell had been rumored to have a mistress before he married. Nothing unusual about that, of course. But from the look of things, Maxwell's mistress was anything but in the past.

After dinner, Isabel rose from the hostess's chair to lead the ladies out of the dining room, leaving the gentlemen to their port and cigars, and it was all Gavin could do not to heave a sigh of relief.

Lucien moved down the table to sit beside him, sharing a rueful grin. "At least we have a few minutes of peace from the muslin company, and I intend to enjoy every instant. Are you going to pour that port or only stare at it, Gavin?"

Gavin filled his own glass and handed the decanter on. "Are all the ladies of the *ton* quite so determined?"

"Some of them are more so. Or their mothers are, which is even worse. Now you understand why I avoid London parties at all costs. I just never expected Uncle Josiah to play me false like this, bringing the hounds right into the house."

"I suppose it's good practice," Gavin said. "Dealing with them a few at a time."

"I'd rather *not* deal with them. I'm locking my bedroom door tonight, and I advise you to do the same."

Not a bad idea. Since Emily wouldn't be appearing beside his bed again, looking like a delightful phantom in her white nightdress, he might as well make certain no one else could surprise him. He doubted the Carew sisters would be as open-minded as Emily was about lessons in making love. At least, he suspected, their views regarding proper conduct on the morning after would be very different from Emily's.

He was not looking forward to his lonely bed. The tall, carved four-poster had felt very empty in the early-morning hours after Emily had slipped away to her own room. Feeling noble because he had successfully resisted the urge to complete the act—and leave her with no questions whatever about what lovers did—was little consolation.

Still, leaving her maidenhead intact had been the right thing to do, for Emily was obviously rethinking her options. The carriage that had delivered the lady who might be Maxwell's mistress had also brought a young man whom Emily clearly knew. Though she hadn't flirted with the young Baron Draycott as she had with Lancaster at the Fletchers' party, it had been apparent to Gavin that she was enjoying the baron's company in the drawing room before dinner. She had smiled and leaned ever so slightly toward him to share an observation, as though she was feeling quite serious about the young man.

Gavin looked across the table to where the Earl of Chiswick was chatting with Draycott. "Friend of the family?" he asked Lucien in a low voice.

"Who? Draycott? His sister was at school with mine, I think—so he went around a bit with Emily when she first had her come-out."

"She seemed happy to see him this afternoon."

"Did she? I suppose she might have missed him, though she never complained when Father discouraged him from setting his sights on her. Father said it was because Draycott has so little brain, but I always thought he was set on Emily bringing a bigger title into the family than a mere barony."

"Lancaster has no title at all, but the earl seems to think he would be a good match."

"Well, things changed, what with Philip and all," Lucien said cryptically. "Now Father might think even Draycott would be a good thing for Emily."

Gavin let his gaze drift over the young baron. "He looks like a lamb, with all that unkempt curly hair."

Lucien's laugh sounded more like a snort. "That, my friend, is the newest style. But he *is* a bit of a sheep—Emily would have her own way on every question."

Gavin wondered if that was what she wanted. But at least the choice was still hers; he had done the right thing, and he knew it.

Now if he could just stop the frustrated state of his own body from causing him to have second thoughts about that decision. Not that it mattered anymore. She would not be coming back.

❀ ❀ ❀

After dinner, the Carew sisters tried out the duke's pianoforte, while Lady Stone, with a single shrewd glance at Isabel, drew Lady Murdoch aside to a pair of chairs in a corner. "For I'm certain you know all the gossip, my dear Elspeth," she said, "and it will never do if the *ton* finds out that I do not!"

With the others occupied, Emily was free to go straight to her sister's side. "Lady Murdoch is a cat," she said frankly. "But what's wrong with you? It isn't as though *you* want Maxwell—and in any event, she's the one who's flirting. Maxwell isn't doing anything to encourage her."

"I have no idea what you are talking about, Emily."

Emily felt as if a door had been slammed on her hand. She bit her lip and hoped the evening would not drag on interminably. Who would have expected she'd find herself defending the Earl of Maxwell—and to his wife, of all people?

Over the tinkle of the pianoforte, she couldn't help but hear Lady Stone's pointed questions as she interrogated Lady Murdoch about the doings of the *ton*.

Eventually, Lady Murdoch seemed to have had enough. "Much as I have enjoyed our conversation, Lady Stone, I must not ignore our host's nieces." She rose. "Lady Isabel—"

Emily took a deep breath and stepped between Isabel and Lady Murdoch. "I don't recall my Uncle Josiah ever mentioning you, Lady Murdoch. How is it you know the duke?"

"My husband is an old friend of Weybridge's. I am his representative to honor the duke's birthday, since Murdoch's health does not allow him to travel."

"*Old friend.*" Lady Stone's laugh sounded like a carpenter's rasp. "That's the truth! Murdoch isn't as old as Weybridge, of course, but he's hardly a puppy."

Beside Emily, Isabel murmured, "He's rich, of course. *Very* rich. And she fulfilled her duty admirably, because nine months and one day after the wedding, Lady Murdoch presented her husband with an heir. So now she's free to once again seek out more amiable company."

Once again? Emily sucked in a long, soundless breath. Obviously, Isabel had heard the gossip that had been circulating even before Emily had left London, linking Maxwell's name with Lady Murdoch's. Or possibly there were new stories going around—ones that Emily, in her backwater village, had not yet heard. No wonder Isabel's nose was out of joint, with her husband's mistress sharing the same roof.

"You're not making things better by letting her see that you care," Emily whispered.

Isabel didn't seem to hear the advice—but she did smile at Lady Murdoch and make a comment about a mutual acquaintance, and the awkward moment passed.

Blessedly, the gentlemen did not linger over their port. The duke retired directly to his bedroom—and that was just as well, Emily thought. By tomorrow, Isabel would be calmer and less likely to confront Uncle Josiah to ask why he had invited Lady Murdoch—and with his uncertain state of health, such a showdown would be more than just unpleasant; it might be dangerous.

With no special entertainment planned and a long day of travel behind them, the new guests were easily encouraged to seek their beds early.

"How thoughtful of you to suggest it, Lady Emily," Lady Murdoch purred. "Above all things, I crave a restoring..." She paused and then directed a sultry smile at Maxwell. "...sleep."

Yesterday, Emily herself might not have caught all the underlying meanings in that single suggestive word. Now—after just one night in Gavin's bed—she understood exactly what sort of invitation Lady Murdoch was issuing, and she wondered if Maxwell would accept.

Not that it was any of her business what he did—except that it concerned Isabel.

Suddenly Emily felt warm, as though a pair of skilled and knowing hands gently caressed her body. She turned her head to see Gavin watching her.

Though he was standing between the Carew sisters, his eyes were dark and intent and focused on Emily. He held her gaze for a moment, and then with no hurry, he looked slowly down her body. Her sea-green dimity gown seemed to evaporate as he studied her, and goose bumps rose on her skin as though she was indeed naked.

This morning he had seemed almost eager to be rid of her, but now...Was it only her imagination, or was he issuing an invitation? Not that she had any intention of acting on it, even if that was what he meant. She refused to put herself in the position of begging a reluctant man.

But he didn't look reluctant.

An embarrassing gush of warmth rippled through her body and pooled between her legs. But that, she told herself firmly, would go away. She just wouldn't look at him anymore. She would go up to her room, to her own bed, and to sleep.

Two hours later, she had to admit the truth. Her room was lonely, her bed felt cold, and there would be no sleep. Merely lying down reminded her of being with him—of the way he had gently laid her on his bed and joined her there. Every time she tried to close her eyes, she could feel Gavin's hands on her, stroking and caressing, sending flickers of sensation over her skin—flickers which built to ripples and then to waves. But unlike ripples of water in a puddle, moving rhythmically outward from the source, these waves gathered, concentrating at her core until the emptiness there was more than she could stand. Though she tried to satisfy herself, the effort left her frustrated beyond bearing, unable to capture even the faintest echo of the magic she had felt the night before.

She didn't realize she'd made a decision until she was standing at Gavin's door. She hesitated there for an instant, as flighty as a butterfly—but the sound of a door quietly closing somewhere across the gallery sent panic through her veins. She turned the knob and pushed hard in her eagerness to get out of sight. The door swung a few inches and stopped with a sort of *whoof*. Puzzled, she leaned against it.

Gavin, with his hand still gripping the matching knob, looked around the edge of the door. "I must say this is a surprise."

Emily blinked up at him, too startled at finding him there to think clearly. He was obviously on his way out. But he was wrapped in a dark dressing gown, which surely meant he wasn't going down to join the other gentlemen at some pastime. And he wasn't carrying a candle.

"Oh," she said finally, trying to be delicate. "Are you on your way to visit a lady?"

He raised one eyebrow. "No, Emily, I was planning to knock on every door up and down the gallery and ask if anyone had a volume of sermons I could borrow, to bore me to sleep. Are you mad? Of course I was going to visit a lady!"

She told herself she was neither surprised nor disappointed. "Then I mustn't get in your way. I'm only here because I heard a door close somewhere and I didn't want to be caught so far from my room."

The glimmer of his eyes, reflecting the faint glow of moonlight falling through the glass panels in the roof far above their heads, took her breath away. "You are a terrible liar, Emily. If you weren't coming here, what are you doing on this side of the gallery?" His hand closed hard on her arm and he tugged her into his sitting room. With the door closed, he leaned against it and pulled her into his arms. "Ninny. I was coming to see you."

His mouth was hot against hers, demanding, certain. Her breasts ached, and wet heat surged between her legs. "You said we shouldn't," she reminded, almost incoherently.

"Yes, I did—and I seem to recall you agreed with me. In the light of day, that decision made perfect sense. But I gather you couldn't sleep either?" His hands skimmed her body with easy familiarity. "I assume you're not here because you're looking for a book of sermons."

"No. I want you to do…*everything*…again." He pressed her more tightly against him, and the hard bulge of his erection against her belly was all the answer she needed. "But…"

He went still. "But what, Emily?"

"Last night you didn't—" She didn't know how to say it, so she licked her lower lip instead.

His gaze focused on the tip of her tongue. "If you mean that I didn't take your virginity, no, I didn't. And I never intended to."

Sadness drifted through her. "So that means we didn't really become lovers, did we?"

"Of course we did. What are you talking about?"

"Will you, tonight?"

He swallowed—though Emily thought it was more of a gulp—and said, "No."

"But why not? If that's what lovers do?"

"Because there is no practical way to assure that you wouldn't become pregnant. Well—there is, mostly, but I… uh…I don't have what I'd need to protect you. And while taking a lover is one thing, I doubt you're willing to scandalize your village, or your family, with a child."

She considered that. "Then if you don't have—whatever it is—that means there isn't a mistress waiting for you in the village, is there?"

"Emily, you are always a surprise. You didn't really believe I'd stashed a doxy in the inn—did you?"

"No." Her voice wavered. "Though I did wonder a bit today, when you were gone so long. But it's nice to know for certain. You really were coming to my room?"

"I really was—in the hope that you were as uncomfortable as I am. Though I was prepared to swear I was sleepwalking, if you didn't welcome me."

"I would have welcomed you," she whispered, and he growled a little and picked her up to carry her to his bed.

Just as she had requested, he did *everything*, all over again—and then, while she was still dreamily basking in the afterglow of her climax, he took hold of her hand and taught her to satisfy him.

She stroked him gently until he gritted his teeth and cupped his fingers around hers to urge her on, and she watched in awe as the first tiny droplet pearled. Moved by an instinct she did not begin to understand, she leaned over him and touched the tip of her tongue to the opening of his penis.

He growled, and Emily pulled back in shock. "No," he said thickly. "That's...that's wonderful." He threw back his head and groaned in release.

A surge of energy swept over Emily. If she could do this to him—make him lose control...She was thrilled—and stunned—with the realization of this newfound power, and eager to explore. What else might she be able to do? He had nearly driven her mad—it would be only fair if she returned the favor.

Afterward, he nestled her close to his side, and Emily listened to his heartbeat slow gradually to normal. "That was wonderful, Gavin. When can we do it again?"

His penis twitched against her belly. "Apparently, just about any time," he said dryly. "The truth is that I want so much to be inside you that I don't trust myself."

Warily, she lifted her head from his chest. "You aren't going to send me back to my room just to protect yourself, are you? Because I don't want to go."

"Then you must promise not to tempt me any further." He considered. "And if I forget my pledge, just lift up this lovely, perfect knee…" His hand slid down her thigh to cup her kneecap. "And hit me hard, right here." He bent her leg and demonstrated, though gently.

Emily laughed. "As if I would. That would *hurt*."

"Exactly my point." He kissed her kneecap and released her, then shifted her a bit, cupping her against his body, and nuzzled her shoulder. "And in the meantime, I'm going to distract myself by exploring all the other bits of you—the ones that don't make me think of plunging myself inside you."

Emily was pretty much convinced there weren't any bits like that. At least, she hadn't found any part of *him* yet that didn't tempt her to pull him down to nestle within her.

But then, she was no expert—and she wasn't about to argue the point.

❉   ❉   ❉

With Lady Murdoch present in Weybridge Castle, Maxwell would not be setting foot in his wife's bedroom tonight. Isabel was certain of that, yet every sound sent her heart fluttering for fear that she might be wrong after all.

And there were so many sounds that she was constantly in turmoil. She had never before realized the castle constantly creaked. Or perhaps her hearing was so magnified tonight that she heard things she never would have noticed before. Would she be able to hear him leaving his own room to seek out his mistress?

That would be a good thing, she told herself, for she would know for certain he would not be coming to her.

If she was truly fortunate, she was already pregnant, and when Maxwell's heir was born, she would be in the same position as Lady Murdoch—with her obligations fulfilled, she could take a lover. And because she would have met every one of her husband's conditions, she would be absolutely free—with a home of her own and an income more than adequate for all her needs.

Doubt assailed her. Their bargain was hardly an easy one, but could it be as simple as that? Had she overlooked something? Made an assumption that might come back to haunt her?

She took her jewel case from the wardrobe. There was little enough in it of value—her mother's pearls, a pair of earbobs set with brilliants, a brooch that had been a gift on her sixteenth birthday from Uncle Josiah and his duchess. The most important item in it, in Isabel's mind, was the single sheet of paper that she had tucked safely away at the bottom.

She tipped the contents out on the coverlet and unfolded the page of contract terms that Maxwell had written out. It all seemed direct, straightforward, plain and simple. And yet something about the agreement didn't feel right.

She almost laughed at the insanity of that thought. How utterly foolish of her—*nothing* about an agreement of this sort was right!

Behind her, Maxwell spoke. "Are you deciding what jewels to wear for the ball, my dear?"

Intent on their contract, Isabel had not consciously heard him come into the room. Yet she didn't feel the jolt of surprise she normally did. Somehow, even as she had explained to herself that he would not seek her out tonight, she had known better. She had understood, deep down, that the matter of his heir was so important to him that he would not be deflected from his goal.

She wondered how Lady Murdoch would feel about that.

Isabel glanced over her shoulder at him, trying to block his view as she scrambled her few treasures—and the contract—back into the jewel case. "I am setting a new fashion," she said airily. "With no jewels, my dress will receive the attention it deserves rather than being only a background to a hodgepodge of ornaments."

"Then your gown must be beautiful indeed—but if you plan to wear no jewels, how odd it is to sort them. Are you certain you were not reviewing our agreement, instead?"

"Well, that, too." She closed up the case and shifted her position on the edge of the mattress to face him. "You see, Maxwell, the truth is I feel...different."

He settled onto the bed next to her. Though he left a few inches between them, Isabel's skin prickled at his nearness. There was only the thickness of his dressing gown, and her nightdress, separating them.

"And by *different*, I suppose you mean pregnant?"

To Isabel's relief, his voice was absolutely calm. She hadn't expected this to be quite so easy—but perhaps he was eager to grasp the opportunity to spend his time with Lady Murdoch instead. "I expect that's what it means, yes."

He leaned a little closer and stretched his hand over her belly. His palm rubbed gently against the linen of her nightdress and warmed the flesh beneath. "And this odd feeling is centered right here, where our child would grow?"

Isabel nodded. "Exactly. Therefore, there is no longer any need to..." She hesitated and added delicately, "to spend your energy on me."

"How very convenient that would be for you. But since you have never been pregnant before, how can you be certain?"

Taken off guard, she had no answer. She shifted her feet on the carpet. Suddenly his hand on her belly seemed to burn. *This isn't going to be so easy after all.*

His voice, low and soft, stirred the tendrils of hair around her ear as he whispered, "Have you considered the possibility, Isabel, that the odd feeling in your womb might be desire?"

She snapped, "More likely it's dread!"

He smiled. "No, or you would not respond to lovemaking as you do. There is nothing unladylike about admitting you have physical needs—or that I satisfy them. In any case, since it is far too soon to know for certain that you are pregnant, and because I prefer not to take the risk of losing another month in case it turns out that you are not, I intend to...as you say...spend my energy on you at every opportunity."

The heat of his hand sank deeper into her flesh, until her insides seemed to have melted. She fidgeted under his touch, and he gently kneaded her belly, his fingertips scorching a pattern on her skin.

"Fine," she said between clenched teeth. "Get it over with, then." She flung herself back on the bed and pulled up her nightdress to better accommodate him.

He laughed softly. His hand slipped down to stroke her curls, and he slipped a finger inside her. "Your body can't lie," he whispered. "You're wet and slick and eager for me."

What was it he had said? Something about how she must have been tempted at times to take a lover. *Think of one of those men, if you like, while I make love to you. I don't mind if you pretend.*

"Eager? Not for you," she said coolly.

He moved over her, nudging her legs apart, settling himself against her with the head of his penis barely sliding inside her body. "Tell me," he whispered against her ear. "Describe him for me—your dream lover."

Her mind went blank. She could think of nothing, only feel the spot where they were so nearly joined as she waited for him to take her. She gasped in a feeble effort to regain her senses.

I don't mind if you pretend…

He didn't mind if she dreamed of some other lover, because he must be doing the same himself. What if she asked him to describe the woman he imagined when he closed his eyes? But she didn't need to ask. The picture was just as clear in her mind as it must be in his, of Lady Murdoch—playful and willing, sprawled out under him, her supple body cradling him.

Pain shot through her at the thought, followed by the urge to wound him. "His hair is golden as ripe wheat. And his eyes are blue—like a summer sky."

Maxwell nibbled her earlobe and palmed her breast. Her nipple peaked, thrusting against his hand. "Does he have a name, this dream lover of yours?"

Warily, she said, "Why would I tell you?"

"Why not? It's not an offense I can call him out for, you know—being your fantasy lover. As long as he's never touched you..." He trailed his tongue down her throat, between her breasts, and on to her navel. "Does he do this, when you pretend?"

"No. And I don't want you to, either." She would not allow a repetition of what had happened last night, when he had driven her wild with his tongue. He had wanted to make a point then, and he had done so. But that sort of conduct did not lead to a pregnancy, and that was all either of them was interested in. "This whole thing would be much easier if you just got on with it—with no distractions."

"Interesting, that you don't want to talk about your fantasies." His voice rumbled against her stomach as he worked his way lower. "What a very dull and predictable man your dream lover is, Isabel."

She threw up her hands to clutch a pillow and pretended not to notice what he was doing. If she denied him the satisfaction of reacting to his caresses, then he would soon tire of the effort. He could try to repeat what had happened the night before, but if she refused to cooperate...

She had to admit, however, that it was easier to make a resolution than to keep it, for he didn't give up lightly. Finally she gasped, "Why are you doing this? Why not just—take me?"

He shifted his attention to her breasts, licking and nipping. "I'll take you when I'm ready, Isabel—and when you are. And as for why, I told you that already—to make it easier for you to conceive. Surely you wish that, too. The sooner you are with child…"

The sooner she was pregnant, the sooner his heir would be born, and the sooner she would have Kilburn all to herself and never have to deal with him again. All of those were things to be wished for—and yet…

Isabel closed her eyes and tried to picture that golden-haired, blue-eyed man she had told him about—but the dream lover would not come into focus. She tried to picture any other man, for surely having anyone else in her bed would be preferable to having her husband there, with his mouth warm and slick on her breast, his breath tantalizing her skin, his hand toying with the curls between her legs…then delving beyond, slipping a fingertip inside her and then withdrawing, only to dart a little deeper with the next stroke, and the next.

She couldn't stop herself—and when she pressed upward against his hand, Maxwell smiled. "You can't deny me, Isabel—or yourself."

Only then did he slide very slowly inside her, branding her with his heat. He seemed even bigger and harder than ever before, though it didn't seem possible that he could be—unless the difference was Lady Murdoch's actual presence, making it easier for him to picture her.

"Are you thinking of…" At the last moment, she swallowed the name. She didn't want him to know that she had recognized Lady Murdoch for what she was. Isabel would pretend to be above it all.

No, that wasn't accurate—for she wasn't pretending. She *was* above it all. Nothing about this situation mattered, as long as there was an end to it.

"Thinking of…?" Maxwell murmured.

Isabel tried to sound matter-of-fact. "You must think of your mistresses when you're inside me."

He stopped moving for a moment, as if he was considering the question. "Mistresses?" he mused. "No. At least, only one at a time."

She wanted to hate him. She wanted to lie rigid beneath him and deny him any response. But slowly, stroke by stroke, he tantalized her, until finally when he thrust hard and came deep inside her, she shuddered, and clenched around him, and screamed her own release.

Chapter 12

There was nothing uncomplicated about making love to Emily. Or, more accurately, the real problem was that Gavin's urges were all too plain—and the woman in his arms was far too willing to accommodate his desires. Finally, in a last-ditch effort to keep his promise to himself that she would leave his bed still a virgin—no matter how fragile the distinction might be—Gavin resorted to conversation.

The idea was simplicity itself. Women always wanted to natter on about nothing after they had sex, and their chitchat was always a mood-killer. Since his mood could stand some killing just now, he would encourage her to talk, and that would be the end of the problem.

"Talk?" Emily said doubtfully. "You want to *talk*? About what?"

He rolled onto his back and laced his fingers together beneath his head. "Anything. Whatever you'd like."

She stretched and her breast brushed against his side. "Anything?"

Gavin groped for a topic that would bore him senseless. "What do you think of the new guests?"

Emily propped herself up on an elbow. "You want to gossip about the Carew sisters and Lady Murdoch and Lady Stone?"

"Of course," Gavin lied. "These people are important to the duke, or he wouldn't have invited them. Therefore it is to my benefit to understand them. Who better to explain it all than you?"

She seemed to accept his logic and curled up once more against his side. If she'd been glued to him, she couldn't have fit more closely. "The Carews are only accidental guests, of course." She frowned. "At least, that's the way it was made to sound, but it is a bit too much to believe, don't you think? That they just happened to be visiting their uncle right now?"

"Why? Is there something special about them?"

"Their father is heir to the Earl of Kilchurn—and he is one of the wealthiest men in England. I wonder if Uncle Josiah is hoping that one of them might catch Lucien's eye."

"I think the duke would have given up the idea of matchmaking for Lucien long ago."

"But he did sort of promise Lucien that he would help make his fortune. I wonder if that might have been what Uncle Josiah meant. Marrying one of the Carew sisters would let Lucien be completely independent of our father."

Gavin yawned. "Plus it's the sort of match Chiswick couldn't turn up his nose at. What about your fortune?"

"Mine? What do you mean?"

"I can't think young Baron Draycott is a bosom companion of the Duke of Weybridge—so why is he at this party if not because of you?"

Emily sat up. "You think Uncle Josiah invited him to make a match with *me*? But that's—"

He rolled onto his side so he could see her better and waited patiently, trying to interpret the series of expressions that crossed her face. Irritation—yes, he was all too familiar with that one. But the others baffled him. Finally he could stand it no longer and attempted to finish her sentence himself. "Brilliant? Wise? Foolish? Devious?"

"Annoying," she said. "And insulting. I'd never have considered marrying Draycott, so it's a bit of a facer if Uncle Josiah thinks that's the best I can do, after—" She turned her back to Gavin. "Never mind. It hardly matters what Uncle Josiah thinks of my marriage prospects. It doesn't matter what *anyone* thinks of them."

"Because you're never going to marry." Her spine felt rigid against his chest, and Gavin was nearly certain she was crying—though the only sound that escaped her was a tiny sniff. He scooped her closer, spooning her body against his, curving himself around her. "What happened, Emily? Tell me, my dear."

Gradually she relaxed, and after a long while she began to speak. "My first Season was almost over, and Isabel was to marry Maxwell in June, just before the *ton* left London. With her so close to being settled, my father turned his attention to getting me married off. Even though I believed I'd met every unattached man in London, none of them seemed just right. Then Philip Rivington began to court me, and he was at least young and exciting, and he seemed more likely to be compatible than some of the others had. And Father approved. That was important to me, for you must have observed how rare it is to win my father's approval."

"I noticed," Gavin said dryly.

"My betrothal to Philip was announced in the newspapers on the day of Isabel's wedding."

Her voice was so soft that Gavin had to lean his cheek against her hair to hear.

"That very night, Philip was challenged to a duel. He met the challenger just before dawn the next morning— and Philip was killed."

Gavin frowned. "So because your betrothed died, you gave up on the entire idea of marriage?" But if she hadn't even loved Philip Rivington, why had his death—tragic though it sounded—affected her so strongly? He must be missing something, for this straightforward story didn't seem to fit with what Lucien had hinted about a scandal and a mystery surrounding Emily. "Why did they duel?"

She took a deep breath, which pushed her nipple against the palm of his hand, sending tingles all the way up his arm. "Because of the sister of the young man who issued the challenge. Philip had gotten Miss Lester with child, and she said he had promised to marry her. But then my father offered him a dowry so tempting he could not turn down the opportunity to marry me instead."

"So he abandoned the mother of his child?" And by dying, Philip Rivington had abandoned Emily too—leaving her behind to face the scandal and gossip that should have come to rest on him. No wonder the entire idea of marriage left her cold. Why couldn't her father understand that, and leave the poor darling alone?

Gavin kissed her hair, snuggled her closer, and held her tenderly until she sighed like a tired child and slept in his arms.

He would let her sleep for a while, for it would be cruel to drag her back into wakefulness and send her to her cold and lonely bed with the painful memory of her betrothal so freshly stirred up. Let her rest a bit first, for this might be the only slumber she got tonight. As for himself—he expected his own anger would keep him riled until morning.

A good thing it is that Philip Rivington is dead, or I'd have to kill him myself.

He intended to keep watch for the first hint of dawn. As soon as the sky began to lighten, and well before the servants started to stir, he would awaken Emily and take her back to her room.

He only vaguely heard his bedroom door open, and by the time he roused enough to react, it was too late. The bed curtains that he had pulled slid back with a hiss. Gavin reared up and banged his head on something hard. He did his best to shield Emily from view, but even the still-faint light of early morning that flooded across the coverlet from the long windows near the bed made it impossible to conceal her presence.

Warily, Gavin looked over his shoulder. The back of his head had hit the edge of the silver tray that held his morning tea, and Benson was doing some fancy juggling to keep the teapot and cup from bouncing off.

Finally, with the china once more safe, the valet spoke. "Good morning, my lord. It promises to be a sunny day."

Was the imperturbable Benson pretending he couldn't see them tangled together in the bedclothes?

"Perhaps, sir," he went on calmly, "you would like me to fetch another cup, for your guest?"

❉ ❉ ❉

Clean living must be getting to be a habit, Lucien told himself when he woke with a start just as dawn cracked over the eastern horizon. He shaved with cold water left from the previous night's ablutions and scrambled into his clothes without bothering to ring for his valet. The boot boy was making his rounds to deliver newly cleaned shoes to each bedroom door as Lucien crept out onto the gallery. On the lower floor of the castle's new wing, footmen were clearing out cinders and ash and delivering fresh coals, while maids polished and cleaned and swept the public rooms.

No need to tiptoe, for that would make a gentleman look sneaky even if he had nothing to hide. If he walked across the hall with a bit of a swagger, everyone would assume he was merely going out for a ride to clear a head left murky by last night's port.

Lucien whistled a fragment of a tune, to reinforce the idea that his conduct was perfectly normal, and pulled open the door of the breakfast room in the faint hope that something already on the sideboard would be portable enough to tide him over. Ham and a slice of bread would do nicely.

The Earl of Chiswick laid down his newspaper. "Off for another adventure, Hartford?" he asked. "By the way, did you lame one of the duke's horses yesterday?"

Lucien bristled. "I most certainly did not. What sort of horseman do you think I am?"

"Don't fly into the boughs with me, young man. That was the only explanation I could generate for why you were gone so long. But if you were not walking miles to lead an injured horse back to his stable, then how, I wonder, did you entertain yourself for so many hours away from the castle?"

You must learn to think before answering. If he'd admitted to laming an animal, the inquisition would be over by now. Besides, it usually wasn't anything a rider did that caused a horse to go lame. Why had he so quickly assumed that Chiswick intended a slur on his horsemanship?

Because he always assumes the worst of me.

To get out of this spot, Lucien needed a convincing answer—right now. "I found myself entranced by the beauty of the countryside, Father."

Chiswick's tone was dry. "Congratulations on your newfound enjoyment of country life. I assume you're going out for another deep breath of fresh air right now."

Please don't offer to accompany me. "I plan to ride, yes. I find the atmosphere quite refreshing." He hoped that sounding like a prig would accomplish his purpose.

Chiswick turned the page of his newspaper. "Is it only the environs of the castle that excite you, or do you embrace the country in general?"

Wariness swept over Lucien, for that hadn't sounded like an ordinary, casual question. Could Chiswick have guessed at yesterday's tryst in the linden grove at Mallowan? Was it possible Lucien and Chloe had been observed? Would it deflect suspicion if he openly admitted to having ridden onto Sir George Fletcher's land, or would the confession only confirm some intuitive sense of Chiswick's that his son was up to no good?

Before Lucien found an answer, his father went on. "I ask because I find myself hopeful that you are finally ready to come home to Chiswick and begin learning to manage the estate."

"Uh, *no*." The refusal was out before Lucien could stop himself, and he groped wildly for a plausible excuse. Chloe's lovely face, her wide-set green eyes, that lush golden hair, sprang into his mind. "I mean…your new wife will not want anyone around to interrupt the honeymoon."

"Nonsense," the earl said crisply. "Any wife of mine will soon learn who the master of the house is. My countess will do exactly as I say."

Lucien couldn't keep control of his tongue. "Did my mother obey you in everything, sir?" He didn't remember ever hearing his parents quarrel, that was true, but surely he recalled discussions—perhaps even heated ones.

"Of course she obeyed me."

"Then no wonder she died," Lucien said under his breath. "It must have seemed the only way to escape."

Chiswick stared at him. "*What* did you say, Hartford?"

Lucien reminded himself that this was no time to pick a quarrel with his sire. Whatever had happened to the late countess was long past; the only thing Lucien could do right now was to help Chloe escape the same fate. No wonder she was willing to put her life in the hands of a soldier. No wonder she was willing to abandon her home and her parents and run away in the hope of finding freedom. No wonder she hadn't hesitated to threaten Lucien himself.

He could not bear to see her smothered by the Earl of Chiswick's rules.

But if he was to help her, Lucien must not give his father cause to draw out this discussion. Lucien simply had to escape, and soon, if he was to meet Chloe as they had arranged. He could not leave her waiting for him, and he could not risk his father deciding to ride out with him as some strange form of discipline. If swallowing his rash words was the price, then Lucien would eat them, instead of ham and bread, for breakfast.

He met Chiswick's cold gaze straight on. "Nothing important, sir."

Chiswick held his gaze for a long moment. "Do not think this is the end of the matter, for we will discuss the question of estate management, and soon. It is high time for you to learn how to preserve your heritage for future generations. I have indulged you for far longer than I should have done—"

Indulged? Lucien's jaw dropped. How his father could call his pittance of an allowance an *indulgence...*

"—by allowing you to spend so much time with your friends in London. However," Chiswick added dryly, "I believe your stay there has achieved the main purpose, which was to illustrate for you how large an income it will take to pay for the sort of life you seem to want. I believe you must agree with me that it will require a great deal more blunt than you currently command."

Chiswick had never put it quite that way before. Instead, he had always made it sound as though Lucien was to be imprisoned on the estate, condemned to the sort of point-less exercises he'd hated as a child when the governess and later his tutor had ruled over him. But when it came down to guineas and shillings—well, that did put a differ-ent color on the matter. And he might not be absolutely tied to the estate.

Still, as Lucien made his escape, he thought wryly that only a discussion with Chiswick could make a man look forward to the meeting Lucien would soon have with Chloe—especially since there was no guessing what she might cozen him into doing this time.

*　*　*

In the dim light of early morning, Isabel woke slowly, stretching luxuriously against the crisp linen sheets. Though she would never admit it to Maxwell, in the last few days she had become aware of her body in ways she had never known before. The way he touched her seemed to have sensitized her to every sort of stimulus. She felt an entirely new sensual enjoyment of fabrics, for instance—not only the texture of linen and lace against her skin but the sheen of fine muslin when light played across it, and the scent of lightweight wool snuggled around her throat when she rode. And every touch made her feel more alive somehow, as if she had grown more sensitive in every way.

"Hello," Maxwell murmured.

She gave a little shriek and turned her head so fast she almost cracked her neck. He was lying on his side, watching her, and his eyes were bright and not in the least sleepy. But why was he here? How was it possible that she had actually *slept* with him there beside her? Why hadn't her instincts warned her that unlike the previous nights, when he had simply gone away after he finished with her, this time he had stayed in her bed?

"But it's morning!" she protested.

243

"Amazing that the sun came up as usual." He didn't move. "I was just lying here with nothing to do but think, Isabel, and I find myself wondering…why did you demand Kilburn? Why not something else? Maxton Abbey, for instance?"

She wriggled farther away from him and higher in the bed, sitting up against a stack of pillows. "The ghosts of three hundred years' worth of earls would haunt you if you tried to break the entail on the abbey."

"There are other properties—the London house, for instance. You do so love London."

She shrugged. The sheet slid down from her shoulder. She grabbed for it, but too late—she saw his gaze focus on her breast, and heat swept over her. "That was simply practical. The London house does not produce an income."

"There's the hunting lodge."

She tucked the top hem of the sheet tightly under her arms to hold it in place. "Same problem—no income."

"You could have rented it out."

"I wouldn't know where to begin. And as for living there—well, the truth is I don't like hunting all that much."

"I thought you were eager to join the Beckhams' party last week."

That was when you were due to come back to the abbey, and I'd have seized any opportunity to leave. "I didn't see hunting as the main attraction of the Beckhams' party."

"You're suggesting one of the men there is the one you long for." He seemed only mildly interested.

She was on dangerous ground. He could easily find out exactly who had been on the Beckhams' guest list…Not that he would bother, Isabel reminded herself. Her flirtations, such as they were, could not matter to a man who felt not the least inclination to jealousy. Still, she reached for a safer subject. "I told you from the beginning, Max—since Kilburn was my dowry, it was the natural choice."

"I suppose so. But is that the only reason you asked for it? I have larger estates. More lucrative ones."

"I like Kilburn—I always have. But I asked for it because it seemed only right that I benefit from the property I brought into the marriage. Is that so hard for you to understand?"

"Yes, it is. I wondered..." Maxwell broke off and moved his pillows around to achieve a better angle to watch her. "How did you learn to like it so much? You never lived there, did you? Despite the fact that your father is a shrewd negotiator, I got the impression he never gave that estate much more than a cursory thought."

"He found it a nuisance," Isabel admitted. "Because it's located so far from Chiswick, it was difficult to manage."

"So my instinct was right—it wasn't such a sacrifice after all for him to give it up. Why did he own it, if the estate was such a problem for him?"

A better question, Isabel thought, was why Maxwell cared. "Kilburn was my mother's dowry, too—or, rather, her inheritance. She grew up there."

"And that is how you came to like it so much?"

"She took us there to visit our grandparents in the summers, when we were little."

"Your father didn't go?"

"Never, that I recall. Just Lucien and Emily and me, and our mother. We didn't even take a governess. Because it was so long a trip, we would stay for weeks. Grandpapa made up stories for us and taught us to fish, and Grandmama fashioned dresses for our dolls, and told us about being a lady-in-waiting to the queen, and taught us to curtsey. I remember my mother lying in a long chair on the terrace—just lying there, smiling—while we played on the lawn."

"You were happy at Kilburn," he said softly.

She nodded. "I suppose I was. I didn't know I even remembered so much from those summers. By the time I was ten years old, my grandparents had died. Mama took us only once after that, but she was very sad—and already ill, too, I think, though I didn't realize it then."

"Very touching," he said softly. "No wonder you remember it fondly. I'm glad I asked. And I'm glad you will have it one day." He leaned over her and took a long, deep kiss—the sort of kiss, Isabel knew, that always led to other things.

"You can't," she said firmly.

"I assure you there's no law against making love in the morning. But if you feel strongly about the matter, very well."

She was wary. "You mean it? You'd stop because I—"

"All you have to do is show me that you don't want to." He kissed her again, and then lazily began stroking her, from the sensitive patch of skin under her ear to the arches of her feet. The sensation of cool sheets against her skin had been stimulating, but the mere brush of warm hands was arousing. And when he shifted from touching her to tasting her earlobes and her breasts, Isabel moaned despite herself.

"I wish you'd go back to thinking," she muttered.

He smiled and whispered, "Are you certain you don't want to make love?" His voice resonated through her, and she shivered.

Isabel fumbled for sanity, as well as for an excuse he might accept. "Martha will be coming in at any moment with my morning chocolate."

"No, she won't. I instructed her that from now on she is not to disturb you in the morning until she is summoned. So if preferring not to shock your maid is your only objection…" He didn't wait for an answer but slipped a finger inside her. "As I expected—and I like this answer much better."

He moved over her, and though she had no conscious intention of helping him, Isabel opened her legs. He smiled and slid inside her, so deeply that he seemed to stretch her more than ever before, and slowly began to thrust.

Long minutes later, when he was finished and she was still shivering from the force of her own climax, he did not withdraw but settled himself more firmly inside her, rested his lips against her hair, and went completely still.

"Maxwell," she said finally. "What are you doing?"

He didn't open his eyes. "I'm following the directions we were given on our wedding day. *With my body I thee worship.*"

Annoyed, she struck back. "It goes on after that, you know. *With all my worldly goods I thee endow.*"

"All part of a single bargain, Isabel—one that you are finally living up to. As soon as you've fulfilled your end of the deal, I will honor mine, and Kilburn will be yours."

"Fine." She wriggled a little in irritation. "Are you finished?"

He raised his head and looked down at her. "No, I don't believe I am."

Even as he spoke, she felt him growing hard again, stretching and thickening inside her. To her surprise, she was so aroused that before he even began to stroke her once more, she clenched around him in her own release.

He took her slowly, and left her panting and dizzy and almost whimpering with satisfaction. When he left her, she sank into the mattress, too luxuriously relaxed to move.

"Sleep," he told her. "I'll instruct Martha that your hot chocolate can wait. By the way, I like it when you call me Max."

Isabel's eyes flew open. "I didn't!"

"Yes, you did." He paused beside the bed as he tied the belt of his dressing gown. "Thank you for telling me about Kilburn, and why you asked for it."

"That again?" she murmured. "I told you…"

"Because it seemed to me when you made your proposition that your goal must be to present me with a bargain I could not possibly accept."

Her almost-boneless state of relaxation gave way to tense wariness. Maxwell's conclusion was perfectly correct, which meant he knew her far better than she had counted on. But why was he bringing this up now?

"If that was the case, however, why did you not ask for Maxton Abbey, my dear? Why didn't you suggest trading my heir for my largest estate?"

"Don't be ridiculous, Maxwell. It's the family seat. You couldn't—"

"Exactly, Isabel. That would truly have been a bargain I could not have agreed to."

The bottom fell out of Isabel's stomach. Why had it not occurred to her to raise the stakes even higher? She had been so certain he wouldn't give in to *any* demand that she hadn't even considered asking for more. Besides, there were limits to what was credible.

"Instead," he went on softly, "you asked for Kilburn, an estate you love and one to which I feel no personal attachment. I am left to wonder why you chose to make your terms so palatable to me. Did you want this to happen? Do you—despite all your denials—want to give me my heir?"

❁   ❁   ❁

Looking as though he owned the entire stock of patience in the world, Benson stood beside the big gold-draped bed holding the tea tray and waiting—exactly as he had every morning since they had arrived at the castle—for Gavin to prop himself up against the headboard, ready to take his tea cup in hand.

Emily made a noise that was just short of a screech and dived under the blankets.

Gavin punched a pillow, but the move did not lessen his frustration. "You didn't see anything, Benson."

"Certainly not, sir."

Emily's voice was muffled. "We were only talking!"

"Indeed, my lady," Benson said. "I didn't doubt it for a moment." He set down the tray on the bedside table, poured tea into the single cup, and handed it to Gavin. "If I might make an observation, sir…It would seem you and the young lady are in a bit of a pickle."

"Noticed that, did you?" Gavin said dryly. "Despite not seeing anything?"

"I assume you intended for Lady Emily to return to her room before the household began to stir. Since that time is past, I believe I can be of some service."

"Benson, if you can fix this one, I'll double your pay."

"An increase in remuneration would be most welcome, sir, but it is not necessary. I am simply doing my duty. I shall—reconnoiter, I believe they would say in the army, and return in a few minutes. The young lady might be ready to depart at that time." Soft-footed, he crossed the bedroom and went out.

"Emily," Gavin said. "Time to get up."

"I'm *never* coming out. Benson hates me, and I don't trust him. He'll probably tell everyone he sees and gather a crowd in the gallery."

"If he hated you, that's the last thing he'd do." Gavin tugged the blankets back and handed her the teacup. "Drink. It's hot and sweet—good for you when you've had a shock."

"Why?" Her hand shook as she took the cup. "I mean Benson."

"Because if he passed the word, your father would come down on us with the force of all Napoleon's cannons and you'd find yourself married before the day was out."

Without seeming to notice what she was doing, Emily sipped. "That *is* hot. How does he...Never mind. It would mean he'd never be able to get rid of me, yes—but are you certain he understands that?"

"Oh, I think he grasps the major points," Gavin said dryly. He took the empty cup out of her hand and set it back on the tray, then retrieved her nightdress from where it had landed on the carpet. "I don't know how he'll manage it, but I have confidence he'll slide you back into your room as slick as…"

Benson reappeared just as Gavin was tying the belt of Emily's dressing gown. "Lord Hartford is stirring," he said. "Lord Chiswick has gone downstairs. There is, as yet, no sign of Lady Isabel, and of course no movement around the duke's chambers. I shall look out into the gallery once more to be certain. Then if all is clear, I will signal you, Lady Emily, and walk with you back to your room."

"And how is that supposed to help the situation?" Emily asked suspiciously.

"If anyone appears, or if we hear voices, you must simply stop walking and turn to face me. I'll do the rest."

Emily rolled her eyes.

"Remember Napoleon's cannons," Gavin said softly.

"Well, I don't want to end up married," she snapped, and took a deep breath. "All right, Benson—let's go."

Chapter 13

Chloe was already in the linden grove when Lucien's gelding picked his way between the trees. She seemed lost in thought, and Lucien was almost into the sunny glade when she heard his approach and swung around, plainly startled. A tinge of fear in her face quickly gave way to anticipation, and she hurried toward him. "Tell me—did all go as planned?"

Lucien swung down from his saddle, trying to find an answer that was both truthful and honest. He supposed it would be accurate to say that indeed everything had gone as she had planned it. All she had asked of him was to put her letter directly into the hands of the captain, and Lucien had done exactly that. But would it be honest to say that much and nothing more?

Should he tell her about his suspicions? Should he confide the nagging ache inside him, which warned that Captain Hopkins had no intention of acting on the request she had made in her letter?

A request, he would be wise to remember, that Lucien himself was not supposed to know about in detail.

"Lucien," Chloe said slowly, "if you didn't do as I wanted…"

The threatening note in her voice would have amused him had the matter been less serious. "Your letter has been delivered, exactly as you asked."

"You saw Captain Hopkins yourself? You didn't leave my message with his batman, or…"

"I laid it into his hands, and I watched him open it."

She closed her eyes and released a long breath. "That's all right, then." She sat down on the log and patted the spot beside her. "Now tell me what he said—*exactly*—after he'd read my letter."

Why, Lucien wondered wearily, did lovesick girls always want precise details? He couldn't remember every word the captain had said. Not that there had been many of them, for the captain seemed to be a man of few words. But Lucien could hardly tell Chloe that her beloved had grunted rather than speaking.

Was that why Lucien had come away from the army encampment with so many doubts? Because Captain Hopkins hadn't regaled him with poetic phrases of love about Chloe? If that was all that was bothering him, then Lucien was being a bit of a clunch to suspect that the captain might not be the knight in shining armor that Chloe plainly pictured.

After all, why should the captain confide in a stranger? Chloe, who knew Lucien a great deal better than the captain did, had not gushed out her feelings or trusted him completely with her plans.

Of course Chloe and her captain felt strongly about each other. Girls simply didn't arrange elopements with men they didn't love—or with men who they weren't certain returned their feelings.

Lucien knew he should dismiss his doubts, tell Chloe what she wanted to hear, and get himself back to the castle before the day was too far advanced. He'd done everything she asked; if she had wanted him to be more involved than that, she would have come straight out and told him what she planned to do. He could—he *should*—walk away now.

And yet there had been something about the way the captain had looked at Lucien, after he had opened and glanced at Chloe's letter, that had made Lucien's insides go tight with apprehension. The captain had not looked excited that the woman he loved would soon be his. He had not seemed anxious to get started on the many preparations that would be necessary for an elopement.

In fact, he had not looked like a man who had just received good news. Instead, he had looked annoyed.

And for good reason, Lucien admitted. Chloe hadn't seemed to realize that the captain would have to arrange with his superiors to be absent from his post for a week at the very least. He must also find, hire, and pay for a post-chaise. He must pack for himself, provide the necessities for his bride, and get himself to Weybridge Castle on the appointed night—whether the timing Chloe had chosen was convenient for him or not.

Yes, Lucien admitted, the captain could be pardoned if he felt a bit put out over his bride's blithe assumption that all she had to do was snap her fingers to set an elopement in motion.

Still, Chloe had demonstrated immense faith and trust by placing her future in the hands of the captain. What if he didn't live up to her expectations? What if he didn't show up at Weybridge Castle on the night of the duke's birthday ball with a post-chaise and four, ready to flee with her to Scotland?

Chloe's voice was firm. "What—*exactly*—did he say?"

"He seemed surprised," Lucien said carefully.

"Well, of course he was surprised. When he rejoined his regiment last winter, we had no idea that so drastic a step as elopement would be necessary." She tipped her head to look up at him with a flash of defiance, as if she expected him to try to argue her out of the idea.

Lucien knew better. "You expect me to be scandalized that you're planning an elopement? I'm not a fool, Chloe. What else could you possibly be up to?" *Besides, I read your letter.* No—much wiser not to admit that transgression. "Go on."

"I was certain that in a year or two—by the time Captain Hopkins could sell his commission—if I made it clear I had found no one I liked better, my father would withdraw his objections to our marriage."

"And then Chiswick came to call. When was that, by the way?"

"I believe there was no thought of matching me with the earl until the last few weeks. I have had no opportunity even to tell Captain Hopkins about the arrangement."

"Because a gently bred young woman has no way to send off secret communications to a suitor her parents do not approve of. Yes, I quite understand why he was surprised today when I turned up with a letter. You believed your father would change his mind about your suitor? Didn't it even occur to you that it might be necessary to elope?"

"Of course it did."

Lucien knew he should have found it reassuring to find that only the timing, and not the elopement itself, had come as a shock to the captain. But something still didn't feel right.

"Every girl whose suitor is not welcomed by her family speaks wildly of running away," Chloe said airily.

Lucien gritted his teeth. "*You* were the one who talked of running away? What did the captain say? Did he urge you to act right then?"

"Of course he didn't. He was certain that, given time, my father would drop his objections. But why should all that matter, now that the situation has changed?"

Lucien was damned if he knew. But the question nagged at him.

Chloe bounced up from her perch on the log. "I have a favor to ask."

"Another one? No—no more favors. Look for someone else to be your messenger this time."

Chloe laughed. "I don't need a messenger."

Her smile had been stunning enough, Lucien thought, but the gleeful peal of her laugh was enough to pull the free will right out of a man and leave him helpless. He looked into her face—that small triangular face with the catlike eyes was now alight with amusement—and heard himself say, "What is it?"

"You don't have to go anywhere," she assured him. "At least nowhere that's out of your way. I only want you to take some things to the castle for me."

The request seemed simple enough, but some last remnant of common sense made him say, "What sort of things?"

"Things that are precious to a young woman. Things I don't want to lose when I leave my parents' home for the last time. Things I will need for a long trip and a wedding."

The sadness in her voice tugged at his heartstrings. Trying not to show it, he cleared his throat. "Not big things, I hope, or you should have warned me to bring a wagon."

"No—well, not exactly big. I suppose I might hide a few things in my hatbox when we come to the garden party this afternoon. But if you will take my valise now, it would help me a great deal. I can hardly walk through the castle in my ball gown, carrying my case, without rousing suspicions."

"I should think not. But you can't seriously intend for me to ride back to Weybridge with your valise balanced on the saddle in front of me. What exactly would I say to anyone who saw me and wondered why I've taken to carrying luggage around?"

"No one needs to see you. If you take the back lanes, you'll come into Weybridge at the far end of the garden. Just leave the valise under a bench in the garden folly—you know, the little folly that's directly beside the lane—before you ride on to the stables."

The folly at the base of the garden, where she had instructed Captain Hopkins to meet her. It wasn't a bad plan, Lucien conceded. The back lane was secluded and far enough from the castle not to draw notice. She could wait out of sight in the garden folly, protected from the weather and from casual observers, until the captain appeared. The entire area would be dark and quiet, yet the lane was wide enough to bring a chaise and four through. And on a night when carriages were coming and going from far and wide at all hours, one more chaise and four would probably not be much noticed in the confusion around the castle, or even in the nearby villages.

"You'd be harder to trace, you know, if you didn't head straight for Scotland," he heard himself say.

"That's why we'll leave before the dancing is finished."

"How are you going to manage to get away from the ballroom?"

"Oh, that should be easy. I can't tell you how pleased I was that the duke has invited us to stay overnight at the castle rather than return home after the ball ends. I shall retire to my bedroom with a headache, and that will give me a head start of—oh, at least a few hours. If I'm fortunate, I won't be missed until morning."

Lucien thought she was optimistic to hope that Lady Fletcher wouldn't look in on a supposedly ailing daughter, but it was hardly his place to argue the point. *If it were me, I'd wait till dead of night—till Lady Fletcher is all tucked in.* Of course, in the wee hours a chaise was more likely to be noticed and remembered by the few other people who were on the roads. Chloe might have it right after all.

Idly, he kicked at a pile of bright leaves that had gathered by the log seat. "Do you think your parents will refuse to receive you at Mallowan after this? You're their only child. Surely—"

Chloe said dryly, "Oh, no, I'm certain they'll be delighted. I will only have insulted the Earl of Chiswick by refusing to marry him *and* the Duke of Weybridge by using his birthday ball to run away with a penniless soldier. So I'm sure my parents will be happy to welcome me back and turn over my dowry to my husband."

Lucien thought he knew now what had been nagging at him. "Captain Hopkins is penniless?"

"He was hoping for the American war to continue for a few more years so he could win advancement in the ranks. He might even have made his fortune there, but it was not to be."

"Chloe, if he has no money, how in hell do you expect him to show up at the castle with a chaise and four?"

"Don't swear at me, Lucien! My father considers Jason to be penniless, but he's not. He has his army pay, of course, and a hundred a year from his uncle."

Lucien gaped. "*A hundred a year?* Chloe!" Suddenly his own allowance sounded huge. A hundred guineas a year wouldn't pay Lucien's tailor.

"In any case," she said stubbornly, "he only has to get here. I have money enough for the trip and to last us for a while. And I have an income left me by my grandmother that my father cannot stop, no matter what. We'll manage."

Lucien was speechless. The girl was foolish, innocent, completely naive—and well on the road to ruining herself.

Still, Lucien couldn't help but admire her determination. He was actually growing fond of this feisty, snappy young woman who refused to give up, who took her fate into her own hands, who was willing to scandalize society and alienate her own parents to escape an unpalatable marriage.

And who could blame her for that?

"You know," Chloe said softly, "I thought you might not come this morning."

"I gave my word," he said a bit sharply. "The word of an Arden. Why wouldn't I keep it?"

"Only that yesterday it seemed the young ladies were quite willing to entertain you. I thought you might forget about me." She smiled. "Now if you'll take my valise, I must hurry back to the manor and get ready for the garden party, or my mother will be sending out grooms to look for me. Remember—put it under a bench in the folly." She pulled a big case out from behind a tree.

Lucien pictured himself riding across the estate while balancing that in front of him, and sighed. Then he bent over her hand and raised it to his lips. She smelled of lavender and sunshine.

Chloe knew Captain Hopkins, he reflected, while Lucien did not. It was possible that Lucien might have been entirely wrong about the soldier. Maybe Captain Hopkins's silence after he read Chloe's letter had not been irritation but only caution. Maybe he had been careful what he said only because he thought Lucien an ordinary messenger, not realizing that he was in on the secret. Maybe the captain had already turned his attention to planning how he could carry out Chloe's wishes. Maybe he had every intention of waiting in the dark back lane with a chaise and four to sweep her away to live happily ever after.

If she truly loved her soldier, and if he loved her, then the loss of her parents and her reputation might be worth the price. Lucien hoped, for Chloe's sake, that it would be enough.

"Do you have a particular bench in mind?" he said dryly. "Or will any one of them do?"

❋ ❋ ❋

The castle's normal early-morning noises rose from downstairs, sounding incredibly loud to Emily's oversensitive ears. She swore she could hear the swish of a housemaid's dress, the rattle of coal being dumped on a fire, the clang of a serving fork striking the marble surface of a sideboard. But the gallery was blessedly empty and absolutely quiet, except for the whisper of her steps and Benson's on the wide wooden planks.

As they rounded the first corner, safely away from Gavin's rooms, Emily began to relax. "It looks as though I did not require your assistance, Benson," she said softly. "What a pity it is that you may not be able to claim double wages after all."

He did not answer. Instead, he seized her arm and swung her around to face him.

"Mr. Benson!" she sputtered, furious that he had dared to touch her. But he had already gone immobile once more, hands straight at his sides, head bent in deference. She stared at him, puzzled.

Behind her, a calm, deep voice said, "Emily? What is the meaning of this?"

She gulped and looked over her shoulder, meeting the quizzical gaze of the Earl of Chiswick as he stood at the top of the staircase.

"Why are you wandering around the gallery in your nightclothes?"

I'm sleepwalking, Emily thought wildly. Wasn't that the excuse Gavin had considered using? But her father would instantly see it as the faradiddle it was.

"Has Athstone's man accosted you, Emily?"

Benson cleared his throat. "Beg pardon, my lady. My lord, if I might enlighten you—"

"Yes," Chiswick said coolly. "Please explain yourself— Benson, is it?"

Explaining would be good, Benson. Especially since I haven't the shadow of an idea what you're going to say.

Benson bowed slightly. "My lord, Lady Emily heard a sound earlier—a sort of thud, as she has just described it to me. She thought it came from the duke's rooms and was afraid it meant he might have fallen."

"A thud," Chiswick repeated evenly.

"Yes, my lord. A thud—as though some large object had struck the floor. She immediately came out of her room to inquire, but she naturally hesitated to disturb the duke or his man, in case the sound had *not* come from the duke's rooms. Of course, her sensibilities are too delicate to permit her to go lightly into a sickroom."

If Benson keeps going on about me like this, any minute now I'm going to have to faint dead away to prove just how delicate I am.

"When she saw me coming out of Lord Athstone's rooms after delivering his morning tea, my lord, she asked that I go and check on the duke in case something has gone awry."

Emily had to admire Benson's glib delivery. At least the tale he was telling about why she was in the hall in her dressing gown was semiplausible, which was a great deal more than could have been said about any story she'd have created. She wondered if Benson had ever considered penning one of the three-volume romantic stories that were so popular in the lending libraries.

"I was just seeing her back to her room before doing as she requested, my lord. But it might be better if you were the one to inquire about the duke's health."

Emily gulped. That was going too far—a mere valet sending Chiswick to check on the duke, especially when he knew quite well there was nothing wrong. Had Benson run mad?

Nervously, she twisted her toes against the cold boards of the gallery floor and waited for Chiswick to lay into Benson with the sharp side of his tongue.

Instead, Chiswick seemed to dismiss the valet entirely, and his gaze came to rest on Emily's feet. "You must indeed have been concerned about your uncle, to have come out without your slippers. Go to your room immediately, before you catch a chill."

Ignoble though it might be to run, Emily beat a quick retreat. Once inside her own bedroom, she leaned against the door for a while, trying to get her breathing under control, and then dived under the covers of her cold bed.

She tossed and twisted for half an hour, but finally gave up the idea of sleep and rang for her maid. Better to face the music straightforwardly than to huddle in her room and worry about what her father might say. If he had seen through Benson's ruse…

Besides, she was starving. Why had no one ever mentioned that taking a lover increased one's appetite at least threefold?

Just as she crossed the entrance hall, Gavin caught up with her. "Good morning, Lady Emily," he said formally, and bowed over her hand. His warm breath tickled her wrist, and the gentle brush of his fingertips brought back memories of the night and made her midsection go as gooey as cheese held over an open flame.

He might as well be holding *her* over an open flame. Worse, he knew exactly the effect he was having, for Gavin's eyes danced with glee.

"You left your slippers behind," he murmured. "Apparently you kicked them off in a hurry last night, and they slid under my bed."

Her cheeks flamed. "I'm certain you'll think of some creative way to return them."

"I plan to make souvenirs of them. I could tuck one under my pillow to dream on."

"You wouldn't! The chambermaid…she'll find it when she straightens your bed." Too late, she saw Gavin's grin. She bit her lip, annoyed that she'd reacted exactly as he'd expected.

"She might think I have very small, delicate feet."

"And that you like to wear pink slippers?" Emily's gaze dropped to the toes of his top boots, polished to a gleam that was almost mirror-bright. The boots were beautifully made, but the feet inside them were anything but small and delicate—as she was certain any female in the castle would have noticed.

"Well?" Gavin said, offering his arm. "I understand that you arrived safely and I must therefore double Benson's wages."

She said tartly, "You'd be wise to keep an eye on him. Any servant who can lie so glibly—and to my father, of all people—can't be entirely trustworthy in other areas."

"He's never lied to me."

"But he's so very good at it—how would you possibly know?"

He smiled. "Don't fret, my dear. Benson's very clear about where his loyalties lie."

Emily sniffed. If that was what Gavin wanted to believe, there was no point in trying to warn him. She'd done all she could. Loyalty! Benson had faced down a peer of the realm and lied through his teeth!

Only to protect me.

No, that wasn't quite factual. Benson hadn't been protecting Emily; he'd been protecting his employer. Gavin was correct about that much: Benson would do whatever was necessary to advance Gavin's interests. To protect him.

The valet hadn't stepped into the mess this morning to preserve Emily's reputation, for Benson didn't care a rap about her. He had been saving his master. Looking back, she could even see that he had taken his cues from Gavin. Benson wasn't the one who had been most anxious to get her back where she belonged without consequences; Gavin had been far more edgy and worried than the valet was.

Your father would come down on us with the force of all Napoleon's cannons, and you'd find yourself married before the day was out.

But if that had happened, it wasn't only Emily who would have ended up married. Gavin would have been drawn into the coil as well. Both the master and the manservant had foreseen that complication and acted swiftly to avoid it.

And she was glad of it, Emily told herself fiercely. Very, *very* glad.

* * *

As the door closed behind her husband, Isabel sat bolt upright in bed and tugged furiously at the bellpull to summon her maid. Her delicious lassitude was gone, blown away by Maxwell's parting comments.

Did you want this to happen, Isabel? Do you—despite all your denials—want to give me my heir?

What an absolute unmitigated ass her husband was! How arrogant did a man have to be, anyway, to assume that a woman was so swept away by his lovemaking that she could think of nothing else? No, it was even worse than that. He believed that even before he had ever made love to her, Isabel had schemed and planned how best to lure him into her bed. He was convinced she had done all this on purpose, that the bargain she proposed had been nothing but a strategic maneuver.

She buried her face in her pillow and shed a few angry tears. Then she pounded her fists on the mattress and shrieked.

Isabel didn't realize Martha had already come into the room until the maid jerked in surprise and almost pulled the bed hangings down on Isabel's head. "Ma'am? My lady? Are you all right?"

"Perfectly fine," Isabel said icily. "But I do not wish to lie abed with chocolate this morning, Martha. Is my blue walking dress fit to be seen?"

"I washed and ironed it myself just yesterday, my lady. But—"

Isabel slid out of bed and reached for a wrapper. "Yes, Martha, I know that dress is hardly elegant, and it's not the sort of thing I'd choose to wear for my uncle's garden party. But you of all people know my wardrobe is seriously limited." At least Maxwell had stopped tearing up her clothes, after that one ruined dinner gown, or she would be in desperate straits by now.

"Not quite so limited as yesterday, ma'am."

"What do you mean?" As Isabel turned toward her dressing table, her gaze fell on a gown hanging on the wardrobe door. A walking dress—one she had never seen before.

The dress was primrose yellow, a color that had always flattered Isabel's midnight-dark hair and made her hazel eyes look bigger and brighter. Though the style was simple, the puffed sleeves and slightly scooped neckline were the very latest fashion. The muslin was the lightest she had ever seen, for even the stray air current she caused as she moved toward the wardrobe set the deep flounce at the bottom of the skirt swaying. At the hem, around the neckline, and scattered across the skirt, flowers had been embroidered in a slightly darker yellow.

"Where did that dress come from, Martha?"

"I brought it up just now. The seamstresses finished the decorative stitching only this morning. There's a note, my lady."

Isabel put out a hand for the message, but she was still looking at the dress. "How generous of Uncle Josiah, to provide this as well as the ball gown," she murmured. "And to make it a surprise…" She opened the page.

In spiky black writing—nothing like the duke's—were a few words. *Just a trifling gift, in appreciation for all you plan to give me. I will enjoy seeing you wear this for your uncle's garden party.* There was no signature, but none was necessary.

Isabel sputtered. If Maxwell thought he could turn her up sweet with a dress—as though she could be bought off with mere clothes—she would soon disabuse him of that notion.

She crossed the room and flung open the connecting door, and only when she stood on the threshold did she stop to think that it might have been wise to plan what she wanted to say.

But he was not there. His valet was near the washstand, rhythmically stropping a razor, and he turned politely. "My lady?"

Isabel was puzzled. Had she lost track of time? She'd thought only a few minutes could have passed since he had left her bed—not long enough for him to dress and go out.

Before she could embarrass herself by asking his valet where Maxwell was, a little flurry behind her drew Isabel's attention back to her own room. Martha stood holding the open door to the gallery for Emily, who was wearing a new pale-pink walking dress—cut differently from Isabel's but also in one of the latest styles.

"My dear, however did you manage it?" Emily twirled around, showing off the narrow skirt. "I came up from breakfast to find this lying across my bed. I thought your pockets were just as much to let as mine are."

Isabel bit her lip. "I didn't manage anything."

"But the note said the dress was a gift from you."

"It wasn't me," Isabel said. "It was Max—" She choked back the rest of the name.

How perfectly calculating he was, to have included Emily in his gift. By giving her sister a dress, Maxwell made himself look both generous and thoughtful. By claiming that Emily's gown was a gift from Isabel instead of from him, he presented himself as sensitive—too well-mannered to embarrass his sister-in-law by offering such a personal gift.

Emily frowned. "Isabel? Since when do you call him *Max*?"

Isabel coughed and said irritably, "Since the frog in my throat kept me from finishing the word. Don't be ridiculous, Emily."

If she refused to wear the gown he had provided, Isabel would look foolish—especially when Emily was turned out neat as a pin—and Maxwell would be entertained by her stubbornness. But if she did wear it, he'd not only have the satisfaction of seeing her decked out in a gown he had chosen, but he'd be amused because he had outmaneuvered her.

He wouldn't laugh at her—not openly; he was too much the gentleman for that. But in the last few days she had learned his expressions—and from the glint in his eyes and the tiny curve of his mouth, she would know exactly how much he was enjoying himself at her expense.

Chapter 14

✤

By midday, the courtyard of the castle bustled with carriages coming and going. The sweeping lawn was alive with tents and marquees, with tables full of food, and with musicians strolling among the early guests. Looking out over the scene from the drawing room terrace, Gavin heard snatches of lively songs and occasional trills of laughter, and once in a while the gentle breeze brought the scent of roasted meat to his nose, along with something that smelled like warm apples and cinnamon.

He leaned against the terrace rail and frowned as he observed the crowd. The women all looked similar. True, the ladies were decked out in light-colored muslins, while the estate women had generally chosen brighter colors, but every one of them showed off her best dress and an elaborate hat. Only a closer look at details like gloves and frilly parasols showed true distinctions between the classes. And, of course, the different ways in which each group walked—the ladies almost mincingly, the estate women with confident strides.

The men were much easier to distinguish. Gentlemen arrayed in bright coats and carefully tied cravats strolled—sometimes within jostling distance—past young men who were tanned and broad-shouldered from their work in the fields, most wearing loose shirts and no coats or neckcloths.

From the long windows of the drawing room, Lucien said, "I'll wager you've never seen anything quite like this before."

"No," Gavin said. "Nor would I have expected to see it, here at the castle. The guests are an interesting mix."

Lucien came to stand beside him. "You mean because some of them are estate people rather than ladies and gentlemen? I thought you Americans believed everyone to be equal."

"We do. I just didn't think the duke did."

"He doesn't. But if you're surprised he invited his tenants to mix with the gentry of the neighborhood…" Lucien shrugged. "It's a garden party. A holiday for the estate's people."

"Does he do it often?"

"I don't think there's any regular schedule. But this is the first I've attended in years, so I might be wrong."

Gavin sensed another person on the terrace even before the Earl of Chiswick added, "There's one thing you're correct about, Hartford—you don't know what you're talking about. The annual garden party for all is a Weybridge tradition, as you would know if you paid the slightest attention to family habit and customs." He looked past his son to Gavin. "The duke asked me to send you to him in the library, Athstone. I believe he would like you to accompany him through the grounds as he greets his guests."

Making certain I understand what a big job it is to be master of the castle, more likely.

The Fletcher party was just arriving as Gavin crossed the hall. Sir George greeted him heartily; Lady Fletcher gabbled on about how handsome he looked; Chloe's gaze was darting all over the room as if she was trying to take in everything at once.

"You seem quite excited, Miss Fletcher," Gavin said indulgently.

She stared at him a moment, her eyes suddenly wide and dark. "No—of course not." Her voice was high and breathless.

The girl was on the edge of panic, Gavin realized.

"I mean," she went on, with more composure, "I expect to enjoy this little gathering, as I do all parties. So amusing of the duke to have a garden party."

He considered telling her that a young woman who affected boredom was also boring to others. But he suspected the comment would only call Lady Fletcher's attention to her daughter's odd conduct and earn Chloe a scold—and it would be cruel to do that when the girl was at her wits' end. What on earth was bothering her?

Of course, even if she had been truly bored, Gavin might be the only one who found a young woman's ennui to be tedious. Baron Draycott didn't, that was clear—for as Gavin walked on toward the library, young Draycott paused for an instant in a theatrical pose at the foot of the staircase and then rushed across to Chloe. "My dear Miss Fletcher—how lovely to see you here!"

A good thing it was that Emily didn't want the baron, Gavin told himself. It might prove difficult to keep that young man on the string.

Wrapped up in his thoughts, he turned the knob and stepped into the library. After the brilliant sunshine of the terrace and the light-reflecting marble lining the hall, the library seemed dimmer than usual. The heavy velvet drapes were drawn, and the duke's wheeled chair stood near the fireplace.

Empty.

Not far from the chair, a body lay sprawled across the hearthrug. For a moment, in the dim light, Gavin couldn't see any movement. He sucked in a long breath, and the weight of the entire castle seemed to descend on his shoulders.

"Ever think about knocking before you barge into a private room?" the Duke of Weybridge asked irritably.

He sounded perfectly normal—in other words, testy—but it took Gavin a moment to get himself back under control. "Your Grace, how did you end up on the hearthrug?"

"Don't just stand there and talk down at me, Athstone."

Gavin had to step over one of the duke's hounds to reach the old man. The animal, crouched practically nose to nose with the duke, held a soggy knotted-rope toy in his mouth as if he had brought it over to the fallen man, expecting his master to play tug-of-war.

The dog raised his head and uttered a low growl as Gavin neared, and he said calmly, "That's enough out of you, Balthazar." The animal stared at him for a moment longer, dropped his nose as if he was ashamed of himself, and rolled onto his back.

"Never saw him do that before," the duke said. "Been making up to my dogs, have you?"

"Yes, sir—and with more success than I've had at making up to you, I might add." Gavin gave the hound a perfunctory scratch on the belly before he bent over the duke. "If you can put your arms around my neck, sir, I'll lift you back into your chair."

"No, no," the duke said. "Call my man. He'll be somewhere about. That's what he's for."

The real question, Gavin thought, was why the valet wasn't right there, guarding against this very sort of accident. Was the servant enjoying a rare respite? Gavin couldn't exactly blame him for that. Still...

"Nonsense, sir. You shouldn't lie on a hard floor any longer than you already have. And you shouldn't be left alone even for the few minutes it would take for me to find someone to go looking for him. Everyone in the castle is busy today."

He slid his hands gently under the old man's arms and lifted. Gavin had never lacked for strength, but getting the duke back into his chair took more effort than he'd anticipated. Though his body looked small and frail, Weybridge had more muscle than Gavin would have expected from an invalid. But hadn't Lucien, or someone, said that the decline in the duke's health had been recent and sudden?

"Are you comfortable now, sir?"

"*Comfortable*? I'm tied to a chair with wheels, and you ask if I'm comfortable? No, I'm not—I need to sit up straighter or I'll go sliding off."

The hound whined a little and edged closer to the chair, nudging the duke's hand with the rope toy.

Gavin shooed him away and adjusted the old man's position.

"That'll do for now," the duke said grudgingly. "I called for you to go out on the lawn with me. It's your opportunity to meet all the people of the estate. Plus a good many of the neighboring families, of course."

"Is it my imagination, sir, or do the majority of those families include young ladies?"

"What if they do?"

"I only wondered if there were some you would like me to notice in particular," Gavin murmured.

"If I did, I wouldn't tell you about it," the duke snapped. "Thankless lout that you are, you'd go out of your way to make a bad impression."

"And here I thought that the better you came to know me, the more you would appreciate my strong qualities."

"I might, if I saw any. Let's not sit here all day, Athstone!"

At least when the old man is snarling, he isn't feeling sorry for himself.

Gavin wheeled the chair the length of the new wing of the castle, past the dining room, smoking parlor, and billiard room, to a door that led out to the lawns. Two footmen on duty there snapped to attention, and Gavin waited quietly at the door as they maneuvered the duke's chair outside and carried it down a flight of wide stone steps to the grass.

From the smoking room behind Gavin came a low voice. "It'll all be settled tonight, you'll see. By tomorrow you'll be wishing me happy."

Gavin recognized the voice, for he'd last heard it only a few minutes ago by the main entrance. Lancaster—and he was talking of marriage.

Gavin told himself a scrap of overheard conversation didn't mean Lancaster was still fixed on Emily. The man sounded very sure of himself, and of the lady's answer—so that might mean he'd turned his attentions to some other woman, one who welcomed his courtship.

"Shouldn't you be out there on the lawn wooing?" the other man in the smoking room said. "Lady Emily doesn't seem the sort to stand for being ignored."

"I'm not ignoring her," Lancaster replied. "Just waiting for the appropriate moment."

From down on the lawn, the duke called, "Are you coming, Athstone, or do you plan to stand there all day?"

Gavin realized he had already taken a step toward the smoking room. But it was just as well that he couldn't go barging in, demanding to know Lancaster's intentions. The last thing he needed to do was behave like the girl's guardian.

Nevertheless, as they made the circuit of the lawn, Gavin had to force himself to pay attention to the duke's introductions, to make small talk, to show interest. "I'm so sorry to be boring you, Athstone," the duke said irritably. "Would you like me to go back inside for my nap now, so you can find your own entertainment? Or I could commandeer Lucien here to push me around."

Lucien was standing nearby, holding a glass of ale, but he didn't seem to hear—he was looking out across the crowd as if mesmerized. Curious, Gavin tried to figure out what Lucien was looking at, but instead his gaze fell on Emily.

At last, he thought with a warm rush of relief. He could at least warn her to be on guard.

She responded to his beckoning wave with a smile and began to stroll toward them—though she was taking her own sweet time about it. Gavin forced himself to be patient while she worked her way through the crowd with a word and a smile for everyone, and even a hug here and there.

Tonight, Lancaster had said. *It'll all be settled tonight.* Surely that meant nothing would happen before then.

"I feel like heading out to the folly at the very end of the garden," the duke said. "I haven't been out there in months."

A few feet away, Lucien jerked to attention, and ale slopped over the rim of his glass.

"What ails you, Hartford?" the duke grumbled. "I suppose that means I'm stuck with my heir—since I don't want a glass of ale tipped down my neck."

"Emily's coming to greet you," Gavin said. Too late, he realized that he hadn't used her proper title.

The duke didn't seem to notice. "I must say my two nieces are quite the prettiest girls here."

There could be no argument about that, Gavin thought. He'd seen Isabel earlier, and she was lovely indeed. But Emily was more beautiful yet; she seemed to glow with contentment. Amazing how much a new dress could do for a lady's confidence.

Doubt jabbed through him. Was it only the dress that had put luminescence in her face, added brilliance to her eyes? Was it possible her quiet joy today was because of Lancaster?

She curtseyed to the duke. "You have no idea how wonderful it is to see you outside, Uncle Josiah—and enjoying your party!"

When a stout old gentleman came up to the duke, Gavin drew Emily aside. "Have you seen Lancaster?"

"Only from a distance, and I'm doing my best to avoid catching his eye. Why?"

"Then there's no new understanding between you?"

She laughed. "Gavin, what have you been drinking?"

"I just…" The old gentleman was saying his good-byes to the duke, and Gavin said hastily, "I need to talk to you. Lancaster's plotting something, and—"

"What could he possibly be plotting? Uncle Josiah's getting impatient."

"How can you tell? He always acts that way."

The stout old gentleman bowed to the duke and moved away.

"Also," Emily added, "Lady Murdoch is headed in this direction, and I caught a glimpse of Lady Fletcher as well." She tossed a smile at Gavin, then linked her arm in Lucien's and whisked him down a nearby path.

"You wish to go to the folly, I believe you said?" Gavin asked quickly. "Point the way, Your Grace."

As he trundled the wheeled chair along the graveled paths, Gavin tried to smother his fears.

It'll all be settled tonight, Lancaster had said.

That meant Emily would be all right through the rest of the day, he assured himself. But when Lancaster said *tonight*, what did he mean? Before dinner? During the ball? After the dancing was over, in the small hours? Just before dawn?

And what made the man so certain he would prevail, that he could convince Emily to marry him after all?

❖ ❖ ❖

As Gavin went off to the library to answer the duke's summons, the Earl of Chiswick nodded a dismissal to Lucien and turned back toward the drawing room.

Lucien cleared his throat. "Sir, if I might have a word with you?"

"You wish to converse with me, Hartford?" Chiswick frowned up at the sky. "Did I miss the sun rising in some other direction besides the east, this morning?"

Lucien bit his tongue. "I was thinking about what you said earlier, about family customs and traditions. And also about estate management." He thought he caught a flash of surprise in the earl's face and was heartened by it; it wasn't often anyone could startle the Earl of Chiswick. "I am not the fool you think me, Father. Someday Chiswick will be mine, and I wouldn't like to make a bad job of running it. But before I agree to come back and spend my time learning about the estate, I have some terms to set out."

Chiswick raised both eyebrows. "Oh, do tell me what you demand," he purred. "This should be amusing."

"First, there must be a sizeable increase in my allowance."

"Whatever for? You will have no expenses beyond your tailor."

"If I am taking on additional responsibility, it is only fitting that I be able to maintain my position—and that includes keeping my rooms in London as well as a carriage. Which brings me to the second condition—I will not be tied to the estate. I must be free to come and go as I wish, without asking permission from you or anyone else. If I want to spend time in Town, or visit my friends..."

"Including the wastrel set headed by your friend Aubrey? Yes, Hartford, I do know who you associate with. Tell me—exactly how does this proposal of yours differ from the current situation? For I must tell you, I don't see any advantage for myself in agreeing to your terms."

"I'm not going to make myself a slave to Chiswick," Lucien snapped. "The idea of being trapped there—never able to leave—makes me queasy."

"But as long as you have the freedom to come and go as you please, your intention would be to spend the majority of your time at Chiswick?" The earl's voice was very soft.

Lucien hesitated. His father had laid a trap there some-where, he'd wager—but he was damned if he could see it. "That is what I intend, yes, but—"

"And what of your objection to sharing the estate with my new wife? That matter has not changed in the few hours since you expressed your reservations."

But Chloe won't be there.

Lucien's mind went blank. *Oh, God—did I say that out loud?*

Chiswick maintained his customary calm, and Lucien found if he was careful he could breathe again. He must not let on that anything had changed; he must not hint that the earl's marriage plans were doomed to come to nothing. "You convinced me that she will not interfere."

Chiswick's eyes narrowed. "Did I? There seems to have been a remarkable improvement in my powers of persuasion."

"But I still think it would make a difficult situation for a pair of newlyweds, if they had to share their home with a grown son."

"How thoughtful of you to consider my comfort, Hartford. I'm sure you have a solution in mind?"

Make it sound good, Lucien. Improvise. "I might move into the dower house."

"You want your own establishment?"

"You keep telling me I'm old enough to set up my nursery," Lucien pointed out. "Managing my own roof would be a good start."

"No wonder you demanded a larger allowance." Chiswick tapped his fingers on the stone railing. "You have made an interesting proposal. I'll consider it. And I have a few terms of my own."

Lucien waited for the hammer to drop, but before Chiswick had gathered his thoughts, Sir George Fletcher burst through the double door between drawing room and terrace, and his bluff, hearty greeting made it impossible to continue a serious conversation.

Sir George was so obviously pleased with the world that Lucien had a very hard time keeping himself from warning the man that trouble was brewing, or hinting that he shouldn't count on the Earl of Chiswick becoming his son-in-law.

But Lucien knew if he breathed even a single word, he'd betray Chloe. Her father would step in and prevent her from trying to elope. She would consider Lucien a traitor, and she'd be right.

However, would things turn out any better for Chloe if he stood aside and let her plan proceed? If Captain

Hopkins came to get her tonight and took her straight to Scotland, what then? Would her new husband expect her to follow the army? How could anyone think that an exquisite girl like Chloe, brought up in the midst of luxury, could trail along after her soldier from one army camp to the next? Chloe was special—she deserved to be treated gently.

Lucien realized grimly that the real reason he was so suspicious of Captain Hopkins was not because he feared the man would ignore her plea for help. He was afraid the soldier might after all sweep up in a chaise and four tonight and carry Chloe away.

*   *   *

The garden party had barely started, with only the first few guests wandering up and down the paths and checking out the entertainment and food in the tents and marquees, when Isabel's internal warning system went off. The nape of her neck itched and her nerves began to quiver.

A moment later her husband murmured into her ear, "You look lovely wearing my gift, Isabel. How do you plan to thank me for it?"

Isabel had to fight off the sudden and irrational urge to lean back against him, to draw his arms around her. She took a step away and turned to face him. "I do not regard it as a gift."

He paused with her hand half-raised to his lips. "What do you think I intended? If you're suggesting I meant it as payment for services received—"

Her cheeks felt hot. "I consider it nothing more than a replacement for the gown you ruined. Therefore no thanks are required, since you were merely paying a debt."

"Ah, yes. That abominable dinner gown you insisted on wearing over and over. I had almost forgotten what fun it was to tear you out of it."

And now you've reminded him. Isabel gritted her teeth. *What a fool you are!*

"I hope you've kept other old dresses for me to practice on. No, don't tell me—for it doesn't matter. If I may treat your wardrobe as I like, I shall not mind replacing it regularly, my dear." His gaze slid down over her bodice as if he was considering where best to start ripping.

Isabel gave a little whoosh of irritation and turned her back on him. "Lady Fletcher, I hoped you would soon arrive. Mrs. Meeker—the housekeeper, you know—has assigned you and Sir George the burgundy suite. It's at the southeast corner of the new wing and looks out over the courtyard. Miss Fletcher will be directly next to you."

Chloe took a deep breath. "Dear Lady Isabel, I wonder if I might be moved to somewhere in the back of the castle instead. The noise, you know—carriages coming and going. I'm afraid I wouldn't be able to sleep."

"Nonsense, my dear," Lady Fletcher said. "You mustn't act like a troublesome child. I'm sure the castle is quite full, and Lady Isabel has many more important things to do than shuffle room assignments."

Was that a plea in Chloe's eyes? Isabel wondered what the girl could possibly be up to.

"Besides," Lady Fletcher went on, "you'll be dancing to the wee hours—and even after the ball is over, I warrant you'll be too excited to sleep, so the carriages cannot possibly disturb you. I know—we'll make a second party of it, drinking chocolate and reliving all the excitement. Just the two of us—unless Lady Isabel and Lady Emily would like to join in?"

"We'll see," Isabel said. She found she didn't mind Chloe after all—the girl was really rather endearing—but she'd rather be roasted on a spit than sit on a bed and gossip with Lady Fletcher about who had danced with whom, and who had exchanged melting looks, and who had slipped away from the ballroom for a minute too long to be quite proper. She'd rather spend another night with Maxwell.

The thought came so naturally that Isabel almost didn't notice, and when she did, she had to laugh at herself. As though she had a choice in where—and how—she spent her nights!

* * *

Emily had kept an eye out for Mr. Lancaster all through the party, intending to avoid him—but after Gavin's comment, she was intrigued enough to seek him out. *Lancaster's plotting something.* That accusation covered a great deal of territory, and it made her curious. What had sparked Gavin's suspicion and made him warn Emily?

Young Baron Draycott came up to her as she was scanning the lawn for Lancaster. "If you're looking for Lord Athstone," he said, "I believe he and the duke were—"

"Why would I be looking for Athstone?" Her voice sounded sharper than she'd intended, and Draycott looked startled. Emily took a firm grip on herself. She was both annoyed and a little frightened by his observation—if Draycott had reason to link her name with Gavin's, she shuddered to think what her father might have observed. Had she not been as careful as she'd thought?

"I assumed you'd be looking for your uncle," Draycott said, "only it would be much easier to spot Athstone instead of the chair, because he's so tall."

"Oh." Emily felt as if someone had stuck a pin in her and let all the air out. "That makes sense. I've already greeted my uncle, however, so I have no need to notice Athstone's height."

She couldn't help looking, though. Her gaze drifted across the garden until she spotted Gavin, halfway between the castle and the unique little folly. Even from a distance, there could be no mistaking Gavin—not only his height but the breadth of his shoulders made him stand out. His strength was apparent, too, from the easy way he was pushing the duke's chair over the gravel path.

Draycott cleared his throat, and Emily shook herself a bit and turned back to him, startled to see that Lancaster had joined them.

"Lady Emily," he said with a deep bow. "I am delighted to see you again. I hope to win a dance with you at the ball this evening." He kissed her hand with exactly the right degree of deference, and moved off before she could do more than nod politely.

Lancaster's plotting something, Gavin had said. It seemed more likely Gavin was seeing things that didn't exist, for Lancaster was being perfectly proper. Even distant.

She wondered if Gavin had some misguided notion that she needed protecting—or a conviction that it was his place to look after her.

A good deal later she was outside the main marquee, trying not to yawn over an interminable tale being told by an old crony of the duke's, when Isabel caught up with her. "Emily, do you know where Uncle Josiah is? I haven't seen him for half an hour at least."

"The last I knew, Gavin was taking him down to the folly. Why, I have no idea. But surely he's back inside by now, resting."

Isabel chewed her lower lip. "I just want to be certain he's all right. I saw them headed in that direction, and a little later Lady Murdoch said she was going down to chat with Uncle Josiah. But she hasn't come back. What if she's annoying him?"

"I think Uncle Josiah would put her in her place, Isabel."

"Or what if something happened and Gavin couldn't leave him to get help?"

"Then he'd send Lady Murdoch to fetch someone. Oh, all right, Isabel. I'll walk down if it makes you feel better."

Isabel shook her head. "I'll go to the folly. But will you check the castle and see if he's there? It's possible I just didn't see them come back."

Emily thought the whole thing silly, but it was a good excuse to escape from the crony. As she crossed the lawn, she noticed that Mr. Lancaster was so busy flirting with one of the Carew sisters that he didn't even nod as she passed. Just wait till she had a chance to talk to Gavin again about his idiotic suspicions—she'd have enjoyed catching him down in the folly and tearing into him.

The castle was cool and dim and quiet compared to the garden party, and she stopped in the hall outside the billiard room for a moment to let her eyes adjust. "Chalmers?" she called as a dark-clad figure crossed the hall. "Is that you?"

The moment the man turned toward her, Emily recognized him.

"No, my lady," Benson said. "I believe the butler is currently engaged with the footmen who are replenishing food in the tents outside. If I may be of assistance?"

"Do you happen to know if the duke has returned to the castle?"

"Yes, ma'am. He is in his rooms."

"Thank you." Emily turned to go back outside, and the valet stepped into her path. "You presume, Benson. Because you did me a favor this morning doesn't mean you're allowed to—"

Benson coughed. "My lady? I beg your pardon, but I recall nothing of the sort."

Emily knew she should be grateful for his discretion—but instead she felt a wave of color wash over her face. What had she been thinking, to refer to that mortifying trip back to her bedroom? Even the valet displayed more common sense than she did.

"My apologies, my lady, but I have a message for you from his lordship."

She paused in midstep. "From Athstone? What now?"

"Since he is otherwise engaged, his lordship asked me to convey to you his concern that Mr. Lancaster may have designs on you."

"Is that all? He already told me as much—and you may inform his lordship that he has mistaken the situation. I have spoken to Mr. Lancaster and everything is quite normal."

She brushed past Benson and went back to the garden party. The first thing she saw was Gavin, halfway across the lawn with a Carew sister on each side of him. One of them seemed to have said something hilarious, for as Emily watched, Gavin threw back his head and laughed.

He was *otherwise engaged,* all right. So he'd assigned his servant a troublesome duty, then wiped the problem from his mind.

So much for her concern that he might feel responsible for her! Emily was glad she'd learned the lesson so easily—for it was perfectly clear that to Gavin, she was no more than a passing thought.

❀ ❀ ❀

Lucien finally managed to break free from a crashing bore—an old friend of the duke's who had pinned him up against a brick wall for half an hour while he recounted every embarrassing incident from Lucien's childhood visits to the castle.

With a relieved sigh, he settled himself on the stone coping surrounding a gently splashing fountain near the main marquee, where he had a good view of a group of girls eating ices. One of them was Chloe Fletcher, and though he tried not to stare, Lucien couldn't keep his gaze from drifting back to her every time he forced himself to look away. He hoped that her laugh didn't sound as uncomfortable to those girls as it did to him. But they didn't know her as well as he did; they might not even suspect that anything was wrong.

Lady Stone, the old gossip, started past him and paused, her beady black gaze intent on his face. "You look as though you're longing to have one of them." She nodded toward the girls.

Lucien choked. "I beg your pardon, ma'am?"

"The ices. What did you think I was referring to, Hartford? The girls?" She gave a rusty laugh. "What has the youth of today come to?"

Belatedly, Lucien rose from the low stone wall and bowed, careful not to spill his glass of ale. Perhaps if he acted as if he hadn't heard that last jibe, she would move on.

Instead, Lady Stone settled herself on the wall as if she intended to stay all afternoon. She planted her ebony cane in the grass at Lucien's feet, propped her folded hands on the knob, and surveyed the girls. "Chloe Fletcher is very young to be a stepmother."

She was obviously fishing for information, and Lucien was not about to venture into those troubled waters by giving an opinion.

"Especially when the stepchildren-to-be are all older than she is. She's barely nineteen. What are you now, Hartford? Twenty-six, twenty-seven?" Lady Stone shook her head. "It's too bad of your father, you know, even to think of marrying her. I never would have expected it of him, considering how badly he's missed your mother all these years. He's hardly been the same man since Drusilla died."

Lucien bit his tongue hard to keep from giving Lady Stone his own unadulterated opinion.

"Besides, Chiswick doesn't need to add Sir George Fletcher's land to his holdings."

He frowned. "What do you mean?"

"Think about it, young man. Sir George's estate is not entailed. He's only a baronet, a rank he earned by some kind of service to the crown long ago. His title will end with him, and Chloe is his only natural heir. Whoever marries her will own Mallowan one day."

Lucien sucked in a deep breath. Finally he understood what he'd seen in Captain Hopkins's eyes that day in the army stables when he'd handed over Chloe's letter. The expression had been so fleeting Lucien hadn't had time to recognize it—but now it all came clear in his mind. As the captain realized that his hopes had been dashed and his patience had been for nothing, he had looked chagrined.

Captain Hopkins had hoped to marry Chloe the heiress. But it would be a different thing altogether to elope with Chloe the disowned daughter, and live on her minuscule allowance with no hope of inheriting her father's rich acres. A poor bride was not an attractive proposition to an ambitious young man who had only his army pay and a hundred guineas a year.

This explained everything. The captain's instant flash of annoyance when he had read Chloe's letter. The fact that he had not sent back any message for Lucien to deliver to her. The way the captain had merely grunted at Lucien instead of thanking him or raving about his lovely bride-to-be.

Lucien allowed himself a moment of pure triumph, basking in the conviction that he had been right all along about Captain Hopkins's intentions. Lucien was as certain of it in his own heart as if the man had told him outright that he had no intention of showing up tonight.

But his triumph quickly gave way to uncertainty. How could he possibly break this news to Chloe? She would never believe him. She would listen, and shake her head, and tell him that he didn't know Captain Hopkins—and she would be right. How could Lucien persuade her that he had read the man's character more accurately in just a few minutes than she had in however many weeks or months she had known him?

Besides, with her freedom at stake—when giving up her dream of eloping with her soldier would mean she was once more caught in a betrothal to a man she detested, with no escape in sight—everything in her would want to trust Captain Hopkins. She would not lightly be swayed from believing in him, and in her plans.

Even if somehow Lucien could convince her not to go out to the folly tonight, part of her would always wonder whether her lover had come after all and found her to be the unfaithful one.

So though he was as certain as it was possible to be that Captain Hopkins would not appear in that dark back lane tonight with a chaise and four ready for a trip to Scotland, Lucien was also positive that Chloe would not be dissuaded from her plan. It would do no good to tell her what he had discovered; she would have to face the truth for herself. She would no doubt wait in the folly until her heart broke rather than believe that her lover might not come for her.

But maybe there was still something he could do to ease the pain.

"Yes, indeed," Lady Stone said. "The only possible conclusion is that it's a love match."

Lucien had the vague impression that she'd been talking to herself the whole time, working through a convoluted line of logic on her way to an incredible conclusion. But who was this fount of gossip talking about? Could she possibly know about Chloe and Captain Hopkins?

"A love match?" he said unsteadily.

"Stop woolgathering, Hartford." Lady Stone rapped him across the knuckles with her fan. "I mean Chiswick and your soon-to-be stepmother. As far as I can see, there's no other way to account for it. But you look shocked—so tell me, is there some factor I've overlooked?"

Chapter 15

❧

As Isabel followed the path through the gardens to the folly at the far end, she kept her eyes open for guests who seemed uncomfortable or lost. Not many had come so far, and before long she was able to simply enjoy the quiet.

She knew she was probably fretting over nothing, to worry so about Uncle Josiah. But why had the duke wanted to come all the way out here anyway, so far from his guests?

Uncle Josiah had looked much healthier in the last couple of days than he had on the evening the family had arrived. Probably that was just the effect of having something to think about besides his illness, and some entertainment that was livelier than the usual castle routine. However, the fact that he felt somewhat better might have prompted him to attempt too much.

The folly stood on a little knoll that commanded some of the best views on the entire estate. An octagonal structure that looked like an oversized lantern, it had a steep slate roof with deep overhangs. Its open sides were partially sheltered by trellised wisteria vines, which provided shade and windbreak all year, as well as glorious aromas in the summer.

Isabel heard voices coming from the folly—a woman's laughing tones—and she hastened her step in case Lady Murdoch was annoying the duke.

Then a man's voice cut across the laughter. But it wasn't Uncle Josiah's voice, and it wasn't Gavin's.

The Earl of Maxwell was in the folly, with Lady Murdoch. Isabel's husband—with the woman who had been rumored to be his mistress.

Isabel stopped in a secluded spot behind a row of tall, thick boxwood. She had no intention of eavesdropping, she told herself. Besides, nothing could happen, for Uncle Josiah was there, too. Wasn't he?

Through the vines, she caught a glimpse of a bright-red skirt, and very close to it, a deep-blue coat—the one Maxwell had been wearing. And there were no other voices.

Lady Murdoch and Maxwell. No wonder he hadn't been anywhere on the castle lawn. Only now did Isabel realize she'd been watching for him. She wondered if she had suspected this, when Lady Murdoch announced that she planned to seek out the duke. Why else would Isabel have had that sudden and overwhelming fear that something might have happened to Uncle Josiah, except that it had formed an excuse to come all the way down here and see for herself? Why had she insisted on coming, when Emily had volunteered?

Because you wanted to know. And now what are you going to do about it?

"Isn't your tedious little bride with child yet, Max? Do hurry it up—because now that I've provided my husband with his heir, I'm free to do as I like. And what I'd like is…"

Her voice dropped, but Isabel had no difficulty in filling in the rest of the sentence.

"You'd risk losing your husband's money by flaunting a lover in front of him, Elspeth?" Maxwell sounded good-humored, almost lazy.

"I expect we'd need to be discreet." Lady Murdoch's laugh sounded just a bit forced. "But Murdoch is Scottish, you see. All that lovely money and he won't let go of a single farthing. So it doesn't matter whether I please him or only myself—all I'll have is my marriage portion. But at least I could have you."

Isabel gritted her teeth as the flash of red skirt moved even closer to the dark-blue coat.

It was only a moment later—though it seemed forever to Isabel—when Lady Murdoch said, "What's wrong, Max? You haven't gone sentimental on me, have you?"

Isabel's breath caught. If he wasn't seizing the lure Lady Murdoch held out, why not? Was it possible that Maxwell intended to honor his vows?

She knew better than to let her thoughts wander in that direction, of course. More likely he was delaying only because he wanted to make certain that his *tedious little bride* was pregnant before he devoted himself to a lover.

"What is it, Max? You're not *still* feeling guilty about that young woman, are you? Miss Lester?"

Isabel fought off a dizzy spell. She hadn't heard that name in a very long time. But what had Maxwell to do with the young lady Philip Rivington had ruined? Maxwell had been drawn into that duel only because he was Philip Rivington's friend—and that, Isabel thought, was bad enough. Surely he had no other involvement with the young woman Philip had seduced.

Lady Murdoch sounded accusing. "You're still sending her money—aren't you?"

Foreboding descended on Isabel like fog, so dense and gray and heavy that she could barely breathe.

"It is none of your business what I do with my money."

"Just because she was supposed to be a lady, and ladies are expected not to get themselves with child, is no reason for *you*..."

"It's little enough to do for her and the child, since I am responsible for her situation."

Isabel clutched her arms tightly across her body and wished she had never come down the path to the folly. Each word seemed to tear deeper into her heart.

"Oh, Max," Lady Murdoch soothed, "don't be so silly about this. How foolish you're being—what would people say if they knew? She got *herself* into this mess, after all. A sensible female would have taken care not to get with child."

"A sensible female like you, Elspeth?"

Lady Murdoch laughed. "Yes, darling, a sensible female like me. You needn't be afraid that *I'll* saddle you with a by-blow. Now come here, Max—and kiss me."

Blind with pain, Isabel turned back toward the castle, and with the last of her self-control she slipped silently away.

❂ ❂ ❂

The duke dismissed Gavin at the bottom of the stairs, as soon as the two burly footmen appeared to carry his chair up the long flight to the gallery. "I've had enough of your company for one afternoon, Athstone. Go back out to the garden and take care of my guests."

The man was exhausted but far too proud to admit it. Or else, Gavin thought as he looked out over the lawn, the duke agreed that garden parties were the most boring activity on the face of the earth. He must have forgotten that fact when he'd planned this one, or surely he'd have used the excuse of his illness to avoid it.

The annual Weybridge garden party was a tradition, the Earl of Chiswick had said. He made it sound as though the castle itself would collapse if the party wasn't held on schedule. But then that might not be such a bad thing, Gavin thought. If there was no castle, there wouldn't be a place to hold garden parties, much less balls—and the upcoming dance promised to be every bit as dull as the garden party, only warmer and more crowded.

He descended the wide stone steps to the lawn and plunged once more into the throng, nodding and smiling and chatting, till he ended up near the big marquee and spotted Lucien sitting on the edge of the low stone basin of a fountain. Gavin dropped down beside him. "Where did you find that glass of ale?"

Lucien shook his head a little as if he were just waking up, and he looked at the glass, apparently surprised to see what he was holding. "Around front, in the courtyard. The innkeeper brought a barrel, but he's keeping it under wraps. Favored customers only."

"Thanks. I'll be back in a few minutes." But Gavin didn't move, because as he scanned the crowd, he saw Emily with Lancaster and young Baron Draycott. Apparently, Benson hadn't yet been able to pass along the message to her, or surely she wouldn't be standing there making eyes at the man.

Lucien stood up suddenly. "I'll bring you a glass. If you go out to the courtyard yourself, half the crowd will notice and probably follow you. The heir, you know—everyone's watching you."

"And here I thought my main job was to flirt with every unmarried woman within twenty miles."

Lucien grinned. "That, too." He saluted Gavin with his glass and strolled off.

Gavin looked back at Emily. Lancaster had gone, leaving her with Baron Draycott. That was interesting, Gavin thought. Was it possible he'd read too much into the fragment of conversation he'd overheard? Or maybe Lancaster had known he was standing there just outside the smoking room door and had been goading him. The duke had called Gavin's name from the foot of the steps—Lancaster could have heard that and decided to have a little fun.

There was nothing he could do about it now—or, rather, he'd done everything he could by warning Emily. Surely she would take care of herself. And what could Lancaster do in the middle of a garden party, anyway?

The Carew sisters sidled by with their eyes modestly cast down, and he rose to bow politely just as one of them lost her shoe and seized his arm to steady herself. Gavin smothered a sigh and helped her back into her footwear, and wished he were still trundling the duke's chair around the garden.

*   *   *

A by-blow. A side-slip. A bastard…

As soon as she was away from the folly, Isabel found a stone bench in a secluded corner of the garden, as far as she could get from the laughter and joy of the party. She barely felt the cold of the shaded stone seeping through her fine new dress. She was making a mental list of all the names, from euphemistic to blunt, for a child born out of wedlock—because occupying her mind with semantics for a while let her avoid thinking too deeply about what she had overheard.

But the respite from her pounding thoughts was fleeting.

Maxwell sent money to a young lady who had borne a child without being married—because, he had flatly told Lady Murdoch, he was responsible.

All this time, Isabel had despised Philip Rivington—because he had been a cad and a fool, because he had destroyed Emily's life, because he had ruined Isabel's own marriage. But now it seemed that Philip Rivington had not been the guilty party after all—because Maxwell was.

Isabel had never before wondered why Philip Rivington had met his challenger in a duel rather than seek some other, more honorable solution. If he *had* been the father of Miss Lester's child, he could have muddled through the mess by breaking off his betrothal to Emily and marrying the young woman he had seduced. Even Miss Lester's irate brother would have agreed to a quiet marriage, no matter how much he despised Philip Rivington, because the alternative was worse—a scandalous duel, a ruined sister, and a bastard child.

But if Maxwell had been the father instead, he would have had no such option—for by the time the challenge was issued, he had already married Isabel.

For the first time, she considered the odd timing of that duel. She'd always thought it purely coincidence—annoying and inconvenient, but coincidence nonetheless—that her new husband's friend had been called out to face justice on the very night after her wedding. But since it was also the day that Emily's betrothal had been publicly announced, she had never questioned which event might have been the actual trigger.

But what if it should have been Maxwell instead who faced that pistol at dawn—and Philip Rivington had stepped into his shoes, taken the blame—and paid the price?

You have to ask him. You have to know the truth.

Her entire body shuddered away from the confrontation. They were finally beginning to find their way to a sort of peace, but now she would have to upset that fragile balance…

Isabel pulled herself up short. What was she thinking? There was no peace between them, no balance. Only a bargain—a straightforward swap. How had she, even for a moment, forgotten that?

Because you wanted to forget.

She gasped as the harsh truth struck home. Sometime in the last few days, she had stopped thinking of the benefits she would get from their bargain—full possession of Kilburn and complete independence from her husband—because the fact was she didn't want to leave him after all.

Maxwell's reasoning, annoying though she had found it, had been correct. Though she hadn't admitted it even to herself, Isabel could no longer deny the facts. She *had* deliberately set out to make their marriage real. She wanted to be his wife. She wanted to give him his heir.

Sometime in the last year, even while she had been constantly telling herself she wanted nothing to do with Maxwell, she had fallen in love with her husband...only to find out now, in the most painful way possible, that she had never known him at all.

❖ ❖ ❖

Even though he'd scarcely taken his eyes off Chloe all afternoon, Lucien almost missed her signal as she left the group of girls she'd been sitting with under the edge of the marquee and started off toward a quieter corner of the garden by herself. In fact, he wondered for a moment if she'd acquired some sort of tic, the way she was tossing her head around.

Oh. She must be beckoning for him to join her.

He groped for an excuse to walk away from Gavin and finally mumbled something about getting his cousin a glass of ale. But instead of heading for the courtyard and the innkeeper's barrel, Lucien took a path that paralleled the one Chloe was on, watching her progress from the corner of his eye. Only when they were out of sight did he push through a hedge and come up next to her.

She wheeled around to face him. "What in heaven's name is wrong with you, Hartford?"

He hadn't expected an attack. "Nothing. Why?"

"Then stop watching me! Someone will notice and wonder why you're so interested."

"Why wouldn't I watch you? You're quite pretty, you know."

She turned a little pink and seemed—to Lucien's relief—to calm down. At least her voice was lower and steadier. "I forgot to ask you this morning. Did he give you a time?"

"Give me a...? Oh, you mean Cap—"

"Shush! Someone could be listening."

"We're in the middle of the knot garden, Chloe."

"With hedges all around, so someone could be lurking on the other side. Anyway, we mustn't be away from the party for long. Did he tell you what time he'll be here?"

"No," Lucien said honestly. *And he didn't tell me anything else, either—this fortune-hunting soldier of yours.*

Chloe lifted her pinky finger to her mouth and nibbled at her nail. "He won't be late, I'm certain, for he'll want to put a great deal of the journey behind us before anyone realizes I'm gone. So of course I don't want to keep him waiting."

"Not good for the horses," Lucien agreed, "standing around in the damp air."

Chloe rolled her eyes. "It will already be dark by the time the dancing starts, but I must at least make an appearance at the ball. My mother would never believe that even the most dreadful headache could make me give up the entire evening. Then I'll have to go back upstairs, after I make my excuses and leave the ballroom."

"Why? I left your valise in the folly, just as you requested—tucked under the bench farthest from the castle."

She rewarded him with a smile, but it was far from her best one; she was obviously distracted. Lucien was disappointed. He hadn't realized that he looked forward to her smiles.

"Because I'll have to stuff something into my bed to make it look as if I'm lying there sound asleep, or else my mother will want to come in after the ball and share all the gossip."

"My sisters used to do that sort of thing."

Chloe seemed not to hear him. "I wouldn't like to keep Captain Hopkins waiting, but I should stay at the ball till the last possible moment."

"Yes, because it would be a shame to miss any of the fun."

"Don't be sarcastic, Lucien. The sooner I leave, the more likely it is that I'll be missed before we can get well away. I wish he had told you when he'd arrive."

"I don't suppose he knew how long it would take a post-chaise to get here."

"To be safe, I'd better make my move after the very first country dance."

Lucien was still thinking about her smile—and realizing that if Captain Hopkins showed up tonight, he would never see her smile again. He would probably never see Chloe again, for the orbits of an earl's heir and a woman who had eloped could never cross.

He couldn't bear the thought. Still, it was cruel of him to wish for her hopes to be dashed solely because he didn't want to give up her smile.

All this might work out for her after all, Lucien told himself. He might be imagining Captain Hopkins as a villain because he didn't want to see another side of the man. But maybe the captain *wasn't* just a fortune-hunting soldier. Maybe he loved Chloe enough to do without her father's money. There would be nothing incredible about that, for Chloe Fletcher was eminently lovable.

I love her that much. Why shouldn't he?

For a moment Lucien didn't even hear what he was thinking, and when the knowledge hit him, he staggered a little.

"Are you all right? Lucien Arden, have you been swilling ale all afternoon?"

I love Chloe Fletcher.

Her laughter. Her feisty attitude. Her determination not to be traded off in marriage. Even the smooth way she'd maneuvered him into helping her. God help him, he loved all of her.

But he couldn't even confess his feelings, for Chloe had already made her choice.

*   *   *

Isabel sat on her out-of-the-way bench until the cold stone and the chilly breeze drove her back inside. In her bedroom, Martha was waiting with a bath prepared and a scold on the tip of her tongue. "Staying out in that damp air," she muttered. "It'll be a wonder if you don't catch your death. And now there's hardly time to get you ready for dinner, much less do justice to your new ball gown."

Isabel paid no attention. The warm water did not soothe her; her bones still felt cold when she climbed out of the tub and stood listlessly by the fire as Martha rubbed her down with a rough towel. Even the new ball gown Uncle Josiah had provided couldn't lift her spirits tonight, beautiful though it was. Layers of white silk and net drifted around her as she moved, and the silver spangles that were scattered across the skirt twinkled in the candlelight.

"How beautiful you are," Martha said.

Isabel dutifully looked in the mirror. "I suppose so."

The maid frowned. "If you're coming down with some ailment, my lady—"

Only a troubled heart, Isabel almost said. "I'm fine, Martha."

"You don't look…Oh," Martha said, and smiled. "I see. I should have known. Well, as long as you don't wear yourself out, dancing can't hurt the babe."

"I'm not pregnant." *I refuse to be pregnant.* But sadness swept over her at the thought that there might never be a child.

Martha shrugged and went to answer a knock.

Emily swept in. "You're not ready yet, Isabel? I couldn't wait—I was so excited about putting on this gown."

Isabel could see why. The deep rose-pink of Emily's gown reflected in her cheeks and made her big brown eyes dark and mysterious. *While I just look washed out.*

Though, when she looked closer, it seemed to her that Emily's excitement might not be rising out of joy but something else instead. Was her color not quite natural? And was it sadness rather than exhilaration that had made her eyes so dark?

Martha put the last pin in Isabel's hair and added a spray of tiny white roses—no doubt the very last of the season—and Isabel glanced at the result and nodded curtly. Just as she stood up, she caught a flash of movement behind her in the mirror, and she braced herself.

"Aren't you even going to wear Mother's pearls?" Emily asked. "You look lovely, but that neckline cries out for something, Isabel. You can't just leave it bare."

Maxwell came to stand beside Isabel. "I should think not."

For a moment she saw the two of them side by side in the mirror. He had chosen a black coat tonight, with black satin knee breeches—but his shirt, waistcoat, and neckcloth were just as pure a white as Isabel's gown. They looked like a matched set—the perfect couple.

Appearances can be misleading.

"I hope you will wear this." He held out a velvet-covered box.

Isabel wanted to dash it in his face. But then she would have to explain herself, admit what she had heard in the folly, and confront him—and she was not ready to do any of those things.

Besides, she could not make a scene in front of her sister, and obviously Emily had no intention of going away; she was already peering at the box, longing to see what was inside.

Isabel did not reach out, and finally Maxwell snapped the latch and turned the open box toward her.

Emily gasped.

Against the dark satin lining of the box, the inch-wide band looked like a narrow river of diamonds, the stones set so closely together that there seemed to be no break between them.

"Quite nice," Isabel said coolly.

Maxwell frowned and lifted the necklace from the satin.

Isabel turned her back, hoping to forestall him. "Martha, if you will help me?"

But Maxwell himself laid the necklace around her throat and fastened the clasp, his fingers warm against her nape. Isabel thought for a moment that even with Emily in the room, he might bend his head and kiss her, and she tensed at the thought. He let his hands rest on her shoulders instead and turned her toward the mirror.

The main section of the necklace fit closely around her throat—so closely, Isabel thought, that it just might choke her—while a few larger stones in pendant settings dripped down almost to the swell of her breasts.

She kept her voice absolutely level. "I shall take the greatest care of it, my lord, and return it to you unharmed at the end of the evening."

Emily was goggling at her as if she couldn't believe her eyes.

For a moment, Isabel considered which would be more uncomfortable—being left alone with Maxwell or with Emily. Fortunately, neither was likely to happen, for the clock on the mantel announced it was time to go down for dinner. She linked her arm in her sister's and led the way downstairs.

As they reached the drawing room door, Maxwell said, "A moment, Isabel." His voice was deep, calm, and inexorable.

Isabel's insides froze. Surely he wouldn't ask her to explain her attitude while Emily was present…though even with an audience, he usually managed to get his point across without quite causing a scene.

But why should she assume he meant to confront her? He had no way of knowing she had been outside the folly this afternoon, eavesdropping on that damning conversation. Her own guilty knowledge—and the uncertainty of what she was going to do about what she had heard—was making her sensitive; that was all.

Besides, Maxwell could hardly be surprised at her lack of reaction to the diamond necklace. After the way he had seemed to expect favors in return for a dress, Isabel would have to be a fool not to wonder what reward he expected for presenting her with diamonds. Of course she hadn't thrown herself on him with hugs and tears of glee.

And if she *had* been so foolish as to read some deeper meaning into a diamond necklace, he would probably have told her—whether it was true or not—that the jewelry was only rented and not hers to keep.

"I see you already have your card for the ball," he went on. "I should like first choice of this evening's dances." He held out a hand for Isabel's dance card.

Numbly, she handed it over and watched, seething, as he wrote his name on three different lines. Had he selected those particular dances ahead of time, she wondered, or chosen them at random?

He put the card back into her hand and solicitously closed her fingers over it. "Or were you thinking, my dear, that I might wish to ask for something else instead?"

Isabel didn't even try to answer, but brushed past him to go into the drawing room. They were almost the last of the group to arrive, and Isabel felt as though every eye in the place was on her.

Almost every eye. From her chair near one of the fire-places, Lady Murdoch looked over the edge of her fan, past Mr. Lancaster and on beyond Isabel, coming to rest on Maxwell. When she smiled at him, Isabel was reminded of a lioness who had just sighted a particularly juicy bit of prey.

Then Lady Murdoch's eyes widened and her gaze swept back to Isabel and focused on the necklace. For an instant, shock flooded her face.

She's just as surprised as I was.

For the first time, Isabel wondered why Maxwell even had such an elaborate necklace with him. He must have brought it from London, for there was nowhere within a day's journey where he could buy such a thing, and there hadn't been time for him to send an order all the way back to the city. But why would he have tucked such elaborate jewels into his luggage?

As a gift for a mistress, Isabel thought. No wonder Lady Murdoch was looking daggers at her. She thought the necklace should have been hers.

But if it had been Maxwell's intention to give the necklace to his mistress, why was Isabel the one who was dripping with diamonds tonight?

❄   ❄   ❄

Guests were still streaming through the ceremonial entrance to the old section of the castle, then making their way into the ancient great hall to bow to the Duke of Weybridge and wish him a happy birthday, when the master of ceremonies announced the start of the first country dance. The duke waved Gavin away from the receiving line to where the dancers were forming into two columns running almost the entire length of the great hall.

Gavin took his place near the center, opposite the elder Miss Carew, and glanced down the row to where Emily stood across from young Baron Draycott.

Between the small orchestra tuning up and his own distraction, he almost didn't hear Miss Carew say, "I wonder why the duke has never added a ballroom. Don't you think it odd that the castle doesn't have one?"

To Gavin's relief, the music started just then, so he could merely nod instead of having to answer. She was right, after all—the absence of a ballroom *was* odd, since the damned castle seemed to have at least two of everything else. Not that he felt the lack; he hadn't even been able to count all the rooms as yet. Why would anyone feel the need to add a ballroom, to be used at most once a year?

Only a few minutes into the dance, the complex steps brought him face-to-face with Emily. As they wheeled around together, he asked, "Is Lancaster on your dance card?"

"What concern is it of yours?"

The music surged on and the figures moved them away from each other.

A bit later, as they repeated the steps, he stayed silent. But Emily said, "If you really want to know who I'll be dancing with tonight, perhaps you should send Benson to look me up and inquire." She flashed a smile—though he thought it was more of a grimace—and was gone.

That hadn't gone well. What was wrong with her, anyway? She'd seen firsthand that he was stuck to the duke's side at the garden party, so why didn't she seem to realize that he had only brought Benson into the picture so she would have all the warning it was possible to give her?

The man had rescued her just this morning, so surely she wasn't fearful of what he might do. True, she still seemed to have her suspicions of Benson, but...*I'll just have to catch her alone.*

But she was never alone. Her dance card must be crammed full—for when Gavin asked for it after the first country dance so he could claim a waltz later in the evening, Emily merely gave him a pitying smile and shook her head. "I'm quite occupied with other gentlemen tonight, you see. I'm interviewing to see who I want as my next lover, so I must take advantage of every opportunity."

Before he could find his voice, she'd slipped away—and the next time he saw her on the floor, she was dancing with Lancaster.

Gavin gritted his teeth and wished that he hadn't been quite so noble after all. If he had done as she'd asked and taken her virginity, she wouldn't be looking for another lover, and he could have better protected her from adventurers like Lancaster.

He frowned, because something about that logic didn't feel quite right—but before he could sort it out, the music changed and he had to mind his steps.

❖ ❖ ❖

As the first country dance began, Lucien found himself at the extreme end of the line of dancers and paired with the younger Miss Carew, while Chloe, partnering the Earl of Chiswick, was in the thick of things right in the center of the ballroom. Only for an instant in the entire half hour of the dance was he able to touch her hand and look into her eyes, before the figures swept them apart once more.

He couldn't help thinking that this might be the only time they would ever dance together—and to have such a special moment be gone in the blink of an eye was painful.

He tried not to watch for her as the music ended and everyone milled about the floor, changing partners for the next dance, so he was startled to see her cutting across the great hall straight toward him. "Chloe," he said. "What—?" Too late, he realized that the Earl of Chiswick was still beside her.

Chloe brushed past Mr. Lancaster and Lady Murdoch as they left the floor. She stopped in front of Lady Fletcher, who was sitting with Lady Stone only a few feet from Lucien.

"Mama," she said, "I'm sorry, truly I am, and I fear I'm insulting the dear duke—but I have a terrible headache and if I don't lie down, I'm afraid I will be ill."

She did look pale, Lucien thought, and he wouldn't be surprised if her head really was hurting.

Lady Fletcher seemed reluctant to give up her conversation with Lady Stone, though she clucked a little over her daughter. "My dear, you've looked forward to this ball. Surely if you just sit somewhere for a moment you'll be better. I'm certain Lord Chiswick will keep you company."

Chloe looked even more ill, though Lucien wouldn't have thought it possible. "No, Mama, I must lie down. You'll make my apologies to the duke?"

Her voice cracked, and Lucien winced. He hadn't even considered how difficult this moment would be for her; she was saying good-bye to her mother forever, but she wasn't even able to say the words.

Chloe curtseyed to Chiswick. "I thank you, of course, my lord." She put a hand to her forehead.

"Poor child," Lady Fletcher said absently, and turned back to Lady Stone. "I've never known her to have a megrim before—at least not when there's an entertainment she enjoys. You were telling me about the very strange behavior of your companion, ma'am?"

Emily tugged at Lucien's arm. "The dancers are forming up for the next set, and you did write your name on my card. Besides, you can't stand in the middle of the room, practically next to Father, and ogle Chloe Fletcher. People notice these things, and you're making a cake of yourself."

Horrified, Lucien could only stare at her.

"I mean your conviction that she set out to marry so far above herself," Emily said impatiently. "You're being a corkbrain if you still think she's anything but a pawn, Lucien."

"I thought you didn't like her."

"Not at first, but now…The music's starting, so come along."

He couldn't concentrate on the dance, and to Emily's obvious aggravation he kept missing his steps and messing up the turns.

He could think only of Chloe, sitting by herself out in the folly, in the dark and the chill. He wouldn't even know until morning if Captain Hopkins had kept the assignation she had made.

Even then, he realized, he would not know for certain whether she was safe. She would just be gone—with nothing to nothing to show whether Captain Hopkins had appeared. What if someone else found her out there?

Lucien tried to dismiss that fear, for what was the likelihood someone else would come along that back lane in the dark of night and stop to visit the folly? That was the reason she had chosen the location, after all—the loneliness of the spot. Still, Lucien couldn't quite shake the apprehension that swept over him.

And what if his instinct was right and Captain Hopkins didn't come? How long would she sit there and wait, growing colder by the moment? What would she do when she finally gave up, as she must sooner or later? She could hardly limp back into the castle, valise in hand, and pretend that she hadn't tried to run away.

What kind of a gentleman are you, Lucien Arden—letting a lady sit out there in the cold by herself?

He stuck out the dance because to walk off the floor in the middle would call far too much attention to his behavior. But the moment the music stopped he seized Emily's arm. "If anyone asks about me, just say I've…oh, say I'm tired of dancing and I'm going to scare up a card game somewhere."

She made a face. "I'd object, but the way you were stumbling over your feet, it's probably for the best if you don't make any other partner miserable tonight." She wheeled around and collided with Gavin. "Not *you* again. Did you hear Lucien say he'd rather play cards? You should join him."

Lucien didn't wait to hear the answer.

All the activity was centered in the great hall tonight, so the new wing of the castle was largely empty. Even the footmen who normally manned the doors had been moved to duty in the great hall. Lucien pretended not to notice a pair of waiters carrying trays from the kitchen, because asking why they were strolling through the public rooms instead of taking the back stairs would only make his departure something to remember. For the same reason, he didn't stop to find a greatcoat. Stepping out for a moment's fresh air was common at a ball. But to bundle up as if he were going for a cross-country walk would draw attention.

The full moon was past, but the night was clear and the garden paths were not hard to follow despite the deep shadows cast by trees and hedges and statues. A brisk five-minute walk brought him to the folly, and he approached carefully, not wanting to frighten her.

But the folly was empty.

Lucien could not believe his eyes. He would have wagered his entire year's allowance—pittance though it was—that Captain Hopkins would not show up. But it appeared the soldier had not only answered Chloe's summons but had been waiting for her. She could not have been many minutes before Lucien on that lonely garden path.

She was gone, far out of his reach, and Lucien would never see her again. Now that it was too late, he was entirely clear about what he should have done. He should have thrown himself at her feet and told her he adored her. She might have laughed at him; she might even have felt pity for him. But he should have offered her the choice. Now he would never have the chance.

He flung himself down on the farthest bench from the castle, the one where just this morning he had stashed her valise. At least he knew she had been right here—kneeling beside this bench to retrieve her belongings.

His heel hit something hard, and he bent double to check the dark hollow under the bench. Just as his hand touched a leather-wrapped handle, he heard a rustle from the path—a step on the gravel.

"Captain Hopkins?" Chloe said softly. "Is that you?"

Lucien stood in the shadowed folly—and a well-named bit of architecture *that* was, he thought irritably—holding Chloe's valise and feeling like a prize fool. She had told him she must return to her room, to leave her bed looking occupied. Maybe she had even stopped to change into something more suitable for traveling, for she wouldn't want to trail across England in a ball dress.

And all the time he'd spent practically wailing about his lost love…What a nodcock he was!

"No," he said. "It's just me."

"Lucien?" Her steps pattered quickly up the stairs to the folly. "What are you doing here?"

There was something odd about her voice. Disappointment, no doubt. "You intend to elope with the man, but even to his face you call him *Captain Hopkins*?"

"My mother still calls my father Sir George."

"Well, you call me Lucien."

"That's different. We're like partners. Why are you here, anyway?" She pulled her dark cloak more closely around her throat and settled onto the bench.

Stop stalling and just tell her. But now that the moment was upon him, the words stuck in Lucien's throat. A roundabout route would be better. He could hint at his feelings, testing how she reacted, before he exposed his heart entirely.

He sat down next to her. "Because even if your soldier comes, it would be a mistake for you to run off with him."

A stray moonbeam struck her face, highlighting the tight lines between her brows. "What do you mean, *even if he comes*? Why do you think he won't? What did he say to you? Why didn't you tell me this before?"

"Calmly, now. He—uh—he didn't actually say anything."

"Then—"

"I mean, he didn't utter more than a few words—none of them to the point. And he looked unhappy, as though he was annoyed at the entire idea of eloping."

"You're saying you only have a *feeling* to go on?"

Lucien loosed a deep breath. He had known she'd be hard to convince. "Wait and see. He's not coming, Chloe."

"He has to come. I've gone too far now to back out."

"No, you haven't. We can walk back to the castle right now. You can return to the ball. All you have to do is tell your mother that a few minutes of rest cured your head-ache, and—"

"And I'd be right back in the mess I was in before—betrothed to your father."

"I guess I'd forgotten that part," Lucien admitted.

The silence drew out for a bit. "If there's some other way, Lucien, I wish you would help me find it."

"Sir George doesn't seem such a bad sort. Surely if you told him you're so miserable you thought of running away with a penniless soldier—"

"He'd lock me in my room and move up the wedding date. He hates Captain Hopkins—even mentioning his name would make my father lose all reason."

Lucien paced the three steps across the folly's stone floor and back. "All right. What if you were to run away with someone else?"

"You mean tell my father I'm unhappy enough to elope with—who?"

"Don't tell your father anything. We go back to the castle right now, and we enjoy the rest of the ball." Lucien was planning as he spoke. "Then tomorrow morning, we go for a ride—separately, of course, but we can meet up in the village and..."

Chloe's voice sounded oddly choked. "If you're suggesting that we run away together—you and I—Lucien, you can't mean it."

The plan—such as it was—did sound foolish. "Look, Chloe, I know you love Captain Hopkins. But I swear he's not what you think he is, and you'd be miserable with him. And poor as well—don't forget *poor*."

She took a deep breath. "I don't think I do. Love him, I mean. I liked him well enough, and last winter I thought I'd like to marry him. But it's not as if I've missed him since. Still, I'm committed, now. And if he comes tonight..."

"He's not coming."

"I just..." She sounded distracted. "It's not as though I have a great many choices."

You can choose me.

Just as Lucien opened his mouth to assure her that he did indeed mean it—that all she had to do was say the word and he would run away with her to the ends of the earth—the scratch of gravel on the path below brought his head up.

"It's the captain," she whispered. She sounded terrified.

Lucien put his hand gently over her mouth.

A large shadow—no, two shadows—loomed up in the door of the folly, and the Earl of Chiswick said calmly, "I hear you went looking for a card game, Hartford. I don't suppose you'd like to deal us in—Sir George and me?"

Chapter 16

❧

*N*o matter who she was dancing with, Emily couldn't seem to escape from Gavin's cool scrutiny. How typical it was of the man to act like a dog in the manger! Apparently he didn't want her himself, or he wouldn't have delegated his valet to pass along messages—but he didn't seem to think she should so much as speak to any other man.

Even his lovemaking now looked entirely different to Emily. He'd been happy enough to fulfill her fantasies—up to a point. But he'd made certain she couldn't possibly limit his options by presenting him with any nasty consequences. The heir of the Duke of Weybridge wasn't about to tie himself down with a scandal-plagued wife and an unwelcome baby, so he'd passed off his failure to take her virginity as a noble act of self-sacrifice.

You're not being fair, a little voice whispered in the back of her mind. Whatever the reason he'd sent Benson to talk to her, Gavin wasn't avoiding her now. And he'd been protecting her by not risking a pregnancy...

He was, however, devoting a lot of attention to the Carew sisters. Why had she told him they were heiresses, anyway?

Next time she'd choose her lover more carefully. She would find someone she could enjoy without risk. And in the meantime, she was going to revel in dancing.

Young Baron Draycott presented himself as her partner for the next dance, but just as they were forming the set, Mr. Lancaster came quietly up beside her and said, "If I might have a word, Lady Emily."

"I'm afraid I don't have a dance left on my card, sir."

"My loss; I should have acted earlier. But in fact…" He dropped his voice further. "This is a private matter, and a very sensitive one. It concerns Miss Fletcher."

"Chloe?" Emily tipped her head to one side and surveyed him for a moment before turning to Draycott. "My lord, I am afraid we must miss our dance," she said. The baron nodded, and Emily let Lancaster draw her behind a pillar. "Well? What is going on?"

"You may know that she told her mother of a headache and left the ball?"

"What of it? A shame, but—"

"I have reason to believe there was no headache. And I gather she has stolen away to one of the quiet rooms in the new wing of the castle." He cleared his throat and whispered, "With your brother."

Denial was on the tip of Emily's tongue—how utterly silly it was to think that Lucien would sneak away with Chloe, of all people—until she remembered the way he had stared at the girl, and how he had stumbled through a dance as though he had something much more important on his mind. Perhaps he still thought he could talk sense into her.

Lancaster nodded. "I see you understand exactly what I mean."

"Chloe left the ball quite a long time ago."

"That's why I thought it best, for the sake of Miss Fletcher's reputation, to come to you rather than to her mother, or to Chiswick."

Emily shivered at the idea of her father finding Lucien and Chloe together—no matter how innocent the circumstances.

"If you are the one to find them," Lancaster went on, "the incident can still be kept quiet. But if anyone else were to stumble across their assignation…"

"Thank you," she said. "I'll go and make a discreet search."

His brow wrinkled. "Do you think it wise to go alone? With two of us, the search would go faster."

Emily hesitated, then peeked around the pillar at the dancers. No one seemed to have missed her. "We can go out this way and through a back corridor to the new wing."

"Lead the way," Lancaster said.

She quickly checked each room along the corridor, with little hope of finding the wayward couple; this area was too close to the crowd to be truly private. In the new wing of the castle, she methodically worked her way from room to room down one side of the central hall while Lancaster took the other. Just as she was beginning to fear that Lucien might have completely lost his mind and taken Chloe upstairs for a more private chat, Lancaster beckoned to her from outside the door of the smoking room.

Emily turned the knob as quietly as she could. With any luck, she'd be inside with the door closed before there was any outcry.

The room was dim, and she paused just inside the door to let her eyes adjust as well as to listen for telltale noises. But the room felt empty.

Lancaster had followed her in. Puzzled, Emily said, "What made you think they were here?"

"I didn't," he said quietly. "But now *you're* here."

She took a quick step toward the door, but he was on guard, and he stretched an arm around her and dragged her against him. Unable to keep her footing, she hung off balance, pressed against him so intimately that she was afraid to take a breath.

He chuckled and lifted her slightly off her feet. His erection nestled into the hollow between her legs, held away only by the thin gauze of her skirt and the satin of his knee breeches. "But you mustn't worry, Lady Emily," he whispered against her ear. "Just as soon as I'm done, I'll marry you."

❖ ❖ ❖

As the two men loomed over them, Chloe screeched in horror.

Lucien said, as much to himself as to her, "It'll be all right. Everything will be all right."

She managed to get her voice back. "Oh? And just *how* is everything going to be all right?"

As Sir George Fletcher alternately sputtered and yelled, Lucien grew ever more certain that Chloe's headache was more than a convenient fiction, for his own skull was pounding.

The curious thing was that the Earl of Chiswick hadn't said a word after that flippant greeting. Which was in no way a relief, for—in Lucien's experience—silence only made Chiswick more deadly.

Or had that strange old gossip Lady Stone been right about this being a love match…at least on the earl's side? Was it possible Chiswick was truly hurt by the idea that his prospective bride would rather ruin herself by running away than go through with the wedding?

No, Lucien couldn't believe that—and it didn't matter much, anyway. If the earl felt such fondness for Chloe, why hadn't he tried to win her over? Why hadn't he wooed her, instead of dealing only with her father? Chiswick had lost his opportunity; it was time for someone else to step in.

"I am shocked," Sir George ranted. "*Shocked* to find my daughter entirely alone with a man in compromising circumstances—"

Lucien cleared his throat, loudly.

"Young lady, your mother is having hysterics all over the castle at finding you gone."

Lucien said, "Sir—"

"I don't suppose the earl here would have you after this, unless I were to serve up your head on a platter. And believe me, miss, when I say I am tempted!"

Lucien raised his voice. "Sir George!"

"The only good thing I can say about your judgment is that at least you had enough sense not to elope with that fortune-hunting soldier I forbade you to ever see or communicate with again!"

Lucien stuck two fingers in his mouth and whistled, and Chloe clapped her hands over her ears. Sir George stumbled into a confused silence.

The Earl of Chiswick put one foot up on a bench, leaned his elbow on his knee, and—seeming completely at ease—said, "I prefer not to know where you learned to do that, Hartford. I gather you have something to say?"

"I do." Lucien deliberately stepped between the two men and Chloe, blocking their path to her. "You can stop browbeating right now, both of you. Chloe is not going to become a countess."

"Certain of that, are you?" Chiswick murmured.

Sir George brightened. "My lord, do you mean you would still—?"

Lucien cut across him. "She will absolutely not marry you, Father. And let's not pretend that this scandal doesn't bother you. If Lady Fletcher is having hysterics in the castle—"

"Only quiet ones." Chiswick didn't move, but somehow his posture eased. "However, you suppose correctly, Hartford. Miss Fletcher may consider herself entirely free."

Chloe plopped down on the bench as though her knees had given way.

Sir George looked downcast for a moment, and then his face hardened again. "Free? I don't think so. After this behavior, my girl, you have to marry someone, and you'll be lucky if even the stable boy will have you!"

"She doesn't," Lucien said calmly. "If you were to say that you have been with her the entire time, Sir George, no one would dare contradict you. But if she wants to marry..." Lucien turned to face Chloe. "It would be my honor to wed her myself."

❀ ❀ ❀

Maxwell had signed his name—that bold, black, arrogant slash of a name—across three lines on Isabel's dance card. He had claimed three dances—the maximum that any gentleman, even a husband, could request of a lady in a single evening.

The first, the country dance which opened the ball, had been unavoidable—but at least in the swirling mass of dancers, changing partners every minute or two, she could pretend not to be dancing with him at all.

But the next he had claimed would be a waltz. Isabel did not know if she could bear to swirl around the floor in his arms, on display for the world. Once—during their courtship—she had enjoyed waltzing with him. But now...

What if Maxwell were to treat the dance as some kind of seduction?—which of course he would. To a man who could turn a thorny plant in a conservatory—or even a plateful of kidneys in a breakfast room full of people—into a lovemaking tool, a waltz would be no challenge whatever.

He would enjoy holding her, watching her, tantalizing her, reminding her of intimacies shared. But for her, the dance would be torment. She could not bear being face-to-face with him for endless minutes, looking into his eyes, unable to breathe a word about the subject uppermost in her mind for fear someone might overhear or the ever-vigilant gossips in the crowd might notice that Lady Maxwell was behaving strangely.

She would have to make an excuse—even if it required pretending to sprain her ankle. But she would not pretend any longer than she must. As soon as the ball was over and they were alone, Isabel would bring this game of his to an end—she would challenge him about Miss Lester and her child.

She wondered how Maxwell would act when he found out she knew. He might deny it all and try to bluff his way through. Or he might argue that what had happened in his past had nothing to do with his wife. Or he might actually be relieved to have it out in the open; since he had already admitted to Elspeth Murdoch that he was responsible, perhaps he felt guilty enough to tell his wife as well. He might even expect that a confession would be followed automatically by understanding and forgiveness.

If that was the case, Maxwell would soon learn differently—for understanding and forgiveness were hard to find in a heart that felt like a lump of lead.

* * *

The silence in the folly was so thick that Lucien could barely breathe. Still, asserting himself to his father felt good. What was it Chloe had told him, long ago? *No wonder your father gives you no respect, if you never stand up to him.* She might have been right.

Sir George looked suspicious. "I can't allow the match. Not unless you're able to show me that you can take care of her."

"I assure you I can do better than the stable boy could," Lucien said cheerfully.

"But no better than that soldier fellow. What do you have of your own, anyway? Nothing, I wager, that doesn't depend on your father's goodwill."

Lucien's sense of well-being vanished with a pop, for Sir George was right. Lucien's allowance was hardly large enough for him alone; it couldn't be stretched to support a wife. And he was dependent on his father even for that much. Now that he'd stolen the earl's bride…

"Damnation," he said.

"I wondered how long it would take for the drawbacks to strike home," the earl murmured. "And speaking of home, and your plans to return to Chiswick—where does this leave us?"

Lucien's head swam. He'd no doubt made a mull of that possibility, too. If he was no longer welcome at Chiswick, if the job of learning to manage the estate was no longer open to him…he had no idea what he would do.

He saw a gleam of anticipation in Chiswick's eyes. What was it his father expected of him now? Maybe the mess could still be salvaged, if Lucien apologized. Begged. Groveled. Gave up Chloe…

No—never that.

Lucien squared his shoulders and said, "I am still your heir, Father, and I do not believe you wish to see the estate suffer through my ignorance. But if you cannot find it in your heart to forgive me, then I must ask Chloe for her patience while I establish myself. I can learn estate management elsewhere—on some other gentleman's land, as a steward or…"

Chiswick snorted. "No one else would teach you properly."

Lucien held his breath.

"I have conditions," Chiswick said quietly.

"So do I," Lucien countered.

"Yes, yes—larger allowance, freedom to come and go."

"No, Father. The most important condition is that my wife be treated well."

"Are you going to have a wife, Hartford?"

"If she'll accept me. Surely you cannot object, Father. If you considered Chloe an eligible bride for you, then she is more than good enough for me."

After a long pause, Chiswick said, "It appears we have a great deal to talk about tomorrow, Hartford—but nothing, I think, that we cannot negotiate. Sir George, you may announce a betrothal."

Triumphant, Lucien turned to smile at Chloe. She looked lost and scared, and remorse rushed over him. "I'm sorry, my dear. We're doing everything backward, it seems—but will you marry me?"

"You don't mean it, Lucien." Her voice was unsteady. "You can't possibly see me as anything more than an interfering nuisance."

He reached for her hands and held them tightly against his heart. "I love you, Chloe."

She chewed at her lower lip. "Even after the way I blackmailed you?"

Lucien started to cough, trying to drown her out. Chloe shot a guilty look at her father.

Sir George bellowed, "Blackmail?"

Chiswick's lips twitched. "We might be wise not to pursue that line of investigation, Sir George. In fact, it would be a good idea to leave these two alone."

"Absolutely not," Sir George said.

"They *are* betrothed...and the sooner we put that word about, the less gossip will fly concerning how the two of them vanished from the ballroom."

As the two men walked off together, Lucien could hear Sir George grumbling for a long time. He waited till they went out of earshot and then tried without success to find his voice. He felt stiff—afraid to move, afraid to speak. Somewhere down the lane, a night bird called.

Chloe looked at her hands, still firmly planted against his chest. "Do you really care for me, Lucien? Or did you say all that because you feel sorry for me—since I can't even elope and get it right?"

"It's a good thing you *can't* get it right, for I wouldn't want to have to fight Captain Hopkins over you. Plus you'd still have to reimburse him for the cost of the post-chaise, since I haven't that much money in my pockets." He lifted Chloe's hands to his shoulders and put his arms around her.

Her breath was coming quickly. Finally she lifted her face to his, but she still looked hesitant.

Lucien remembered what Aubrey had said about the chorus girl he'd been pursuing, on the night before Lucien left London for Weybridge Castle. *Never let a woman know how interested you are.*

Well, what did Aubrey know about love, anyway?

Lucien slowly tightened his hold, drawing her closer. Sometimes, he thought, words only got in the way. So he kissed her instead, long and softly.

She was perfect. She fit so very nicely in his arms, and when she tilted her chin just the slightest bit, her mouth was at precisely the right angle.

Chloe's eyes suddenly seemed to reflect the stars. "I didn't know what it could be like, to be kissed. Oh, Lucien, I so hoped for this—but I thought you couldn't possibly want me."

He didn't know what to say, so he kissed her again.

A long while later, she giggled and said, "How funny—someday I'll be a countess after all!"

For just an instant, Lucien's gut clenched. Had he been correct from the start, and she was so intent on being a countess that she'd flung herself in his path?

No. She couldn't glow that way, or kiss him so sweetly, if she were pretending. In any case, she was the only one for him.

"Not for a while yet." A good many years, he hoped. He had a lot to learn before he was ready to step into the Earl of Chiswick's shoes.

Besides, he was beginning to have a sneaking suspicion that given the right conditions, he just might grow fond of his father.

❂   ❂   ❂

Drafty though the great hall must be in winter, when it was filled with dancers and onlookers and candles and lamps, the room was unpleasantly warm. When Gavin finished a dance—his second with the elder Miss Carew—he would have given anything to wander outside for a breath of fresh air. Unfortunately, he suspected Miss Carew would be quite willing to go along with him, despite—or perhaps because of—the risk to her reputation, so he walked her around the perimeter of the room instead.

"I suppose I should return to Lady Stone," Miss Carew said with a dimpled smile. "Though she's quite a lenient chaperone, she does like to hear that my sister and I have enjoyed ourselves. And I shall tell her what an excellent dancer you are, my lord."

That was a humbug and Gavin knew it—there were definite differences in an English country dance from what he was used to in Baltimore, and despite Emily's instruction, he had trouble finding his place in some of the figures.

Miss Carew peeked up at him through her lashes. "I know it's not proper for a lady to ask a gentleman," she whispered shyly, "but I should very much like to waltz with you later. I saved the supper dance."

Gavin was in luck, however, for just then they arrived in the corner of the great hall where Lady Stone was sitting next to a very tight-faced Lady Fletcher.

"Lady Stone," Miss Carew began. "We've had such a lovely—"

"Not now, child. Run away and occupy yourself with something else."

Foreseeing that within seconds, Miss Carew would come up with an activity that involved him, Gavin bowed to the ladies and moved as far away as possible. Outside air sounded even more inviting.

The Earl of Chiswick intercepted him. "Athstone, where's Emily?"

"Why should I know?" Gavin turned to look across the floor, where dancers had gathered in small groups as they waited for the orchestra to begin playing again. "I think she was dancing just now." As a matter of fact, he knew she had been dancing, for he seemed to have a magnet inside him that was always drawn in her direction. But he wasn't about to admit that to Lady Emily's father.

"I must talk privately with Lady Fletcher, and I need Emily to pry her away from the unrepentant gossip she's sitting with, without causing a scene."

Gavin was barely listening. How odd that he couldn't spot Emily's rose-colored dress or her golden-brown hair anywhere in the room. His gut tightened, and he looked again—this time for Lancaster. But neither of them was in sight.

It'll all be settled tonight, Lancaster had told someone this afternoon. *By tomorrow you'll be wishing me happy.*

The cad must have made his move. But how much time had passed? How long had Gavin dawdled around the edges of the great hall?

He almost blurted the news to Chiswick—but explaining it all to Emily's father would take time that would be better spent in looking for her. Besides, Chiswick had spent the last year trying to marry her off, including negotiating with the very man who might have compromised her now. Emily wouldn't thank him for adding that complication.

"I'll find her," Gavin said, and only realized how harsh he'd sounded when he saw the Earl of Chiswick's eyebrows draw together in concern. "Wait here. I'll bring her to you."

And as he began to search the castle for Emily, he asked himself why he hadn't made her truly his when he'd had the chance.

❂   ❂   ❂

By the time Isabel noticed the gleeful buzz which indicated a scandal in the making, whispers were surging from group to group around the great hall like an epidemic of yawns at a musicale. Usually Isabel tried to ignore that sort of excited chatter—but she had just finished a strenuous country dance with young Baron Draycott when she heard one of the Carew sisters whisper to the other, *"Lady Fletcher…She fainted dead away when they told her about Chloe!"*

Isabel pulled away from the baron and hurried to the corner where she had last seen Lady Fletcher. She was still occupying the same chair, but her head was thrown back, her eyes were closed, her face was as white as Isabel's dress, and her feet were stretched out almost to the edge of the dance floor. She looked as if she'd fainted while in the midst of a temper tantrum.

Lady Stone waved a vinaigrette under Lady Fletcher's nose, while Sir George hovered helplessly nearby.

Isabel picked up more whispers from the people who had crowded around. *"Chloe's simply gone…" "Nowhere to be found…" "I wonder what Chiswick will do…"*

"Nonsense," Isabel said loudly. "Miss Fletcher retired to her bedroom with a headache."

"You're a bit behind the times, Lady Isabel," Lady Stone said mildly. "Lady Fletcher, sit up now and smile. A betrothal is good news—even if Sir George was a bit clumsy in how he broke it to you."

Lady Fletcher groaned and blinked owlishly up at her husband. "You can't have understood what happened, Sir George. Chloe has ruined herself—hasn't she?"

"No, no," Sir George said hastily. "It's just that she's betrothed to Hartford instead."

Isabel felt the floor lurch under her. "Chloe—and *Lucien*? But that's outrageous. Where's my father? Does he know?"

"Oh, yes." Lady Stone didn't look up. "Chiswick went off looking for Lady Emily so she could break the news gently to Lady Fletcher. But Sir George couldn't wait, so he blurted it out." Lady Stone patted Lady Fletcher's hand. "Men are sometimes *so* annoying."

The music started again, and the dancers in the crowd drifted away onto the floor.

Maxwell strolled up to Isabel. "I believe this is our waltz."

She frowned. "No, it's not. You claimed the supper waltz, not this one."

"Have you been keeping track? Counting until the next dance we can share? I talked a friend into giving me his dances with you."

Her fear for Lucien already had Isabel balanced at knife's point, and Maxwell's easy assumption that she was eager for his attentions pushed her over the edge. "Why?" Her voice was low, but hard. "Because Lady Murdoch is already out there? I suppose if you can't dance with her, at least you can be close to her. Is that it?"

Maxwell's eyes narrowed. "Isabel, one would think you might be jealous."

"One would be wrong. After the ball is over, we will discuss your mistresses—all of them. I will not talk to you until then—and don't think I'll allow anything more than talk."

She turned her back on him. Somewhere in this crowd, she thought, there must be someone who could tell her the truth about Lucien and Chloe. She only hoped it wouldn't be the Earl of Chiswick that she had to ask.

Chapter 17

❦

*P*anic would get him nowhere, Gavin knew. Searching the castle's countless rooms could take hours, but he didn't have that sort of time. Emily might have mere minutes before her life was forever changed. He needed to think like the quarry he was hunting. Where would Lancaster go? Where would *he* feel confident and safe?

Gavin took a few seconds to ponder. Of the half-dozen possibilities that came to mind, which was the right choice? He might not have the opportunity for a second try, so he must make the correct call the first time.

He closed his eyes for an instant to concentrate and then set off, walking as quickly as he could without drawing attention to himself. At least he hoped no one would notice—though he was certain the Earl of Chiswick wouldn't stand in the ballroom and wait for him to return. With any luck, however, Gavin would have found Emily long before her father caught up with her.

Nothing in the new wing of the castle seemed out of place, and all the rooms were quiet. For once, Gavin would have been pleased to catch a glimpse of a servant, but tonight every one of the castle's massive staff was busy in the great hall or down in the kitchens. The main door had been locked so the footmen who were normally on duty there could assist guests at the entrance to the great hall instead. The new wing was deserted, which made it a perfect spot for seduction—forcible or otherwise.

He walked straight to the smoking room and flung open the door. It banged against the wall, and across the room, on a settee facing the fireplace, Lancaster raised his head to check out the disturbance.

An instant later, Gavin reached over the back of the settee, intending to grab the man's collar and drag him off Emily. But his fingers closed on air as Lancaster rolled away, howling as he curled up on the carpet in a fetal position with his hands clutched over his private parts.

Gavin braced both hands on the settee and looked down at Emily just as she lowered her knee and began to smooth her skirt.

"Thank you for the lesson, Gavin. It came in quite handy just now." Though her words were calm, her voice shook a little.

Gavin said dryly, "I'm happy to provide a distraction so you could make your move."

In the firelight, he could see that her dress was askew and tendrils of hair straggled around her face. He thought she had never been more beautiful than in this moment of defending herself.

"Are you all right?" Despite his best efforts, his voice cracked.

She stood up, shaking out her dress, and made a face. "A little rumpled, as you can see. Nothing more."

Relief flooded him, followed a bare instant later by a tidal wave of anger. "Why the hell didn't you believe me? I *told* you he was plotting something!"

Over the whimpers still coming from the hearthrug, Gavin heard voices and footsteps in the hall. Chiswick, no doubt—and here was Emily all mussed and manhandled. Even though her attacker hadn't succeeded and was now mewling on the floor, Lancaster had still managed to compromise her—and in the eyes of society, the only remedy was marriage.

Gavin hadn't even realized he'd been in a sort of fog— for days, he suspected—until the mist suddenly cleared. His future unrolled before him, as pristine and lovely as the view from his bedroom window of the sweeping hills and lakes and fields and rivers of Weybridge.

Gavin reached over the settee, seized Emily's wrists, and dragged her around and into his arms. He smothered her protest with a long, deep, hungry kiss—an embrace more passionate than anything he'd allowed himself in the two nights they'd spent together.

And a good thing, too, or he would never have let her out of his bed.

From the corner of his eye, Gavin saw two men appear in the doorway, but he didn't care. The only thing that mattered was the woman in his arms. No. The important point was *saving* the woman in his arms. No matter what it took—even if she was likely to turn him into mincemeat later.

He went on kissing her until he was reasonably certain that her voice was out of commission, and he was very careful to keep her pressed so tightly against him that she couldn't move her knee.

Behind him, one of the men cleared his throat, and Gavin slowly released Emily's mouth and turned his head.

He didn't have to pretend to be dazed; his head was swimming with lust. But he was genuinely startled, because the man next to the Earl of Chiswick was the Duke of Weybridge—and he was standing.

"You're *walking*, Your Grace?" Gavin congratulated himself. Considering the circumstances, his voice sounded pretty normal.

"When Chiswick told me you seemed to think Emily was in danger, riding around in a chair was a waste of valuable time." The duke folded his arms across his chest, and his index finger tapped out a rhythm on his elbow. "I hope you can explain yourself, Athstone."

"I don't believe I actually said she was in danger," Gavin said. "And she wasn't."

Chiswick moved closer and peered over the settee. "Why is Lancaster sniveling on the hearthrug?"

"That was a misunderstanding." Gavin looked the earl straight in the eye. "He overheard us and thought Emily was...reluctant. When he interrupted, I may have overreacted."

"Remind me not to get into a *misunderstanding* with you, Athstone," Chiswick murmured. "At least not until we've reviewed the rules of the boxing ring."

"Yes, sir. I need hardly add that the reason for the enthusiastic embrace was that Emily has just made me the happiest of men."

Emily, who seemed not to have been breathing, gasped and began to squirm.

Gavin held her a little more tightly. "I apologize for not asking for your daughter's hand ahead of time, my lord, but I'm sure you understand that we were—uh—carried away by the moment. Shall we talk in the morning about arrangements for the wedding? Emily, you might just nod to your father now—assure him that everything is all right." He paused. "Emily?"

The duke grunted. "And what about *my* permission, Athstone? I seem to recall you were to consult me about your choice of a wife."

"Yes, sir. I regret that I cannot do as you asked. No doubt you are correct in believing that Emily will make my life hell—"

Emily gulped. "You said *what*? Uncle Josiah, how could you—"

Gavin raised his voice to drown her out. "But it is my life. So—with all due respect, Your Grace and your lord-ship—since Emily and I are now betrothed, would both of you please just *go away*?"

* * *

Everything had happened so quickly that Emily's head was spinning. Had she really nodded her agreement to marry Gavin? She must have done something of the sort, or surely her father and uncle would not have left her there with him. It wasn't that she minded being held, but he was clutching her so tightly, with his body wrapped almost around her, that she could barely breathe. She wriggled a little.

"Emily," Gavin said quietly. "If you promise not to put me on the floor next to Lancaster, I'll let you go now."

Breathlessly, Lancaster said, "Much as I'd like to see that, I'd rather get out of range." He climbed slowly to his feet. "My congratulations, Athstone, for reeling in Lady

Emily's dowry. That kind of money is the only reason a man would put up with such a shrew. Glad I was able to help by telling you all about it." He left the room, still hunched over.

Emily said, "I promise."

Very slowly, Gavin eased his hold. As soon as she could move, Emily jerked her knee up, hard and fast—and missed, for suddenly he was holding her at arms' length. "That was naughty of you, my dear."

"I'm not your dear, and Lancaster's not on the floor anymore, so you wouldn't have been next to him. Why do you think I'd tell you the truth, when you just lied your head off to me?"

"I understand you're angry, but—"

"Angry? I am so far beyond angry..." She stopped, swallowing hard. She *had* nodded to her father, agreeing to the betrothal; she remembered it now—because, for just a few minutes while Gavin held her, kissed her, and schemed to protect her, she had hoped that he meant it. That he cared for her.

You fool. You fell in love with him.

Her voice was quiet. "You said once there was nothing about me that you admired."

"No, *you* said it. And even if it had been true at the time, I found, on closer acquaintance, that—"

"Oh, yes, on closer acquaintance you found something to admire—the same thing Lancaster wanted. So he told you all about my dowry. You may as well admit it, Gavin."

"You'd take that cad's word for anything?"

"It's not a matter of taking his word. The whole thing is obvious, now that I think about it. You've done to me exactly what Lancaster was planning to do—force me into marriage for the sake of my dowry. No wonder you came bursting in here to *save* me! You had to act quickly, or he'd have beaten you to the prize."

"That was a rescue, Emily—not a competition."

"You'd like me to think that, wouldn't you? I couldn't have been more wrong about you. Tell me—how large a bribe did it take to interest you? Has my father increased the amount even more?"

"I'd be the last to know."

"I don't believe you. Not now." She stared up at him. "Gavin, I trusted you! I thought you wouldn't be attracted by my dowry because you have no need of it. But that's not true, is it?"

He leaned against the back of the settee, folded his arms across his chest, and pasted a patient expression on his face.

Fury raced through Emily's veins. How dare he be so calm? Just because he thought he'd won…Well, she'd make certain he knew he wasn't fooling her. "You may be the heir of the Duke of Weybridge, but that fact doesn't give you anything but a courtesy title. You'll be dependent on Uncle Josiah for handouts and an allowance. You *do* need my money to support you. So you caught me in a bad spot, and you forced me into this—the same way Lancaster intended to do. "

She ran out of breath. She was almost afraid to look at him, for he'd been too quiet. Surely he should have argued, defended himself.

"Yes," he said quietly. "I did force you."

Emily's heart sagged.

"Though I have to say, if I'd been the one who had you under me on that settee, you wouldn't have been reluctant."

Damn him, he was right—and that made her feel even worse. How could she know all this and still want him?

"As I see it, Emily, because of your own actions you have no choice but to marry someone."

The last little shred of hope that he might truly have wanted this—wanted *her*—curled up and died deep inside her. "Wait a minute. *My* actions?"

"You were fool enough to go off alone with Lancaster."

"I only went because he told me—" Memory flashed over her. "Oh, no! Lucien's in trouble. He's taken Chloe off somewhere, and if our father finds them—"

"There's nothing we can do about Lucien. Even if Lancaster was telling the truth, which I doubt, Chiswick won't murder his heir. Whatever else your father may be, he's hardly impulsive." He reached out a hand to her. "One way or another, you must give up this mad dream of independence, Emily. I want you to marry me."

Stubbornly, she shook her head.

"Very well." Gavin pushed himself upright. "Since Lancaster is your choice—"

"He's not my choice! I don't want—"

"—To marry anyone. I know. By the way, feel free to consult your father and your Uncle Josiah about whether they agree with you, or with me, about the need for you to marry."

Emily felt a flush climb her cheeks.

"If you'd prefer Lancaster to me, I'll find him. I'll even be happy to explain to him that strictly speaking, you're still a virgin. Though I must admit when he laughs at me for being such a fool, I may be sorely tempted to finish the job you—"

"Gavin!"

"Sorry, I got distracted there for a moment. I was merely making the point that he won't quibble over marrying you."

A little hiccup of a sob escaped her, and she shook her head in despair.

"You don't want Lancaster?"

"Of course not. But I don't want to marry you, either—and you don't want to marry me." Just saying the words made her throat feel raw.

"You're wrong there, for I do want to marry you. I fell in love with you that first afternoon when you snipped at me over your title."

He sounded almost matter-of-fact. Surely, she thought, he should be flattering her, making up to her—not reminding her of embarrassing moments.

"Emily, I'm so deeply in love with you that I want to make you a duchess someday—and for a man who has never quite taken to the idea of being a duke, that's a considerable change."

She stole a look at him. He was smiling, and there was a softness in his eyes she'd never seen before. She couldn't get her breath.

"There's something else you should know," he said quietly. "It's true that the duke's solicitors found me laboring in a farm field."

"I heard Uncle Josiah say something about that," she muttered.

"I was helping to bring in a crop for a friend who had been injured and couldn't do it himself. But that's not what I do—what I used to do—for a living. I wasn't a farmhand, and I don't need your dowry."

She looked at him doubtfully.

"Even if your Uncle Josiah leaves every penny of his private fortune to charity, we can get along. I sold all the real estate, because I knew it would be too hard to take care of it from the far side of the Atlantic Ocean in case I ended up staying here. That's why it took so many months for me to show up in England."

Her breath stuck in her throat. "You owned..."

"Mostly houses. A few business properties—not the businesses in them, only the buildings. But that was a sideline. I spent most of my time running the shipping lines. I still own my share, and I plan to keep it, but I turned the day-to-day management over to my partner when I decided to come to England. Just in case—"

"In case you ended up staying." She shook her head in disbelief. "You really thought you might not want all this?"

"I almost didn't come at all—except my curiosity wouldn't let me stay away. A castle, a title...who could resist taking a look? Now I know making that trip was the best decision of my life. Not because of the castle or the title. Because of you." He reached out to brush a curl back from her face.

Emily noticed that his hand was unsteady.

"I should warn you, though, that I'm not as well off as your uncle."

"Nobody is," Emily said quietly.

"If you want a castle of your own—well, that might be more than I can afford. But the fact is I'd be happy with you in a cottage in Barton Bristow."

Emily sniffed and fumbled for a handkerchief. "It's a very small cottage. I'm afraid you wouldn't fit."

Gavin handed her a big white square. "So what are we going to do?"

She blew her nose quietly and then toyed with the linen, folding it precisely so she didn't have to look at him. "I suppose," she said very quietly, "in that case, we'll just have to live in *this* castle."

         ❂ ❂ ❂

Isabel couldn't find Lucien or Chloe or Emily anywhere. Even the Earl of Chiswick and the Duke of Weybridge seemed to have disappeared.

She was distracted for a moment when she spotted the duke's wheeled chair sitting empty in the most secluded corner of the great hall. But she concluded the footmen might have carried the duke upstairs without it. Isabel was only surprised that Uncle Josiah had stuck it out for so long. He'd had a very strenuous day—by the time he gave in and retired, he might have been too exhausted even to sit upright any longer.

She made a full round of the great hall and came back to the little knot of onlookers still gawking at Lady Fletcher and whispering behind their hands.

Lady Stone had put the vinaigrette away and was discussing some sort of wager with an elderly gentleman of military bearing.

He shook his head. "You'll have to do better than that, Lucinda."

"Oh, all right. I'll give you four to one, you chiseler." She broke off and looked past Isabel. "Here they come."

Isabel swung around, expecting to see Emily, or Lucien. Instead, the Earl of Chiswick came slowly across the great hall, pushing the duke in his wheeled chair and pausing here and there to speak to someone in the crowd. Far from being an exhausted hulk, Uncle Josiah had more color in his face than he'd displayed all week.

Mr. Lancaster came up beside her. "What's all the excitement about?"

Lady Stone answered. "It appears that Hartford and Miss Fletcher are to be married."

He snickered, and then gave way to a belly laugh. "Now *that's* funny."

Isabel wasn't about to ask him to explain the joke. She moved aside and surveyed the room again. Surely by now Emily should have reappeared. Where could she have gone?

"Tell me, Chiswick," Lady Stone rasped. "Did I do well to bet on young Athstone?"

The earl bowed. "I am pleased to announce that my daughter Emily is betrothed to Lord Athstone."

Emily and Gavin, Isabel thought with a wave of pleasure. She'd thought for days they would make a good combination, and Emily was eminently suited to be a duchess. Isabel was so delighted at the news that she momentarily forgot her own troubles.

Then Lancaster spoke up, loud enough to be heard even above the orchestra. "The truth is that Chiswick found Athstone with Lady Emily...ahem...*in flagrante delicto* in the smoking room. But of course he's not going to tell you that part."

Isabel's joy dried up in an instant. If Emily was being forced into this marriage, the gossip tonight would be only the start. And this time all the talk would be much more difficult to bear.

But why take Lancaster's word for it? Perhaps Isabel's first instinct had been right and Emily was happy. "How would *you* know?"

"I was there, Lady Isabel." His voice had the ring of truth. "It was quite a scene."

Beside Isabel, Maxwell murmured, "What a rare party this has been. Lucien stealing your father's promised bride, Athstone compromising Emily, or possibly vice versa...Do the Ardens actually go looking for scandal, or does it just naturally cling to you?"

Isabel turned on him. "Can I possibly make it any plainer that I would like you to go away?"

"No, you've been quite clear," Maxwell said easily. "But my name is on your card and the supper waltz is just starting."

"I am not going to waltz with you, Maxwell."

"Very well." He started a low and unusually courtly bow— but before Isabel knew what was happening, he draped her over his shoulder and straightened up, his arm tight around her knees and her head dangling down his back.

"What are you *doing*?" she shrieked.

"Improvising. There have already been two scandals at this ball, so why not another one?"

He carried her straight across the center of the great hall, scattering the dancers, and through the back rooms toward the new wing. On the staircase he slowed down a bit, but when he reached Isabel's bedroom he was still breathing easily.

Which was more than Isabel could say for herself, since it was difficult to get adequate air when she was upside down with a shoulder directly under her diaphragm.

He dropped her on the bed and straddled her hips to hold her there, sitting back on his heels so he loomed over her. "I wouldn't advise struggling unless you intend to turn that dress into rags. What was it again that you wanted to talk to me about after the ball? Ah, yes. Mistresses."

"I'd be happy never to talk to you again," Isabel said.

He braced his hands above her shoulders and leaned over her. His lips brushed hers and she turned her head away. All she accomplished, however, was to put her ear right next to his mouth, so he traced the outline of it with the tip of his tongue.

She gritted her teeth. "Stop it!"

"I didn't think you could make that resolution work for long," he whispered straight into her ear. "The not-talking part, I mean. But I'd be happy to make love to you first, if—"

"No! Get off me!"

"You have to promise to stay here and listen."

Isabel considered and gave a jerky nod.

Maxwell rolled to one side, pulling her with him so they lay face-to-face, only inches separating them. "It's pretty clear Lady Murdoch is your main concern. Right?"

She didn't bother to answer.

"First, I didn't arrange for her to be here. She wasn't invited—her husband was, because he's an old friend of your uncle's, and she seems to have borrowed his invitation. Second, I did have a *tendre* for the lady a long time ago—before she was married and before I acquired enough common sense to realize that beauty doesn't make up for a grasping nature. She is not and has never been my mistress."

"She'd like to be," Isabel muttered. "And now that she's given her husband his heir—"

"Neither her wishes nor Murdoch's heir are any concern of ours. There's only one heir in the world I'm interested in."

Isabel's eyes brimmed with tears, and she turned her head away, trying to hide them.

"But the fact that she bothers you, my dear…"

"She doesn't. I mean—she's not the only thing that bothers me."

"Then it's Kilburn?" He sighed. "It's true I wanted the property your dowry included, and your father made marrying you a very intriguing proposition when he dangled not only Kilburn in front of me, but the rest."

"*The rest*? He gave you more than just Kilburn?"

"Your father never told you? I suppose that's no surprise. Chiswick has always played his cards close to his chest. But don't worry. Keep your word, and you'll finally have what you've wanted all this time." He sounded almost bitter.

Beauty doesn't make up for a grasping nature, he had said a few minutes ago about Elspeth Murdoch. Did he think that phrase described Isabel too?

But why should she feel guilty for trying to provide for herself? She wasn't the one whose conscience was burdened with a ruined mistress, a secret child, the death of a friend…

"It's not Kilburn, either." She had to steady her voice before she could go on. "You say you're only interested in your heir, but what about the other child? Miss Lester's child?"

He went as still and cold as a frozen lake. "That doesn't have anything to do with you."

"Yes, it does!" She surged up from the bed and onto her feet. "It was bad enough when you left me on our wedding night to stand up as a second to the scoundrel who disgraced my sister. You betrayed me, and you betrayed Emily."

"And I've been sorry for it ever since." He sat on the edge of the mattress. "Philip Rivington was my friend, Isabel."

"Quite a good friend, it seems. Close enough to die for you!"

Her words fell in a silence as deep as a chasm. "What are you talking about?"

"I was outside the folly this afternoon. I heard it all—everything you told Lady Murdoch. Odd that it never occurred to me until today to wonder why Philip Rivington fought that duel—why he didn't just marry Miss Lester instead. But if the real father of her child couldn't marry her, because he was already married..." She gulped. "Already married *to me*..."

Maxwell's face went white. "You think I sent Philip out to take a bullet for me?"

"Why else would you have left your bride on your wedding night—unless you had no choice?"

"I *didn't* have a choice. Philip swore to me that he was innocent."

"You believed him?"

"He assured me Miss Lester had lied to her brother when she said Philip had seduced her—that it must have been a gardener or a footman or a stable boy who got her with child, but she didn't want to admit it. It wouldn't be the first time a gentleman was accused without proof." His tone was dry. "Or the last, it seems."

But Isabel had heard the evidence, in his own words. Hadn't she?

"It wasn't until the bullet struck and he knew his time was short that Philip admitted the truth. With his dying breath, he finally owned up. He took advantage of that girl, he seduced her, and he promised marriage. It was a promise he never intended to keep."

She stared at him.

Almost casually, Maxwell said, "I wondered why Elspeth asked me to meet her in the folly today, when there were so many more convenient places. But how did she get you to come all that way, so you could conveniently overhear what she phrased so carefully in order to mislead you?"

"It wasn't only what *she* said. You told her you were responsible."

"Yes, because I feel responsible. I believed Philip and I supported him—and I was absolutely wrong."

Isabel felt dizzy.

"If he had told me the truth, or if I had taken the time to ask more questions, I would have prevented that duel. I would have forced Philip to offer marriage to the young woman he had ruined. She would have had a reluctant cad for a husband, but perhaps she would have preferred that. At least she'd have been able to choose."

Try as she might, Isabel could hear nothing in his voice but sadness—and truth.

He closed his eyes for a moment as if picturing the scene in his mind. "Could you see Elspeth this afternoon—in the folly?"

"I glimpsed that bright red skirt of hers. Why?"

"That means she could see you, too, in your yellow dress. Her timing was perfect. Well, at least we know how we were played for fools." He stood up. "I hope you'll be able to sleep. I don't expect I will."

He was leaving her—and God help her, she didn't want him to go. But she had accused him of cowardice, of dishonor…*It wouldn't be the first time a gentleman was accused without proof,* he had said. *Or the last.*

Isabel's hand went to her throat, where a massive lump made her breathing jerky. "Max, wait."

He turned to look at her, stern and solemn. "What is it, Isabel?"

Her feet seemed to have taken root in the carpet. She couldn't move, and she didn't know what to say. "The necklace." She fumbled with the catch, and when the river of diamonds came free she thrust it at him.

Carelessly, he shoved it into a pocket.

Isabel rubbed her throat. "You'll keep your word? About Kilburn?" As soon as the words were out, she wanted to bite her tongue off, for she'd done it again—questioning his honor.

He swore under his breath. "I shall keep my word."

"And you'll hold me to mine?"

"I don't know," he said slowly.

Isabel's heart sank, and her shoulders sagged.

"Yes, damn it—I *will* hold you to your bargain. On the day my son is born, I will sign Kilburn over to you. Then your duty will be finished and you can do as you like. Take a lover. Take a dozen lovers."

She whispered, "I don't want a lover."

"Do you think I care, Isabel?" He was almost shouting. "Maybe you're lucky and you're already pregnant, and this entire discussion is pointless!" He flung open the door between their rooms.

"I hope not," she whispered. "I hope I'm not pregnant."

He seemed to freeze. "Because you can't face the idea of carrying my child?"

"No." Carefully, wary of her trembling knees, she eased around him until she was between him and the door. "I am so sorry for what I said to you."

"No doubt you are—because you risked everything when you accused me, didn't you?"

"That's not...Don't you see? If I didn't care about you, Max, none of it would matter. Not Elspeth Murdoch. Not Miss Lester or her child. You're my husband, and...and you've made me love you." She had to stop for a moment and fight to draw a breath. "I don't mean to be a nuisance about it, but...I had to tell you just this once. I had to explain why I was so angry—and why I'm so sorry now that I didn't trust you."

He hadn't moved.

That gave her a little more hope. "Max," she whispered, "please. Will you just hold me for what's left of the night? Just hold me."

"I can't hold you and not make love to you."

"I don't mind," she whispered. "You were right. I like—"

"Isabel, why do you think I was so willing to promise you Kilburn?"

She shrugged. "I don't know. Because you want an heir, and that was the price."

"No. Because it doesn't matter which one of us owns that property."

She was trembling. "I don't understand. If you didn't mean to keep your promise—"

"It's what I *didn't* promise that's more important, Isabel."

She searched her memory, but she couldn't find the hidden snare. She shook her head in confusion, and then an ugly suspicion reared up. "Unless...If you mean you don't intend to let me even see my child..."

He said, "You can take the baby with you to Kilburn. I don't mind."

She frowned. That casual dismissal didn't sound at all like the man who had trapped her in her own bargain, the man who had said his heir was everything to him.

"Because if you're at Kilburn, Isabel, I'll be there, too. I never promised I wouldn't follow you."

Isabel gasped.

"The morning after our wedding, when I came home to you—"

"It was hardly morning," Isabel pointed out. "I'd heard all about the duel—and your part in it—*hours* before you showed up. And you'd been drinking."

Maxwell nodded. "You're right. And you were right then, too—about all of it. Philip betrayed us all. I understood why you were hurt, and I—well, the truth is I agreed with you. I was so in the wrong, to leave you on our wedding night. To automatically side with Philip rather than asking the difficult questions. How could I come straight to my bride after that and ask you to understand? Ask you to forgive me, when I couldn't forgive myself?"

"You could have told me the truth."

"I was still reeling from what Philip had done—I couldn't even put into words what an ass I had been, how easily he had fooled me." He rubbed a hand across his brow as if his head hurt. "Perhaps if I had courted you differently—if we hadn't been so formal, if we'd gotten to know each other better before the wedding..."

"But it wasn't that kind of an arrangement." Her voice felt stiff. "It wasn't as if ours was a love match."

"No, it was a sensible one—though I expected with time we'd become comfortable together, as we built a family. I think you expected that, too."

She nodded, jerkily.

"Even while we railed at each other that day—and while I felt your every word doubly hard because I had said it all to myself as I sat there on the ground while Philip died—I expected that our trouble would pass."

"But it didn't."

"By the time I was thinking clearly again, it was too late. Your anger had hardened into hatred, and you couldn't even bear to be in the same room with me."

Isabel shook her head, more in sadness than in disagreement.

"The worst part was that I understood how you felt. So—much as I wanted things to change, and much as I regretted the mess I'd made of our marriage, before it ever had a chance—I didn't know how to start. And though I hadn't been wise enough to treasure you as I should have done from the beginning, once I couldn't have you, I wanted you even more."

She clenched her hands together, trying to still the tremors that rocked her body.

"Even though I expected this week at Weybridge would be more of the same, I couldn't stay away. I had to try *something.* At least here you couldn't run away from me."

"I'd have liked to," she admitted.

"Then over tea on the very first afternoon, you threw out a challenge."

"I didn't!"

"Oh, but you did, Isabel. You said you wanted only what was fair—and that's what I wanted, too."

"You wanted an heir." The words tasted bitter.

"No—I wanted an opportunity to start over. And since behaving like a gentleman didn't get me far last time around, I thought perhaps *not* behaving like a gentleman—and showing you the benefits of marriage—might."

She felt herself coloring.

"So yes, I'll hold you to your promise, because it's the best excuse I can think of to stay close to you. I will follow you wherever you go, whether you want me or not, because I love you, Isabel. I'll spend every day for the rest of my life convincing you that we should be together."

A wave of gratitude and confidence swept over her, and she stepped into his arms. "Then follow me," she whispered. "Please, Max—follow me."

❂   ❂   ❂

As he kissed Emily, Gavin realized that the settee in front of the fire was looking more and more inviting—but the last fragments of his common sense reminded him that the smoking room wasn't nearly private enough for what he'd like to do. After a particularly long and arousing kiss, he raised his head and said unsteadily, "Your room or mine?"

"Actually..." Emily said shyly.

He tried not to groan. "You don't want to go back to the ball, do you?"

She shook her head. "Everyone would be watching us and talking. It's just that ever since that first night with you, I haven't been able to stop thinking."

Gavin felt every danger signal in his body go off in a chorus.

"Someday, Gavin," she said wistfully, "will you make love to me on the billiard table?"

❀ ❀ ❀

As the ball wound down and the sky began to lighten in the east, the Duke of Weybridge—whose health and stamina seemed to have been miraculously restored—shared a glass of brandy and a cigar with the Earl of Chiswick in front of a hastily made-up fire in the library. The windows were open and the morning air was fresh and bracing. Harnesses jingled in the courtyard as the last of the carriages pulled away.

Weybridge rose to refill his glass and stretched luxuriously. "It's a relief to be out of that chair." With a hopeful wag of the tail, one of the dogs pushed his rope toy into the duke's hand, and he set his cigar into a glass dish before dropping onto the carpet to wrestle. "Athstone almost caught me playing like this with the dogs this afternoon. The cub thought I'd fallen, but he wouldn't even go call my man to help me—he insisted on picking me up himself and tucking me back in my chair. He's a good man, my heir. Emily will be in safe hands."

Chiswick said unsympathetically, "I told you it wasn't necessary to tie yourself to a wheelchair and pretend you were decrepit in order to make the younger generation think about their futures. None of them can see past the ends of their noses anyway."

The duke shook his head. "You may as well admit it, Chiswick. Your offspring positively enjoy thinking they've pulled the wool over your eyes."

"Foolish of them to believe they can," Chiswick muttered.

"On the other hand, they respect me too much to carry on if I'm watching—so I had to take myself out of the picture so they were free to act. Anyway, you can't argue with the results."

"Oh, now you're taking all the credit?" Chiswick snorted. "If I hadn't stepped in, you'd have had to make good on your promise—and a pretty penny it would have cost you to live up to those birthday-gifts-in-reverse you dangled over their heads."

"They all received perfectly fine gifts in the end," the duke said. "Not quite what they expected, of course, but far better for them than mere money—and exactly what I promised. Happiness for Emily; a much more pleasant life for Isabel; a proper place in society for Lucien."

Chiswick swirled the brandy in his glass. "If you're wise, Josiah, you won't point out to Lucien that he could have held out for a curricle instead of a wife."

The duke didn't look at him. "You don't mind that he's to marry Chloe Fletcher? She didn't touch your heart?"

"God, no. After I lost Drusilla…" Chiswick cleared his throat roughly. "I miss her—but I think she'd be proud of what we accomplished this week, you and I." He drained his glass. "Anyway, what would I do with a teenaged bride? She'd have killed me within a week. Another brandy, Josiah—to celebrate?"

He topped off their glasses just as the sun rose over Weybridge Castle.

Acknowledgments

pecial thanks go to: writing buddies Elaine, Rachelle, Cecily, and Lynda Gail—you guys are wonderful. To my agent, Christine Witthohn of Book Cents Literary Agency, and my editor at Montlake Romance, Kelli Martin. To Shannon and Jenny, for your hard work and invaluable comments on the manuscript. To Margaret—I appreciate your friendship and our long, therapeutic walks. To the readers who asked for another Regency romance. And to Michael—just because.

About the Author

❧

*L*eigh Michaels is the award-winning author of more than eighty romance novels, which have been translated and published in 120 countries, and in more than twenty-five languages. She was born and raised in rural Iowa and was only a teenager when she wrote her first romance novel (which she subsequently burned, along with the next five books she would write). Since then, six of her novels have been finalists for RITA awards, and she received two Reviewer's Choice awards from *Romantic Times*. She is also the 2003 recipient of the Johnson Brigham Award. In addition to her prolific writing career, Leigh also teaches romance writing, and is the author of *On Writing Romance*, which has been called the definitive guide to writing romance novels. Leigh currently resides in Ottumwa, Iowa, where she and her photographer husband enjoy watching white-tailed deer and wild turkeys that visit their property.

Made in the USA
Charleston, SC
28 September 2012